D0325491

GABE

NEW YORK TIMES BESTSELLING AUTHOR
LORI FOSTER

Recycling programs
for this product may
not exist in your area.

ISBN-13: 978-1-335-40656-9

Gabe
First published in 2000. This edition published in 2021.
Copyright © 2000 by Lori Foster

Taking the Boss to Bed
First published in 2015. This edition published in 2021.
Copyright © 2015 by Joss Wood

This edition published by arrangement with Harlequin Books S.A.

For questions and comments about the quality of this book,
please contact us at CustomerService@Harlequin.com.

Harlequin Enterprises ULC
22 Adelaide St. West, 41st Floor
Toronto, Ontario M5H 4E3, Canada
www.Harlequin.com

Printed in U.S.A.

CONTENTS

Lori Foster is a *New York Times* and *USA TODAY* bestselling author of more than one hundred titles. Lori has been a recipient of the prestigious *RT Book Reviews* Career Achievement Award for Series Romantic Fantasy and for Contemporary Romance. For more about Lori, visit her website at lorifoster.com.

GABE

Lori Foster

Chapter 1

"Isn't he just the absolute sexiest thing you've ever seen?"

"Hmm. And thank heavens for this heat wave. I love it when he leaves his shirt off." A wistful, feminine sigh. "I swear, I could sit here all day and look at him."

"We *have* been sitting here all day looking at him."

Gabe Kasper, pretending to be asleep, had to struggle with a small smile. Life was good. Here he was, sprawled in the warm sun, letting the waves from the weekend boaters gently rock the dock, with a fishing pole loosely held in one hand, a Van Halen hat pulled low over his eyes and a gaggle of good-lookin' women ogling him. He had not a care in the world. Man couldn't ask for much more satisfaction out of living.

"He is *so* gorgeous."

"And wicked lookin'. I dearly love those whiskers on his chin."

Aha. And here his brother Jordan had sworn the whiskers looked disreputable and tried to convince him to shave. Jordan could be such a stuffed shirt sometimes.

"I like that golden hair on his body, myself."

Gabe almost chuckled out loud. He couldn't wait to tell his brothers about this. Now that the two eldest were married and off-limits, Gabe and Jordan, the only two single ones left, got even more attention. Not that he was complaining. Female adoration was one of those things that couldn't really go to excess, at least, in his opinion.

"I don't mind tellin' you, Rosemary, it made me nervous when the first two brothers got married off. I cried for two days, and I was so afraid they'd all end up doing it. Heck, besides dying to have one of them to myself, those brothers were the biggest tourist draw we had here in Buckhorn."

Gabe bit the side of his lip. He'd just keep that little tidbit to himself when he did the retelling. Hell, his brothers' egos—Morgan's especially—were big enough as it was. No need adding to them. No, he'd just stick to sharing the compliments about himself.

"And Gabe is the biggest draw my boat dock has. With him sitting there, no one wants to get their gas or bait anywhere else. I keep thinkin' I ought to pay him or something."

"Ha! You're just hoping to get a little closer to him."

"No, I just wanna make sure he doesn't take his sexy self off to some other dock."

"Amen to that!"

Giggles erupted after such a heartfelt comment and Gabe sighed. He had no intention of switching loyalties. Hell, Rosemary's daddy had been letting him hang out on his docks since he was just a grasshopper and had first noticed what a pleasing thing it was to see females in bikinis. This place felt almost like a second home now. And since Rosemary's daddy had passed away, he felt honor bound to stick around and help out on occasion. The trick was to keep Rosemary from getting marriage minded, because that was one route his brothers could travel alone, thank you very much.

"It amazes me that those brothers aren't full related. They all look different—"

"But they're all gorgeous, I know. And they're all so...*strong*. My daddy used to say it took a hell of a woman to raise boys like that. I just wish they didn't live so far out on that land. Thinking up a good excuse to visit isn't easy. Not like accidentally running into the other men here in town."

Gabe did smile at that, he couldn't help himself. He and his brothers—he refused to think of them as half brothers—had often joked about going into town to see who was looking for them. Usually some female or another was. But by living out a ways, they could always choose when and if they wanted to get friendly. It had been helpful, because once they'd hit their teens, the females had come on in droves. His mother used to claim to keep a broom by the front and back doors to beat the women away. Not that any of them minded overmuch, though his two new sisters-in-law were sure disgruntled over all the downcast female faces since the two weddings had taken place.

Gabe was just about to give up feigning sleep when a new female voice joined the others over by the gas pumps.

"Excuse me, but I was told Gabriel Kasper might be here." It was more a statement than anything else, and rather…strident to boot.

Female, but not at all local.

This new voice wasn't soft, Southern or sweet. She'd sounded almost impatient.

Gabe decided just to wait and see what the lady was up to. It wasn't unusual for someone female to be looking for him, and most everyone in these parts knew that in the summer, you could find him by the lake more often than not. He resisted the urge to peek at the owner of the voice and kept his body utterly relaxed.

"Whatdya want Gabe for?" That suspicious tone was from Rosemary, bless her sweet little heart, and Gabe vowed to take her to dinner real soon.

There was a beat of silence, then, "I have personal business to discuss with him."

Oh, great, Gabe thought. That'll get the gossip going. What the hell kind of personal business could he have with a woman he didn't know? And he was certain he didn't know her. She didn't sound at all familiar.

"Well, he's right there, but he's relaxin', and he won't thank you none for disturbing him."

"I appreciate your warning."

Well used to the soft thud of sneakers or bare feet on the wooden planks of the dock, Gabe almost winced when the clack of hard-soled shoes rang over the water.

He ignored it, and ignored the woman he could feel hesitating next to his lawn chair. The breeze stirred and he caught a light feminine scent, not really perfume, but maybe scented shampoo. He breathed deeply, but otherwise remained still.

He heard her clear her throat. "Uh…excuse me?"

She didn't sound so confident, and he waited, wondering if she'd shake him awake. He felt her hesitate, knew in his gut she was reaching for his naked shoulder…

And the fishing pole nearly leaped out of his hand.

"Son of a bi—" Gabe jolted upright, barely managing to hang on to his expensive rod and reel. His feet hit the dock and he deftly maneuvered the rod, going with the action of the fish. "Damn, it's a big one!"

Rosemary, Darlene and Ceily all ran over to his side. "I'll grab the net!" Rosemary said.

Ceily, who usually worked the diner in town, squealed as the fish, a big ugly carp, flipped up out the water. Darlene pressed to his back, peering over his shoulder.

Gabe slid over the side of the dock to the smooth, slick, moss-covered concrete boat ramp, bracing his legs wide to keep his balance while he struggled with the fish. Rosemary, a fisherwoman of long standing, didn't hesitate to slip in beside him. She held the net at the ready. Just as Gabe got the carp close enough, she scooped him with the net. The fish looked to weigh a good fifteen pounds, and she struggled with it while Gabe tried to reach for the net and hold onto his pole.

But then Rosemary lost her footing and Gabe made a grab for her and they both went down, splashing and cursing and laughing, too. The rod jerked out of his hands and he dove forward to grab it, barely getting ahold and soaking himself thoroughly in the process. The other two women leaped in to help, all of them struggling to keep the fish and the rod while roaring with hilarity.

When the battle was over, Gabe had his fish, and a woman, in his lap. Rosemary had settled herself there while Darlene and Ceily hung on him, both struggling to control their raucous laughter. He'd known all three of them since grade school, so it wasn't the first time they'd played in the water; they felt totally familiar with each other and it showed. A long string of seaweed clung to the top of Gabe's head, and that started the women giggling again.

Gabe, enjoying himself, unhooked the big fish, kissed it—making the women smack at him—then tossed it back.

It was then they heard the tap, tap, tap of that damned hard-soled shoe.

Turning as one, they all peered at the woman who Gabe only then remembered. He had to shade his eyes against the hot sun to see, and it wasn't easy with three women draped over his body.

Silhouetted by the sunshine, her long hair looked like ruby fire. And he'd never in his life seen so many freckles on a woman before. She wore a crisp white blouse, a long jean skirt and black pumps with nylons. *Nylons in this heat?* Gabe blinked. "Can I help you with somethin', sugar?"

Her lips tightened and her arms crossed over her

middle. "I don't think so. I was looking for Gabriel Kasper."

"That'd be me."

"But… I was looking for Gabriel, the town hero."

Darlene grinned hugely. "That's our Gabe!"

Ceily added, "The one and only."

Gabe rolled his eyes. "That's nonsense and you all know it."

The women all started in at once, Ceily, Rosemary and Darlene assuring him he was all that was heroic and wonderful and more.

Little Red merely stared in absolute disbelief. "You mean, *you* are the one who rescued those swimmers?"

He gently lifted Rosemary off his lap and cautiously stood on the slick concrete. The women had gone silent now, and Gabe could see why. While they looked downright sexy in their colorful bikinis, loose hair and golden tans, this woman looked like the stern, buttoned-up supervisor of a girls' prep school. And she was glaring at them all, as if she'd caught them having an orgy in the lake, rather than just romping.

Gabe, always the gentleman, boosted each woman to the dock, then deftly hauled himself out. He shook like a mongrel dog, sending lake water flying in cold droplets. The woman quickly backed up two steps.

Rosemary plucked the seaweed from his hair and he grinned at her. "Thanks, sweetie. Ah, would you gals mind if I talk to…" He lifted a brow at Red.

"Elizabeth Parks," she answered stiffly. She clutched a notepad and pencil and had a huge purse-like bag slung over one shoulder, stuffed to overflowing with papers.

"Yeah, can I have a minute with Ms. Parks?" He had the sneaking suspicion Ms. Parks was another reporter, and he had no intention of chatting with her for more time than it took to say thanks but no thanks. "I won't be long."

"All right, Gabe, but you owe us for rescuing your fish."

"That I do. And I promise to think up some appropriate compensation."

Giggling again, the women started away, dragging their feet every step, sashaying their sexy behinds. But then two boats pulled in and he knew that would keep them busy selling gas and bait and whatever other supplies the vacationers wanted. He turned to Red.

"What can I do for you?"

Now, without the sun in his eyes, Gabe could see she had about the bluest blue eyes he'd ever seen. They stood out like beacons among all that bright red hair and those abundant freckles.

She flipped open her bag and dragged out a folded newspaper. Turning it toward him, she asked, still with a twinge of disbelief, "Is this you?"

She sounded suspicious, but Gabe didn't even have to glance at the paper. Buckhorn, Kentucky was a small town, and they looked for any excuse at all to celebrate. The town paper, *Buckhorn Press,* had used the changing of a traffic light for front-page news once, so it was no wonder they'd stuck him in there for a spell when he helped fish a few swimmers out of the path of an unmanned boat. It hadn't been even close to an act of heroism, but if changing traffic lights was important, human endangerment was outright momentous.

"Yeah, that's me." Gabe reached for his mirrored sunglasses and slipped them on, then dragged both hands, fingers spread, over his head to smooth his wet hair. He stuck his cap on backward then looked at the woman again. With the shades in place, he could check her over a little better without her knowing.

But the clothing she wore made seeing much impossible. She had to be roasting in that thick denim and starched cotton.

She cleared her throat. "Well, if it's really true, then I'd like to interview you."

Gabe leaned around her, which made her blue eyes widen, and fetched a can of cola from the cooler sitting beside his empty chair. "You want one?"

"Uh, no, thank you." She hastily stepped back, avoiding getting too close to him. That nettled.

After popping the tab on the can and downing half of it, Gabe asked, "What paper do you write for?"

"Oh. No, I don't—"

"Because I'm not interested in being interviewed again. Every damn paper for a hundred miles around picked up on that stupid story, and they blew it all out of proportion. Folks around here are finally about done razzing me, my damn brothers included, and I'm not at all interested in resurrecting that ridiculous business again."

She frowned at him, then snapped the paper open to peruse it. "Did you or did you not dive into the water to pull three people, a woman and her two children, out of the lake when a drunken man fell out of his boat, leaving the boat unmanned?"

Gabe made a face. "Yeah, but—"

"No one else did anything, they just sort of stood there dumbfounded while the boat, without a driver, began circling the hapless swimmers."

"Hapless swimmers?" He grunted at her word usage. "Any one of my brothers would have done the exact same thing, and in fact—"

"And did you or did you not then manage to get in the boat—" She glanced up. "I'd love for you to explain how you did that, by the way. How you took control and got inside a running boat without getting chewed to bits by the prop. Weren't you at all scared?"

Gabe stared at her. Even her lashes were reddish, sort of a deep auburn, and with the sun on them, the tips were turned to gold. She squinted against the glare of the sunshine, which made the freckles on her tipped-up nose more pronounced. Other than those sprinkled freckles, her skin was smooth and clear and...

He shook himself. "Look, sugar, I said I didn't want to do an interview."

She puckered up like someone had stuck a lemon between her lips. "My name is Ms. Parks, or Elizabeth, either will do, thank you." After that reprimand, she had the audacity to say, "All the others wanted to be interviewed. Why don't you?"

She stood there, slim brows raised, her pencil poised over that damn notepad as if she expected to write down his every profound word.

Gabe cursed. Profound words were not his forté. They took too much effort. "What others?"

"The other heroes."

He could see her long hair curling in the humidity even as they spoke. It hung almost to the top of her behind, except for the front which was pulled back with a huge barrette. Little wispy curls, dark with perspiration, clung to her temples. The longer hair was slowly pulling into corkscrew curls. It fascinated him.

The front of her white blouse was beginning to grow damp, too, and Gabe could detect a plain white bra beneath. Damn, it was too hot to be all trussed up like that. What the hell kind of rigid female wore so many clothes to a vacation lake during the most sweltering heat wave of the summer season?

He didn't care what kind of female. "All right, first things first. I'm not doing any interview, period. Two, I'll admit I'm curious as to what the hell you're talking about with this other heroes business. And three, would you be more comfortable in the shade? Your face is turning berry red."

If anything, her color intensified. It wasn't exactly a pretty blush, more like someone had set a fire beneath her skin. She looked downright blotchy. Gabe almost laughed.

"I, ah, I always turn red," she explained, somewhat flustered. "Sorry. Redheads have fair skin."

"And you sure as certain have redder hair than most."

"Yes, I'm aware of that."

She looked stiff, as if he'd insulted her. It wasn't like her red hair was a state secret! A body could see that hair from a mile away.

He had to struggle to keep from grinning. "So whatdya say? You wanna go sit in the shade with me? There's a nice big piss elm hanging over the water there and it's cooler than standing here on the dock in the sun, but not much."

She blinked owlishly at him. "A what elm?"

"Piss elm. Just sorta means a scraggly one. Come on." She looked ready to expire on him, from flustered embarrassment, heat and exasperation. Without waiting for her agreement, he grabbed his cooler, took her arm in a firm grip and led her off the dock, over the rough rock retaining wall and through the grass. One large root of the elm stuck out smoothly from the ground and made a nice seat. Gabe practically shoved her onto it. He was afraid she might faint on him any minute. "Rest there a second while I get you a soda."

She scrambled to smooth her skirt over her legs, covering as much skin as possible, while trying to balance her notepad and adjust her heavy purse. "No, thank you. Really, I just—"

He'd already opened a can. "Here, drink up." He shoved the drink into her hand and then waited until she dutifully sipped. "Feel better?"

"Uh, yes, thank you."

She acted so wary, he couldn't help but be curious about her. She wasn't his type—too pushy, too prim, too...*red*. But that didn't mean he'd let her roast herself in the sun. His mother would hide him if she thought he'd been rude to a lady, any lady. Besides, she was kinda cute with her prissiness. In a red sort of way.

Gabe grabbed another cola for himself, then sat on the cooler. He looked at her while he drank. "So, tell me about these heroes."

She carefully licked her lips then set the can in the grass before facing him. "I'm working on a thesis for college. I've interviewed about a half dozen different men who were recently commended for performing heroic acts. So far, they've all had similar personality types. But you—"

"No fooling? What type of personality do heroes have?"

"Well, before I tell you that, I'd like to ask you a few questions. I don't want your answers to be biased by what the others have said."

Gabe frowned, propping his elbows on his knees and glaring at her. "You think I'd lie?"

She rushed to reassure him. "No! Not consciously. But just to keep my study pure, I'd rather conduct all the interviews the same way."

"But I've already told you, I don't want to be interviewed." He watched her closely, saw her frustration and accurately guessed that wasn't typical behavior of a hero. *What nonsense.*

After a long minute, she said, "Okay, can I ask you something totally different?"

"Depends. Ask, then I'll see if I want to answer."

"Why'd you throw the fish back?"

Gabe looked over his shoulder to where he'd caught the carp, then back. "That fish I just caught?"

"Yes. Why fish if you're not going to keep what you catch."

He chuckled. "You don't get out by the lake much, do you?"

"I'm actually not from around here. I'm just visiting the area—"

"To interview me?" The very idea floored him, and made him feel guilty for giving her such a hard time.

"Yes, actually." She took another drink of the soda, then added, "I rented a place and I'm staying for the month until school starts back up. I wanted to have all my research together before then. I'd thought I was done, and I was due a short vacation, but then I read the papers about you and decided to add one more interview."

"So you're working during your vacation?" He snorted. That was plain nuts. Vacations were for relaxing, and the idea of wasting one to pester him didn't make sense.

"Yes, well, let's just say that, hopefully, I'm combining my vacation with an interview. I couldn't resist. Your situation was unique in that every time you were quoted, you talked about someone else."

"I remember." The people he'd talked about were more interesting than anything he had to say about himself.

"You went on and on about how brave the two little kids were…"

"They were real sweet kids, and—"

"…and you lectured something fierce about drinking and water sports."

"This is a dry lake, which means no alcohol. That damn fool who fell out of his boat could have killed someone."

She gave him a coy look, surprising the hell out of him with the natural sensuality of it. She was so starchy, he hadn't been at all prepared. "But you keep saying the situation wasn't dangerous."

"It wasn't. Not to me." She looked smug, and she wrote something on her paper, making him frown.

He decided to explain before she got the wrong idea. "Hell, I've been swimming like a fish since I was still in diapers. I was in this lake before I could walk. My brothers taught me to water-ski when I was barely five years old, and I know boats inside and out. There was no risk to me at all, so there's no way anyone in their right mind can label me a hero."

"So you say. But everyone else seems to disagree."

"Sweetheart, you just don't know Buckhorn. This town is so settled and quiet, any disturbance at all is fodder for front-page news. Why, we had a cow break out of the pasture and wander into the church-yard sometime back. Stopped traffic for miles around so everyone could gawk. The fire department showed up, along with my brother, who's the sheriff, and the *Buckhorn Press* sent all their star reporters to cover the story."

"All their star reporters?"

He grinned. "Yeah. All two of them. That's the way things are run around here. The town council meets to vote on whether or not to change the bulbs in the street lamps and last year when Mrs. Rommen's kitty went missing, a search party was formed and we hunted for three days before finding the old rascal."

She wrote furiously, which annoyed the hell out of Gabe, and then she looked up. "We?"

He tilted his head at her teasing smile, a really nice smile now that he was seeing it. Her lips were full and rosy and... He frowned. "Now, Ms. Parks, you wouldn't expect me to avoid my civic duty, would you? Especially not when the old dear loves that ugly tom-cat something fierce."

She grinned at him again, putting dimples in those abundant freckles, making her wide mouth even more appealing, before going back to her writing. Gabe leaned forward to see exactly what she was putting on paper, and she snatched the paper to her chest.

"What are you doing?" She sounded breathless and downright horrified.

Gabe lifted a brow. "Just peeking at what you consider so noteworthy."

"Oh, I'm sorry." She lowered the paper, but the damage had been done. Dark smears of pencil lead were etched across the front of her damp white blouse.

Gabe nodded appreciatively at her bosom while sipping his cola. "Looks like you'll need to be cleaned up." He said it, then stood. "You should probably head on home to do that."

She quickly stood, too. "But I haven't asked you my questions yet."

"And you won't. I don't want to be interviewed. But just for the hell of it, I turned the fish loose 'cause it's a carp, not that good for eating and a real pain to clean being as they have a mud vein. Bass is more to my tastes. Which doesn't matter any when you're fishing just for the fun of fishing, which is usually how I do it. You should try it sometime." He looked her over slowly. "Cuttin' loose, I mean. It's real relaxing."

He turned to walk away and she trotted to keep up with him. "Gabriel… Mr. Kasper…"

"Gabe will do, unless you're thinking to ask more questions." He said it without looking at her, determined to get away before he noticed anything about her besides her lips, which now that he'd noticed he couldn't stop noticing, or how nicely that starched shirt was beginning to stick to her breasts in the humidity. He still couldn't tell for sure, but he suspected a slight possibility that she was built rather nice beneath all the prim, stiff clothing. And that was the kind of suspicion that could distract a man something awful.

Only she wasn't the kind of woman he wanted to be distracted by. She had an obvious agenda, while he avoided plans and merely enjoyed each day.

"Gabe, really, this isn't a lengthy interview. There's no reason for you to be coy."

He had to laugh at that. Shaking his head, he stepped on the dock and looked at her. He could have sworn he saw another long red tress snap into a curl right before his eyes. Her whole head was beginning to look like corkscrews. Long, lazy, red corkscrews. It was kinda cute in a way... Hell, no. No, it was not cute.

"I've never been called *coy* in my life. I'm just plain not interested in that foolishness." He skimmed off his sunglasses and hat, and placed them on his chair, then tossed a fat inflated black inner tube into the lake. "Now, I'm going to go cool off with a dip. You can either skim out of those clothes and join me before you expire from the heat, or you can go find some other fool to interview. But no more questions." He started to turn away, but belatedly added, "Nice meeting you." Then he dove in.

He was sure his splash got her, but he didn't look to see. At least not at first.

She stood there for the longest time. He was strangely aware of her presence while he hoisted himself into the center of the inner tube and got comfortable. Peeking through one eye, he watched her stew in silence, then glare at him before marching off.

Finally. Let her leave.

Calling him a hero—what nonsense. His brothers were real heroes; even those kids that had kept their cool and not whined could be considered heroic little devils. But not Gabe Kasper. No, sir.

He started to relax, tipping his head into the cool water to drench his hair and lazily drifting his arms. But his neck snapped to attention when he saw Little Red stop beside Rosemary. She pointed at Gabe, then pulled out her damn notepad when Rosemary began chattering. And damn if Ceily and Darlene didn't wander closer, taking part.

Well, hell. She was gossiping about him!

When he'd told her to interview someone else, he meant someone else who wouldn't talk about him. Someone not on the lake. Hell, someone not even in Buckhorn—not even in Kentucky!

Rosemary's mouth was going a mile a minute, and he could only imagine what was being said. He ground his teeth in frustration.

A couple of women in a docked boat started flirting with him, but Gabe barely noticed. He stared at Rosemary, trying to will her to clam up, but not wanting to appear too concerned about the whole thing. What was it with Red, that she'd be so damn pushy? He'd explained he wasn't a hero, that she didn't need him for her little survey or whatever it was she conducted. But could she let that go? Hell, no.

One of the women from the docked boat—a really

nice inboard that cost more than some houses—dove in and swam over to him. Gabe sent her a distracted smile.

It was in his nature to flirt; he just couldn't seem to help himself, and he'd never yet met a woman who minded. This particular woman didn't. She took his smile as an invitation.

Yet anytime he'd gotten even remotely close to Red, she'd frozen up like he was a big water snake ready to take a bite. Obviously she wanted into his head, but nowhere else.

Strange woman.

She walked away from Rosemary with a friendly wave, and Gabe started to breathe a sigh of relief—until she stopped a few yards up the incline where Bear, the repairman who worked on boat engines for Rosemary, was hanging around. Gabe helped the man regularly, whenever things got too busy, but did Bear remember that now? Gabe snorted. The old whiskered cuss looked at Red warily, then glanced at Gabe, and a smile as wide as the dam spread across his wrinkled face. Just that fast, Little Red had her pencil racing across the paper again.

"Damn it." Gabe deftly tipped the inner tube and slid over the side into the water. The sudden chill did nothing to cool his simmering temper. Keeping his gaze on the meddling female, he swam—dragging the inner tube—to the dock. But just as he reached it, so did the woman from the boat.

"Ah, now you're not planning to leave just when I got here, are you?"

Gabe turned. He'd actually forgotten the woman, which was incredible. She stood waist deep in the shallow water and from what he could see, she was built like a Barbie doll, all long limbs and long blond hair, and so much cleavage, she fairly overflowed her skimpy bikini bra. She should have held all his attention, but instead, he'd been thoroughly distracted by an uptight, overly freckled, redheaded wonder of a woman who jumped if he even looked at her.

Gabe glanced at Red, and their gazes clashed. He'd thought to go set the little darling straight on how much prying he'd put up with, but he reconsidered.

Oh, she was in a hot temper. Her blue-eyed gaze was glued to him, and her pencil was thankfully still. It was then Gabe realized his female swimming companion had caught hold of his arm—and Red disapproved mightily. She was looking like a schoolmarm again, all rigid, her backbone straight. Well, now. That was more like it.

Gabe turned to the blonde with a huge smile. This might just turn out to be fun.

Chapter 2

Elizabeth narrowed her eyes as she watched Gabriel Kasper fairly ooze masculine charm over the woman draped at his side. And the woman *was* draped. Elizabeth snorted in disgust. Did all women want to hang on him? Rosemary, Darlene, Ceily and this woman. They seemed to come from all around just to coo at him. No wonder he seemed so…different from the others.

The men she'd interviewed so far had been full of ego over their heroics and more than willing to share their stories with any available ear. They were rightfully proud, considering they'd behaved in a brave, out of the ordinary way that had directly benefited the people around them. Some of them had been shy, some outrageous, but not a one of them had refused her an interview. And not a one of them had so thoroughly ignored her.

No, they'd hung on her every question, anxious to share the excitement, thrilled with her interest, but in a purely self-satisfying way. They certainly hadn't been distracted with her as a woman, eyeing her up and down the way Gabriel Kasper had. She wondered if he thought she was stupid, or just naive, considering the way he'd looked at her, like he thought she wouldn't notice just because he wore sunglasses. Not likely! She'd felt his gaze like a tactile stroke, and it had unnerved her. The average man just didn't look at her that way, and men like Gabe never gave her a thought.

But then Gabe had dismissed her, and that she was more than used to. Except with the heroes she'd interviewed, the men who wanted their unique stories told.

Damn, Mr. Kasper was an enigma.

"Don't mind that none, miss. Gabe always gets more'n his share of notice from the fillies."

Elizabeth snapped her attention to Bear. His name suited him, she thought, as she looked way, way up into his grizzled face. "I beg your pardon?"

He nodded toward the docks, where Gabe and the woman were chatting cozily. Elizabeth curled her lip. It was disgusting for a woman to put on such an absurd display, especially right out in the open like that. And for Gabe to encourage her so… Good grief, he had a responsibility to the community as a role model after all the attention they'd given him.

"Has he acted any different since becoming a town hero?" During her research, Elizabeth had discovered that people heralded for valor quickly adapted to all the fanfare and added interest thrown their way.

Bear chuckled. "Not Gabe. Truth is, folks in these

parts have pretty much always looked up to him and his brothers. I don't think anyone doubted Gabe would do something once he noticed what had happened. Any one of his brothers would have done the same."

"He mentioned his brothers. Can you tell me something about them?"

"Be glad to!" Bear mopped a tattered bandanna around his face, then stuck it in his back pocket. "The oldest brother, Sawyer, is the town doc, and a damn good one to boot. He takes care of everyone from the newborns to the elders. Got hisself married to Honey, a real sweet little woman, about a year back. And that cut his patient load down considerable like. Seems some of the womenfolk coming to see him weren't really sick, just ambitious."

Bear grinned, but Elizabeth shook her head in exasperation.

"Right after Sawyer is Morgan, the sheriff, who generally looks like he just crawled right off a cactus, but he's as nice as they come as long as you stay on his good side." He leaned close to whisper, "And folks in these parts definitely stay on his good side."

"Lovely." Elizabeth tried to picture these two respectable men related to Gabe, who looked like a beach bum, but she couldn't quite manage it.

"Morgan up and married Honey's sister, Misty, just a bit after Sawyer married. He smiles more these days—that is, when she doesn't have him in a temper. She does seem to enjoy riling that boy."

It was a sure sign of Bear's age that he'd call a man older than Gabe a boy.

"Then there's Jordan, the best damn vet Buckhorn

County has to offer. He can sing to an animal, and damned if it won't sing back! That man can charm a bird out of a tree or lull an ornery mule asleep. He's still a bachelor."

Good grief. Elizabeth could do no more than blink. Doctor, sheriff, vet. It was certainly an impressive family. "What does Gabe do for a living?"

Bear scratched beneath his chin, thinking, and then he looked away. "Thing is, Gabe's the youngest, and he don't yet know what it is he wants to do. Mostly he's a handyman, sort of a jack-of-all-trades. That boy can do just about anything with his hands. He's—"

"He doesn't have a job?" Elizabeth didn't mean to sound so shocked, but Rosemary had told her Gabe was twenty-seven years old, and to Elizabeth's mind, that was plenty old enough to have figured out your life's ambition.

"Well…"

She shook her head, cutting off whatever lame excuses Bear was prepared to make. "I got the impression from a few things Rosemary said that he worked here."

A cold, wet hand clamped onto her shoulder, and Elizabeth jumped, then whirled to see Gabe, dripping lake water, standing right behind her. His grin wasn't pleasant, and she wished that she hadn't gotten engrossed in what Bear had to say, that she'd kept at least part of her attention on Gabe.

She looked around him, but his newest female companion was nowhere to be found. Which, she supposed, accounted for his presence. Surely if any other woman was available he'd still be ignoring her.

Gabe nodded to Bear, more or less dismissing him,

then pulled Elizabeth around and started walking a few feet away. In a voice that only barely bordered on cordial, he said, "Well, Miss Nosy, I do work here, but I'm not employed here. There's a definite difference. And from now on, I'd appreciate it if you kept your questions to yourself. I don't much like people prying into my personal life, especially when I already told 'em not to."

Elizabeth gulped. No amount of forced pleasantness could mask his irritation. She tried to inch away from his hot, controlling grasp, but he wasn't letting go. So she simply stopped.

Gabe turned to face her. They were once again standing in the bright sun, on a gravel drive that declined down the slight hill, used to launch boats into the lake. The glare off the white gravel was blinding. She had to shield her eyes with one hand while balancing her notepad, pen and purse with the other. Looking directly at him both flustered and annoyed her. He was an incredibly...*potent* male, no denying that. Standing there in nothing more than wet, worn, faded cutoffs—and those hanging entirely too low on his lean hips—he was a devastatingly masculine sight. A sparse covering of light brown hair, damp from his swim, laid over solid muscles in his chest and down his abdomen, then swirled around his navel. He was deeply tanned, his legs long, his big feet bare. He seemed impervious to the sharp gravel and the hot sun. And as she watched, his arms crossed over his chest.

"You be sure and let me know when you're done looking so I can finish telling you what I think of your prying ways."

The heat that washed over her face had nothing to do with the summer sun and everything to do with humiliation.

"I'm sorry. It's just that you don't look like the other men."

He sighed dramatically. "I take it we're talking about the other supposed heroes?"

"Yes."

"And how did they look?"

Elizabeth hesitated, wondering how to explain it. She couldn't just say they had all been fully dressed, because thinking it made her blush more. At the moment, Gabe Kasper looked more naked than not, and even the jean shorts didn't help, considering they were soaked and clinging to his hard thighs, to his… *Don't go there*.

She cleared her throat. "They were all more…serious. They have careers they take great pride in, and they enjoyed telling their stories."

"But I told you, I don't have a story to tell."

"Your friends disagree."

His arms dropped and he scowled at her. Strangely, Elizabeth noticed he was watching her mouth instead of looking into her eyes. It made it easier for her because staring directly at him kept her edgy for some reason. There was so much expression in his eyes, as if he wasn't just looking at her, but really seeing her. It was an unusual experience for her.

But with him looking at her mouth, she felt nervous in a different way, and without thinking, she licked her lips. His gaze shot to hers, and he stared, eyes narrowed, for two heartbeats while she held her breath and felt faint for some stupid reason. She gulped air and fanned her burning face.

Relaxing slightly, he shook his head, then said, "Look, Lizzy—"

"Don't call me that. My name is Elizabeth."

"And as long you're disregarding my wishes, I think I'll just disregard yours. Besides, Lizzy sorta suits you. It sounds like the proper name for a red-haired girl."

Elizabeth wanted to smack him. But since he'd come right out and all but admitted he wanted to annoy her, she decided to deny him the satisfaction. When she remained silent, he smiled, then continued. "This is all foolishness. Now I'm asking you nicely to let it drop."

"I can't. I've decided you'll make a really good contrast to the other men in my study. See, you're very different, and I can't, in good conscience, leave out such an important factor in my study. In order for the study to be accurate, I need to take data from every angle—"

He raised a hand, looking annoyed enough for his head to explode. "Enough of that already. This is your summer break, right?"

She watched him cautiously. "Yes."

"So why work so damn hard on summer break? Why not just cut loose a little and have some fun before going back to school?" He looked her over again and judging by the tightness of his mouth and the expression in his eyes, obviously found her lacking. "You're so prissed up, you have to be sweltering. No one puts on that many clothes in this heat."

Her shoulders were so stiff they hurt, and her stomach was churning. How dare he attack her on such a personal level? "Obviously someone does. I consider my dress totally appropriate."

"Appropriate to what?"

"To interviewing a hero."

His head dropped forward and he groaned. "You are the most stubbornest damn woman…."

"Me? You're the one who refuses to answer a few simple questions."

Their voices had risen and Gabe, with a heartfelt sigh, took her arm again and started farther up the gravel drive.

"Where are we going?" She had a vague image of him dragging her off and wringing her neck. Even a hero could only be pushed so far, and with the way everyone worshiped him, she didn't think she'd get much help.

"We're drawing attention and it isn't the kind of attention I like."

With a sneer she couldn't quite repress, she asked, "You mean it isn't purely female?"

Glancing her way, he grinned. "That's right."

"Oh, for heaven's sake!"

"Here we go. Have a seat."

Luckily, this time it wasn't a root he wanted to perch her on. The rough wooden picnic table was located beneath a tree—not an elm—and though it was partially covered with dried leaves, acorns and twigs, it was at least shaded.

Elizabeth had barely gotten herself settled before Gabe blurted, "Okay, what is it going to take to get you to back off?"

He wanted to bargain with her? Surprised, but also

hopeful because she really did want to add his story to the others—he was proving to be the exception that broke the hero mold she'd mentally formed—Elizabeth carefully considered her answer. Finally, she said, "If you'd just answer five questions…"

"I'll answer one. But it'll cost you."

Her relief died a short death. "How much? I have a job, but it's barely enough to pay my tuition so I couldn't offer you anything significant—"

He looked so totally and utterly appalled, she knew she'd misunderstood. His expression said so, but in case she hadn't caught on, he leaned close, caging her in with one arm on the picnic table, the other on her shoulder, and said through his teeth, "You actually think I'd take money from you?"

Elizabeth tried leaning back, but she didn't have much room to maneuver, not without toppling over. "You…you said you don't have a job."

"Wrong." He looked ready to do that neck wringing she'd worried about. "I said I'm not employed here. For your information, Red, I more than pay my own way. Not that my financial situation is any business of yours."

"But…" It was one of the questions in her survey, though luckily this time she had the good sense to forfeit it. "Of course not. I didn't mean to suggest—"

"If you want me to answer a question, you'll have to loosen up. And before you start widening those big blue eyes at me again, I'm not suggestin' an illicit affair."

Her heart almost stopped, but for the life of her she wasn't entirely sure if it was relief or disappointment she felt. No one had ever offered her an illicit affair, and the idea held a certain amount of appeal. Not that she'd ever accept, of course, but still… "What, exactly, are you suggesting?"

"A swim. In the lake. Me and you."

The big green murky lake behind her? The lake he'd pulled that enormous fish out of—then thrown it back so it was still in there? The lake where any number of things could be living? Never mind that she didn't even own a bathing suit, the thought of getting into that lake positively terrified her. Hoping against hope, she said, "I don't understand."

"It's easy, Lizzy. I want you here tomorrow, same time, wearing a swimsuit instead of all that armor. And I want you to relax with me, to take a nice leisurely swim. Maybe if you loosen up a bit, I won't even mind so much answering a question for you."

To make certain she understood before she agreed to anything, she asked, "And in exchange, you'll answer my questions?"

"No, I'll answer one question. Just one. Any question you like. You can even make notes in that damn little book of yours." He eyed her mouth again, then shook his head. "And who knows, if all goes well, maybe we can work out another deal."

"For another question?"

He shrugged, looking reluctant but strangely resigned.

Elizabeth had the sneaking suspicion he was trying to bluff her, to force her to back out. But she was fascinated. Such unusual behavior for a hero! She could almost imagine the response she'd get from this thesis—if anyone even believed it. But there had to be some redeeming information there, something that would make her research all that more complete, valuable and applicable.

In the end, there was really only one decision she could make. She held out her hand, and after a moment, Gabe took it.

His hand was so large, so tanned. And he felt hot. She gulped, shored up her courage, and with a smile that almost hurt, she said, "Deal."

He couldn't believe he was running late.

If anything, he'd planned to be on the dock, sunning himself, a man without a care, when she arrived. Truth was, he felt strangely anxious. He grinned at the novelty of it.

"You've been doing a lot of that this morning."

Gabe turned to his brother Sawyer. "What?"

"Smiling like a fool."

"Maybe I have good reason."

"And what would that be?"

"None of your business." Gabe, still grinning, finished running caulk around the windowpane then wiped his hands on a small towel. "That should do you, Sawyer. From now on, don't let kids play baseball in your office, hear?"

Honey hustled up to his side with a tall glass of iced tea. Bless her, he did like all the doting she felt compelled to do. Having a sister-in-law was a right nice thing. "Thanks, Honey."

"What are you so happy about, Gabe?"

Uh oh. He glanced at Sawyer, saw his smirk and concentrated on drinking his tea. Sawyer knew without a doubt that he wouldn't even consider telling Honey to mind her own business. By virtue of being female, she was due all the respect his brothers didn't warrant. He just naturally tempered himself around women—well, all but Red. She seemed to bring out the oddest reactions from him. Damned if he wasn't looking forward to seeing her again.

What would she look like in a bikini?

"There he goes, grinning again."

"Actually," Gabe said, ignoring his brother, "I was just thinking of a woman." That was true enough, and not at all uncommon. In fact, Honey gave him a fond look of indulgence, patted his shoulder, then went to her husband's side. Sawyer sure was a lucky cuss. Honey was a sexy little woman—not that he thought of her that way, her being in the family and all. But he wasn't blind. She was a real looker, and best of all, she loved his brother to distraction.

Sawyer gave a grievous sigh. "He's in lust again. Just look at him."

That drew Gabe up short. Lust? Hell, no, he didn't feel lust for Little Red. Amusement maybe, because she was unaccountably funny with her freckles and her red corkscrew curls that hung all the way down to her fanny.

And frustration, because she simply had no idea how to accept no for an answer and she trussed herself up in those schoolmarm clothes, to the point a guy couldn't even tell what he was seeing.

Maybe even annoyance, because her stubbornness rivaled his brother Morgan's, and that was saying a mouthful. But not lust.

He grunted, earning an odd look from Sawyer.

His invitation for a swim was simply his way of keeping the upper hand. And thinking that, he said to Sawyer, "If a funny little red-haired woman tries to talk to you about me, don't tell her a damn thing, okay?"

Sawyer and Honey blinked at him in confusion, but he didn't bother to explain. He hurried off. Knowing Red, if he was too late, she'd give up on him and go home. She wasn't the type of woman who'd wait around, letting a guy think she'd be happy to see him when he did show up. No, Red would probably get her back all stiff and go off asking questions of every available body in the area.

And he really didn't want anyone filling her head with that nonsense about heroes. Best that he talked to her himself. And that was another reason he'd engineered the date. No, take that back. Not a date. An appointment. Yeah, that sounded better. He'd arranged an appointment so that at least she'd get her stupid story straight.

Hell, he had plenty of reasons for seeing her again, and none of them were about lust.

He did wonder what she'd look like in a bikini, though.

She was still in full armor.

Gabe frowned as he climbed out of his car and started down the hill. Judging by the color of that long braid hanging almost to the dock, the woman with her back to him was one Miss Elizabeth Parks. And she wasn't wearing a bikini. He consoled himself with the fact that at least she was waiting for him. There was a certain amount of masculine satisfaction in that.

The second he stepped on the dock, she turned her head. He noticed then that she was sitting cross-legged instead of dangling her feet in the water. She had her shoes and frilly little white socks on. Socks in this heat? He stopped and frowned at her. "Where's your swimsuit?"

She frowned right back. "I have it on under my dress. Surely you didn't think I'd drive here in it? And you're late."

She turned away and with her elbows on her knees, propped her chin on a fist and stared at the lake.

Gabe surveyed her stiff back and slowly approached. He wasn't quite sure what to expect of her, so he said carefully, "I'm glad you waited."

With a snort, she answered, "You made it a part of the deal. If I want to ask you one measly question, I had to be here." She waved a dismissive hand. "I figured you'd show up sooner or later."

Not exactly the response he'd hoped for. In fact, she'd taken all the fun out of finding her still here. "Well, skin out of those clothes then, so we can get in. It's hot enough to send a lizard running for shade. That water's going to feel good."

She didn't look at all convinced. Peering at him with one eye scrunched against the sunshine and her small pointed nose wrinkled, she said, "The thing is, I'm not at all keen on doing that."

"What?"

"The swimsuit thing. I've never had much reason to swim, and this boat dock is pretty crowded...."

"You want privacy?" Now why did that idea intrigue him? But it was a good idea, not because he'd be alone with her. No, that had nothing to do with it. But that way, if she asked her dumb hero question, no one else would be around to contradict him.

He liked that idea. "We can take a fishing boat back to a cove. No one's there, at least, not close. There might be a few fishermen trolling by, or the occasional skier, but they won't get near enough to shore to look you over too good." He gave her a crooked grin. "Your modesty will be preserved." *Except from me.*

Her face colored. "It's not that I think I'd draw much attention, you understand. It's just not something I'm used to."

With the way she managed to cover herself from shins to throat, he didn't doubt it. "No problem. The cove is real peaceful. I swim there all the time. Come on." He reached down a hand for her, trying not to look as excited as he suddenly felt. "Do you know how to swim?"

She ignored his hand and lumbered to her feet, dusting off her bottom as she did so. "Not really."

Rather than let her get to him, he dropped his hand and pretended it didn't matter. But he couldn't recall ever having such a thing happen in his entire life, and he knew right then and there he didn't like it worth a damn. "Then you'll need a flotation belt. There's some in the boat. You got a towel?"

"My stuff is there." She pointed to the shore where a large colorful beach towel, a floppy brimmed hat and a pair of round, blue-lens sunglasses had been tossed.

Next to the pile was her infamous notepad, which made him frown.

Gabe had his towel slung around his neck, his mirrored glasses already in place and his hat on backward. He carried a stocked cooler in his free hand. "Let's go."

He led her to a small metal fishing boat, then despite her efforts to step around him, helped her inside. The boat swayed, and she nearly lost her balance. She would have fallen overboard if he hadn't held on to her.

He managed not to smirk.

He tossed her stuff in to her, then said, "Take a seat up front and put on a belt. If you fall in, it'll keep you from drowning until I can fish you out."

"Like you did the carp?"

Her teasing smile made his stomach tighten. "Naw, I kissed the fish and threw him back in for luck." He glanced at her, then added, "I wouldn't do that to you."

Her owl-eyed expression showed her confusion. Let her wonder if he meant he wouldn't kiss her or he wouldn't throw her back. Maybe keeping her guessing would take some of the edge off her cockiness. He hid his satisfaction as he stepped into the boat and tilted the motor into the water. He braced his feet apart, gave the rip cord a tug, and the small trolling motor hummed to life.

After seating himself comfortably, he said, "We won't break any speed records, but the ride'll be smooth."

"Is this your boat?"

"Naw. Belongs to Rosemary. But she lets me use it whenever I want."

"Because you do work around the dock for her?"

Tendrils of hair escaped her long thick braid and whipped into her face. She held them back with one hand while she watched him. The dress she wore was made like a tent—no shape at all. From what he could see, it pulled on over her head, without a button or zipper or tie anywhere to be found. The neck was rounded and edged with lace, and the sleeves were barely there. But at least it was a softer material, something kind of like a T-shirt, and a pale yellow that complemented her red hair and bright blue eyes.

Gabe pulled himself away from that distraction and reminded himself that lust had nothing to do with his motivation today. He smiled at her. "Is that your question?"

"What?"

"Your one allotted question. You want to know about me working at the boat dock?"

Her frown was fierce. "Just making conversation."

"Uh-huh. You know what I think? I think you figured you'd sneak a whole bunch of questions in on me and I wouldn't notice."

She bit her lips and looked away. Gabe couldn't help but laugh out loud, it was so obvious she'd been caught. Damn, but she was a surprise. She sat there with her little feet pressed primly together—those damn lacy ankle socks somehow looking kind of sexy all of a sudden—while her snowy white sneakers got damp with the water in the bottom of the boat. Her hands were clasped together in her lap, holding onto her big floppy hat, her eyes squinted against the wind and sun. Her freckles were even more noticeable out here on the lake. She wasn't exactly what you'd call a pretty woman, certainly not a bombshell like Sawyer's Honey or Morgan's Misty. But there was definitely something about her....

"Where are we going?"

She sat facing him in the boat, so he pointed behind her to where the land stretched out and the only living things in sight were a few cows grazing along the shoreline. The man-made lake was long and narrow, shaped a lot like a river with vacation cabins squeezed into tight rows along both sides. Several little fingers of water stretched out to form small coves here and there, only a few of which were still owned by farmers and hadn't been taken over by developers. The land Gabe lived on with his brothers had a cove like that, a narrow extension of the main lake, almost entirely cut off from the boating traffic since it was so shallow. But it made for great swimming and fishing, which was what the brothers used it for.

Though they didn't have any cows there, it was peaceful and natural and they loved it, refusing to sell no matter how many times they were asked and regardless of the offer. They jointly owned a lot of property, and in two spots runoff from the main lake had formed a smaller lake and a pond. Gabe intended to build a house on that site some day.

"We're going *there?*" Lizzy asked, interrupting his thoughts. She sounded horrified.

Gabe bobbed an eyebrow. "It's real private."

"Are the cows friendly?"

"Most bovines are. You just don't want to walk behind them."

"They kick?"

She sounded appalled again, so he had to really struggle to keep from laughing. "Nope. But you have to be real careful where you step."

"Oh."

Slowing the motor, Gabe let the boat glide forward until they'd rounded the cove and nudged as far inside as possible. Someone in years past had installed a floating dock, but it had definitely seen better days. It tended to list to one side, with three corners out of the water and one corner under, covered by moss. But at least it was a good six feet square and didn't sink if you climbed on it.

Gabe threw a rope around a metal cleat on the side of the dock. It was strange, but his heart was already pounding like mad—he had no idea why—and he had to force himself to speak calmly.

He looked at her, saw her shy, averted gaze and felt the wild thrum of excitement. He swallowed hard. "This is as far as we get, so you can skin out of that dress now."

She peeked at him, then away. "Why don't you go ahead and get in, then I'll…inch my way in?"

"Have you ever driven a boat?"

"No."

"Do you know how to start it?"

She glanced dubiously at the pull start for the motor, then shook her head. "I don't think so."

He nodded. "So at least I know you're not plotting on getting me overboard then taking off."

Her eyes widened. "I wouldn't do that." She chewed her lip, looking undecided, then admitted, "It's just that

I hadn't figured on how to go about stripping off my clothes out here in the open."

"With me and the cows watching?"

"Right."

He could have offered a few suggestions, but that would be crass. Besides, he was afraid his suggestions would offend her. Likely they would.

Oh, hell, he knew damn good and well they would.

"All right. I'll turn my back. But don't take too long. You can put your folded things on the cooler so they won't get wet." Before he could change his mind, he turned his back, stepped on a seat and dove in. He heard her squeal as the small boat rocked wildly.

The water was shallow, so he made the dive straight out, and seconds later his head broke the water. He could easily stand, so he waded to the dock, keeping his head averted, then rested his folded arms over the edge of the aged wood. He could hear her undressing.

"The water feels great." His voice shook, damn it.

"It's…green."

He cleared his throat. "Because of the moss." She probably had her shoes off already, and those ridiculous, frilly, feminine little socks that looked like they'd come from a fetish catalogue, though he doubted she knew it. He pictured her wearing those socks—and nothing else. The picture was vague because he had no idea what the hell her body looked like, but the thought still excited him. Dumb.

Did she only have on the dress, or was she wearing other stuff over her suit? He cleared his throat and mustered his control. "Aren't you done yet?"

"Well…yeah."

His head snapped around, and he stared. She stood there, pale slender arms folded over her middle, long legs pressed together, shoulders squared as if in challenge. And her suit wasn't a bikini, not that it mattered one little bit.

"Damn, woman." The words were a choked whisper, hot and touched with awe. It felt like his eyes bugged out of his head.

She shifted nervously, uncrossing and recrossing her arms, taking her weight from one foot to the other, making the supple muscles in her calves and thighs move seductively.

Gabe had no idea if she blushed or not because he couldn't get his gaze off her body and onto her face.

The one-piece suit was simple, a pale lime green, and it covered enough skin to make a grandma happy. But what it left uncovered…

Her plump breasts made his mouth water with the instinct of Pavlov's dog. High, round…he wondered for a single heartbeat if they were real or enhanced. He stared, hard, unaware of her discomfort, her uncertainty. Nothing in the suit suggested it capable of that incredible support. There were no underwires, no lined bra cups. The suit was a sleek, simple design, and it hugged her like her own skin.

The visible outline of soft nipples drew him, making his imagination go wild. He wanted to see them tight and puckered, straining for his mouth.

Breathing deeply, he traced her body with his gaze, to the shaping of her rib cage, the indention of a navel, the rounded slope of her mound.

Heat rolled through him, making his nostrils flare.

He could easily picture her naked, and did so, torment-ing himself further.

Surely even the cows were agog. She had the most symmetrically perfect feminine body he'd ever seen, and the lake water no longer felt so cool. His sex grew thick and heavy, hot. It was unexpected, this instanta-neous reaction he had to her. Women didn't affect him this way. He'd learned control early on and hadn't had an unwanted erection since his teens. He chose when to be involved; he did not get sucked into a vortex of lust!

But there was no denying what he felt at this mo-ment. It annoyed him, with himself, not her. She did nothing to entice him, other than to stand there and let him look his fill.

Just as he'd suspected, her freckles decorated other parts of her body, not just her face. Her shoulders were lightly sprinkled with them—and her thighs. His heart-beat lost its even rhythm. Damn. He hadn't known freckles could be so incredibly sexy.

One thing was certain, he was sure glad he'd brought her here so that every guy on the lake wasn't able to gawk at her.

Hell, he was doing enough gawking for all of them.

Pulling himself together, he cleared his throat again and looked at her face. Her head was down, her long braid hanging over a shoulder, touching a hipbone. He bit his lip, feeling the heavy thumping of his heart, the tautness of his muscles. "Lizzy?"

Her arms tightened around herself. "Hmm?"

Belatedly he understood her anxiety at being on display. He felt like a jerk, and tried for a teasing tone despite the urgency hammering through him. "You comin' in or not?"

"Do I get a choice?"

He didn't hesitate. "No."

Slowly her gaze lifted to his. "You'd better be worth this."

Oh, he'd show her just how worthwhile he could— No, wait. Wrong thought. He hadn't brought her here for that. He'd brought her here to convince her to forget about her silly ideas of heroism.

He scowled with determination, but his carnal thoughts seemed less and less wrong with every second she stood there, her small body the epitome of sexual temptation. He unglued his tongue and said, "Come on. Quit stalling."

She licked her lips and he groaned, practically feeling the stroke of her small pink tongue.

She glared at him suspiciously, then looked over the side of the boat, looked at him and licked her lips again. "How?"

Without even thinking about it, he found himself wading to the boat, holding up his arms and inviting her into them.

And just like that, she closed her eyes, muttered a quiet prayer and fell in against him.

Chapter 3

Gabe found his arms filled with warm, soft woman. It wasn't the first time, of course, but it sure felt different from any other time. Unexpectedly, her scent surrounded him. Lizzy smelled sweet, with a unique hint of musk that pulled at him. Her fingers were tight in his hair, her arms wrapped around his head in a death grip. His mind went almost blank. He could feel her firm, rounded bottom against his right forearm where he'd instinctively hooked her closer, to keep her from falling when she'd jumped in against him. His left arm was around her narrow waist, his large hand splayed wide so that his fingers spanned her back.

More momentous than that, though, was the fact that his face was pressed between her breasts. They certainly felt real enough. Jolted by the sexual press of her body, he froze, not even breathing. She was wrapped around him like a vine, but she didn't seem to notice the intimacy of their position.

Gabe noticed. Damn, but he noticed.

He shifted the tiniest bit so that his hand could cuddle a full, round cheek, and felt the shock of the touch all the way to his throbbing groin. She panted, but not with excitement.

"Lizzy?" His voice was muffled, thanks to having his face buried in lush breasts. His hand on her bottom continued to caress her, almost with a will of its own.

Her arms tightened, her legs shifting to move around his hips in a jerky, desperate attempt to get closer to him. The movement brought the open, hot juncture of her thighs against his abdomen, and he sucked in a startled, strangled breath. If they were naked, if he slipped her down just a few inches, he could be inside her.

He was losing his grip on propriety real fast.

"Lizzy," he said, speaking low to keep from jarring her, "you're afraid of the water?"

Her growled, "No...*yes*," almost made him smile. Even now, she tried to hide behind her prickly pride.

"It's okay. There's nothing in here to bother you." Nothing but him, only she didn't need to know that.

"I've never...never swam in a lake before."

Her lips were right above his ear. She sounded breathless, and her voice trembled. "There's nothing to be afraid of," he crooned, and then, because he couldn't help himself, he turned his face slightly and nuzzled his nose against the plump, firm curve of her breast.

She screamed, making his ears ring. In the next instant, she launched herself out of his arms and thrashed her way wildly to the floating dock. The back view of her awkward, hasty climb from the water didn't do a thing to cool his libido. She seemed to be all long legs and woman softness and enticing freckles. The suit, now wet, was even more revealing. Not more revealing than a bikini, but that didn't seem to matter to his heated libido. He watched her huddle on the dock, wrapping her arms around herself, then hurriedly survey the water.

He owed her an apology. That made him disgruntled enough to grouse, "I'll be deaf for an hour. You screech like a wet hen."

Lizzy shook her head, and her teeth chattered. "Something touched me. Something brushed against my leg!"

Gabe stalled. So she hadn't screamed over his forwardness? From the looks of her, he thought, seeing how wild-eyed she appeared, she probably hadn't even noticed that he was turned on, that he'd been attempting to kiss her breast. Making a small sound of exasperation, Gabe said, "It was probably just a fish."

She shuddered in visible horror. "What kind of fish?"

He looked around, peering through the water, which was stirred up from her churning retreat. "There." Pointing, he indicated a small silvery fish pecking at bubbles on the surface of the lake.

Lizzy carefully leaned forward on her hands and knees, making her breasts sway beneath the wet green suit. "Is it a baby?"

He kept his gaze glued to her body. His tongue felt thick and his jaw tight. "No. A bluegill. They don't get much bigger than that."

Her gaze lifted and met his, forcing him to stop staring at her body. "What'd you expect," he asked, "Jaws?"

Her face heated. To Gabe, she looked sexy and enticing and adorable, perched on the edge of the floating dock, her bottom in the air, her eyes wide and her cheeks rosy. Her brows angled. "Are you laughing at me?"

"Nope." He waded over to her then leaned on his forearms. No way could he join her on the dock. His wet cutoffs wouldn't do much to hide his erection. "I didn't realize you were afraid of the water," he told her gently. "You should have said something."

After a deep breath, she sat back. She drew her knees up and wrapped her arms around them. "I was embarrassed," she admitted with a sideways look at him. "I hate being cowardly."

"It's not cowardly to be unsure of things you're not familiar with."

"Will you still answer my question?"

Annoyed that she wouldn't forget her purpose for even a minute, he shrugged. "Get it over with."

Her blue eyes lit with excitement, and she dropped her arms to lean toward him. Her nipples, he couldn't help noticing, were long and pointed.

She smiled. "What were you thinking when you went into the water to save those kids?"

"Thinking?"

"Yes. You saw they were in trouble, and you wanted to help. What did you think about? How you'd get them out, the danger, that your own life wasn't important…"

"Oh, for pity's sake. It wasn't anything like that."

Forgetting that he needed to stay in the water, he levered himself up beside her on the dock in one fluid movement. The dock bobbed, making her gasp and flatten her hands on the wood for balance. Water sluiced off his body as he dropped next to her then shook his head like a wet dog. Lizzy made a grab for him to keep from getting knocked in, but she released him just as quickly and frowned at him.

"So what was it like?"

He leaned back on his elbows and surveyed the bright sun, the cloudless sky. "Hell, I don't know. I didn't think anything. I saw the boat, saw the kids—and just reacted." Before she could say anything about that, he added, "Anyone would have done the same."

"No one did do the same. Only you."

He shrugged. "I'd already gone in. There was no reason for anyone else to."

"You were quicker to react."

"Maybe I just noticed the problem first."

When she shifted to face him, Gabe again eyed her breasts. He felt obsessed. Would her nipples be pink or a rosy brown?

She touched his arm. "Were you afraid?"

Annoyed by her persistence, he leaned back on the dock, covering his eyes with a forearm. "That's another question." Gabe wondered if she even realized he was male. He had a raging hard-on, he'd been staring at her breasts with enough intensity to set her little red head on fire, and she hadn't even noticed. He snorted. Or maybe she just didn't care. Maybe she found him so lacking, so unappealing, he could be naked and it wouldn't affect her.

Her small hand smacked against his shoulder. "Not fair! You didn't even really answer the first question."

He lowered his arm enough to glare at her. "You didn't really swim, so we're even."

Mulish determination set her features, then she turned to the water. Distaste and fear stiffened her shoulders and, amazed, Gabe realized she was going to get in.

"Lizzy…" He reached for her shoulder.

"If a snake eats me, it'll be on your head!" She stuck a toe in the water.

Smiling, Gabe pulled her back. "All right. I'll answer your question."

The tension seemed to melt right out of her. "You will?"

He sighed long and loud to let her know she was a pest. *Yeah, right.* "It beats seeing that look of terror on your face." He flicked her nose as he said it, to let her know he was teasing.

She paid him no mind, speaking to herself in a mumble. "I wish I had my notebook."

Gabe came to his knees, caught the line holding the boat secure and pulled it in. It was a stretch, but he was able to reach her bag and hand it to her. "There you go."

Her smile was beatific. "Thank you."

He gave her a gentlemanly nod. She didn't notice his body, but at least she appreciated his manners. "No problem. Not that I can tell you anything interesting enough to write down."

The look of concentration on her face as she pulled out her notepad told him she disagreed. Gabe thought how cute she was when she went all serious and sincere.

Not that a cute, redheaded virago should have interested him. Beyond making him unaccountably hot, that was.

Nose wrinkled against the glare of the sun, she looked at him and said, "I'm ready."

She looked ready, he thought, unable to keep his mind focused on the fact that he wasn't interested. Posed on the dock as she was, she made a fetching picture. Her long legs were folded to the side in the primmest manner possible, given her body was more bare than not. She tilted her head and pursed her lips in serious cogitation. The bright sunshine glinted off her hair, showing different colored strands of gold and amber and bronze. Midway down, her braid was darker from being wet, and it rested, heavy and thick, along her side. Her skin shone with a fine mist of sweat, intensifying her sweet scent so that with every small breeze he breathed her in.

His skin felt too hot, but not because of the sun.

Gabe wondered what she'd do if he eased her backward and covered her with his body. Would she scream again? He groaned, causing her to lift one brow. She hadn't screamed last time because of him. No, she hadn't even noticed his attention.

"What's wrong?"

Other than the fact he was attracted to a woman who shouldn't have appealed to him and didn't return the favor? He groaned again. "Not a thing." Once again he reclined on the small dock, crossing his arms behind his head. He was too long for the thing, so he let his knees stick over the side and hung his feet in the water. "Let's see. What did I think? Well, I cursed. I know that."

Pencil to paper, she asked, "What did you say?"

"It's not something to be repeated in front of a lady."

"Oh. I understand."

She scribbled quickly across her paper, making Gabe curious. But he already knew she wasn't about to reveal her words to him. "Thing is," he admitted, "I don't really remember thinking anything. I saw the kids and the woman, saw the boat, and I just dove in. I knew they could get hurt, and I knew I could help." He shrugged, not looking at her. "It's no more complicated than that."

"So," she said, her eyes narrowed in thoughtful speculation, "your heroism was instinctive, like a basic part of you?"

"It wasn't heroism, damn it, but yeah, I guess it was instinctive to just dive in and do what I could."

"Did you even think about the danger to yourself?"

Here he was, Gabe thought, lounging in front of her, half naked, and she hadn't even looked at him once. He knew, because he'd been watching her, waiting to see what she'd do when she saw he was aroused. She'd barely noticed him at all except to give him her disapproving looks.

It nettled him that she was on this ridiculous hero kick. He was a man, same as any other, but that obviously didn't interest her at all. He wanted her interest, though he shouldn't have. But looking at her made him forget that she wasn't his type, that he didn't care what she thought, that he was only here today on a lark, as a way to pass the time and have some fun.

He wasn't used to a woman being totally oblivious to his masculinity, and he damn sure didn't like it.

He wouldn't, in fact, tolerate it.

Speaking in a low, deliberately casual tone, he reminded her, "That's another question. I told you I'd answer one."

"But…"

"We could make another deal." He closed his eyes as he said it, as if it didn't matter to him one way or the other. The ensuing silence was palpable. He felt the dock rock the tiniest bit and knew she was shifting. In nervousness? In annoyance? If he looked at her, he'd be able to read the emotions in her big blue eyes. But he didn't want to see if it was only frustration that lit her gaze. He waited, held his breath.

And finally she said, "All right. What deal?"

He opened his eyes and pinned her, his heart pumping hard, his muscles twitching. "I'll answer another question—for a kiss."

She blinked at him, her long, gold-tipped lashes lazily drifting down and up again, as if she couldn't quite believe what he'd said. "A kiss?"

"Mm." He pointed to his mouth. His gaze never left her face, watching her closely. Anticipation, thick and electric, hummed in his veins. "Right here, right now. One question, one kiss."

She shifted again. The lake was still, the only sounds those of a cow occasionally bawling or the soft splash of a frog close to shore. Lizzy nibbled her lips—lush, wet lips. Her gaze, bright and direct, never left his face.

She drew a deep breath that made her breasts strain against the clinging material of the suit.

Her blue eyes darkened and her words, soft and uncertain, made him jerk in response.

"What…" she whispered, her breath catching before she cleared her throat and started again. "What if I kiss you twice?"

At least he was smooth-shaven today, Elizabeth thought as she watched Gabe's face, saw his eyes glitter and grow intent. She felt tense from her toes to her eyebrows, struggling endlessly to keep her gaze on his face and off his lean, muscled body. He was by far the most appealing man she'd ever known—and the most maddening.

When he continued to watch her, his eyes heavier, the blue so hot they looked electric, she made a sound of impatience. "Well?"

In husky tones, he asked, "Two kisses, hm?"

Much more and she'd be racing for the shore. She couldn't take his intensity, the way he stared at her, stroked her with his gaze. Her breasts felt full, her belly sweetly pulled with some indefinable ache. What could he possibly hope to gain with his present attitude? She didn't for a minute think he was actually attracted to her. For one thing, men simply didn't pay that much attention to her. More often than not, she could be invisible for all the notice they took. Secondly, she still remembered his reaction when they'd met. Gabriel Kasper had found her amusing, annoying and, judging by the way he'd looked her over, totally unappealing.

Perhaps, she continued to reason, he only hoped to

intimidate her! That would certainly make sense. She swallowed hard and refused to back down. She needed his knowledge. She craved the information that would make her understand what special qualities created a hero. Or a heroine.

His mouth, firm and sensual, wholly masculine, twitched slightly. "Two kisses, two questions."

It was what she'd wanted. And then he added, "Ten kisses, ten questions—but understand, Lizzy, I'm only a man. Kisses are all I can barter and remain a…gentleman." He turned his head slightly toward her, and his voice dropped. "Or does that matter?"

She stiffened. Did he suggest her kisses could make him lose control? Not likely! Mustering her courage, she asked, "Why are you doing this?"

"This…what?"

She waved a hand at his lazy form. "This game. Why trade for kisses? Why trade at all? Is it really so hard to answer a short interview?"

His jaw tightened, and he shut his eyes again. After a moment, still looking more asleep than alert, he said, "You need to loosen up a little, Red. It's a nice afternoon, the sun is warm, the water's cool. We're all alone. Why not play a little?" He looked at her, his gaze probing. "Is the idea of kissing me so repulsive?"

She filled her lungs with a deep breath. So she was just a game, a way to pass the time. The arrogant jerk. She'd have to remember to make a note of that, that some heroes were not always perfect in their behavior, some of them enjoyed toying with women.

She straightened her shoulders, refusing to let him intimidate her. "No, not at all."

"Then we don't have a problem, do we?"

The only problem, evidently, was her inhibition. But in the face of all she could learn from him, did her reserve really matter? Suddenly determined, she squelched her nervousness and said with firm resolve, "Okay, a kiss for a question."

She waited, braced for his sensual assault, but Gabe simply continued to watch her. Not by so much as the flick of an eyelash did he move. Her stomach cramped the tiniest bit and she lifted an eyebrow.

She was both disappointed and relieved when she asked, "You've changed your mind?"

With one indolent shake of his head, Gabe crooked a finger at her. "C'mere, Red. You're going to do the kissing, not me."

In reaction to his potent look, more than her stomach cramped, but the feeling wasn't at all unpleasant.

"Oh." She looked at his gorgeous body stretched out in front of her—and started shaking. His shoulders were wide and bunched with muscles, as were his biceps. The undersides of his arms were smooth, slightly lighter than the rest of his skin. She'd never considered a man's armpits sexy before—just the thought was ludicrous—but she'd never seen Gabriel Kasper's. Seeing the hair under his arms was somehow too intimate, like a private showing. She looked away from that part of him.

His chest, tanned and sprinkled with golden brown hair, had the lean hard contours that spoke of a natural athlete. Her pulse fluttered.

His abdomen was flat, sculpted, and if his underarms were too personal, his navel was downright sexual. The way his body hair swirled around it, then became a silky line that disappeared into the very low waistband of his shorts… Her eyes widened.

With his wet cutoffs clinging to his body, there was no way to miss his obvious arousal. Fascinated, she couldn't help but stare for a moment. Never, not in real life, anyway, had she seen an erection. Heat exploded inside her, making her cheeks pulse, her vision blur.

Her gaze flew to his face, desperate, confused, *excited.* His grin, slow and wicked, taunted her. He didn't say a word, and she knew he was waiting for her to back down.

She couldn't. Not now, not with him challenging her. But…

Licking her lips, Elizabeth croaked, "Are you sure we should do this?"

He shrugged one hard shoulder in a show of negligence. "No one will see. Don't be a coward, Lizzy. It's just a kiss."

Just a kiss. She remembered how those women on the dock had hung on him, how every woman who passed in a boat had stared at him with hunger. He was used to kissing, used to so much more. She couldn't recall any other man in all her acquaintance ever demanding such a thing from her. No wonder she was at a loss as to how to proceed. She preferred to arm herself with knowledge, to learn from a book what she didn't understand. But she hadn't known to research this particular theme. She frowned with that thought. Were there books to help you bone up on kissing a sexy-as-sin, half-dressed reclining man?

She eyed him warily. "Why don't you…sit up?" The

idea of leaning over him, of being that close to so much masculine flesh, flustered her horribly.

Without hesitation, Gabe shook his head. "Naw, I'm already comfortable. So quit stalling."

He was right; the quicker she got it over with, the better. Like getting a tooth pulled, it meant just a flinch of pain, and then you were done.

Not giving herself time to think about it, she slapped one hand flat on the dock beside his head, bent down and brushed her mouth over his in a flash of movement. She straightened just as quickly and, avoiding his gaze, put her pencil to paper. Her voice shook slightly, but she ignored the tremor as she asked, "Now, when you leaped into the water with the runaway boat, were you afraid?"

"No."

She waited, her pencil ready, but he said no more. Elizabeth rounded on him, her nerves too frazzled for more games. "That's an awfully simplified answer."

He gave her a wry look. "It was an awfully simplified kiss."

Unable to help herself, she looked at his mouth. Her lips still tingled from the brief contact with his. It took all her concentration not to lick her lips, not to chew on them. Her heartbeat was still racing too quickly, her stomach was in knots of anticipation...no! Dread, not anticipation. She had to be philosophical. "You mean, if I made the kiss longer..."

So softly she could barely hear him, he said, "Why don't you give it a try and see?"

She could do this! She was not a fainthearted ninny.

Determination stiffened her spine. Sensual awareness sharpened her senses. She gave one quick nod.

Laying the pencil and paper aside, she bent, clasped her palms over his ears to anchor both him and herself, then kissed him for all she was worth.

Never having done much kissing, she had no idea if she was doing it right. But she mashed her mouth tightly to his, turned her head subtly so their lips meshed, and sighed. Or maybe it was more a growl filled with resolution.

His lips felt firm, warm. This close, his scent was stronger, drifting over her, making her insides fill with a new and unexpected need. He was so hot, his skin where they touched almost burning her. Her chin bumped his, their noses rubbed together, and her wrists rested on his silky hot shoulders. She stopped moving her mouth and simply breathed deeply.

Gabe groaned, then promptly laughed, startling her enough that she sat up and stared at him in hurt and confusion.

With a small smile, using only one rough finger, he stroked her bottom lip. His words were as gentle as his touch, and just as devastating. "You haven't done much kissing, have you, Lizzy?"

Indignation would be misplaced; obviously, he could already tell she was inexperienced, so why should she deny it or be embarrassed? He could see what she looked like, had even used the same insulting taunt of Red she'd heard in grade school. He could probably guess at the other names—freckle face and scarecrow. And no doubt he understood the way she'd been ignored in high school, when all the boys were chasing cheerleaders with bubbly personalities and model faces.

None of that hurt her anymore. She had found more important things to do with her time. With an accepting shrug, she agreed. "Pitifully little, actually." And even that was an exaggeration.

Amazingly, his smile turned seductive. He came up on his right elbow, wrapped the fingers of his left hand around her nape and pulled her close. Against her mouth, he whispered, "Then allow me."

His tongue... Oh gracious. His mouth opened hers with almost no effort. His tongue touched, teased, not really entering her mouth, but making her crazed with small licks and tastes, softly, wetly stroking. She held herself very still so as not to disturb him or interrupt his progress.

Slowly, in infinitesimal degrees, he pulled his mouth away. His hand still held her neck, his fingers caressing, and he stared at her mouth. "You're not kissing me back, Lizzy."

"I..." She hadn't realized he wanted her to. All her senses had been attuned to what he was doing, not what she might do. "Sorry."

With a groan, he took her mouth again, not so gently this time, a hungry greed coming through to curl her toes and make her fingers go numb. Elizabeth leaned into him, tilted her head the tiniest bit to better accept his mouth. She braced her hands against his chest, then jerked at how hot his skin was, the way his chest hair felt on her palms. Her breasts tingled, and below her stomach an insistent tingling demanded her attention.

She panted, and this time when his tongue touched her mouth, she captured it, stroking her tongue against him.

She wasn't sure if it was her heartbeat or his that rocked her. His hand left her head and captured her elbow. She found herself being slowly lowered to the dock, but she didn't care; she just wanted him to go on kissing her like this, creating the overwhelming turmoil inside her. She liked it. She liked him—his taste, his hardness, his scent.

His chest crushed her breasts, but not uncomfortably. It helped to ease the ache there, but then the ache intensified, especially when he moved, abrading her taut nipples. She gasped.

He was braced over her with his elbows on either side of her head. Tentatively, uncertain how far she should go, Elizabeth placed her hands on his back. His tongue stroked deeply and she moaned, arching into him.

Gabe pulled away with a curse. He stared into her eyes, his face so close she could see his individual lashes, and then with another soft curse he sat up and gave her his back.

She struggled for breath, not certain what had happened, if she'd done something wrong. She pressed her palms flat on the rough wooden dock and tried to secure herself. Her head was spinning, her heart beating so wildly she thought it might punch right out of her chest. Her lungs felt constricted, and she couldn't get enough air, which forced her to pant. And there was the most delicious tingling sensation deep inside her.

Gabe ran a hand through his hair, but he kept his

back to her. She could see the straight line of his spine, the shift of his muscles as he, too, breathed deeply, quickly. With his attention elsewhere, she devoured him with her eyes. His skin was bronzed, testimony to how much time he spent on the lake, and a striking contrast to his fair hair and burning blue eyes. His damp shorts rode low on trim hips, but all she could see was tanned flesh.

Abruptly he shifted and speared her with a look, as if he'd sensed her regard. Over his shoulder, his gaze razor sharp, he growled, "Ask your damn question."

Still gasping, Elizabeth tried to gather her wits. Question? Her muddled mind came up with one reply. "Are you tanned all over?"

No sooner had the words left her mouth than she realized her mistake. Gabe's eyes widened comically. There was a moment of startled hesitation, then he threw his head back and laughed, the sound bouncing off the placid surface of the lake to return to her again and again, making her brain hurt and her face throb with heat.

Appalled, she started to sit up, but just that quick, Gabe caught her shoulders and pinned her in place.

"Where are you going?" he asked, his voice a husky rumble. His mouth was still slightly curled in amusement.

Elizabeth tried to think. "I… I meant to ask you—"

"I know what you meant," he growled around another smile. "You want me to skin off my shorts so you can get a good look at my backside, just to appease your curiosity?"

Yes. "No, of course not!" He loomed over her, making rational thought impossible. But then, everything about Gabriel Kasper, from their first meeting to now, had been impossible.

"Liar." There was no insult in the accusation. In fact, he said it with amused affection, like an endearment. Then he kissed her again, softly, slowly. Elizabeth felt a constriction in her chest that had nothing to do with the way he held her and everything to do with the realization of all she'd missed in life.

The kiss wasn't consuming, but sweetly sensual. As Gabe lifted his head, he looked at her breasts, gently crushed against the hard planes of his chest. A slight tremble went through him as he swept one fingertip over the upper swell of each breast. "Are these real, sweetheart?"

Her breath strangled at the feel of his hot, rough finger stroking her there, in a place no man had ever touched. Eyes wide, she muttered, "What are you talking about?"

"You have such a sexy body." That taunting fingertip dipped slightly into her cleavage, causing her heart to pick up a quick, almost frantic beat. "And these breasts…so plump when you're so trim everywhere else. So soft when you're mostly firm. I just wondered if Mother Nature had really been so generous, or if you'd had a little help."

She stared at him, her mind blank, unable to think while he was touching her. She was aware of the sun hot against her skin, of the slight breeze that stirred the humid air, of the gentle lapping of the lake on the shore. But all of it was overshadowed by Gabe and the blue flare of his eyes.

Grinning, Gabe murmured, "Maybe I should just find out on my own?" His fingers spread over her chest, just below her collarbone, and jolted her into awareness.

She caught his wrist and stared at him hard. "They're real!" Then, because she was embarrassed over his attention, she muttered, "What a stupid question."

Gabe easily freed his hand from hers and wrapped his fingers around her skull, stroking her hair, smoothing it. "You must have never gone braless in your life."

Heat washed over her face, then down to her breasts. "Of course I haven't."

His thumb rubbed her cheekbone, the corner of her mouth. He shifted, his chest moving over hers, pressing. "Such a little innocent. Such a surprise." He looked at her mouth.

"Gabe?"

"Just one more," he whispered, husky and deep.

She thought to tell him that he'd owe her a lot of conversation for this, that she had plenty of questions he was going to have to answer, but the moment he took the kiss, she forgot all that.

His hand slid down her side to her waist, shaping her, measuring her, it seemed, then drifted to her hip. His touch was sure, his fingers rough, callused. He met bare skin on her upper thigh and made a raw sound of pleasure, causing her to quiver in response.

"So soft," he growled, his mouth against her throat, leaving damp kisses, sucking softly. Overwhelmed, alive, she tipped her head back to make it easier for him. His grip on her thigh tightened, and with little direction from him, she bent her knee and lifted one leg alongside his. The position neatly settled him into the cradle of her hips. She vaguely wondered why she didn't feel crushed, because he was so big, so hard.

He pushed, nestling closer, and his erection rubbed her in the most intimate spot imaginable. She gasped; he groaned.

She'd never felt a man on top of her before. The sensation was...*wonderful*. Scorching, enveloping, gratifying and at the same time stirring new needs.

Gabe dipped the tip of his tongue into her ear. That sensation, too, was astounding. How could such a simple act be so incredibly erotic? She heard his harsh breathing, felt his hot, moist breath and the hammering of his heart. He licked her ear. Stunned for just a moment, she froze, trying to take it all in.

He kissed her again. His mouth ate at hers, his teeth nipping, his tongue stroking. She melted, no longer capable of rational thought, simply reacting to what he did and how he did it.

In the next instant he was gone, sitting up beside her.

Elizabeth blinked in shock, uncertain what had happened or why he had pulled away so abruptly. She lay there, her eyes open but unseeing, trying to assimilate her senses. Gabe never hesitated. He caught her arms just above her elbows and jerked her upright so that she, too, was sitting, although not quite as steadily as he. It took a lot of effort not to flop down. She felt boneless and flushed and limp. Mute, she stared at him.

He gave her a grim, somewhat apologetic look and then she heard the motor. They both turned to stare at the entrance to the lake.

Seconds later a small fishing boat similar to the one

they had used rounded the bend into the cove. Two older men, goofy hats hooked with a variety of lures perched on their heads, concentrated on the long fishing lines they had dragging in the water. Their voices were barely audible over the steady drone of the trolling motor.

They looked up in surprise when they noticed Gabe. Almost as one, their gazes turned to Elizabeth, and she felt herself turning pink with embarrassment. Good grief, could they tell what she and Gabe had been doing? Would they be able to look at her face and see it all?

Gabe moved, leaning forward to block her from view. He waved at the men, who waved back and continued to stare at them until their boat nearly went aground. With a disgruntled curse, the man in the back redirected their course and they puttered out of sight.

Gabe turned to her, his gaze probing and direct. Unable to look away, Elizabeth thought how unfair it was that he could completely snare her with just a look. Eyes so light and clear a blue should have appeared cool, not fiery and passionate.

His fair hair shimmered beneath the sunshine, mussed from his swim—and from her fingers. Every muscle in his tensed body was delineated, drawing her eyes. He watched her so intently, she almost flinched.

Swallowing hard, Elizabeth tried to think of what to say. It was nearly impossible to muster a straight, businesslike face after that…that… She didn't know what to call it. It was certainly far more than a mere kiss. Admittedly, she lacked experience, but she was certainly not stupid. She knew the difference between kissing and what they'd just done.

It wasn't easy, but she reminded herself of her original purpose, her continued purpose. All her life she'd struggled to deal with the idiosyncrasies of heroism, why some had those qualities and some did not. Having heroism gave you the ability to change lives, lacking it could leave you forever empty.

She met Gabe's eyes and cleared her throat. "Well, after that, I expect an entire explanation for my thesis."

She hadn't meant to sound so cold and detached; what she really felt was far different from those simple emotions. She'd only meant to stress the point of what they were doing and why.

Gabe's eyes darkened, narrowed, the heat leaving them as if it had never been there. His jaw flexed once, then stilled. He stared at her mouth and said, "You'll get it."

Chapter 4

He wanted to shake her, to… God, he'd never had the inclination to do any more than make love with a woman, laugh with her, tease. But Lizzy had him crazed.

He'd all but taken her on the damn dock, out in the open, on the lake, for crying out loud.

And she'd have let him.

He sensed it in his bones. He knew women, knew how they thought, what they felt, when they were turned on and how to turn them on. Little Red had been wild. She'd bit his bottom lip, sucked on his tongue, lifted her hips into the thrust of his… She'd strained against him, trying to get closer, and her fluttering heartbeat had let him measure each new degree of her excitement. She'd been on the ragged edge. He could have slipped his fingers past the leg band of her suit and stroked her over the edge with very little effort.

But now she watched him as though it had never happened, demanding answers to questions that were beyond stupid.

"I need to cool off." With no more warning than that, Gabe went over the side of the dock. He swam down until he touched the bottom, feeling around for a shell. When he surfaced, Lizzy was hanging over the edge, watching for him anxiously. He pushed wet hair from his face and forced himself not to eye her breasts.

"You scared me!" She stared at him in accusation, looking like a wild woman. Thanks to his hands, long strands of hair had escaped her thick braid in various places, giving her a woolly-headed look, like a damn red thistle. Her smooth cheeks were flushed, making the freckles more pronounced. Her lush mouth, which had felt so hot and hungry under his only moments before, was pressed into a severe line.

Gabe almost laughed. Hell, she wasn't even pretty, not really, and she sure as certain didn't have the right temperament to lure a man. So why had he reacted so strongly?

"Here." He handed her the shell, watched her sit back, bemused, to look it over. "It's just a mussel. The bottom of the lake is littered with them. I dated a girl for a while who used to find live ones and eat them raw."

Lizzy's head jerked up, and she dropped the shell. Her lip curled in a way that made her look ready to vomit. No, she looked far from pretty right now.

Gabe laughed out loud. "Gross, huh? I couldn't quite

bring myself to kiss her again after that. I kept thinking of what had been in that mouth. Have you ever seen a live mussel? They're sort of slimy and gray."

She covered her mouth with a hand, swallowed hard, then sat back and glared at him some more. "Are you going to stay in there, or will you get out and answer my question?"

"Answer one for me first, okay?"

Her blue eyes widened, and he had to admit that they, at least, were beautiful. No matter her mood, her eyes were a focal point in her face, vivid and filled with curiosity and intelligence. He liked the color, dark and deep, unlike his faded, washed-out color. With the sun reflecting off the lake, he could see green and black and navy striations in her irises, lending richness to the unique color. As he studied her eyes, her pupils flared, reminding him how quickly she'd gotten aroused with him.

Arousing Little Red was fun, indeed. And from what he could tell, she could use a little fun in her life. Maybe it'd take some of the starch out of her spine and some of the vinegar out of her speech.

He propped his crossed arms over the edge of the dock, facing her and smiling into her stern face. "Where'd you get that suit?"

Bemused, she looked at herself, then at him. She plucked nervously at the material by her waist. "I... well, I hadn't owned a suit before this. You insisted we needed to swim, so I had to go get one last night. But I couldn't see spending a lot of money on one when this would likely be the only time I wore it. So I grabbed the cheapest one I could find."

"The cheapest one-piece?"

Her lips trembled, fascinating him. "I'm not exactly the type to wear a bikini."

"Why not?" His voice dropped despite his effort to sound dispassionate. "You have an incredible body, Lizzy." He was serious, but he could tell by the way her eyes darkened and she looked away that she didn't believe him.

"Lizzy?" She wouldn't look at him. His heart softened, felt too thick in his chest. Very gently he asked, "When was the last time you looked at yourself naked?"

Her head snapped up, her cheeks hectic with hot color. Her mouth opened twice, but nothing came out. Finally she glared and said with acerbity, "Why do you deliberately try to embarrass me? Is that your idea of fun, to make me feel…feel…"

"Feel what, sugar?" His hand was a scant inch from her small foot, and he caught her ankle, using his thumb to caress her arch. "Shy? You shouldn't. There's not a woman on this lake that looks better in her suit than you. Why don't you know that?"

Her auburn brows snapped down so fiercely, he expected her to get a headache. "I don't know what you're up to, Gabriel Kasper, but I'm not blind. I'm well aware of how I look, and if it wasn't for you and your ridiculous stipulations, I wouldn't be here now, sitting in this ridiculous suit!"

"You've enjoyed yourself," he felt compelled to remind her, then held on tight when she tried to draw her foot away.

"It was…unexpected." She looked prim and righteous, and he felt his blood heating in masculine reaction to her silent challenge. "As you've already surmised, I haven't done much kissing in my lifetime. I looked at this as sort of a...a learning experience."

Gabe grinned, his thumb still brushing sensually over her foot, making her stiffen. "So I'm sort of a class project, huh? Will you write another thesis? What I did over the summer vacation?"

Like a small volcano erupting, she jerked away and scrambled out of his reach. Her hands flattened on the dock to push herself upright, then she squealed and lifted a finger to her mouth.

Gabe watched her antics with curiosity. "What are you doing?"

"I'm leaving," she grumbled, still looking at her finger. "I realize now that you have no intention of answering my questions, and I can't afford to waste the time with you otherwise."

So he was a waste of time? Like hell! He'd make her eat those words. Gabe levered himself onto the dock, and his weight set it off kilter, causing Lizzy to tilt into him. Her attention was still on her finger.

"I'll answer your damn question, so quit frowning."

She gave him a skeptical, disbelieving look, then went back to frowning.

"What's wrong with you? Did you hurt yourself?" He leaned over her shoulder to see her hand, and as usual, she pulled it close to her chest as if protecting it from him.

"I have a splinter, thanks to you." As an afterthought, she added, "It hurts."

Gabe wrested her hand away from her body and looked at the injured finger. A jagged piece of wood was imbedded under the pad of her middle finger. "Damn. That sucker is huge."

She tried to pull her hand free. She did that constantly, he realized, always pulling away from him. Well, not constantly. When he'd been kissing her, she'd strained against him.

"I can get it out."

"No!" She tugged again, finally gaining her release. "I can take care of it after I get home. If you're ready to leave?"

Gabe chewed the side of his mouth. "Actually, no, I'm not ready to leave. You have a question for me, and I'll answer it. But first let me take care of this."

"Gabe…"

"Stop being such a sissy. I won't hurt you."

Her chin firmed, her lips pursed, and then she thrust her hand toward him. "Fine. Do your worst."

Without hesitation, Gabe lifted her finger to his mouth. He heard Lizzy gasp, felt her tremble. Probing with his tongue, he located the end of the splinter, then carefully, gently closed his teeth around it. It pulled out easily.

He smiled at her, still with her hand close to his mouth. "There. That wasn't so bad, was it?"

She had that glazed look in her eyes again, like the one she'd had before the fishing boat had interrupted. Unable to help himself with her looking so flustered and shivering, he held her gaze and kissed her fingertip. Her pupils dilated, her lips parting. Damn, but she was quick to react—which made him react, too.

It was if they were connected by their gazes, an intimate hold that he'd never quite experienced before.

Gabe touched the tip of his tongue to her finger and heard her inhalation of breath. Her eyes grew heavy, her lashes dipping down. He drew her finger into his mouth and sucked softly. With a moan, she closed her eyes.

Damn, it was erotic. *She* was erotic. Moving her finger along his bottom lip, he said, "Being in the water is second nature to me. It never scares me."

He was shocked by how husky his voice had become, but still, it jarred her enough that her eyes opened. Gabe dipped his tongue between her fingers, licked along the length of one. "I'm as at home in the water as I am on land. Especially this lake. I never once considered there was any danger to me, because there wasn't, so I wasn't afraid."

"Oh."

He moved to her thumb, drawing it into his mouth and tugging gently, just as he might with a breast. The thought inflamed him.

"After the kids and their mother were out of the way, I didn't have time to think or be afraid. I just reacted."

"I... I see."

Her voice was so low and rough he could barely understand her. She watched him through slitted eyes, her body swaying slightly. "I learned to drive boats when I was knee-high to a grasshopper. I started working on boat motors when I was ten, knew more about them than most grown men by the time I was fourteen."

He licked her palm, then the racing pulse in her wrist.

"Because I knew what I was doing, there was no danger, no reason to be afraid."

"I see."

Her eyes were closed, her free hand curled into a fist, her breasts heaving.

"Therefore," Gabe added, as he started to lower her once again, "I'm not what you'd call a hero at all."

Her back no sooner touched the dock than she bolted upright. Her head smacked his chin with the force of a prizefighter's blow. She blinked hard, rubbed her head and scowled at him.

After working his jaw to make certain she hadn't broken anything, Gabe asked, "Are you all right?"

"You've given me a concussion."

He smiled. "I have not." Then: "Why'd you get so jumpy?"

"I need to write everything down before I forget it."

Rolling his eyes, Gabe said, "So you're finally satisfied?" No sooner did the words leave his mouth than he looked at her spectacular breasts, saw her pointed nipples and knew true satisfaction was a long way off. Not that she'd ever admit it.

Her gaze downcast, she said simply, "I'm satisfied—for that question. But I have so many more." Looking at him, a soft plea in her gaze, she asked, "Will it really be so difficult to let me get some answers?"

Damn, he wanted her. He wanted to see that look on her face when she was naked beneath him. It defied reason and went against everything he knew about his preferences and inclinations. She was so far from the type of woman who usually caught his eye that it was almost laughable.

But it didn't change the facts.

Gabe chucked her chin. "I'm willing if you are."

"Meaning?"

There was a note of caution in her tone that made him smile with triumph. "Meaning as long as we stick to our original bargain, I'll answer your questions. One kiss per question."

Lizzy turned her head to stare at the lake. There was a stillness about her that he hadn't seen before, and it made him uneasy.

"Because this is important to me," she said without inflection, "I'll agree if you insist. But what we've just been doing...that was more than kissing." She turned her big blue eyes on him and added, "Wasn't it?"

Sure felt like more to him! But he'd never admit that to her. He had a feeling that if she knew how she'd turned him on, how close he'd gotten to losing all control, she'd never agree to see him again, much less let him kiss her. "It's not a big deal, Lizzy. You don't have to worry for your reputation or your chastity."

Her lips tightened, giving her a wounded look. Gabe cursed. He'd wanted to reassure her, not make light of their mutual attraction. "I didn't mean..."

"Why?" She turned to face him. "Why is it so important for you to toy with me?"

"I'm not toying with you, damn it."

She obviously didn't believe him. "Do you enjoy seeing me flustered, embarrassed? Do you enjoy knowing this is all very strange to me?"

A direct attack. He hadn't been expecting it, no more than he'd anticipated her vehemence. He watched her, but she once again avoided his gaze. After some thought, Gabe said honestly, "I like you. And it's for certain I like kissing you." She made an exasperated sound, but he continued. "You're different from the women I know around here."

"You mean I'm odd?"

He laughed at the suspicious accusation in her tone and look. "No, that's not what I mean. I've known most of the women in these parts for all of my life. They're entirely comfortable with me and with their own sexuality."

She slanted him a look. "I'm odd."

"No, you are not!" He tucked a long tendril of hair behind her ear, still smiling. "You're a…contradiction. Sweet and sassy—"

"What a sexist remark!"

"—and pushy but shy. You intrigue me. I guess it's tit for tat. Just as you seem to want to know what makes me tick, I want to know what makes you tick. It's as simple as that."

"It doesn't feel simple."

"That's because you're evidently not used to men paying you attention." She didn't answer his charge, and he frowned. Catching her chin and bringing her face around to his, he asked the question uppermost in his mind. "Why is that, Lizzy?"

She shook her head, her lips scrunched together.

"I figure you must be…what? Twenty-two?"

She looked at the sky. "Almost twenty-three."

"Yet you had no idea how to kiss. What girl gets through high school these days, much less college, without doing some necking?"

She glared at him and growled, "Redheaded, freck-led, gangly girls who are shy and bookish, apparently."

Gabe took a telling perusal of her body. "Sweetheart, you're not gangly. Far from it."

She stared at him hard for at least three heartbeats, then asked with endearing caution, "Really?"

Tenderness swelled over him, taking him by surprise. "Didn't your mother ever tell you that you'd filled out real nice?"

She clasped her hands in her lap and shook her head. "My mother died when I was twelve."

Gabe scooted closer to her and put his arm around her sun warmed shoulders. He didn't question his need to hold her, to touch her. "Friends? Sisters?"

Shaking her head, she explained, "I'm an only child. And I didn't really have that many friends in school." As if admitting a grave sin, she added, "I was always very backward until recently."

Gabe squeezed her gently. "You're hardly a robust conqueror now."

"I know. It's not easy for me to do all these interviews, but they're important, so I do them." Her expression turned mocking. "Most of them have been fairly quick and simple."

"Then it's a good thing you ran into me, huh? Because lady, if anyone ever needed shaking up a little, it's you."

"I need to complete my thesis."

"You have the rest of summer break, right?"

She nodded warily, obviously uncertain of his intent.

"So why don't we indulge each other? I'll answer any questions you have, and in return, you'll let me convince you how adorable you are in that bathing suit."

Her chin tucked in close to her chest. "Convince me...how?"

"By what we've already been doing. I won't ever push you further than you want to go, you have my word on that. But I can promise there'll be more kissing." His hand cradled her head. "You won't mind that so much, will you, Lizzy?"

She didn't reply to that, and she didn't look convinced. In a slightly choked voice that gave away her tension, she said, "I need you to be more specific than that."

Gabe chewed it over, trying to think of how to couch his terms so she would be reassured. "Okay, how's this. I'll answer a question and you'll cut loose a little, my choice of how. And before you start arguing, first I want you to go to a drive-in with me. You ever been to the drive-in?"

"With my father when I was young. I didn't even know they still had them."

"You're in for a treat!" *And I'm in for a little torture.* "We can go over to the next county, to the Dirty Dixie." He bobbed his eyebrows. "They play fairly raunchy movies—which will probably be another first for you, right?"

Looking dazed, she nodded.

"Perfect. How about this Friday? That's two days away, plenty of time for you to get used to the idea." *And plenty of time for him to get a better grip on himself.*

She hesitated once again and Gabe held his breath. Then she nodded. "All right. Where should I meet you?"

"Ah, no," he told her gently, knowing she wanted

to keep him at a distance and knowing, too, that he wouldn't allow it. "You'll give me your address and phone number. I pick up the women I take on dates, Lizzy, I don't *meet* them."

She seemed to consider that, then shrugged in feigned indifference. Taking up her pencil, she jotted her address and phone number. Gabe accepted the scrap of paper, then slipped off the edge of the dock and waded to the boat to put it in his cooler for safekeeping.

Lizzy, watching him in the water, said, "I'm renting the upstairs from this nice single mother. She has two young children and needed the extra money."

Gabe knew she was prattling out of nervousness. He hated to see an end to the day, but he checked his waterproof watch and saw it was time to go. "We'd better head back. I have some work to do."

"I thought you didn't have a job."

Looking at her from the other side of the boat, he gave her a wide grin. "Angling for another question? All right, I can be generous." He propped his forearms over the metal gunwale and explained, "I don't have a regular job, but I have more work than I can handle. I'm sort of a handyman and this time of year everyone needs something built, repaired or revamped. And that's all I'm telling you, so get that look out of your eyes."

"Spoilsport."

Gabe maneuvered the boat close to the dock. "Since I now know you're afraid of the water—something you should have told me right off—I'll be gallant and hold the boat steady for you to climb in."

"You won't expect me to get in the water again?"

He shook his head at her hopeful expression. "Oh, I imagine we'll get you used to it little by little. After all, what's the use of taking a vacation near a lake if you don't want to get wet? But for today you've had enough."

She couldn't quite hide her relief. "Thanks."

Using exaggerated caution, she scooted off the dock and into the boat. Gabe watched the way her long legs bent, how her breasts filled the snug suit, how her bottom settled neatly on the metal seat, heated by the sun.

Damn, he was in deep. And he couldn't even say why. In the normal course of things, a woman like Ms. Elizabeth Parks shouldn't have appealed to him at all. She was uptight, pushy, inexperienced…but she was also funny and curious and she had about the sweetest body he'd ever seen.

With a muttered curse against his fickle libido, Gabe hauled himself over the side of the boat, which made her squeal and grab the seat with a death grip. "You can thank me Friday night," he told her, and wondered if he'd be able to keep his hands off her even then. Two days didn't seem like near enough time to get himself together.

But it did seem like an eternity when already he wanted her so bad his hands were shaking.

Gabe felt the sun on his shoulders, smelled the newly mown grass and breathed a deep sigh of contentment. Or at least, he'd be content if he could get a redheaded wonder out of his head. He steered the tractor mower toward the last strip of high grass by rote. He and his brothers had so much property, they only kept up the acres surrounding the house. Beyond that, the land was filled with wild shrubs and colorful flowers and mature trees of every variety. It was gorgeous in the fall, when the leaves changed color, but Gabe liked summer best.

His mother used to accuse him of being part lizard, because the heat seldom bothered him, and he was always drawn to the sunshine.

Life had been different since his two oldest brothers had married. Different in a very nice way. He enjoyed having Honey around. She made the house feel homier in some small indefinable ways, like the smell of her scented candles in the bathroom after she'd been indulging in a long soak, or the way she always hugged him when he left the house, cautioning him to be careful—as if he ran around risking his neck whenever he went out the door.

Gabe grinned. He could still recall how Honey had cried when Morgan had moved to his own house. Never mind that it was just up the hill; she liked having all the brothers as near as possible. It was a huge bonus that Morgan had married her sister, Misty. The two women were very close and managed to get together every day, especially since Misty had given birth to an adorable little girl seven months ago. Amber Marie Hudson was about the most precious thing he'd ever seen. And watching his brother fuss over the baby was an endless source of entertainment.

Females flat-out fascinated Gabe, whether they were seven months, twenty-seven or seventy. He didn't think he'd ever tire of learning more about them.

He was pondering what he might learn from a certain redhead when he saw a car pull into their long drive. Gabe stopped the tractor and watched, a feeling of foreboding creeping up his sweaty back. The car, a small purple Escort, looked suspiciously like the one he'd seen Lizzy park at the docks. He'd noticed because the purple clashed so loudly with her hair.

And sure enough, even from this distance, when she stepped out of the car, there was no mistaking the fiery glint of the sun off her bright head.

Scowling, he put the tractor in gear and headed toward the house. He was aware of a strange pounding in his chest, hoping to intercept her before any of his brothers saw her. Or worse, before Honey or Misty saw her.

But his hopes were in vain. Just as he neared the drive the front door opened and there stood Honey, her long blond hair moving gently in the breeze, her killer smile in place.

Oh, hell.

He watched in horror as Lizzy was evidently invited in, as she accepted and as the door closed behind her. The tractor was too damn slow so he stopped it, turned it off and ran the rest of the way.

His chest was heaving and he was dripping sweat by the time he bolted through the front door. No one was in sight. He hurried down the hallway to the family room, finding it empty. He stopped, trying to listen. A feminine laugh caught his attention, and he raced for the kitchen. He had to stop her before she said too much, before she started in with her questions—before anyone found out he'd been kissing her....

He skidded to a halt on the tile floor. The kitchen

was crowded, what with Honey and her sister and Amber and Sawyer… Gabe stared at Lizzy, seated at the table with her back to him.

Sawyer was looking her over—not politely, but in minute detail. He leaned over Lizzy with his fingers grazing her cheek, so close to her she could probably feel his breath, for God's sake.

Gabe's brows snapped down to match Sawyer's frown, and he demanded, "What the hell is going on?"

Everyone looked up. Honey was the first to speak, saying, "Gabe. I was just about to come get you."

Misty shook her head at him in a pitying way, as if he'd gotten himself into trouble somehow, and Amber cooed at the sound of his voice. Gabe ignored them all to stare at his oldest brother.

Of course Lizzy would have to call at lunchtime, he thought darkly, when everyone was bound to be around. Normally Sawyer would have been in his office at the back of the house, treating patients. Luckily, to his mind, Jordan always ate lunch in town. Morgan used to, too, until he married Misty. Now he was likely to show up any minute. Gabe needed to get Lizzy out of the house before she said too much about their association. He could imagine the ribbing he'd take if his brothers knew he was interested in—as in majorly turned on by—a prickly little redheaded witch with freckles!

His face heated at the mere thought.

Then Lizzy turned to look at him, and he knew the heat in his face was nothing compared to hers.

His frown intensified, but for different reasons, as

he drifted closer, studying her every feature. "Damn, Lizzy, what happened?"

She was bright pink with sunburn, her nose red, her soft mouth slightly puffy. Without thinking about his rapt audience, he knelt in front of her chair and smoothed a wayward tendril of hair gently behind her ear. God, even the tops of her ears were red!

She licked her lips, looking horribly embarrassed and glancing around at the others. "I'm fine, Gabe," she murmured, trying to get him to stand up while sneaking glances at his family. "There's no reason for this fuss."

He paid no attention at all to her words, too intent on discovering every speck of skin that had been reddened. "I thought you had sunscreen on yesterday."

"I did," she assured him, looking more wretchedly miserable by the minute. "I guess it wasn't strong enough, or maybe it washed off in the water."

Sawyer made an impatient sound, recalling Gabe to the fact that he was on his knees in front of Lizzy, treating her like the most precious woman in the world. He jerked to his feet, but he still couldn't take his concerned gaze off her. "Does it hurt?"

"No." She tried a weak smile, then flinched. "Truly. I'm fine."

Sawyer rudely pushed Gabe aside. "I'm going to give you some topical ointment for the sting. In the meantime, stay out of the sun—" and here he glared at Gabe "—and wear very loose clothes. It doesn't look like you'll blister, but I'd say you're going to be plenty uncomfortable for the next few days."

Honey stepped up with some folded paper towels

soaked in cool tea. "This'll help. I'm fair-skinned, too, and it's always worked for me."

Misty leaned close to watch as Honey patted the towels gently in place on Elizabeth's bare shoulders. Gabe realized that Lizzy wore a shapeless white cotton dress, so long it hung to her ankles. He looked closely and could see by the soft fullness beneath the bodice that she wasn't wearing a bra. His heart skipped a beat.

She'd said she never went braless, and her breasts were so firm and round, he believed her. The sunburn must indeed be painful for her to go without one.

To distract himself, he looked around the room and settled on smiling at the baby. At his attention, Amber flailed her pudgy arms from her pumpkin seat on the table, gurgling and blowing spit bubbles. Gabe laughed. "Sorry, kiddo. I'm too sweaty to hold you right now."

Elizabeth watched as he reached out and tweaked the baby's toe, and he knew she was planning on putting that into her little notebook, too. He scowled.

Morgan stepped in through the kitchen door and went immediately to Misty, lifting her into a bear hug that led to a lingering, intimate kiss. The way Misty continued to flush at her husband's touch always tickled Gabe. Morgan had been well and fully tamed.

He turned and hauled Amber out of her chair and against his chest, then nuzzled the baby's downy black hair. Amber squealed as he settled her in the crook of his arm.

Only then did Morgan notice Elizabeth. One dark brow shot up. "Hello."

Misty shook the dreamy look off her face and

smiled. "Morgan, this is Elizabeth Parks, a friend of Gabe's."

Morgan's enigmatic gaze transferred to Gabe, and Gabe felt his face heat again. "She looks done to a crisp, Gabe. I suppose you weren't…ah, paying attention to the sun? Had your mind on…other things?"

Gabe stiffened and said, "You know I can't hit you while you're holding the baby. Care to give her to her mother?"

"Nope." He kissed the baby's tiny ear and with a grin turned to Elizabeth. "Nice to meet you, Elizabeth."

She nodded. "And you, Sheriff."

"You're joining us for lunch?"

"Oh. No, please. I just… I'm sorry to impose. Really." Her attention flicked nervously to Gabe as all his interfering relatives assured her she was no imposition at all. "I just had a few questions, if you have the time."

Morgan pulled out a chair. "Questions about what?"

Gabe stepped forward before she could answer. "Lizzy, I'd like to talk to you. In private."

She stalled, staring at him with a guilty expression.

Sawyer nudged him aside. "I've only got fifteen minutes left before I have to see a patient. You can wait that long, can't you, Gabe?"

He wanted to say no, he damn well couldn't wait, but he knew that would only stir up more speculation. So instead he took the cool towels from Honey and began placing them on Lizzy's shoulders. A thought struck him, and he looked at her feet, set together primly beneath the long skirt. She wore thick white socks and slip-on shoes.

He gave her an exasperated look. "Your feet are burned, too, I suppose?"

Not since he'd met her had Lizzy been so withdrawn. She kept her wide eyes trained on him and nodded. In a tiny voice, she admitted, "A little."

Gabe knelt and very carefully pried off her loose loafers, then peeled the socks off her feet. Like a wet hen, Lizzy fussed and complained and tried to shoo him away. He persisted, despite Morgan's choked laugh and Sawyer's hovering attention.

Her feet were small and slender. Looking at how red they were, Gabe had the awful urge to kiss them better, and instead looked at her with a warning in his gaze. "You should be at home, naked, instead of running around all over the place, asking your crazy questions."

Honey gasped. Morgan guffawed, making Amber bounce in delight. Misty smacked Gabe's shoulder.

But Sawyer agreed. "He's right. Wearing clothes right now is just going to aggravate the sunburn. Taking cool baths and using plenty of aloe, and some ibuprofen for the pain, is the best thing you could do for yourself right now." He glared at Gabe. "Of course if baby brother here had remembered that not everyone is a sun worshiper with skin like leather, there wouldn't be a problem."

Gabe gritted his teeth. "I'm well aware of how delicate a woman's skin is. I thought she had sunscreen on. Besides, we weren't really out in the sun that long."

Lizzy stirred uncomfortably. "Gabe's right. This is my fault, not his. I guess I hadn't counted on the sun's reflection off the lake being so strong."

"Water does magnify the sun," Sawyer agreed, then

propped his hands on his hips and asked in his best physician's voice, "Are you burned anywhere else?"

Lizzy shook her head and at the same time said, "Just my legs." But as Gabe started to lift her skirt he slapped his hands away. Her tone was both horrified and embarrassed. "Don't even think it!"

He grinned. She was behaving more like herself, and he was vastly relieved. He didn't like seeing her so quiet and apprehensive. "Sorry. Just trying to see how bad it is."

She scowled. "Mostly on my knees, and you can just take my word on that, Gabriel Kasper."

Morgan leaned back in his seat, both brows lifted. Everyone stared at them, transfixed. Gabe remembered what he was doing and came to his feet again. How the hell did he keep ending up on his knees in front of her?

After setting a platter of sandwiches on the table, Honey said, "Join us for lunch, okay? What would you like to drink? I have tea and lemonade and—"

"Oh, no. Really, I didn't mean to catch you at a bad time." Lizzy reached for the towels on her shoulders, meaning to remove them. "I can just come back another time if you agree to a short interview."

Gabe let out a gust of relief. "That's a good idea. Come on, I'll walk you to your car."

But Lizzy hadn't even gotten the first towel removed before everyone rejected her intentions and insisted she stay. Hell, they *begged* her to stay, the nosy pests.

Well, they could do as they pleased, Gabe decided, but that didn't mean he had to stick around and take part in it. "I'm going to go shower," he announced, and of course, that was just fine and dandy. No one begged *him* to stick around! Irritated, he stomped out of the room, but before he'd even rounded the corner, he heard Morgan start chuckling, and before long, they were all laughing hysterically.

Everyone but Lizzy.

Chapter 5

Elizabeth bit her lip, not sure what was so funny. She hoped they weren't laughing at her, but then Honey gave her a big smile and said, "Gabe is so amusing sometimes."

Elizabeth had no idea how she meant that, and she didn't ask. She cleared her throat and said, "I'm doing a thesis on heroes for my college major. I've been working on it for some time, and I'd just about finished, then I heard about the boating incident here last summer and decided to add Gabriel to my notes."

Morgan tilted his head. "What boating incident?"

That set her back. His own brother wasn't aware of what had happened? But Misty waved a hand and explained to her husband, "I'm sure she's talking about Gabe saving that woman and her children, right?"

Elizabeth nodded.

"That was right after our wedding. Morgan wasn't paying much attention to what happened around him back then."

Morgan gave his wife a smoldering look. "You're to blame for that, Malone, not me. Can I help it if you're distracting?"

Honey laughed. "Stop it, you two, or you'll embarrass our guest." She sat herself on her husband's lap, and Sawyer wrapped his arms around her. "Gabe is a real sweetheart, Elizabeth. We just enjoy teasing him a little."

Elizabeth could attest to the sweetheart bit. From what she'd found out so far, there didn't live a finer example of the term *lady's man*. She cleared her throat. "So you *do* remember the event?"

"Sure." Honey settled comfortably against her husband's wide chest. To Elizabeth's amazement, Sawyer Hudson managed to eat that way, as if having his wife on his lap was a common occurrence. He quickly devoured three sandwiches, which was one less than Morgan ate. Misty and Honey each nibbled on a half. Since they were insistent, Elizabeth took a bite of one herself. She hadn't realized she was hungry until then.

The sunburn had made her so miserable she'd only wanted to find something to do, to keep her mind off it. Her skin felt too tight, itchy and burning. Clothes were a misery—Sawyer Hudson was right about that. But she simply wasn't used to parading around naked and had decided to take her mind off it by finding out more about Gabe before their trip to the movies.

"Can you tell me about it?" Elizabeth asked after a large drink of icy lemonade. With the cool towels on her shoulders and the uncomfortable shoes off her feet, she felt much better.

"Sure." Honey looked thoughtful for a moment, then turned to Morgan. "You ended up arresting the driver of that boat, right?"

Morgan growled, his tone so threatening that Elizabeth jumped. "The fool was drunk and could have damn well killed somebody. If it had been up to me, he'd have lost not only his boating license, but his driver's license, as well. As it turned out, though, he was banned from the lake, got a large fine and spent a week in jail. Hell, that poor woman was so shook up, Sawyer had to give her a sedative."

Sawyer nodded and his tone, in comparison to Morgan's was solemn. "She thought one or both of her kids would be hurt. She was almost in shock." Then he smiled. "When I got there, I found Gabe with a kid in his arms, one wrapped around his leg, and the woman gushing all over him. The look of relief on Gabe's face when he spotted me was priceless."

Elizabeth reached for her bag on the floor by her chair and extracted her notebook and pencil. "Can you describe it for me?"

"What?"

"The look on his face."

Sawyer appeared startled by her request, then shrugged. "Sure."

It was only fifteen minutes before Gabe rejoined them, his shaggy blond hair still wet and hanging in small ringlets on the back of his neck, his requisite cutoffs clean and dry. Elizabeth had already taken page after page of notes, supplied by all the family members, and she was ecstatic to finally have someone agree with her that Gabriel Kasper's actions had, in fact, been heroic.

When Gabe saw her notebook out, he glared and stomped over to snag the last sandwich on the platter.

Elizabeth drew in a deep breath as he leaned past her, but all she could smell was soap. When Gabe had entered earlier, the earthy scent of damp male flesh warm from the sunshine had clung to him—an enticing aphrodisiac. That wonderfully potent scent, combined with the sight of him, had made her nearly too breathless to talk. She hadn't thought she'd see him today. When she'd called the number Bear gave her, Honey had told her Gabe would be working all day. Elizabeth hadn't realized she meant working around his own home.

She also hadn't realized they'd all make such a fuss about her sunburn. She felt like an idiot for getting burned in the first place. She, better than anyone, knew how easily the sun affected her. She'd even brought along the sunscreen to apply often, keeping it in her bag. But she'd been sidetracked by Gabe and kissing and the erotic feelings he'd engendered. She hadn't thought once about overexposure.

Honey stood to make more sandwiches since Morgan had started prowling around for a cookie and Gabe had only gotten one sandwich. Once his lap was vacated, Sawyer excused himself, saying he'd go fetch the aloe cream he wanted Lizzy to use.

Gabe downed a tall glass of iced tea, and Elizabeth watched his throat work, saw the play of muscles in his arms and shoulders as he tipped his head back. He lowered the glass, caught her scrutiny and frowned at her. He opened his mouth to say something, but at that moment, Morgan thrust the baby into Gabe's arms and he got distracted by a tiny fist grabbing his chest hair.

The contrast between Gabe, so big, so strong, golden blond and tanned, and the tiny dark-haired baby held securely in his arms made Elizabeth's chest feel too tight. She'd have thought a man like him, a Lothario with only hedonistic pleasures on his mind, wouldn't have been so confident while holding an infant. But Gabe not only held the baby without hesitation, he blew raspberries on her soft belly and nibbled on her tiny toes.

Elizabeth decided it was time to make a strategic retreat. She knew, despite his gentle touch with the baby, that he was angry with her. She supposed that negated her deal with him; there'd be no movies at the drive-in. But at least, she told herself, trying to be upbeat instead of despondent, she'd gotten what she wanted. She had an entire notebook full of details, and hadn't that been her single goal all along?

Sawyer reappeared with a large tube of ointment and handed it to Elizabeth. "Put that on every hour or so, or whenever your skin feels uncomfortable. It's mostly aloe. You can keep it in the refrigerator if you like. Drink as much water as you can—rehydrating your skin will help it feel more comfortable. Oh, and take cool baths, not showers. Showers are too stressful to the damaged skin. If it doesn't feel better by tomorrow evening, give me a call, okay?"

Feeling horribly conspicuous, Elizabeth nodded. "How much do I owe you for the cream?"

"Not a thing. I'll take it out of Gabe's hide later."

Since Gabe smirked at that, Elizabeth assumed it was a joke. "Thank you." She glanced at Gabe, then away. "For everything."

Sawyer kissed his wife, his niece and his sister-in-law, then went off to work again. They were a demonstrative lot, always hugging and patting and kissing. It disconcerted her.

Misty and Honey and Gabe all walked her to the door. Gabe was deathly quiet, which she felt didn't bode well since he was usually joking and teasing. As she stepped onto the porch, Honey said, "Misty and I are having lunch in town tomorrow. Would you like to join us? The restaurant where Misty works part-time has fabulous beef stew on Friday afternoons. And afterward, we can all go to the library. I know they must have kept records of the local paper there on file. You could see the firsthand reports of Gabe's—" she glanced at her brother-in-law with a wicked smile "—daring feat."

Gabe gave Honey a look that promised retribution, but she just laughed and hugged him.

Misty added, "It'll be fun."

Aware of Gabe spearing her with his hot gaze, knowing he expected her to turn the women down, Elizabeth nonetheless nodded. "All right. Thank you."

She could have sworn she heard Gabe snarling.

Misty took the baby from Gabe's arms. "Great. If you know where the diner is, we could meet you there at eleven."

"That'll be fine."

"Perfect. We'll see you then!"

Misty and Honey retreated together, and suddenly Elizabeth wished they were still there. Gabe looked ready for murder.

It was his own fault, she decided, refusing to cower. She raised her chin, gave him a haughty look and turned toward her car. Gabe stalked along beside her.

"What are you doing here, Red?"

Uh-oh. He really was angry. "In each of my studies, I've included the accountings of family members whenever possible."

"But you and I had a deal."

Had. She was right, the deal was no longer valid. Disappointment swamped her, but she fought it off. It had been foolish to look forward to her time with Gabe. He was the epitome of a town playboy. He'd amuse himself with her while she was in town, and when she left he'd never think of her.

But she knew already she'd never be able to forget him. Pathetic, she decided, and deliberately tamped down her regret. She opened the car door and tossed in her bag. She hadn't been able to carry it with the strap over her shoulder because of the burn. She was anxious to follow Sawyer's advice and get naked. Her clothes felt like sandpaper against her sensitive skin.

Gabe watched her closely and she managed a shrug. "You never told me I couldn't talk with your family."

"Bull." He leaned closer, crowding her by putting one hand on the roof of her car, the other at the top of the door frame. "You knew damn good and well I didn't want you snooping around. That's why I agreed to answer your questions myself."

With him so close, her heart thundered. Memories washed over her and her belly tingled in response. She couldn't seem to stop staring at his mouth and swallowed hard. "I understand. If…if you want to cancel the rest of it, I won't argue with you."

Gabe stiffened. "Cancel the rest of what?"

The hair on his chest was still slightly damp, as if he'd dried in a hurry. She'd never in her life known a man who paraded around in such a state of undress almost continually. She didn't think he was deliberately flaunting himself for her benefit so much as he was totally at ease with his own body, aware he had no reason for shame or reserve. She curled her hands into fists to keep from touching him.

"The…the drive-in, the…having fun and loosening up." Pride made her add, "I thought it was a dumb plan all along."

He tipped up her chin with an extremely gentle touch. "Oh, no, you don't," he growled. "You're not backing out on me, Lizzy."

"But…" She faltered, caught by the intensity in his gaze. "You're angry."

"Damn right. And we'll discuss my anger tomorrow. At the movies. If you think I'm going to let you breach our deal now, especially after all your damn snooping, you've got another thing coming."

"Oh." Elizabeth couldn't think of anything else to say. Relief was a heavy throbbing in her breasts. "Okay."

Once again she stared at his mouth and felt her lips

trembling in remembrance of how he'd kissed her, how he'd tasted, how hot his mouth had been.

Breathless again, she whispered, "Gabe?" and even she could hear the longing in the single word.

Gabe's nostrils flared and suddenly he cursed. He leaned forward and took her mouth with careful hunger, that single rough finger beneath her chin holding her captive. The kiss was long and deep and Elizabeth grabbed his shoulders, though he didn't return the embrace. His tongue thrust in, hot and wet, and she accepted it, stroking it with her own, moaning softly.

When Gabe lifted his head a scant inch, she said, "Oh, my."

He smiled. "Yeah." There was a husky catch in his voice.

She realized she was practically hanging on him and jerked back. "I didn't mean—"

Again Gabe touched her chin, making her meet his eyes. "You can believe I'd have had you close, Lizzy, if I wasn't afraid of hurting you." His voice dropped and he asked, "Are your thighs burned?"

She couldn't seem to get enough oxygen into her lungs. "A little."

"Your arms?"

"Some."

His mouth barely touched hers. "Your breasts?"

She drew a shuddering breath. "Just…" She sounded like a bullfrog and cleared her throat. "Just the very tops, where the suit didn't cover."

"Want some help with that cream?"

New heat washed over her, making her light-headed. "No! I can manage just fine on my own."

His mouth twitched with a grin. "Spoilsport."

"I should go." She should go before she begged him to help her with the cream, before she attacked his mostly naked body. Before she made a total fool of herself. She had to remember that to Gabe, this was just a game, a way to pass the time while indulging her curiosity. He wasn't serious about any of it. As far as she could tell, he wasn't overly serious about anything.

"All right." Gabe straightened, then gave her another frown. "Don't think I'm not mad over you showing up here. But we'll talk about it when I pick you up for the drive-in, when I'll be assured of a little privacy."

No sooner did he say it than he looked struck by that thought and twisted to look behind him. Elizabeth peered over his shoulder just in time to see a curtain drop and several heads duck out of sight. Gabe cursed.

Unable to believe what she'd seen, Elizabeth asked, "They were spying on you?"

Gabe looked livid but accepting. "Don't sound so incredulous. I'd have done the same."

"You would have?"

"Sure." Then he laughed and scrubbed both hands over his face. "Oh, hell, the cat's out of the bag now. I'm never going to hear the end of it."

"The end of what?" Surely he wasn't embarrassed because he'd been a hero. That didn't make any sense at all.

"Never mind." He turned to her, shaking his head. "Maybe I should just do like Morgan and build my own place. 'Course, Honey'd probably have a fit."

Elizabeth had a hard time keeping up with his switches in topic.

Gabe pointed toward a spot on a hill overlooking the main house. "See that house up there? That's Morgan's. He and Misty moved in there last year. Until then, we all lived in the house together. Morgan lived in the main part of the house with Sawyer and his son, Casey. Have you met Case yet? No? Well, you're in for a treat. Hell of a kid."

She reached for her notebook to jot down the name, but Gabe caught her wrist with a sigh. "Forget I said that. Leave Casey alone."

"But you said…"

"You've done enough meddling, Red."

There was definite menace in his tone. Elizabeth committed the name to memory, determined to write it down as soon as she was away from Gabe. To distract him, she said, "Tell me about these living arrangements."

He gave her a narrow look, then shook his head. "Why not? There's no secret there. I live in the basement. I have my own entrance and it's nicer than most apartments. Jordan lives in the rooms over the garage."

Elizabeth frowned. "Four grown men all live together?"

"Yeah." Gabe squinted against the sun, then his eyes widened and he cursed. "Damn it, here I am, keeping you out in the sun again! Woman, don't you have any sense at all? Get on home."

"But—"

"No buts. I'll give you a family history on Friday. *After* I explain how disgruntled I am with you for trespassing with my family."

Elizabeth huffed. "I didn't trespass. Honey invited me over."

"Yeah, I just bet she did."

Elizabeth sat carefully in the car, trying not to scrape her tender flesh on the seats. Gabe closed her door for her, then leaned in to give her another quick kiss. "Drive careful. And when you get home, get naked."

"Gabe," she admonished, embarrassed by his frank suggestion. She wondered if she'd ever get used to him.

She started the engine and put the car in reverse. Gabe leaned in the window once more. "And Elizabeth?"

She paused. Gabe stared at her unconfined breasts in the loose dress, then whispered, "When you're naked, think of me, okay?" He touched the end of her nose and sauntered away.

Elizabeth stared after him, goggle-eyed and flushed, her heart pounding so hard she could hear it—and dead certain that she'd do exactly as he had asked her to.

Gabe cursed himself the entire way there, but he couldn't make himself not go. He tried to talk himself out of it. He'd even made other plans—then had to cancel them.

He was worried about her, and damned if that wasn't a first. He'd never had a woman consume his thoughts so completely.

But the sunburn was his fault and he felt responsible. Plus he'd yelled at her and she was so sensitive, so inexperienced, she probably felt bad because of it. Besides, he wanted to know what his damn meddling brothers had told her, because they hadn't given him so much as a clue. Even Misty and Honey were staying mum, refusing to reveal a single word.

Gabe squeezed the steering wheel tight and called himself three kinds of a fool, because the bare-bones truth of it was that he wanted to see her. There. He'd admitted it. He liked her and he wanted her.

He pulled into the driveway on the quiet suburban street just outside of Buckhorn County and turned off the ignition. The house was an older redbrick two-story with mature trees and a meticulously trimmed lawn. As he got out of the car, Gabe wondered if Elizabeth had done as ordered and stripped down. Was she naked right now? Maybe lounging in a soothing tub of cool water?

He shoved his hands into his pockets and climbed the outside stairwell to the upper floor at the side of the building. Miniblinds were pulled shut over the only full-size window. That was good, he thought, just in case she was naked.

Gabe rocked on his heels, took a deep breath and knocked. There was no answer. Briefly he considered turning away in case she was asleep. But it was still early, not quite nine o'clock, so he knocked again, harder.

A muffled sound reached him from the other side of the door, and then he heard Lizzy call, "Who is it?"

She didn't sound as if she'd just awakened, but she did sound wary. Probably she didn't get that many callers, especially not at night.

He felt a curious satisfaction at that deduction. "It's me, Red. Open up."

There were more muffled sounds, and finally the door opened the tiniest bit. One big blue eye peeked at him through the crack in the door. "Gabe. What in the world are you doing here?"

Rather than answer that, because he had no answer, he said, "Did I wake you?"

"Oh. No, I was just… Is anything wrong?"

"Yeah." He pushed against the door, and she hastily stepped out of the way. "I wanted to check…on… you." Gabe stared. His gut clenched and his toes curled. Lizzy had her hair all piled up on top of her head, and she wore only a sheet wrapped around her breasts. Loosely. Very loosely. In fact, if it wasn't for one small, tightly clenched fist, the sheet would have fallen. And good riddance, Gabe thought.

He shoved her front door shut with his heel. He knew he should say something, but he just kept staring.

Lizzy cleared her throat. "I was getting ready to put on some more of that ointment your brother gave me. It helps a lot, but it doesn't last all that long."

Gabe looked past her to the open kitchen nook. On the table sat a bowl of water and the tube of ointment Sawyer had given her. "I'll help you."

Her eyes flared wide. She shook her head, making that huge pile of hair threaten to topple. Her shoulders were bright pink, but just on the top, thank goodness. Most of her back, from what he could tell, was fine. But her breasts… Gabe swallowed. The sheet was white and damp in places around her chest; she must have been putting on cool compresses, he decided.

He was a man. He'd act like a man. Gabe put his arm around her sheet-covered waist and steered her toward the tiny kitchen. Her living room was minuscule, holding only a sofa, a single chair and some shelves. A thirteen-inch television was centered on the shelves and around that were some plants. The only other things in the spartan rented room were a few books and two photos. He'd check out the photos later, but for now he wanted to help ease her discomfort.

Her feet were bare and looked adorable peeking out from beneath the sheet. Pink, but adorable. Gabe looked at her breasts again, surreptitiously, so she wouldn't notice. The tops of her breasts, from just beneath her collarbone to somewhere beneath that white sheet, were sunburned.

"Here, sit down."

She remained standing. "Gabe, I'm perfectly capable of taking care of this myself."

"But why should you when I can help? I know it can't be easy to reach your shoulders."

Her mouth twisted, her eyes downcast. Her long auburn lashes left shadows on her cheeks from the fluorescent light overhead. He wanted to kiss her.

"I'll get dressed."

"Don't."

She stared at him, unblinking.

"Please, Lizzy?" He kept his tone cajoling, soothing. "Sit down and let me help, okay? It'll make *me* feel better, I promise."

Still she hesitated, and finally she heaved a sigh. "Oh, all right." She lowered herself carefully into the straight-back chair. "But if you hurt me," she warned, "I'm going to be really angry."

His hands shook as he stared at her shoulders. "I'll be as gentle as I can."

He lifted the tube of cream and realized it was cool. Lizzy must have been keeping it in the refrigerator, just as Sawyer had suggested. He squeezed a large dollop onto his fingertips, then very carefully began smoothing it over her skin. Her head dropped forward and she shivered.

"Cold?"

"It's supposed to be."

"I'm not hurting you?" Her skin was so delicate, even without the sunburn.

"No."

There was a tiny quaking to her voice that made everything masculine in him sit up and take notice. Velvety soft curls on the back of her neck got in his way, and he used one hand to lift them while spreading the cream with the other. Her neck was long and graceful, her hair somewhat lighter here, more like a golden strawberry blond. "Feel better?"

"Mm. Yes."

Gabe looked at her arms, saw they were pink and stepped to her side. He lifted her arm and said, "Brace your hand on my abdomen."

She jerked her hand as if he'd suggested she cut it off. She held it protectively to her chest so he couldn't take it again.

Gabe smiled. "C'mon, Lizzy. Don't be shy. I just want to put the cream on you, and I'm even wearing a shirt. There's no reason to act so timid."

Her spine stiffened. "I am not acting timid! I'm just not used to how you…how you constantly…"

He could imagine what she'd eventually come up with, so he decided to help her. "How informal and comfortable and at ease I am? Yeah, that's true. Touching someone isn't a sin, sweetheart." He pried her arm loose, being careful not to hurt her, then pressed her hand to his abdomen. His muscles were clenched rock hard, not on purpose, but in startling reaction to the feel of her small hand there. "See. That's not so bad, is it?"

A tiny squeak.

Gabe lifted a brow, still covering her hand with his so she couldn't retreat. "What was that?"

Lizzy glared at him and said, "No. It's not…awful."

Laughing, Gabe released her and reached for the cream. "Now just hold still."

He could feel her trembling as he spread the sticky aloe cream up and down her slender arm. She felt so soft, so female, which he supposed made sense. It even made sense that his overcharged male brain immediately began to imagine how soft she was in other, more feminine places, like her inner thighs, her belly and lower.

He felt himself hardening and wanted to curse. Like a doomed man, he continued with his ministrations, torturing himself, but enjoying it all the same.

With only one hand to hold it, her sheet started to slip. Gabe froze as she made a frantic grab for it, his breath held, but she managed to maintain her modesty.

Sighing, he went to her other side, determined to behave himself. He was not a boy ready to take his first woman. He was experienced, mature… There was absolutely no reason for all the anticipation, all the keen tension.

His voice gruff, he said, "You know the drill."

She looked away from him even as she thrust out her arm. Nervously, she said, "I have to admit I'm a little surprised to see you so fully dressed. I was beginning to think you didn't own any shirts or slacks."

He looked at his white T-shirt and faded jeans. The jeans were so old, so worn, they fit like a second skin—which meant that if she bothered to look at all, she'd see he had an erection. Again.

But of course she didn't look. Gabe studied her averted face and smiled. "Are you disappointed that I came fully clothed, Lizzy?"

In prim tones, she replied, "Not at all."

He didn't quite believe her. Sure, he felt the tension, but then, so did she. She was practically vibrating with it. Yet she'd deny any attraction. Most women came on to him with force; this tactic was totally unusual... and intriguing.

She turned her face even more, until her chin almost hit the chair back. Gabe bit his lip to keep from laughing. Elizabeth Parks was about the most entertaining woman he'd ever met. It was probably a good thing she wouldn't be here long or he'd get addicted to her prickly ways.

But until she left, he told himself, he might as well put them both out of their misery.

Chapter 6

Elizabeth didn't quite know what to think when Gabe moved in front of her, insinuating his body into the small space between the Formica table and the chair where she sat. Every one of her nerve endings felt sensitized from the way he'd so gently stroked her. And now his lap was on a level with her gaze.

Her eyes widened. *He was turned on!* It wasn't just *her* feeling so sexually charged. But unlike Gabe, she was the only one uncertain how to continue, or if she even should.

Gabe leaned very close and gripped the seat of the chair in his large hands. Elizabeth yelped when he lifted it and moved it far enough for him to kneel in front of her. Her heart beat so hard she felt slightly sick, her vision almost blurring.

He smelled of aftershave mingled with his own

unique scent. Never in her life had she noticed a man's smell before. She wished she could bottle Gabe's particular aroma—she'd make a fortune. There couldn't be a woman alive who wouldn't love his enticing scent.

His lips grazed her ears and he said softly, "I'm going to finish putting the cream on you, then we're going to do a little experimenting, all right?"

The soft, damp press of his mouth on her temple served as a period to his statement. He phrased his comment as a question, but given the heat suffusing her, it had to be rhetorical.

Her hands opened and closed fitfully on the sheet. "What exactly do you mean?"

Leaning back on his haunches, Gabe stared at her and caught the hem of the sheet. "Your legs are burned, too." His rough palms slid up the back of her calves all the way to her knees, baring them as the sheet parted.

Elizabeth pressed herself back in the chair, her legs tightly clenched together, her toes curled. Good Lord, surely he didn't mean...

The sheet fell open over her thighs, barely leaving her modesty intact. She tried to hold it closed at her breasts and still push his hands away, but Gabe wasn't having it.

"Shhh. Shh, Lizzy, it's all right." He held perfectly still, not moving, not rushing her, waiting for her to calm down and either acquiesce or reject him.

"You're looking at me!" she said, not really wanting him to stop but unable to contain her embarrassment.

"Just your legs, sweetheart. And I've already seen them, right?"

She sucked in a quick, semicalming breath. He was right, in a way. "It just…it feels different."

"Because you're naked beneath the sheet?" His fingers continued to stroke up and down her calves, pausing occasionally to gently explore the back of her knees with a touch so gentle, so hot.

She'd had no idea the back of a knee could be an erogenous zone!

Gabe watched her, waiting for an answer. She forced the words past the constriction in her throat. "Yes, because I'm naked beneath the sheet."

"Am I hurting you, Lizzy?"

She shook her head, heated by the tone of his voice, the careful way he was treating her.

"Do you like this?" He began stroking her again, avoiding her sunburned areas while finding places that were ultrasensitive but nonthreatening.

His hands were so large, so dark against her paler complexion. Working hands, she thought stupidly, rough and callused. She gulped. Words were beyond her, but she managed a nod. She did like it. A lot.

Gabe met her gaze with a smoldering look, his eyes blazing, his tone low and soothing and seductive. "Relax for me, sweetheart. I'm not going to do anything you don't want me to do."

Relaxing was the absolute last thing she could accomplish. Her thoughts swirled as he reached for the cream and squeezed a large dollop into his palm. She had no real idea what he intended, but the look on his face told her it would be sensual and that she'd probably enjoy it a great deal.

Should she allow this? How could she not allow

it? Never in her entire life had a man pursued her. Certainly not a man like Gabe Kasper. She could do her thesis and indulge in an episode that might well prove to be the highlight of her entire life. Who was she kidding, she thought. It was already the highlight of her life!

She squeezed her eyes shut and held her breath, trying to order her thoughts, and suddenly felt his fingertips stroke up the inside of her thigh.

She moaned long and low, unable to quiet the sound. It came as much from expectation as from his touch.

"Look at me, Lizzy."

He was asking a lot, considering how tumultuous her emotions were at the moment. It took several seconds and the stillness of his hand on her leg for her to finally comply.

Gabe was breathing roughly. His mouth quirked the tiniest bit. "I don't know what it is about you, Red, but you make me feel like I'm going to explode." His fingers moved in a tantalizing little caress that made her breath catch. "Have you ever played baseball?"

She blinked, trying to comprehend the absurd question. "I...no."

Gabe nodded. "I'll teach you baseball. But probably not the kind of sport you think I mean." Still holding her gaze, he bent his golden blond head and pressed a soft, damp kiss onto her burned knee. "Much as I'd like to do otherwise, I think we'll just try first base tonight. If you don't like it, say stop and that'll be it. If you do like it, then tomorrow at the drive-in, we'll go to second base. Do you understand?"

He continued to place soft, warm kisses on her skin.

Seeing his head there, against her legs, when no man had ever even gotten within touching distance before, was a fascinating discovery. She couldn't have conjured up something so hot, so erotic, in her wildest dreams.

"I think so." Her throat felt raw, but then she had an absolutely gorgeous hunk of a man kneeling at her feet, staring at her with lust, his hot fingers stroking her leg. "Is what you're doing now considered first base?"

Very slowly, Gabe shook his head. "No, this is just torture for me." He gave her a rascal's grin, and his blue eyes darkened. "For right now, I'm going to just finish putting on the cream. I want you as comfortable as possible. But to keep us both distracted, I'd like to learn a little more about you, okay?"

She probably would have agreed to anything in that moment. She was equally mesmerized and frantic and curious. "All right."

On his knees, Gabe opened his legs so that they enclosed her; his chest was even with her lap. He scooped more of the cream from his palm and began applying it in smooth, even strokes that felt like live fire. Not painfully, but with incredible promise.

"Tell me why you chose heroism for your thesis."

Oh, no. She couldn't explain that, not right now, not to him. She cleared her throat, trying to disassociate her mind from his touch so she could form coherent words. "I'm majoring in psychology. Most of the topics have been done to death. This seemed…unique."

Gabe tilted his head. "Is that right? What gave you the idea for heroism?"

She bit her lip, trying to sort out what she could tell him and what she couldn't. "I've always been fascinated by the stories of people who managed to muster incredible courage or strength at the time of need."

"Like the adrenaline rush? A woman who lifts a car to free her trapped child, a man who ignores burns to rescue his wife from a house fire. Those types of things?"

"Yes." The adrenaline rush that made saving someone important possible. Her throat tightened with the remembrance of how she'd failed, how she'd not been able to react at all, except as a coward.

"Hey?" Gabe finished her legs and carefully replaced the sheet, surprising her...disappointing her. "Are you all right, babe?"

His perceptiveness was frightening, especially when it involved a part of herself she fully intended to keep forever hidden. She went on the defensive without even stopping to think what she was doing or how he might view her response. Meeting his gaze, she said, "I'm not sure I like all these endearments you keep using. And especially not 'babe.' It sounds like you're talking to an infant."

Rather than hardening at her acerbic tone, his expression softened. "There's something you're not telling me, Lizzy."

Panic struck; she absolutely could not bear for him to nose into her private business. He was everything she wasn't, and she accepted that. But she didn't want her face rubbed in it. "I thought you were going to teach me about baseball!"

One side of his mouth kicked up, though his eyes continued to look shadowed with concern. "All right." He touched her chin with a fingertip. "Baseball is something we play in high school, but somehow I think you missed out on that."

His searching gaze forced her to acknowledge that with a nod. "I was very shy in high school."

"There was just you and your father, right?"

"Yes. But we were very close."

Gabe looked at her chest and she felt her breasts tighten in response. "That's good. But it can't make up for all the shenanigans and experiments and playfulness that teenagers indulge in with each other."

"My father," she admitted, willing to give him some truths, "tried to encourage me to go out more often. He was more than willing to supply me with the popular clothes and music and such. On my sixteenth birthday he even bought me a wonderful little car. But I wasn't really interested."

Talking was becoming more difficult by the moment. She knew Gabe was listening, but he also caressed her with his eyes, and she knew what he saw. Her nipples were peaked, pressing against the white sheet almost painfully. But she liked the way he looked at her and didn't want him to stop.

With a bluntness that stunned her, Gabe suddenly said, "I'm going to touch your breasts. That's first base. All right?"

He didn't wait for her permission, but got more of the cooling cream and prepared to apply it her chest. Elizabeth held her breath, frozen, not daring to move for fear he'd stop—and for fear he wouldn't. She was excited, but also cautious. Whenever she'd imagined getting intimate with a man, she hadn't envisioned all this idle chitchat. She'd always assumed things would just…happen. She'd pictured getting carried away with passion, not having a man tease and explain and ask permission.

With the cream in one palm, Gabe closed his free hand around her wrist and gently pried her fingers from the sheet.

"Breathe, Lizzy."

She did, in a long choked gasp. The sheet slipped, but not far enough to bare her completely. Gabe's nostrils flared and his cheekbones flushed. He carried her shaking hand to his mouth and pressed a kiss into her palm, then placed her hand on her lap.

She tried to prepare herself but when she felt the cream on her skin she jumped. Again, Gabe whispered, "Shh…" in a way that sounded positively carnal. She was oblivious to the sting of her burned skin as his fingers dipped lower and lower. The edge of his thumb brushed her nipple.

His gaze leaped to hers, so intense she felt it clear to her bones. He leaned forward to blow on her skin. "I should be shot," he whispered, "for letting your sweet hide get burned like this."

His breath continued to drift over her, making gooseflesh rise, making her shiver in anticipation. His lips lightly touched the upper swell of her right breast. But that wasn't the only touch she was aware of. His hair, cool and so very soft, brushed against her and his hard muscled thighs caged her calves. Against one shin, she felt his throbbing erection.

She moaned.

Gabe nuzzled closer to her nipple, very close, but not quite touching her there. "I like that, Lizzy, the way you make that soft, hungry little sound deep in your throat. It tells me so much."

His lips moved against her skin, adding to her sensitivity. She wasn't used to playing games, and she sure as certain wasn't used to wanting something so badly that her entire body trembled with the need. It wasn't a conscious decision on her part, but her hands lifted, sank into his hair and directed his mouth where she wanted it most.

Gabe gave his own earthy, raw groan just before his mouth clamped down on her throbbing nipple, suckling her through the sheet. Her body tensed, her back arching, her fingers clenching, her head falling back as her eyes closed. It was by far the most exquisite thing she had ever experienced. With her eyes closed, her senses were attuned to every rough flick of his tongue, the heat inside his mouth, the sharp edge of his teeth. She wanted to savor every sensation, store them all away to remember forever. Breathless, she whispered, "It's… it's not like I thought it'd be."

Gabe stroked with his tongue, soaking the sheet and plying her stiff nipple. "No?" His voice was a rough rasp and he sat back to view his handiwork, eyeing her shimmering breasts with satisfaction.

She didn't care. He could look all he wanted as long as he kissed her like that again. Shaking her head, Elizabeth ignored the way some of her hair tumbled free. "No," she admitted. "I used to daydream about a man doing that some day." She stroked his head, luxuriating in the cool silk of his thick hair. "But never a man like you, and it never felt quite that…deep."

His hands settled on either side of her hips, his

long fingers curving to her buttocks. Heavy-lidded, he watched her. "What do you mean by deep?"

Elizabeth placed her hand low on her belly. "I feel it here. Every small lick or suck… I feel it inside me."

Gabe groaned again, then feasted on her other nipple. Elizabeth let her hands drift down his strong shoulders, then farther to his upper arms. She felt half insensate with the pleasure, half driven by curiosity to explore his pronounced biceps. His arms were rigid, braced hard on the chair and her behind.

He leaned back again, his breath heavy, his mouth wet. Still he looked at her body, not her face. "What did you mean, a man like me?"

Elizabeth had to gather her wits, had to force her eyes open. Gabe lifted one hand and, with the edge of his thumb, teased a wet nipple. The sheet offered no barrier at all, and when she looked down, Elizabeth could see that the sheet was all but transparent.

She wanted his mouth on her again.

"I always thought…" She swallowed hard, trying to form the correct words. "I'd hoped that some day I'd get intimate with a man, but I assumed he'd be more like me."

Slowly, Gabe's gaze lifted until he was studying her intently. But his hand was still on her breast, still driving her to distraction. "Like you, how?"

She shook her head. "Boring. Introverted. Something of a wallflower. Homely."

She gasped as Gabe lurched to his feet and glared at her. Her mouth open in a small O, her eyes wide, she watched him, uncertain what had caused that sudden, heated reaction.

Gabe propped his hands on his lean hips, and his chest rose and fell with his labored efforts to gain control. His eyes were burning, his brows down, his mouth a hard line.

He shook his head and made a disgusted sound. "Damn it, Red, now you've gone and made me mad."

Gabe watched her struggle to follow his words. She looked like sin and temptation and sweetness all wrapped together. Her heavy dark red hair was half up, half down, giving her a totally wanton look. Her skin was flushed beyond the sunburn, her eyes heavy lidded with sensuality but somewhat dazed by his annoyance.

It made him unreasonably angry for her to put herself down, though what she'd said had mirrored his earlier thoughts. Looking at her, he doubted any man could think her unattractive. He sure as hell didn't.

Reminded of that, he stalked a foot closer and grabbed her wrist, carrying her hand to his groin. Her mouth fell open as he forced her palm against his erection. "You know what that means, Red?"

She nodded dumbly, so still she wasn't even breathing.

"What? Tell me what it means?"

Her eyes left his face to stare at her hand, then to his face again. "That you're excited."

"Right. Do you think I'd get excited over a homely woman?"

She didn't answer.

He moved her hand, forcing her to stroke him, driving himself crazy. "The answer is no," he said with a rasp. "Now here's another question." The words were forced out through his teeth because Lizzy was no longer passive. Her hand had relaxed, opened, and her fingers curved around him. In a moment of wonder, Gabe realized he was the first guy she'd ever touched.

It was a heady thought.

He wasn't having an easy time controlling himself, but two deep breaths later, he finally managed to say, "Do you think, Red, that this happens to me often?"

"Yes."

That one breathy whispered word nearly made his knees buckle. He released her wrist and stepped back, but she leaned forward at the same time, maintaining the contact. "Well, you're wrong." He nearly strangled when she licked her lips in innocent, unthinking suggestion, her gaze still glued to his crotch. Gabe growled and said, "If you stroke me one more time you're going to see the consequences."

He clenched his fists, tightened his thighs, and luckily she let him go. When he could focus again, Gabe looked at her. Blinking rapidly, Lizzy continued to study his body. Suddenly aware of his renewed attention, she looked him in the eyes and asked, "Can I feel you some more?"

Yes. "No, not right now."

"When?"

He nearly choked on a laugh. "You persistent, curious little witch," he accused.

"You...you don't want me to?"

"I want you to too much."

Her tongue came out to stroke her lips again, making his blood thicken. "Then..."

"Tomorrow," he said quickly, before she could push

him over the edge with her wanton questions. Knowing she wanted him, knowing he'd be the first man she'd ever explored, that she'd learn from him, was possibly the strongest aphrodisiac known to man. "At the drive-in. We'll go to second base, remember?"

Her eyes were dreamy. "You promise?"

Gabe gave one sharp nod while stifling a reflexive groan. He'd never survive. Was she wet right now? He'd be willing to bet she was, wet and hot, and he knew in every fiber of his being that she'd be so tight she'd kill him with pleasure. "I should go."

She came to her feet so fast she nearly stumbled over the sheet. Gabe caught her by the upper arms, heard her sharp intake of breath as his hands closed tightly on her burned skin, and he cursed himself. He released her, but she didn't step away; she stepped closer.

He felt like a total cad. "I can't believe I'm here seducing you when you're in pain." He'd aroused her, but there wasn't much chance of satisfying her without also causing her a lot of discomfort. She was so sunburned that just about any position would be impossible.

Her big eyes stared at him with wonder. "You were seducing me?"

Gabe stared at the ceiling, looking for inspiration but finding none. "What the hell did you think I was doing, Lizzy?"

She said simply, "Playing with me."

"Oh, yeah." A fresh surge of blood rushed to his groin, making him break out in a sweat. He felt every pulse beat in his erection, and ground his teeth with the need to finish what he'd started.

He was so hard he hurt and he knew damn well

he'd have a hell of a time sleeping tonight. "I'll play with you, all right. Playing with a woman's body is about the most pleasure a man can expect. And when a woman has a body like yours... I'm not sure I can live through it."

She stared at him while she chewed on her lips, and he could almost see the wheels turning. Gently, he touched a finger to her swollen mouth. "No, sweetheart, we can't tonight. You're in no shape to tussle with a man, and I'm too damn horny to be as careful as I'd need to be."

Her eyes flared over his blunt language, but he was too far gone to attempt romantic clichés. She touched his chest tentatively. "Would...would you like to just stay and talk for awhile?"

So you can work on seducing me? He knew he should say no, should remove himself from temptation, but he couldn't. She looked so hopeful, so sweet and aroused, he nodded. "Sure. Why don't you go get a dry sheet and I'll pour us some drinks. Sawyer did say you should have lots of fluids."

Her smile was beatific. "Okay."

Gabe watched the sassy sway of a perfect heart-shaped bottom and groaned anew. Damn, she was hot, and her being unaware of it only made her more so.

He found two tall glasses in the cabinet and opened the tiny apartment-size fridge. There was orange juice, milk and one cola. He poured two glasses of orange juice and carried them into the living room. When he set them down, he again noticed the pictures on the shelves and walked closer to examine them.

One was of a much younger Lizzy. Her red hair gave

her away, although in the photo she wore long skinny braids and had braces on her teeth. Gabe grinned, thinking she looked oddly cute. An older woman with hair of a similar color, cut short and stylish, smiled into the camera while hugging Lizzy close. Her mother, Gabe decided, and felt a sadness for Lizzy's loss. No child should ever lose a mother at such a young age.

The other picture was of her father, sitting in a straight-backed chair, with Lizzy behind him. She had one pale hand on his shoulder; neither of them were smiling. Her father looked tired but kind, and Lizzy had an endearing expression of forbearance, as if she'd hated having the picture taken. She was older in this one, probably around seventeen. She was just starting to grow into her looks, he decided. Her freckles were more pronounced, her eyes too large, her chin too stubborn. Added years had softened her features and made them more feminine.

As Gabe went to replace the framed photograph on the shelf, he caught sight of an album. Curious, thinking to find more pictures of her and her life, Gabe picked it up and settled into the sofa. A folded transcript of her grades fell out. As he'd suspected, Lizzy was an overachiever, with near perfect marks in every subject. She'd already received recognition from the dean for being at the head of her class. He shook his head, wondering how anyone could take life so seriously. Then he opened the album.

What he found shocked him speechless.

There were numerous clipped articles, all of them focusing on her mother's death. They appeared to be from small hometown papers, and Gabe could relate because of all the fanfare he'd gotten in the local papers when he'd stopped the runaway boat.

Only these articles didn't appear to be very complimentary. Keeping one ear open for signs of Lizzy's return, Gabe began to read.

Girl fails to react: Eleanor Parks died in her car Saturday night after being forced off the road by a semi. The overturned car wasn't visible from the road, and while Elizabeth Parks escaped with nonfatal injuries, shock kept her from seeking help. Medical authorities speculate that, with timely intervention, Mrs. Parks may well have survived.

Appalled, Gabe read headline after headline, and with each word, a horrible ache expanded in his heart, making his chest too tight, his eyes damp. God, he could only imagine her torment.

Daughter Slow to React: Mother Dies
Unnecessary Death—The Trauma of Shock
Daughter Stricken with Grief—Must Be Hospitalized
Father Defends Daughter in Time of Grief

What could it have felt like for a twelve-year-old child to accept the guilt of her mother's death? Not only had she lost the one person she was likely closest to, but she'd been blamed by insensitive reporters and medical specialists.

Feeling a cross between numbness and unbearable

pain, Gabe carefully replaced the album beneath the photos. He thrust his fisted hands into his pockets and paced. So this was what had her in such an all-fire tizzy to interview heroes. He grunted to himself, fair sick of the damn word and its connotations. How could an intelligent, independent woman compare her reactions as a twelve-year-old child to those of a grown man? It was ludicrous, and he wanted to both shake her and cuddle her close, swearing that nothing would ever hurt her again.

He swallowed hard against the tumultuous, conflicting emotions that left him feeling adrift, uncertain of himself and his purpose. When he heard her bedroom door open, he stepped away from the shelves and crossed the carpeted floor to stare at her with volatile feelings that simmered close to erupting. They weren't exactly joyous feelings, but feelings of acute awareness of her as a woman, him as a man, of the differences in their lives and how shallow he'd been in his assumptions.

Lizzy, wrapped in a very soft, pale blue terry-cloth robe, widened her eyes at him and asked carefully, "Gabe? What's wrong?"

It felt like his damn heart was lodged in his throat, making it hard to swallow, doubly hard to speak. He hated it, hated himself and his cavalier attitude. Gently he cupped her face in his palms and bent to kiss her soft mouth, which still trembled slightly with the urges he'd deliberately created. He'd thought to say something soothing to her, something reassuring, but as her mouth opened and her hands sought his shoulders, Gabe decided on a different approach.

He'd get Lizzy over her ridiculous notions of guilt. He'd make her see herself as he saw her—a sexy, adorable woman filled with mysteries and depth. And he'd make damn sure she enjoyed herself in the bargain.

Chapter 7

Elizabeth felt like she was floating, her feet never quite touching the ground. She said hello to the people she passed on the main street while heading to the diner to meet Misty and Honey Hudson. She hadn't had much sleep the night before, having been too tightly strung from wanting Gabe and from the slight lingering discomfort of her sunburn.

Today it was a toss-up as to which bothered her more. Gabe had stayed an additional hour, but he hadn't resumed the heated seduction. Instead, he'd been so painstakingly gentle, so filled with concern and comfort, it had been all she could do not to curl up on his lap and cuddle. He'd have let her. Heck, he'd tried several times to instigate just such a thing.

By the time he'd left and she'd prepared for bed, she'd been tingling all over, ultrasensitized by the brush of his mouth, the stroke of his fingertips, his low husky voice and constant string of compliments.

He thought her freckles were sexy. He thought her red hair was sexy. Oh, the things he'd said about her hair. She blushed again, remembering the way he'd looked at her while speculating on the contrast of her almost-brown brows and the vivid red of her hair, wondering about the curls on the rest of her body.

He was big and muscular and outrageous and all male. She'd already decided that if he was willing to begin an involvement, she'd be an utter fool to rebuff him. The things he made her feel were too wonderful to ignore.

When she entered the small diner, several male heads turned her way. They didn't look at her as Gabe did, but rather with idle curiosity because she was a new face. She located the women, talking to a waitress at the back of the diner in a semiprivate booth. They all had their backs to her as she approached.

She was only a few feet away when she heard Misty say, "I think he's dumbstruck by his own interest. She's not at all the type of woman he usually goes after and he doesn't know what to make of that."

Honey laughed. "That's an understatement. Sawyer told me Gabe started chasing the ladies when he was just a kid, and he usually caught them. By the time he was fifteen, they were chasing *him*."

The waitress shook her head. Elizabeth recognized her as one of the women who'd been at the docks the day she'd first tracked down Gabe.

"That's nothing but the truth," the woman said. "Gabe can sit on the dock and the boats will pull in or idle by just to look at him. He always accepts it as his due, because it's what he's used to. I remember how he reacted when Elizabeth first showed up there. He didn't like her at all, but then she didn't seem to like him much, either, and I sorta think that's the draw. He's not used to women not gushing all over him."

"I just hope he doesn't hurt her. Gabe is a long way from being ready to settle down for more than a little recreation. But every woman he gets together with falls in love with him."

Misty agreed with her sister. "He's a hedonistic reprobate, but an adorable one."

Elizabeth was frozen to the spot. She wasn't an eavesdropper by nature, but she hadn't quite been able to announce herself. *In love with Gabe?* Yes, she supposed she was halfway there. How stupid of her, how naive to think he'd be truly interested in her for more than a quick tumble. As the women had implied, he evidently found her odd and was challenged by her.

The differences between her and Gabe had never felt more pronounced than at that precise moment. Because she was so inexperienced, not just sexually but when it came to relationships of any kind, she knew she'd be vulnerable to a man's attention. And Gabe wasn't just any man. His interest in her, no matter how short-term, was like the quintessential Cinderella story. Gabe was more than used to taking what he wanted from women, not in a selfish demand, but in shared pleasure. He'd assumed Elizabeth understood that, and that the enjoyment of playtime would be mutual. And it would be. She'd see to it.

A short, humorless laugh nearly choked her…and

drew the three women's attention. Elizabeth mentally shook her head as she stepped forward with a feigned smile. None of it mattered; she still wanted him, wanted to experience everything he could show her, teach her. She wanted to really truly *feel* once again. Since her mother's death and the appearance of the harsh, dragging guilt, it seemed as if she hadn't really been living, that anything heartfelt or lasting had been blunted by the need to make amends, to understand her weakness.

Her heart hurt, but pride would keep her from showing it. She'd accept Gabriel Kasper on any terms, and he'd never know that she dreamed of more. She'd enjoy herself, without regrets, without demands.

Despite her past, she deserved that much.

The waitress, looking cautious, indicated a chair. "Hey, there, Elizabeth. Remember me?"

Again, Elizabeth smiled. "Ceily, from the boat docks, right? Yes, I remember. I hadn't realized you worked here." She carefully lowered herself into her seat and nodded at both sisters. Honey and Misty looked guilty, and Elizabeth tried to reassure them by pretending she hadn't heard a thing. "I hope I'm not too late?"

"Not at all," Misty said quickly. Her baby was sitting beside her in the booth on a pumpkin seat. "I hope you don't mind that I brought Amber along."

Elizabeth leaned over slightly to peer at the baby. "How could anyone ever object to that darling little angel?"

When she'd been a young girl, still fanciful and filled with daydreams, Elizabeth used to imagine someday having a baby, coddling it as her mother had coddled her, but she'd set those fantasies aside when she'd accepted her shortcomings.

Misty beamed at the compliment. "Strangely enough, she looks just like Morgan."

Ceily snorted at that outrageous comment. "Come on, Misty. I've never seen that little doll manage anything near the nasty scowl Morgan can dredge up without even trying."

Honey laughed. "That's true enough. But if Misty is even two minutes late to feed her, she has to contend with scowls and grumblings from both father and daughter. And I have to admit, they do resemble each other then. It sometimes seems to be a competition to see who can complain the loudest."

Misty slid a gentle finger over her sleeping daughter's cheek. "Morgan can't stand it if she even whimpers, much less gives a good howl. I swear, he shakes like a skinny Chihuahua if Amber gets the least upset."

Ceily made a sound of amused disgust. "I never thought I'd see the day when the brothers started settling down into blissful wedlock."

Honey nudged Elizabeth, then quipped in a stage whisper, "Not that Ceily's complaining. I think she's the only female in Buckhorn County who isn't pining for our men."

Being included in that "our men" category made Elizabeth blush, but no one noticed as Ceily broke loose with a raucous laugh. "I know the brothers far too well. We've been friends forever and that's not something I'd ever want to screw up by getting…romantic."

"A wise woman," Honey said, between sips of iced

tea. "I think they all consider you something of a little sister."

Ceily bit her lip and mumbled under her breath, "I wouldn't exactly say that." But Elizabeth appeared to be the only one who'd heard her.

Ceily took their orders and sauntered off. Elizabeth watched her surreptitiously, wondering just how involved the woman had been with the brothers. She was beautiful, in a very natural way, not bothering much with makeup or a fancy hairdo. She looked…earthy, with her light tan and sandy-brown hair. And Elizabeth remembered from seeing her in her bathing suit at the boat dock that Ceily was built very well, with the type of lush curves that would definitely attract the males.

She was frowning when Honey asked, "How's the sunburn?"

"Oh." Elizabeth drew herself together and shrugged. "Much better today. Your husband's cream worked wonders. Would you thank him again for me?"

Honey waved away her gratitude. "No problem. Sawyer is glad to do it, I'm sure."

Misty looked at her closely. "You don't look nearly as pink today. I guess it's fading fast."

Forcing a laugh, Elizabeth admitted, "I can even wear my bra today without cringing."

"Ouch." Misty looked appalled by that idea. "Are you sure you should? This blasted heat is oppressive."

It was only then that Elizabeth realized she was trussed up far more than Misty and Honey were. While they both wore comfortably loose T-shirts and cotton shorts with flip-flop sandals, Elizabeth had put a blouse under her long pullover dress and ankle socks with her shoes.

Deciding to be daring, she asked, "Does everyone dress so casually here? I mean, do you think anyone would notice if I wore something like that?" She indicated their clothes with a nod.

Honey laughed out loud. "Heck, yes. Gabe would notice! But then I get the feeling he'd notice you no matter what you wore. Watching him blunder around yesterday like a fish out of water was about the best entertainment we've had for awhile."

Misty bit her bottom lip, trying to stifle a laugh. "Gabe teased both Sawyer and Morgan something terrible when they got involved with us. Now he's just getting his due."

"But we're not involved." Even as she said it, Elizabeth felt her face heating. She hoped the sisters would attribute it to her sunburn and not embarrassment.

"Maybe not yet, but Gabe's working on it. I've gotten to know him pretty good since Sawyer and I married. He dates all the time, but he never mentions any particular woman. You he's mentioned several times."

Elizabeth didn't dare ask what he'd said. She could just imagine. "I think I'll buy myself some shorts today."

"Good idea. This is a vacation lake. Very few people bother to put on anything except casual clothes."

Ceily sidled up with Elizabeth's drink and everyone's food. Misty was having a huge hamburger with fries, but Honey and Elizabeth had settled on salads.

Misty made a face at them. "It's the breast-feeding, I

swear. I never ate like a hog before, but now I stay hungry all the time. Sawyer says I'm burning off calories."

Honey pursed her lips, as if trying to keep something unsaid, then she appeared to burst. "I wonder if it'll affect me that way."

Misty froze with her mouth clamped around the fat burger. Like a sleepwalker she lowered the food and swallowed hard. "Are you...?"

Honey, practically shivering with excitement, nodded. Elizabeth almost jumped out of her seat when the two women squealed loudly and jumped up to hug across the table.

"When?" Misty demanded.

"In about six months. Late February." Honey leaned forward. "But keep it down. I don't want anyone else to know until I tell Sawyer."

"You haven't told him yet?"

"I just found out for sure this morning." She turned to Elizabeth. "We hadn't exactly been trying not to get pregnant, if you know what I mean, so it won't be a shock. But I still think he's going to make a big deal of it."

Wide-eyed, Elizabeth had no idea what to say to that. She was...stunned that the sisters had included her in such a personal, familial announcement. She'd never in her life had close female friends. She'd always been too odd, too alone, to mix in any of the small groups in school.

But as it turned out, Elizabeth didn't need to reply. Honey and Misty went back to chattering while they ate, and Elizabeth was loath to interrupt.

Finally, they wore down and simply settled back in

their seats, smiling. The silence wasn't an uncomfortable one, and Elizabeth found herself wondering about several things.

Trying to shake off her shyness, she asked, "Do you hope it's a boy or a girl?"

Honey touched her stomach with a mother's love. "It doesn't really matter to me. Amber is so precious—a girl would be nice. But then, Casey is such an outstanding young man that I think a son would be perfect, too."

Using that statement to lead into another question, Elizabeth pulled out her paper and pencil. "Do the brothers have any sisters?"

"Not a one. They only have male sperm, to hear them tell it." Misty had a soft, almost secret smile on her face. "Morgan calls Amber his little miracle."

Honey sighed. "Sawyer even warned me before we were married that I should resign myself to baby boys. The way they dote on Amber, as if none of them had ever seen a baby girl before, is hysterical. I keep telling them she's no different from Casey when he was an infant, but they just look at me like I'm nuts."

Elizabeth grinned at that image. "In a nice sort of way," she ventured cautiously, so she wouldn't offend, "they seem a bit sexist."

"Oh, they're sexist all right! And very old-fashioned, but as you said, in a nice way. They insist on helping a woman whenever they can, but they'd refuse to admit it if *they* needed help."

"Not that they ever do," Honey added. "They're the most self-reliant men I've ever seen. Their mother made sure they could cook and clean and fend for themselves."

Misty leaned forward to speak in a whisper. "Morgan says all he needs me for is to keep him happy." Her eyebrows bobbed. "You know what I mean." Then she settled back with a blissful sigh. "But then he'll show me it's so much more than that. We talk about everything and share everything. He unloads his worries at night over dinner and he says he misses me all day when he's working."

"Do you still work here in the diner?"

"Part-time, just for the fun of it. It keeps Morgan on his toes. He has this absurd notion that every guy in town comes here to eat just to ogle his wife." She laughed. "In truth, there's not a guy around who would look for more than two seconds for fear of incurring Morgan's wrath."

"He has a temper?"

"No, not really."

Honey choked, accidentally spraying iced tea across the table. Alarmed, Elizabeth quickly handed her a napkin. Biting back a laugh, Honey mumbled, "Sorry."

But Misty wasn't offended. "You should talk," she said primly. "Morgan is still bragging about that fight Sawyer had over you."

"What about Gabe?" Elizabeth asked. "Is he a hell-raiser?"

"Gabe? Heck, no, Gabe's a lover, not a fighter. Not that I doubt he could handle himself in any situation."

Elizabeth tried to sound only mildly curious as she pursued that topic. "He has himself something of a reputation, doesn't he?"

Misty shrugged. "I suppose, but it's not a bad one. Folks around here just love him, that's all."

"You know," Elizabeth said thoughtfully as she set aside her pencil and propped her elbows on the table, "I think it's amazing that he did something so heroic and yet he shrugs it off as nothing."

Honey waved her fork dismissively. "They're all like that. They're strong and capable and well-respected and they don't really think a thing of it. To them, it's just how things are—they're nothing special. But I know not a one of them would sit on the sidelines if someone needed help. That's just the way they are."

For over an hour, the women talked, and Elizabeth took page after page of background notes on the brothers, Gabe specifically. If some of her questions had nothing to do with her thesis…well, that was no one's concern but her own.

When the lunch ended and she was ready to go, Elizabeth thanked both women. Misty had her wide-awake daughter cradled in her arms, cooing to her, so it was Honey who touched Elizabeth's arm and said, "I hope we've been some help."

Elizabeth could read the look in Honey's eyes and understood her meaning. She smiled in acknowledgment. "You don't have to worry. I know Gabe is still sowing his wild oats, so while I'm enjoying interviewing him, I'm not going to expect undying love. I'm a little more grounded in reality than that."

Honey bit her lip then shared a look with her sister. Misty sighed. "He really is a doll, isn't he?"

"Yes, he is. But he's a rascal too, and I'm well aware of just how serious he is, which isn't very. Besides, I'm only here for the summer. I have another semester of college to go and then job hunting before I can ever think of getting attached to anyone. Gabe is fun and exciting, but I know that's where it ends."

Misty slid out of the booth to stand before Elizabeth, her brow drawn into a thoughtful frown. "Now, I'm not sure you should rule everything out."

Honey agreed. "He is acting darned strange about all this."

"It doesn't matter." Elizabeth knew they wanted to be kind, to spare her. "I'm not letting anything or anyone get in the way of my goals."

"What are your goals? I know you said you're doing your thesis on the mystique of heroes, but why?"

"I'm hoping to go into counseling. Too often the ordinary person tries to compare herself to the true heroes of the world and only comes up lacking, which is damaging to self-esteem. I'd like to be able to prove that there are real, tangible differences to account for the heroes."

Before either sister could remark on that, Elizabeth asked for directions to Jordan's veterinary office. He was the only brother she hadn't spoken to yet. From what she'd heard, this particular brother was vastly different in many ways, but still enough to melt a woman's heart.

She looked forward to grilling him.

Gabe wrapped his arm around Ceily from behind, then gave her a loud smooch on her nape. "Hey, doll," he growled in a mock-hungry voice.

Jumping, Ceily almost dropped the tray of dirty dishes loading her down, and would have if Gabe hadn't caught it in time.

Rounding on him, Ceily yelled, "Don't do that, damn it! You about gave me a heart attack."

"Shh." Gabe grinned at her. "I don't want anyone to know I'm here."

Ceily seemed to think that was very funny, judging by her crooked grin. "If you're looking for your newest girlfriend, she already left."

Disappointment struck him, and he muttered a low curse that made Ceily's grin widen. "Do you know where she went?"

She took the tray from him and set it in the sink. "Maybe."

"Ceily…"

With a calculating look, she said over her shoulder, "I need a leaking faucet fixed. I can talk while you repair."

Gabe didn't want to waste that much time, but he reluctantly agreed. Ceily was one of his best friends, and she made one hell of a spy. Though she didn't gossip, she always seemed to know anything and everything that was said in her diner. "All right. Show me the sink."

Five minutes later Gabe was on his back, shirtless to keep from getting too dirty, trying to tighten a valve. The job was simple, but Ceily needed new plumbing in a bad way. "I can fix it for now, hon, but we're going to need to make major repairs soon. When's good for you?"

Ceily was at his side on a stool, taking a quick break while business was slow. "You just give me the word and I'll make the time."

Seconds later, Gabe shoved himself out from under the sink and sat up. "All done. So start talking."

Ceily checked the sink first, saw it was dry and nodded. "She went to see your brother Jordan, but she said she's also going to do some shopping." Ceily gave an impish smile. "She wants to dress more casual, like Misty and Honey."

Gabe groaned. Misty and Honey had chic comfort down to a fine art. The women could wear cutoffs and T-shirts and look like sex personified. "I'll never live through it."

Ceily thought that was about the funniest thing she'd ever heard. Gabe used her knee for unnecessary leverage and came to his feet. "You care to share the joke?"

"You don't think it's amusing that the mighty Gabe Kasper, womanizer and renowned playboy, is being struck down by a prim little red-haired wallflower?"

Anger tightened his gut for an instant before Gabe hid it. He didn't like anyone making fun of Lizzy, but he knew Ceily hadn't meant to be nasty. She, like him, was merely surprised at his interest in a woman who was so different from his usual girlfriends.

But then, that was precisely why he felt so drawn to her.

He began lathering his hands in the sink while he gathered his thoughts. Ceily tilted her head at his silence, then let out a whistle.

"Well, I'll be. You really are smitten, aren't you?"

"Smitten is a stupid word, Ceily," he groused. "Let's just call it intrigued, okay?"

"Intrigued, smitten…doesn't matter what you call

it, Gabe, you've still got it bad." She crossed her arms and leaned against the wall. "Care to tell me why?"

Gabe lifted one shoulder in a shrug as he dried his hands on a frayed dish towel. "Lizzy is different."

"You're telling me!"

Gabe snapped her with the towel. "You *are* feeling sassy today, aren't you?"

She yelped, then rubbed her well-rounded hip. There was a time when Gabe would have helped her with that, but he had no real interest in touching any woman, even playfully, except Lizzy. She had invaded his brain, and it was taking a lot of getting used to.

Ceily was still frowning when she said, "It's not every day I get to witness the fall of the mighty Gabe."

Lifting one brow, Gabe announced, "I didn't fall, I jumped."

"So it's like that, huh?"

Gabe propped one hip on the side of the sink and watched Ceily. She was his friend and he'd always been able to talk with her. He loved his brothers dearly, but he could just imagine how they'd react if he started confessing to them. He'd never hear the end of it.

"It's damn strange," he admitted, "if you want the truth. One minute I didn't like her at all, then I was noticing all these little things about her, then I was lusting after her...."

"Uh, I hate to point this out, Gabe, but you tend to lust over every available, of-age woman you meet."

"Not like this." He shook his head and considered all the differences. "You know as well as I do that most of the women have come pretty easy for me."

Her look was ironic. "I have firsthand knowledge of that fact."

Gabe looked up, startled. A slow flush crept up his neck. "I wasn't talking about you, doll." He reached out and flicked a long finger over her soft cheek. "We were both too young then to even know what we were doing."

Ceily's smile was slow and taunting. Despite the fact they'd once experimented a little with each other, their friendship had grown. Gabe was eternally grateful for that.

"As I recall," she purred, teasing him, "you knew exactly what you were doing. And it was nice for my first time to be with someone I trusted and liked."

Gabe felt as though he was choking. Ceily hadn't mentioned that little episode in many years. And never would he point out to her exactly how inept he'd been back then. When she found the right guy, she'd realize it on her own. Curious, since she *had* brought it up, he asked, "Did you ever tell anyone?"

"Nope. And I know for a fact you haven't, so don't get all flustered. Besides, I'm not carrying a torch for you, Gabe. It was fun, but I want more."

Gabe slid off the sink to give her a bear hug. Ceily was a very special person. "I know. And you'll find it. You deserve the very best."

She returned his hug and said with a hoity-toity accent, "I tend to think so." Then she shoved him back a bit. "But I know what you mean. All the women for miles around come running when you crook your little finger."

"Not all." Gabe almost chuckled at the image she

described, but felt forced to admit the truth. "I have been turned down a time or two, you know."

Ceily scoffed. "Never with anyone who mattered."

Gabe stared at her, and her eyes widened. "Oh, wait! Are you telling me Elizabeth Parks turned you down?"

Scowling, Gabe shoved his hands in his pockets. "I'm not telling you anything about Elizabeth. My point was just that most women want me because of my reputation, because they think I'm good-looking or sexy—"

Ceily bent double laughing.

Gabe glared. "Oh, to hell with it. There's no talking to you today."

He started to skirt around her, but she caught him from behind and held on to his belt loops, getting dragged two feet before he finally stopped. Still chuckling, she gasped, "No, wait! I want to hear what it is that she wants from you."

Gabe heaved a deep sigh, then without turning to look at her, he admitted, "She thinks I'm some kind of damn hero and she wants to learn more about me, about my character and my family. She looks at me with this strange kind of excitement and…almost awe. Not for what *we* might do, or for what I might do to her, but for who she thinks I am. Damn, Ceily, no woman has ever done that before. And she hasn't pursued me at all for anything else. If I'd be willing to go on answering her damn questions, she'd be happy as a lark to leave it at that."

Last night, Gabe reminded himself, she'd been more than willing to do other things. But she hadn't come to him, he'd gone to her. He'd set about seducing her when he hadn't found it necessary to seduce a woman in ages.

And even then, he had the feeling that if he'd stuck her damn pencil in her hand, she'd have stopped cold in the middle of his sensual ministrations to start taking notes on his character. Now that he knew why it was so important to her, he not only felt turned on by her physically, he felt touched by her emotionally.

Seduction was a damn arousing business.

Ceily let go of his belt loops and smoothed her hand over the breadth of his back. "Poor Gabe. You really are adrift, huh?"

"I'm gonna turn you over my knee, Ceily."

She laughed at such a ridiculous threat. "No, you won't. Because I can give you some valuable advice."

Very slowly Gabe turned to face her. "Is that right?"

"Yep. You see, I heard Elizabeth tell your sisters-in-law that she has no intention of hanging around here once school starts. She's an academic sort and she has big plans for her life. If you hope to be part of those plans, you'd better get cracking, because I got the feeling that once she's gone, she won't be coming back."

Chapter 8

When Gabe let himself in through the back entrance of Jordan's veterinary clinic, he found Elizabeth and Jordan leaning over an examination table. Their backs were to him, but he could see that Lizzy was cuddled close to Jordan's side, Jordan's arm was around her shoulders, and they were in intimate conversation.

Gabe saw red.

"Am I interrupting?" He had meant to ask that question with cold indifference, but even to his ears it had sounded like a raw challenge.

Jordan looked at him over his shoulder; he was smiling. "Come here, Gabe. Take a look." Then he added, "But be very quiet."

His brother's voice had that peculiar soothing quality he used when treating frightened or injured animals. It was hypnotic and, according to all the women, sexy as hell.

Gabe barely stifled a growl. If Jordan was using that voice on Lizzy, he'd—

A very fat, bedraggled feline lay on the exam table, licking a new batch of tiny mewling kittens. Gabe glanced up at the look on Lizzy's face and promptly melted.

Big tears glistened in her vivid blue eyes and spiked her lashes. As Gabe watched, she gave a watery smile and sniffed, then gently rubbed the battered cat behind what was left of an ear.

Softly, Jordan explained, "She got into a tussle with a neighboring dog and lost. No sooner did she get dropped off than she started birthing. Eight kittens." Jordan shook his head. "She's a trooper, aren't you, old girl?" Jordan stroked his hand down the cat's back, earning a throaty purr.

Lizzy sniffed again. "She's a stray. Jordan says she's undernourished, so we didn't know if the kittens would be all right or not." She peered at Gabe with a worried expression. "They are awfully small, aren't they?"

Gabe smiled. "Most kittens are that tiny."

"And how...yucky they look?"

Jordan chuckled. "She'll have them all cleaned up and cozy in no time. The problem now is getting her into a pen. I hate to move her after she's just given birth, but I can hardly leave her and the babies here on the table."

Lizzy seemed to be considering that. "Do the pens open from the top or the front?"

"Both."

"Then… Well, maybe we could just take the table cover and all, and put her in the pen. I mean, if you hold the two top corners, and Gabe holds the two bottom corners, and I sort of guide it in and make sure no babies tumble out… Would that work do you think?"

To Gabe's annoyance, Jordan smiled and kissed Lizzy's cheek. "I think that's a brilliant idea. Gabe, keep an eye on this batch while I go find a big-enough pen. I'll be right back."

Gabe stepped next to Lizzy. "You've been crying." Just being close to her made him feel funny—adrift, as Ceily had said. He didn't know himself when he was this close to her, and he sure as hell didn't recognize all the things she made him feel.

Lizzy bit her lip, which looked extremely provocative to Gabe. "I've never seen babies born before. It's amazing."

Gabe slipped his arm around her and nuzzled her ear. Keeping his hands, or his mouth, to himself was out of the question. "Did you help Jordan?"

She laughed softly. "Mostly I just tried to stay out of his way."

Jordan said from behind them, "I couldn't have done it without her. She has the touch, Gabe. No sooner did she stroke that old cat than she settled down and relaxed some. I was afraid I was going to have to sedate her, but Elizabeth's touch was better than any shot I could give."

Gabe made a noncommittal sound. He knew firsthand just how special Lizzy's touch was.

Within minutes they had the mother and all her babies cozied up in the pen and set in a warm corner where there was plenty of sunshine and quiet. The mother cat, exhausted after her ordeal, dozed off.

"Will she be all right?" Gabe asked.

Elizabeth answered him. "Jordan said none of her injuries from the dog are significant. He cleaned up some scrapes and scratches, one not too horrible bite, and then she started birthing." Laughing at herself, Lizzy admitted, "When she let out that first screeching roar, I thought she was dying. Jordan explained to me that she was just a mama in labor."

Jordan, trying to slip clean dry bedding in around the mewling kittens, said, "Gabe, why don't you show Elizabeth around the rest of the clinic?"

Lizzy's eyes widened. "Could you? I'd love to see it."

Since Gabe would love to get her alone, he agreed.

Everything about Elizabeth Parks fascinated him—her softness, her freckles, her temper, her awe at the sight of a yapping puppy or a sleeping bird. She was complex in many ways, crystal clear in others. By the time they were done looking around, Jordan had finished with the kittens and he showed no hesitation in embracing Lizzy again.

Gabe wanted to flatten him.

"Come back any time, Elizabeth." He glanced at Gabe. "We can talk more."

"I'd like that. Thank you."

Gabe knew his ears were turning red, but damn it, he didn't want her hanging around Jordan. He didn't want her hanging around any man except himself.

And he still wasn't too keen on her discussing him with everyone. God only knew what she might hear!

She finally stepped away from Jordan and faced both men. "I have to run off now. I have more errands to get through."

She backed to the door as she said it, keeping a close watch on Gabe.

"What errands?" he asked suspiciously.

"Oh, the usual." She reached for the doorknob and opened the door. "The library, the grocery store...a visit with Casey."

The last was muttered and it took a second for it to sink in. Gabe scowled and started toward her. "Now wait just a damn minute—"

"Sorry! Gotta go." She hesitated, then called, "I'll see you tonight, Gabe!"

She was out the door before he could catch her. He would have given pursuit if Jordan hadn't started laughing. At that moment, Gabe's frustration level tipped the scales and he decided Jordan would make a fine target. Slowly he turned, his nostrils flared. "You have something to say?"

Jordan was his quietest brother, but also the deepest. He kept his thoughts to himself for the most part, and tended to view the world differently than the rest of them. He was more serious, more sensitive. Women loved him for those qualities.

What had Elizabeth thought of him?

Gabe waited and finally Jordan managed to wipe the grin off his face. "I'd say Elizabeth Parks is pretty special."

Gabe's muscles tightened until they almost cramped. He hadn't thought her special at first, but now that he did, he didn't want anyone else—anyone male—to think it. "Me, too," he snarled.

Jordan was supremely unaffected by his anger. "Going to do anything about it?"

"It?"

Jordan shook his head as if he pitied Gabe. "You remind me of a junkyard dog who's just sniffed a female in heat. You're trying to guard the junkyard and still lay claim to the female."

"I'm not at all sure I like that analogy."

Jordan shrugged. "It fits. And if I was you, I'd get my head clear real quick."

Because he wasn't sure how to do that, Gabe didn't comment. Instead, he asked, "What did you think of her?"

"Sexy."

That single word hit him like a solid punch in the ribs. He wheezed. "Damn it, Jordan…"

"What? You think you're the only one to notice?" Again, Jordan shook his head. "I've got a waiting room full of clients, so I'll make this quick. No, Elizabeth's sex appeal isn't up-front and in your face. But it only takes about two minutes of talking with her, of watching her move and hearing her voice and looking into those incredible blue eyes to know she's hotter than hell on the inside."

It was so unlike Jordan to speak that way that Gabe was rendered mute.

"If you could have seen how gentle her hands were when she touched that frightened cat, well… You can imagine where a man's mind wanders when seeing that. And the look of discovery on her face when the first kitten appeared, and her husky voice when she's getting emotional…" Jordan shrugged. "It doesn't take a rocket scientist to know those same qualities would carry over into the rest of her life. She's sensitive and tender-hearted and something about her is a little wounded, making her sympathetic to boot."

Gabe rubbed both hands over his face, those elusive emotions rising to choke him.

Jordan slapped him on the back. "Add to that an incredible body… Well, there you have it."

"I'm sorry I asked," Gabe moaned.

Jordan turned his brother around and steered him toward the door. They were of a similar height and build, but Gabe was numb, so moving him was no problem. "Go. I have work to do."

Gabe was just over the threshold when Jordan said his name again. Turning, Gabe raised one brow.

"I talked you up real nice, told her what a sterling character you have, but somehow I got the impression she's given up on you already." Jordan shrugged. "Not that she isn't interested, because I could tell she is. I'm not sure what you've been doing with her, and it's certainly none of my business, but every time she said your name, she blushed real cute."

Eyes narrowed, Gabe muttered, "That's sunburn."

"No, that was arousal. Credit me with enough sense to know the difference."

Gabe started back in and Jordan flattened a hand on his sternum, holding him off. "The thing is," Jordan said with quiet emphasis, "her thoughts are as clear as the written word, and from what I could tell, she's determined that what she feels is only sexual. So if that's not what you want, I'd say you have a problem. One that you better start working on real quick."

It was the second time in one day that Gabe had been given that advice. Without another word he stomped off, his mind churning with confusion. Yes, he wanted more, but how much more? Hell, he barely knew the woman. And she did have an education to finish, one that was obviously important to her.

All he could do, Gabe decided, was take it day by day. He'd get inside her brick wall, get her to talk to him, and maybe, with any luck, he'd find out that Elizabeth wanted him for more than a sexual fling or a college thesis.

But for how much more was anyone's guess.

Elizabeth felt like a puddle of nerves on the drive to the movies that night. In quite a daring move, she'd changed from her earlier clothes into another dress, this one a tad shorter, landing just below her knees, and with a bodice that unbuttoned. She felt downright wanton. Not because the clothing was in any way revealing, but because of why she'd chosen it in the first place.

Thinking of Gabe's hands stealing under her skirt in search of second base or opening her buttons to linger on first base had her in a frenzy of anticipation.

Nervously, she glanced at his profile. He was quiet, his jaw set as he concentrated on driving. His strange, introspective mood seemed to permeate the car. She cleared her throat and said boldly, "Do you realize how many firsts I've had since meeting you?"

He jerked, his gaze swinging toward her for a brief instant. "What's that supposed to mean?"

She had to make him understand, Elizabeth thought. The last thing she wanted to happen, now that she was getting into the novelty of this unique courtship, was for Gabe to feel pressured and back off. His sisters-in-law had been clearly concerned that she might get hurt. Perhaps Gabe would worry about the same thing. But if she reassured him that they wanted the same thing, a pleasant way to pass the time during her visit, with no strings attached, then he'd feel free to continue his wonderful attentions.

And they were wonderful. Gabe made her feel sexy, when all her life she'd felt plain to the point of being invisible. He made her feel feminine when she'd never paid much attention to her softness before, except that it made her weaker, less competent in a crisis. And he made her feel sexually hungry when she hadn't even known such a hunger existed.

"I like your brother."

Gabe shot her a dark look. "Which one?"

"Well, all of them, but I was talking about Jordan. He's different from the rest of you."

Gabe's hands squeezed the wheel tightly. "Yeah? How so?"

"Quieter. More…intense. He's so gentle with the animals. I felt totally at ease with him, and that was certainly a first."

Gabe's jaw locked so hard she wondered that he didn't get a headache. "You're not at ease with me?"

Around Gabe she was tense and so hot she thought she might catch fire. But she wouldn't tell him that. "It was just different with Jordan. And he let me help with that cat. I've never seen babies born before." Her voice softened, but she couldn't help it. Seeing the tiny little wet creatures emerging was a true miracle. "Have you? Seen babies born, I mean?"

"Sure." Gabe glanced at her, then at the road. "Jordan keeps all kinds of pets around the house. We all like animals, Lizzy. He's not different in that."

"But Jordan's… I don't know. More discreet than the rest of you. Softer."

"Ha!" Gabe shifted in his seat, looking disgruntled. "Don't let Jordan fool you! He's quieter, I'll give you that. But he's a man, same as I am."

"Gabe, I didn't mean to draw a comparison." She couldn't understand his reaction. It was almost as if… no. There was no way Gabriel Kasper could be jealous of his brother. She decided to change the subject.

"I had lunch with Honey and Misty today."

Gabe's brows pulled down the tiniest bit. "Did you enjoy yourself?"

"Yes." Elizabeth pleated the edge of her skirt with her fingertips. "I've never really hung out with other women before. It was fun. The things they talk about…"

There was a strange darkness to his eyes as he asked, "What things?"

She shrugged. "Women things." She had no intention of telling him Honey was pregnant. Now that she'd been initiated into the wonders of doing lunch with the ladies, she'd didn't want to do anything to ruin it. When Honey told her husband the news, then Gabe would find out. "Shopping, Amber, men. Things like that."

In a reflexive movement, Gabe's hands tightened on the steering wheel. "What about men?"

"Nothing in particular. Just fun stuff. It was a first for me. I hadn't realized how enjoyable that could be, chatting and laughing with other women. I've never quite fit in like that before, but they're so nice and accepting. I like your sisters-in-law."

Gabe stopped for a red light and turned to face her. "I like them, too. A lot." He tilted his head, studying her, and there was something in his eyes, some vague shadow of consideration. "C'mere, Lizzy."

Oh, the way he said that. It was so much more than an invitation to close the space between them. The heat in his eyes made it more. The low growl of his voice made it more. She looked at the seat where Gabe's large hand rested. Warming inside, she scooted over as much as her seat belt would allow. It was close enough to feel his heat, his energy, to breathe in his wonderfully musky male scent.

Last night she had imagined burying her nose against his neck, drinking him in and tasting his hot skin with her tongue.... She gulped a large breath of air and tried to get control of herself. She was turning into a nymphomaniac!

Immediately, Gabe's rough palm settled on her thigh in a possessive hold that thrilled her.

"How's your sunburn today?" he murmured, gently caressing her.

Staring at his dark hand on her leg, she shrugged. "Much better. It was a little tender this morning, but now I hardly notice it at all."

He slipped his fingers beneath the skirt of her dress and began tracing slow, easy circles on her flesh. Her breathing deepened. "And this? Does this hurt you, Lizzy?"

She shook her head, too startled, too excited to speak.

The light turned green and Gabe pulled away. He used one hand to steer while his gentle fingers continued to pet her bare skin. "Tell me what other firsts we're talking about."

His warm touch was hypnotic and she found her legs parting just a bit so his searching fingers could drift lazily up the sensitive inside of her knee. "Swimming in a lake."

"Oh, yeah." He flashed her a grin. "Think you might want to be daring and try it again sometime?"

This must be old hat to him, Elizabeth thought, as he easily maneuvered the car one-handed while deliberately arousing her with the other. He was such a rogue.

"Yes." She'd try anything Gabe wanted her to. She trusted him.

"Any other firsts?"

"Well, there's…this." She indicated his hand beneath her skirt, slowly inching higher. She sucked in air and concentrated on speaking coherently. "The kissing and touching and the way you…talk to me."

He glanced at her and she said, "I love the way you talk to me, Gabe. No man has ever spoken so intimately with me, much less said the kinds of things you say."

"You've known a lot of fools, sweetheart."

Her smile trembled. "There, you see? And all this business with first base and drive-in movies. I feel like I'm just starting to really see the world."

Gabe squeezed his eyes closed for a heartbeat, and

she added, "You're also by far the most unique hero I've interviewed, so I suppose that's a first, as well."

How in the world she'd managed to string so many words together, she had no idea. Her thoughts felt jumbled, her nerve endings raw. Leaning slightly toward him, she touched his shoulder. "Gabe, can I ask you something?"

Twilight was settling in on the small town, making it almost dark enough to hide what they did with each other. Elizabeth smoothed her hand over his shoulder, then down to squeeze his biceps. She soaked in the feel of the soft cotton T-shirt over solid muscle. Gabe felt so good.

He worked his jaw. "You can ask me anything, babe."

Hesitantly, she explained, "It's sort of a request."

His hand left her as he pulled into a gravel lot behind several other cars, waiting to pay at the drive-in entrance. Elizabeth looked around in wonder. People milled about everywhere, some walking to a concrete-block building that she assumed housed the cameras and perhaps a concession stand. Others leaned in car windows talking to neighbors. Some were sitting outside their cars or trucks or vans, watching the sky darken and the stars appear. The screen was huge, situated in front of row after row of metal poles holding speakers. It fascinated her.

"Ask away."

"Oh." Turning to Gabe, she bit her bottom lip, then because she was unable to look at him and ask her question, she gave her attention to the surrounding lot. "Would it be okay if I touched you, too? I mean, like with first base and second base? Touching you last night…that was another first. I had no idea a man felt so…contradictory."

His Adam's apple bobbed when he swallowed hard. He adjusted his jeans, slouched behind the wheel a bit more and closed his eyes. "Contradictory, how?"

Elizabeth knew her face was flaming. Actually, her whole body was flaming. In a rough, strangled whisper, she said, "Soft in some places, so hard in others. Sleek and alive. I'd… I'd like to feel your chest, under your shirt, and I'd like to feel you…*there,* inside your jeans."

Gabe groaned, then laughed. He rested his forehead against the steering wheel for one second, then swiveled to snare her with his gaze. "Are you absolutely sure you want to see a movie?"

Not quite understanding, Elizabeth glanced at the billboard announcing which titles would be playing tonight. The first movie was *Tonya's Revenge.* Probably an action movie, she decided—not her favorite. But while it didn't sound exactly scintillating, she was very curious. "I'd like to see at least a bit of it, since this is another first for me. Why?"

Gabe hesitated to answer as he pulled up to the small cashier's window and handed over a couple of bills. The attendant, evidently someone Gabe knew based on his greeting and his curiosity as he speared a flashlight into the car to check out Elizabeth, winked and handed Gabe his change. "Enjoy the movie," he said with a wide grin. Gabe answered with a muttered oath.

Elizabeth looked around as Gabe parked the car toward the back of the lot. Already people had set up lawn chairs and blankets or turned their trucks around to relax in the truck beds. Gabe moved as far away from the others as he could.

"You don't want to stay, do you?" Elizabeth didn't want to force him into something he was reluctant to do.

Gabe's frown became more pronounced. "I'm having second thoughts, that's all."

Her stomach pitched in very real dread. "Second thoughts? You mean you don't want to—"

In a sudden move, Gabe grabbed her by the back of the neck and hauled her close, then treated her to a hot, deep, tongue-licking kiss that left her shaken. With his mouth still touching hers, he said, "I want," he assured her in a low growl. "But I'd rather be back at your apartment where I could get you naked and feast on you in private."

Elizabeth could barely get her heavy eyelids to open. Her heart felt ready to burst, her skin too tight, her breasts and belly too sensitive. Breathless, she asked, "And you'd let me touch you, too?"

"Hell, yeah." He kissed her again, short and sweet. "But I don't want you to miss any firsts here, sugar. And every American woman should experience the drive-in at least once. Better late than never, I suppose."

Elizabeth nuzzled his warm throat, just as she'd imagined doing. She luxuriated in his exotic, enticing scent. What would it be like to have that scent surrounding her all night long? Trying to follow the conversation, she asked, "Because the movies are good?"

Gabe grinned, but it was a carnal grin, filled with determination and sultry heat. "No, baby." He held her a little closer, his hand splayed on the small of her back. "It's because getting groped at the drive-in is practically a tradition. You can't really be at the movies without doing at least a little petting. The lights are dim, the movie's boring and all that body heat builds up. It's just natural to get a little frisky."

Elizabeth considered that, then slowly slid both hands up Gabe's chest to his shoulders, then around his neck. "How about if I want to do a lot of petting?"

"Then I'll maybe last through half a movie. *Maybe*." He cradled her head between his hands and rubbed her cheekbones with his thumbs. "But I'm not making any promises, sweetheart, so don't say I didn't warn you."

Chapter 9

She was driving him crazy. Lizzy's sweet, hot mouth opened on his throat and she made a nearly incoherent sound of discovery and excitement. "You taste so good, Gabe. Do you taste the same all over?"

Feeling her soft lips move against his skin, he tightened painfully from toes to scalp. He wanted to let her explore, to take her time and experience everything, but he wasn't sure he'd live through it. "You can find out later," he murmured, and just saying the words almost sent him off the deep end while images of her mouth on his abdomen, his thighs, in between, fired him. He groaned.

She leaned back slightly and looked at the movie. "What?"

There was a breathless excitement to her tone as she anticipated another love scene on the big screen. He'd had no idea Lizzy would be so receptive to the some-what cheesy, low-grade erotic film that was playing. Watching her while she watched the movie, he wedged his palm beneath her breast and felt the frantic racing of her heartbeat.

She amused him. And fascinated him. Grinning, he teased, "Lizzy. I'm surprised you can even see the movie the way we've steamed up the windows."

Her smile was pleased and filled with feminine power. "I'd read about fogging windows in books be-fore, but I thought it was an exaggeration."

Forget amusement. Her naïveté made him rock hard with lust and soft as butter with affection. Bringing her mouth to his, he said against her lips, "Just looking at you is enough to steam the place up," then proceeded to thoroughly feast on her mouth. He'd never tire of her taste, her warmth. The small, sexy sounds she made when he gave her his tongue, or when he coaxed her tongue into his mouth.

She grew quickly impatient with kissing and started tugging on his T-shirt, untucking it from his jeans.

Gabe, always willing to oblige, set her a bit away from him and pulled it over his head. Within a heart-beat she was back, her eyes luminous in the dark inte-rior of the car, her small hands eagerly sliding over his hot skin. Whether on purpose or not, he didn't know, her thumbs brushed over his nipples and he jerked. She stared, wide-eyed, at his reaction, made a sound of discovery and deliberately delved her hands into the hair on his chest again.

"Sweet mercy…" Gabe groaned, knotting his hands against the seat and dredging up thoughts of work, of the lake, anything to try to regain some measure of control.

Then her mouth touched his right nipple and he felt her gentle, moist breath, the tentative flick of her small pink tongue...and he was gone.

"Sorry," he rasped. "I can't take it." He saw the disappointment in her gaze and choked on a strangled breath. Holding her slim shoulders to keep her at bay, he said, "Not here, sweetheart. It's just too much. You're too much. I don't understand it, but..."

She didn't look convinced, so he caught her hand and carried it to his erection, then hissed a painful breath as the contact made his entire body clench.

"You see what you're doing to me?" he asked. He knew his voice was harsh, guttural, knew he'd started to sweat and that his hands were shaking. "It's insane. I've made out in this drive-in hundreds of times, but I've never been this close to losing all reason."

"Really?"

He blinked at her look of wonder, minutely regaining his wits. She honestly had no idea of her appeal or her effect on the male species. "Yeah. I'm sorry, babe, but it's the truth." For the first time in his life, his salacious past embarrassed him a bit. Lizzy was so innocent, so pure, that he felt like a total scoundrel. "My mother should have locked me up or something," he muttered, his long fingers still encircling her wrist, holding her hand immobile against him. "Sawyer told her to often enough. Morgan even tried it a few times. But I was always more wild than not and I was determined to get my fill and..."

He trailed off as he realized how fascinated she was,

soaking up his every absurd word. Good God, he hoped she didn't put any of that in her damn thesis!

Shaking her gently, he added, "Lizzy, listen to me. There's something about you...."

She tilted her head at him in a measure of pity. "What? My freckles? Come on, Gabe. I've never heard of freckles inspiring lust. Or red hair that's too curly. Or..."

Gabe curved his hand around one lush breast. He could feel the warmth and softness of her, the incredible firmness of virgin flesh. "How about a body made for a man?" he growled. "Or a smile that's so sweet I feel it inside my pants."

She gasped.

"Or skin so soft it makes me crazy wanting to feel it all over my body. Or the way you talk, the things you talk about, your innocence and your daring and your—"

She pressed her fingers over his mouth, her eyes squeezed shut. He parted his lips and ran the tip of his tongue down the seam of her middle and ring finger, probing lightly. She snatched her hand away and panted.

"I want you, Lizzy."

Her eyes opened slowly and they glowed. "I want you, too." She gulped in air, then added, "Just for the summer, for this one time in my life, I want to experience everything I've never felt before. When I go back to school and my old life-style and my plans, when I start my formal training, I want it to be with new knowledge. I don't want to be inexperienced anymore. I want to loosen up, as you suggested."

Gabe took her words like an iron punch on the chin. *Just for the summer, just for the summer...*

Damn her, no! He wouldn't give up that easy. But he also didn't want to scare her off. He'd give her everything she asked for and more. He'd drown her in pleasure so intense she'd get addicted. She wouldn't be able to do without him. He'd tie her so closely to him she wouldn't even be able to think about walking away from him.

He had no idea what the murky future held, but for the first time in his life he was anxious about it. A year from now? Who the hell knew? Lasting romantic relationships weren't his forté, but he'd seen his two oldest brothers work it out, and that was nothing short of a miracle. One thing he was certain about: a month from now he'd still be wanting her, today, tomorrow... maybe indefinitely. He wanted, he *needed,* a chance to see what was happening between them.

Gabe reached to the floor of the car and picked up the box of popcorn they'd bought earlier. He put it in her lap. "Hold onto that."

"Gabe?"

He didn't look at her again as he stuck the speaker out the window and hooked it into place on its stand. A lot of people would recognize his car, and they'd know he was leaving early. They'd probably even deduce why. For Lizzy's sake, he hated that, but couldn't think of an alternative. It would be worse if he ended up doing things with her here that he knew damn good and well should be done in private. And his control was too strained. Already he wanted her so bad he felt sweat forming on his naked back and at his temples, though the night had cooled off and was comfortable.

Even without the speaker in the car, he heard the on-screen moaning and looked up. *Tanya's Revenge* wasn't much in the way of evil intent. Gabe figured she planned to physically, sexually wear out her adversary, then gain her revenge—whatever it might be. Lizzy was spellbound. She'd watched every sex scene with single-minded intent.

His heart pounded in his chest as he considered doing all those things to her, and how she would react. "Put your seat belt back on."

Without tearing her gaze from the screen, she obeyed. His car started with a low purr and then they were maneuvering out of the lot. Once the screen was no longer in view, Lizzy turned toward him. He could feel her curiosity, could almost hear her mind working, thinking about what she'd watched and wondering if they'd do things like that together.

"Damn right we will," Gabe said, answering her silent question. Lizzy fanned herself, but otherwise held quiet. They reached her place in record time. In one minute flat they were inside with the door locked and Gabe had her pressed to the wall, giving his hands and his mouth free rein.

Elizabeth held her breath as Gabe's right hand stroked down her side, over her waist, her hip, then to the back of her knee. He pulled her leg upward so that she was practically circling his hips—then he thrust gently.

A moan escaped her. She could feel the fullness and hard length of his erection through his jeans as he deliberately rocked against her in a parody of sex. His mouth, open and damp, moved over her cheek to her arched throat. "I want to be inside you right now, babe. I *need* to be inside you."

"My…my bedroom," she muttered, nearly incoherent, more than ready to accommodate him. But Gabe shook his head.

"You have to do some catching up. I want you to be as hot as I am."

She tried to tell him that she already was, but then his mouth covered hers and his tongue licked past her lips and she could barely think, much less speak.

His hand, rough and incredibly hot, smoothed over her bare thigh to her panties. Elizabeth couldn't stop her instinctive reaction to his hand on her bottom, exploring, first palming one round cheek then gliding inward to touch her in the most intimate spot imaginable.

"Easy," he whispered against her mouth. "Damn, you're wet. You do want me, don't you, sweetheart?"

"Yes…" She felt like she was falling, though her back was flat against the wall with Gabe's hard torso pinning her in place.

"Let's get these out of the way." He released her leg and hooked both hands into the waistband of her panties beneath her skirt. It felt naughty and exciting and achingly sexual the way he went to one knee in front of her to strip off her underclothes. "Step out of them," he instructed.

Like a sleepwalker, Elizabeth lifted first one foot and then the other. Her sandals were still in place, but Gabe had no problem tugging her panties off around them. She waited for him to stand, but he didn't, and she looked down.

His face was flushed, his eyes burning hot as he kneaded the backs of her thighs. He looked at her and didn't smile. Instead he leaned forward and kissed her through her cotton dress, making her suck in a startled, choking breath. Her hands automatically sought his head and her fingers threaded into his cool blond hair.

"Gabe?"

"You smell good," he said, nuzzling into her. Her knees threatened to give out, but his palms moved to cuddle her naked backside, keeping her upright. "So good."

"I… I can't do this." Even as she said it, her hands clenched in his hair, directing his attentions to a spot that pulsed with need. His mouth opened and his breath was incredibly hot, almost unbearable. She felt the damp press of his tongue through her clothes and she cried out.

Gabe shot to his feet in front of her and took her mouth in a voracious kiss meant to consume her. She couldn't breathe, couldn't react, couldn't think. She felt wild, this time lifting her leg to wrap around him without instruction. Both his hands covered her breasts, squeezing a bit roughly, but she loved it, loved him and the way he made her feel.

He started on the buttons of her dress and had them all free within seconds. The bodice opened just wide enough for him to tug it down her shoulders and beneath her breasts. The dress framed her, caught at her elbows and pinned her arms to her sides. "Gabe?" She struggled, wanting to touch him, too.

The dress pulled taut and forced her straining breasts higher. Her nipples were stiff, pointed, and with a low growl Gabe bent and sucked one deep into the heat of his mouth, his rough tongue rasping over her, his teeth holding her captive for the assault.

She screamed. Her body arched hard against his. Gabe switched to the other nipple and his hands went under her skirt, one lifting her thigh, the other cupping over her belly then delving into her moist curls. She knew she was wet, could feel the pulsing of her body. His fingers were both a relief and a torture as he moved them over her hot flesh, stroking, then parting slick, swollen folds.

She pressed her head against the wall, feeling a strange tension begin to invade her body.

"We'll go easy," he promised, but the words were so low, so rough, she could barely understand them. "Right here, sweetheart," he murmured, and she felt a lightning stroke of sensation as one fingertip deliberately plied her swollen clitoris. Gasping, she tried to pull away because the sensation was too acute, but there was no place for her to go.

"Don't fight me," he whispered around her wet nipple, licking lazily. "Trust me, Lizzy."

She couldn't. The feelings were coming too fast, too strong. Her muscles ached and tightened, then tightened some more. Her vision blurred as heat washed over her in waves. She tried to tell him it was too much, but her words didn't make any sense and he ignored them anyway, listening more to her body than what she had to say. His fingertip felt both rough and gentle as he continued to pet her, concentrating patiently on that one ultrasensitive spot, driving her insane.

Her climax took her by surprise, stealing her breath, making it impossible to do more than moan in low gasping pants, going on and on…. Her body bowed, but Gabe held her securely, not stopping his touch, pushing her and pushing her. He moaned, too, the sound a small vibration around her nipple as he sucked strongly at her. His left forearm slipped beneath her buttocks, keeping her on her feet as her knees weakened, forcing her to feel everything he wanted her to feel.

When finally she slumped against him, spent and exhausted, his hold gentled, loosened. She was no longer crushed against his body, but remained in his embrace, gently rocking. His palm cupped her, holding in the heat, and he said, "I can still feel you pulsing."

Embarrassment tried to ebb into her consciousness, but Gabe didn't give it a chance to take hold. He kissed each breast, her throat, her chin. Putting his forehead to hers, their noses touching, he whispered, "That was incredible, Lizzy."

If she'd had the strength she would have laughed. Gabe was a master of understatement. Slowly she opened her eyes and was seared by the heat in his. While she watched, he removed his palm from her and raised his hand to her face. His gaze dropped to her mouth and with one wet fingertip, he traced her lips.

She sucked in a startled breath, but couldn't think of a thing to say. Still watching her, Gabe slowly licked her upper lip, then pulled her bottom lip through his teeth to suck gently. "You taste as sweet as I knew you would."

She couldn't move. Her eyes opened owlishly. Good grief, she'd never been in this situation before, never even imagined such a thing! He hadn't shared intercourse with her, but she supposed this was one form of lovemaking. Only…against her front door? With her panties off and his clothes still on and his magical fingers…

"Cat got your tongue?" he asked while smoothing her hair from her face.

"I…" She swallowed hard. "I don't know what to say."

"How about, 'Gabe I want you.'" His gaze moved over her face in loving detail, his fingers gentle on her temple. She noticed his hands shook.

"Gabe, I want you."

The smile she'd already fallen in love with lighted his face. "Thank the lord. I haven't come in my pants since I was a teenager, but it was a close thing, babe. A very close thing."

"Oh." The things he said, and how he said them, never ceased to stupefy her. She was still considering the image he'd evoked with his words when Gabe scooped her up in his arms and started across the floor. She held on tight, charmed by the gallantry. This was another thing, like fogged windows, that she thought only happened in books.

"Sunburn okay?" he asked. He wasn't even straining to hold her weight.

She sighed, totally enamored of his strength. "What sunburn?"

Gabe laughed, a sound filled with masculine satisfaction and triumph—wholly male, hotly sexual.

Rather than put her on the bed, he stood her beside it, and with no fanfare at all, caught the hem of her dress and whisked it over her head. Her arms caught in the sleeves for just a moment, making her feel awkward, but Gabe wasn't deterred. He freed her easily, then stepped back to look at her.

She still wore her sandals, was her first thought. Second was that the way he looked at her was almost tactile, like a stroke across her belly, penetrating deep to where the need rekindled and came alive once again.

Without a word Gabe kicked off his shoes as he surveyed her body. He unbuttoned his jeans, slid down the zipper and shucked both his jeans and his shorts. Lizzy was given time to look all she pleased—which was a lot. Gabe stood still for her, except to reach out with his right arm and stroke her nipples with a knuckle.

He swallowed at her continued scrutiny. "Put me out of my misery, Red. Please."

His hips were narrow in contrast to his wide chest. His abdomen was hard and flat, his navel a shallow dent surrounded by golden brown hair that felt soft to the touch. His shoulders were straight, his legs long and strong and covered in hair. His groin... She gulped, then reached out to encircle him with her hand and squeezed. So hard and so strong, his erection flexed and he made a small strangled sound. His hands fisted; his knees locked. One glistening drop of fluid appeared on the tip, fascinating her. She spread it around with her thumb, and heard his hissing breath.

"You're playing with fire, babe."

"You're so beautiful," she breathed, then started slightly when he growled and reached for her.

"Come here, Elizabeth. Let me hold you."

But as she stepped up to him he stepped forward and carried her down to the bed. Balanced on one elbow above her, he began exploring her body again.

"I love all these sexy little freckles." He traced around her breasts, skimming just below her puckered nipples, then trailed down her abdomen to her belly button. He dipped his baby fingertip there before moving over her hipbones and her upper thighs. His hand cupped her between her thighs and she groaned, knowing exactly how he could make her feel. "And this fiery red hair," he said. "I've never seen anything like it."

Elizabeth squirmed as he parted her, as one long finger pushed deeply into her.

His gaze met hers. "Does that hurt?" he asked huskily.

She shook her head. "No, please, Gabe." She spread both hands over his chest, reveling in the heat of his skin, the way his heart galloped. She loved touching his nipples and hearing his breath hitch.

"Open your legs more, Lizzy. That's it. Another finger, okay? I want to make sure you're ready, that I won't hurt you."

His words didn't make much sense to her, though she tried to listen closely. She was attuned to his scent, his touch, the warmth of his big body. She turned her face toward him to watch as her hands glided over him.

"I can't wait anymore," he growled.

Good, she thought, already so tense she ached. If she hadn't been so unused to the intimacy, she'd have demanded he get on with it, but she wasn't quite that daring yet. All she could do was try to urge him to haste with her touch.

Gabe reached for his discarded jeans and removed a condom. Curious, Lizzy stroked his body as he slipped it on, letting her palm cup him beneath his erection, where he was heavy and warm and soft. His eyes nearly closed as he groaned, and then he was over her, his entire big body shaking as he forced her legs wide and opened her with gentle fingers.

"Lizzy, look at me."

She did, snared by his beauty, by the savage hunger in his hot blue eyes. He took her in one long slow thrust and she cried out, not in pain but in incredible pleasure. Her hips lifted of their own accord, trying to make the contact as complete as possible.

Gabe slid both hands beneath her bottom and lifted her, pushing deep, retreating, pushing in again, causing the most incredible friction. "Put your legs around me, sweetheart."

She did, crossing her ankles at the small of his back, squeezing him tight. His hairy chest crushed her breasts, and she tried to rub them against him, tried to feel as much of him as she could. The sensation of him being inside her, her tender flesh stretched tight around him, was almost unbearable. The explosive feelings began building again and she struggled toward them, her head tipped back, her eyes squeezed closed.

But then Gabe cursed and paused for one throbbing heartbeat. With another muttered oath he lowered himself to her completely, opened his mouth on her throat and began thrusting hard and fast, his groan building, his body rock hard and vibrating, and Lizzy held him,

enthralled as he came. She forgot her own needs, satisfied to smooth her hands over his damp back, through
his silky soft hair and straining shoulders.

Gabe relaxed against her, breathing deep, his arms
keeping her close, her legs still around him. After several minutes he muttered against her throat, "Sorry."

Lizzy kissed his shoulder. "For what?"

"For leaving you." He leaned up and looked at her
and there was a deeply sated expression to his eyes, a
tenderness that went bone deep. "I'll make it up to you
in just a little bit."

Elizabeth smiled and touched his face. "I'm fine."

"I want you better than fine," he said, and he kissed
her, a long, slow, leisurely kiss. He didn't seem in any
hurry to stop kissing her. After a while he sat up to remove the condom—another first for her! Without much
talking he carried her into the bathroom where they
both soaked in a cool tub. Gabe made her wild with
the way he bathed her, stroked her, teased her. After
that, he seemed insatiable.

She could barely keep her eyes open after two more
climaxes and a lot of new firsts, but when he settled
into the bed with her, she found the foresight to ask,
"Are you staying all night?"

"Yes." He pulled her to his side and pressed her
head to his shoulder.

His assumption that he was welcome amused her,
but then, she wanted him to stay. "Shouldn't you tell
someone where you are so they won't worry?"

"I'm twenty-seven years old, sweetheart. I don't
have to account for myself to my brothers."

"What about Honey? Will she worry?"

He went still, then cursed softly. "Don't move." He padded naked from the bed into the kitchen where her only phone hung on the wall. After a few seconds she heard him say, "I won't be home tonight."

There was a pause. "Yeah, well, I thought Honey might—" He laughed. "That's what I figured. See ya tomorrow."

He came back to bed and settled himself. "You were right. Sawyer said she would have worried." He kissed her forehead and within seconds he was breathing deeply.

Elizabeth stroked his chest, wondering how often he spent the night with women, if this meant anything to him at all, if she had the right to hope he'd stay with her whenever possible.

It was a long time before she, too, dozed off. But thinking of Gabe and how strong and independent and capable he was only served to slant her dreams with miserable comparisons of all the things he was, and all the things she wasn't.

And sometime in the middle of the night, the nightmares returned.

Chapter 10

Gabe was generally a sound sleeper, but then, contrary to popular belief, he seldom had a very sexy, very warm woman cuddled up to his side when he slept. Because he lived with his brothers, and because his nephew, Casey, was there, he hadn't made a habit of flaunting his social life. Having Lizzy at his side was a unique and pleasant experience.

And while he'd had no problem sleeping, he was never at any moment unaware of her curled against him.

When her skin grew warmer and her breathing deeper, he stirred. She mumbled something in her sleep and he turned his head to look at her, making a soft, soothing sound. Her hand suddenly fisted against his chest, and her head twisted from side to side.

Frowning, Gabe came up on one elbow. *"Lizzy?"*

She didn't answer him. He touched her cheek and felt it wet with tears. His heart pounded. "Hey, come on, sweetheart. Talk to me."

In the dim moonlight filtering through the curtains, he could barely make out her features. He saw her mouth move, crying soundlessly, then heard a small whimper, and another, each gaining in volume.

"Lizzy?" Gabe held her closer and stroked her hair. "You're dreaming, sweetheart. Wake up." He made his voice deliberately commanding, unable to bear her unconscious distress.

Suddenly her body went rigid as if she'd just suffered a crushing physical pain. She screamed, harsh, tearing sounds that echoed around the silent bedroom. Her arms flailed wildly and she hit him in the chest, fighting against him, against herself. Gabe pinned her arms down and rolled her beneath him.

"Wake up, Lizzy!"

Sobbing softly, she opened her eyes and stared at him. For one instant she looked lost and confused, her eyes shadowed, then she crumbled. Gabe turned to his side and held her face to his throat. "It's all right. It's all right, sweetheart."

She clutched him, and his heart broke at her racking cries. Gabe felt his eyes get misty and crushed her even closer, wanting to absorb her pain, to somehow be a part of her so he could carry some of her emotional burden.

Long minutes passed before she finally quieted, only suffering the occasional hiccup or sniff. Gabe kissed her temple, then eased her away from him. He kept the lights off and said, "Don't move, baby. I'm going to go get you a cool cloth."

He was in and out of her bathroom in fifteen seconds. When he walked in, Lizzy was propped up in the bed blowing her nose. She had her knees drawn up to her chest, the sheet wrapped around her. The first thing she said was, "I'm sorry."

"Don't make me turn you over my knee when you're already upset." Gabe scooted into bed beside her and manfully ignored the way she tried to inch away from him. He caught her chin and turned her face, then gently stroked her with the damp washcloth. "You have no reason to be sorry, Lizzy. Everyone has bad dreams every now and again."

A long silence threatened to break him and then she muttered, "It wasn't a dream."

Gabe propped his back against the headboard and handed the washcloth to Lizzy. She pressed it over her swollen eyes. Utilizing every ounce of patience he possessed, Gabe waited.

Finally she said, "I'm a little embarrassed."

"Please don't be." He kept his voice soft but firm. "I'm so glad I was here with you." His arm slipped around her shoulders and she didn't fight him as he pulled her close. "I care about you, Lizzy. Will you believe that?"

She nodded, but said, "I don't know."

Rubbing his hand up and down her bare arm, he asked, "Is it so strange for someone to care about you, sweetheart?"

"Someone like you, yes."

"What about someone not like me?"

She went still. "There's…things about me you don't know."

Gabe tightened his hold, anticipating her reaction. "You mean the awful way your mother died?"

As he'd predicted, she jerked and almost got away from him. "What do you know about that?"

"I read the articles you saved."

"How dare you!" She struggled against him, but Gabe held her tight.

"Quit fighting me, honey. I'm not letting you go." Probably not ever. It was several seconds before she went rigid against him. Gabe could feel her hurt, her anger. But he wanted to get past it, and the only way he saw to do that was to force his way. He spread his fingers across the back of her head and kept her pressed to his shoulder. "That's why you're so all-fired determined to understand this nonsense about heroism, right?"

She shuddered, and another choking sob escaped her before she caught herself. "You…you can't understand. You aren't like me. You saw a way to help and you instinctively acted. I… I let my mother die." Her hands curled into his shoulders, her nails biting, but Gabe would have gladly accepted any pain to help her. "Oh, God. I let her die."

Unable to bear it, Gabe pressed his face into her neck and rocked her while she continued talking.

"We were in a car wreck. I… I was changing the radio station trying to find a song Mom and I could sing to. We did that all the time, playing around, just having fun. It was raining and dark. Mom told me to turn the radio down, and I started to, but then a semi came around the corner and Mom had to swerve…"

Her voice had an eerie, faraway quality to it. Gabe wondered how many times, and to how many people, she'd given this guilty admission. The thought of her as a twelve-year-old child, awkward and shy, suffering what no child should ever suffer, made him desperate with the need to fix things that were years too distant to repair.

"The car went off the road and hit a tree. Mom's door was smashed shut, the windshield broken. She was… bleeding. I thought she was dead and I just screamed and got out of the car and crouched down on the gravel and the mud, waiting and numb. Too stupid to do what I should have done."

"Oh, Lizzy." Gabe kissed her temple, her ear. He murmured inanities, but she didn't seem to hear him.

"The nearest telephone was only two miles away. If…if I'd gone for help…she'd have lived if only I hadn't frozen, if I hadn't become a useless lump crying and waiting to be helped when I was barely hurt." Her hand fisted and thumped once, hard, against his shoulder. "She was pinned in that damn car unconscious and bleeding to death and I just let her die." Sobbing again, her tears soaking his neck, she whispered, "By the time another car came by and found us…it was too late."

Keeping her in the iron grip of his embrace, Gabe reached for the lamp and turned the switch. Lizzy flinched away from the harshness of it, but Gabe was so suffused with pity, with pain and mostly with anger, he refused to let her hide. Her ravaged face was a fist around his heart, but he never wavered in his determination. Forcing her to meet his gaze, he said, "You were twelve goddamned years old! You were a child. How in the hell can you compare what a child does to a grown man?"

She looked stunned by his outrage. "I was useless."

"You were in shock!"

"If I'd reacted…"

"No, Lizzy. There is no going back, no starting over. All any of us can do is make the most of each day. You're such an intelligent woman, so giving and sincere, why can't you see that you were an innocent that day?"

"You…you said you read the articles."

"And I also know how the damn media can slant things deliberately to get the best story. One more human death means little enough to them when people pass away every day, some in more horrific circumstances than others. But a human-interest story on a young traumatized girl, well, now, that's newsworthy. You were a pawn, sweetheart, a sacrifice to a headliner. That's all there is to it."

"I let her die," she said, but she sounded vaguely uncertain, almost desperate to believe him.

"No." Gabe pulled her close and kissed her hard. "You don't know that. It was dark, it was raining. Even if, through the trauma of seeing your mother badly injured, you'd been able to run to the nearest phone, there's no guarantee that you'd have gotten there safely, that you'd have found help and they'd have made it to her in time."

She searched his face, then reached for another tissue. After mopping her eyes and blowing her nose, she admitted in a raw whisper, "My dad has said that. But I'd hear him crying at night, and I'd see how wounded he looked without my mother."

Gabe cupped her tear-streaked cheeks, fighting his own emotions. "He still had you." He wobbled her head, trying to get through to her, trying to reach her. "I know he had to be grateful for that."

Her smile trembled and she gave an inelegant sniff. "Yes. He said he was. My father is wonderful."

Relief filled him that at least her father hadn't blamed her. The man had obviously been overwrought with grief. Gabe couldn't begin to imagine how he'd react if something happened to Lizzy. If he ever lost her, he'd—

Gabe froze, struck by the enormity of his thoughts. He loved Lizzy! It didn't require rhyme or reason. It didn't require a long courtship or special circumstances. He knew her, and she was so special, how could he not love her?

He touched the corner of her mouth with his thumb, already feeling his body tense with arousal and new awareness. "You're a wonderful person, sweetheart, so you deserve a wonderful dad."

Her eyes were red-rimmed, matching her nose, and her lips were puffy, her skin blotchy. Gabe thought she was possibly the most beautiful person he'd ever seen. The sheet slipped a bit, and he looked at her lush breasts, the faint sprinkling of freckles and the tantalizing peak of one soft nipple.

He tamped down his hunger and struggled to direct

all his attention to her distress. "Will you believe me that you weren't to blame, Lizzy?"

She bit her lip, then sighed. "I'll believe you don't blame me. But facts are facts. Some people possess heroic tendencies, and some people are ineffectual. I'm afraid I fall into the latter category."

Gabe caught her hips and pulled her down so she lay flat in the bed. He whisked the sheet away. "Few people," he said, while eyeing her luscious body, "are ever given the opportunity to really know if they're heroic or not." He placed his palm gently on her soft white belly. "Personally, I don't think you can judge yourself by what a frightened, shy, injured twelve-year-old did."

She stared at his mouth, firing his lust. "That's... that's why I'm studying this so hard. I want to help other adolescents to understand their own limitations, to know that they can't be completely blamed for qualities they don't possess. We're all individuals."

"And you don't want any other child to hurt as you've hurt?"

Her beautiful eyes filled with tears again. "Yes."

"I love you, Lizzy."

Her eyes widened and she stared. Stock-still, she did no more than watch him with wary disbelief. Gabe had to laugh at himself. He hadn't quite meant to blurt that out, and he felt a tad foolish.

Elizabeth was everything he wasn't. Serious, studious, caring and concerned. She had a purpose for her life, while he'd always been content to idle away his time, shirking responsibilities, refusing to settle down, priding himself on his freedom. She was at the top of her class, while he'd gone from one minor to another, never quite deciding on any one thing he wanted to do in his life. His time in college had been more a lark than anything else; he'd gone because it was expected. He'd gotten good grades because his pride demanded nothing less, but it had been easy and had never meant anything to him.

Lizzy would never consider letting someone like him interrupt her plans. She was goal-oriented, while he was out for fun. She'd told him that she wanted the summer with him, but she'd never even hinted that she might want more than that.

Trying to make light of his declaration—though he refused to take it back—he said, "Don't worry. I won't start writing you poetry or begging you to elope."

She blinked and her face colored, which added to her already blotchy cheeks and red nose, giving her a comical look. Gabe forced a grin and kissed her forehead. Damn, but he loved her. He felt ready to burst with it.

"Have I rendered you speechless, sweetheart?"

She swallowed hard. "Yes." Then: "Gabe, did you mean it?"

"Absolutely." He cupped her breast and idly flicked her soft nipple with his thumb until it stiffened. "How could I not love you, Lizzy? I've never known anyone like you. You make me laugh and you make me hot and you confuse my brain and my heart."

She scrunched up her mouth, trying not to laugh. "How…romantic."

Gabe shifted, settling himself between her long slender thighs. "I'm horny as hell," he admitted in a growl, letting her feel the hardness of his body. "How romantic did you expect me to be?"

She looped both arms around his neck and smiled. "Thank you, Gabe."

"For what?"

"For making me feel so much better." Her fingers caressed his nape, and she wound her legs around him, holding him, welcoming him. "For being here with me now, for saying you love me."

He started to reassure her that he hadn't said the words lightly, that he meant them and felt them down to his very soul. But he held back. Similar words hadn't crossed her lips, and he needed time to get himself together, to sort out this new revelation. So all he said was, "My pleasure," and then he kissed her, trying to show her without words that they were meant for each other whether she knew it yet or not.

He felt as if his life hung in the balance. He needed her, but he didn't know if he could make her need him in return.

Sawyer stood behind him, leaving a long shadow across the planks of wood that extended over the lake. Gabe didn't bother to turn when he asked, "You want something, Sawyer?"

"Yeah. I want to know why you're mangling all those nails."

Gabe looked at the third nail he'd bent trying to hammer it into the new dock extension he was building for his brother Morgan. Normally he did this kind of work without thought, his movements fluid, one nail, one blow. Over the years he'd built so many docks, for his family and for area residents, that he should have been able to do it blindfolded. But he'd hit his damn thumb twice already and he was rapidly making a mess of things.

In a fit of frustration he flung the hammer onto the shore and stomped out of the water, sloshing the mud at his feet and sending minnows swimming away. Sawyer handed him a glass of iced tea when he got close enough.

"From Honey?"

"Yeah." Sawyer stretched with lazy contentment. "She was all set to bring it to you herself, but I figured you might not welcome her mothering right now, since you've been a damn bear all week."

Gabe grunted in response, then chugged the entire glassful, feeling some of it trickle down the side of his mouth and onto his heated chest. "Thanks."

Sawyer lowered himself to the dry grass and picked at a dandelion. He wore jeans and nothing else, and Gabe thought it was a miracle Honey had let him out of her sight. Ever since she'd announced her pregnancy three weeks ago, Sawyer had been like a buck in rutting season. When Honey was within reach, he was reaching for her, and there was a special new glow to their love. Honey wallowed in her husband's attentions with total abandon. It was amusing—and damn annoying, because while their marriage grew visibly stronger every day, Gabe watched the time slip by, knowing Lizzy would be heading back to school soon. Three and a half weeks had passed, and he was no closer to tying her to him than he had been when he'd met her. Not once had she told him how she felt about him, yet their intimacy had grown until Gabe couldn't keep her out of his mind. He had one week left. One lousy week.

It put him in a killing mood.

Cursing, he looked at the clouds, then decided he might as well make use of Sawyer's visit, since it was obvious that's what Sawyer intended by seeking him out. He looked at his oldest brother and said grimly, "I'm in love."

Sawyer's smile was slow and satisfied. "I figured as much. Elizabeth Parks?"

"Yeah." Gabe rubbed the back of his neck, then sent a disgruntled glance at the half completed dock. "I might as well give up on this today. My head isn't into it."

"Morgan'll understand. He's not in a big hurry for the dock, and we've got plenty of room to keep the boat at the house. Besides, he suffered his own black moods before Misty put him out of his misery."

"But that's just it." Gabe dropped down beside Sawyer and stretched out in the sun. The grass was warm and prickly against his back, and near his right ear, a bee buzzed. "I don't see an end in sight for my particular brand of misery. Lizzy is going back to school. I've only got a few more days with her."

"Have you told her you love her?"

"Yep. She was flattered." Gabe made a wry face and laid one forearm over his eyes. "Can you believe that crap?"

A startled silence proved that wasn't exactly what Sawyer had been expecting to hear. Compared to the way he and Morgan had fought the notion of falling in love, it was no wonder Sawyer was taken off guard.

"You've only known her a few weeks, Gabe."

"I knew I loved her almost from the first." He lowered his arm to stare at his brother. "It was the damnedest thing, but she introduced herself, then proceeded to crawl right in under my skin. And I like it. It's making me nuts thinking about her going off to college again, this time with the knowledge that she's sexy and exciting and that plenty of men will want her. She hadn't known that before, you know. She thought she was too plain, and it's for certain she was too quiet, too intense. But now…"

"Now you've corrupted her?"

Gabe couldn't hold back his grin. "Yeah, she's wonderfully corrupt. It's one of the things I love most about her."

Lizzy was the absolute best sex partner he'd ever had. Open, wild, giving and accepting. When she'd said she wanted to experience it all, she hadn't been kidding. Gabe shivered with the memory, then suffered through Sawyer's curious attention. No way would he share details with his brother, but then, there was no way Sawyer would expect him to.

And just as special to Gabe were the quiet times when they talked afterward. He'd shared stories about his mother with her, and in turn Lizzy had told him about her childhood before the accident. Their mothers were exact opposites, but both loving, both totally devoted to their children.

She'd cried several times while talking about her mom, but they were bittersweet tears of remembrance, not tears of regret or guilt. Gabe sincerely hoped she'd gotten over her ridiculous notion that she'd somehow held responsibility for her mother's death. He couldn't bear to think of her carrying that guilt on her slender shoulders.

"How much longer will she be in school?" Sawyer asked.

"Depends." Gabe sat up and crossed his forearms over his knees, staring sightlessly at the crystal surface of the lake. The lot Morgan had chosen to build on was ideal, quiet and peaceful and scenic. But Gabe preferred the bustle of the bait shops, the boat rentals, the comings and goings of vacationers. He'd always loved summer best because it was the season filled with excitement and fun on the lake. He'd invariably hated to see it coming to an end, but never more so than now, when the end meant Lizzy would leave him.

"Depends on what?" Sawyer pressed.

"On what she decides to do. She could easily graduate this semester and be done, but knowing Lizzy she may well want to further her education. She's so damn intelligent and so determined to learn as much as she can."

"We have colleges closer that she could transfer to."

"She's never mentioned doing that." It took him a moment to form the words, and then Gabe admitted, "I don't want to get in her way. I don't want to lure her into changing her plans for me, when I don't even have any plans. I've spent my whole life goofing off, while Lizzy is the epitome of seriousness." He met his oldest brother's gaze and asked, "What right do I have to screw with her life when my own is up in the air?"

Sawyer was silent a moment, and just as Gabe started to expect a dose of sympathy, Sawyer made an obnoxious sound and shook his head. "That is the biggest bunch of melodramatic bull I've ever heard uttered. You don't want to get in her way? Hell, Gabe, how can loving a woman get in her way?"

"She has plans."

"And you don't? Oh, that's right. You said you've screwed around all your life. So then, that wasn't you who helped Ceily rebuild after the fire at her restaurant? And it wasn't you who worked his butt off for Rosemary when her daddy was sick and she needed help at the boat docks? I doubt there's a body in town who you haven't built, repaired or renovated something for."

Gabe shrugged. "That's just idle stuff. You know I like working with my hands, and I don't mind helping out. But it's not like having a real job. I can still remember how appalled Lizzy was when she first came here and found out I wasn't employed. And rightfully so."

"I see. So since you don't have an office in town and a sign hanging off your door, you're not really employed?"

Gabe frowned, not at all sure what Sawyer was getting at. "You know I'm not."

Sawyer nodded slowly. "You know, when I first started practicing medicine, a lot of the hospital staff in the neighboring towns claimed I wasn't legitimate. I worked out of the house so I could be near Casey, and there's plenty of times when I don't charge someone, or else I get paid with an apple pie and an invitation to visit. It used to steam me like you wouldn't believe, that others would discount what I did just because I didn't take on all the trappings."

Gabe scowled. "It's not at all the same thing. You're about the best doctor around." Then anger hit him and he asked, "Who the hell said you weren't legitimate?"

"It doesn't matter now."

"The hell it doesn't. Who was it, Sawyer?"

Laughing, Sawyer clapped him on the shoulder. "Forget it. It was a long time ago and what they thought never mattered a hill of beans to me. And now I have their respect, so I guess I proved myself in the end. But the point is—"

"The point is that someone insulted you. Who was it?"

"Gabe. You're avoiding the subject here, which is *you.*" Sawyer used his stern, big-brother voice, which Gabe waved away without concern. He was too old to be intimated by his oldest overachiever brother. Sawyer didn't mind now that he had Gabe's attention again. "The point is, you damn near make as much money as I do, just by doing the odd job and always being available and being incredibly good at what you do. If it bothers you, well, then, rent a space in town and run a few ads and—" Sawyer snapped his fingers "—you're legitimate. An honest-to-goodness self-employed craftsman. But don't do it for the wrong reasons. Don't make the assumption that it matters to Elizabeth, because she didn't strike me as the type to be so shallow."

"She's not shallow!"

Just as Gabe had ignored Sawyer's annoyance, Sawyer ignored Gabe's. "I have a question for you."

"You're getting on my nerves, Sawyer."

"Have you let Elizabeth know that you'd like things to continue past the summer? Or is she maybe buying into that awesome reputation of yours and thinking you want this just to be a summer fling?"

The rustling of big doggy feet bounding excitedly through the grass alerted Sawyer and Gabe that they were being joined, and judging by the heavy footsteps following in the wake of the dog, they knew it was Morgan and his massive but good-natured pet, Godzilla. Gabe twisted to see his second-oldest brother just as Morgan snarled, "Let me guess. Sawyer is giving you advice on your love life now, too?"

"Too?" Gabe lifted a brow, then had to struggle to keep Godzilla from knocking him over. The dog hadn't yet realized that he was far too big for anyone's lap. Gabe shoved fur out of his face, dodged a wet tongue and asked, "Sawyer gave you advice?"

"Hell, yes." Then: "Godzilla, get off my brother before you smother him." Morgan threw a stick into the lake and Godzilla, always up for a game, scrambled the length of the half-built dock and did a perfect doggy dive off the end. All three men watched, then groaned, knowing they'd get sprayed when Godzilla shook himself dry.

"That damn dog has no fear," Morgan grumbled.

Gabe made a face. "He must get that from you."

Morgan returned his attention to Gabe. "Sawyer fancies himself an expert on women just because Honey walks around with a vacuous smile on her face all the time."

Sawyer's grin was pure satisfaction. "Just because Misty prefers to give you hell instead—"

"She gives me hell because she loves getting me

riled." Morgan chuckled. "She claims I'm a wild man when I'm riled."

Gabe muttered, "You're always a wild man," then had to jump out of the way when Godzilla ran to Morgan and dropped the stick at his feet. Morgan was wearing his uniform, but the shirt was unbuttoned and his hat was gone. He quickly threw the stick again, this time up the hill toward the house and dry land.

"So what's the answer here, Gabe? Does your little redheaded wonder know you're in this for the long haul?"

Sawyer leaned around Gabe to see Morgan. "He told her he loved her."

Morgan raised a brow. "Is that so?"

Gabe wanted to punch them both, but instead he muttered a simple truth. "She's never returned the sentiment."

"Hm." Morgan and Sawyer seemed to be putting their collective brains together on that one until Morgan's cell phone beeped. He took it off his belt and flipped it open. "Sheriff Hudson." He grinned, and his voice changed from official to intimate. "Hi, babe. No, I'm just trying to straighten out Gabe's love life. Seems he's not going to finish my dock until I do." Morgan waited, then said, "Okay, I'll tell him."

To Gabe's disgust and Sawyer's amusement, Morgan made a kissing sound into the phone, then closed it and clipped it on his belt. "That was Misty."

Sawyer laughed outright. "I never would have guessed."

"Gabe, it seems your little woman is headed over to see Jordan, only Jordan told Misty he had to make a house call for an injured heifer and would be away from the office for a bit. Jordan wants you to go over and make his apologies for him."

Sawyer looked at Gabe. "Why is Elizabeth hanging around with Jordan?"

With obvious disgruntlement in every line of his body, Gabe shoved himself to his feet. "Lizzy has some harebrained notion that Jordan is different, somehow nicer than the rest of us."

Morgan and Sawyer looked at each other, then burst out laughing. Gabe ignored them and snatched up his dirt-and sweat-stained T-shirt before Godzilla could step on it. Sitting on a large rock, he shoved his feet into his unlaced sneakers. His brothers were still laughing. "It's not that funny," he told them, then grinned when Godzilla threw himself into Morgan's lap, his tongue hanging in doggy bliss. Morgan made a face, resigned, and rubbed the dog's shaggy ears.

Sawyer wiped his eyes, damp from his mirth. "Elizabeth doesn't know Jordan very well, does she?"

"If you mean, has she ever seen his temper," Gabe asked, "the answer is no. I got the feeling she doesn't think Jordan *has* a temper."

Morgan choked, but there was admiration and pride in his voice when he said, "Jordan is so damn sly. He hides it well. Most women don't realize that he's only civilized on the outside."

"As long as you don't mess with his animals, or anyone he cares about, he keeps it together. But get him on one of his crusades..." Sawyer shook his head in wonder at the way his middle brother could handle himself when provoked.

Even Gabe grinned at that. Jordan gave the impression of a quiet peacemaker—and to some extent, he was. But when quiet tactics didn't work, he was more than capable of resorting to what would. "He does seem to like championing the underdog, doesn't he?"

Morgan stroked Godzilla's wet back. "Literally."

After yanking on his shirt, Gabe faced his brothers. He had his hands on his hips and a nervous chip on his shoulder. "I'm going to ask Elizabeth to give us a chance. I'm going to tell her how things'll be." He pointed an accusing finger at both of them. "But if this backfires on me, I'm coming back and kicking both your asses."

As Gabe strode away, Sawyer yelled, "Good luck."

Morgan muttered loud enough for Gabe to hear, "Never thought I'd see the day when Gabe would have women troubles."

Gabe sincerely hoped today wasn't the day, either, because he just didn't know what he'd do without Ms. Elizabeth Parks in his life.

Gabe found Lizzy pacing outside the front of Jordan's clinic. Her hands were clasped together, her expression frightened. Not knowing what had happened, Gabe left his car in a hurry and trotted toward her. Lizzy looked up, saw him and relief flooded her entire being.

She ran to him. "Gabe, something's wrong!"

Gabe reached for her shoulders, but she pulled away and sprinted toward the clinic door. "Listen to the animals. They're never that noisy. They're all making a racket."

Gabe could hear the whine of dogs, the screech of cats. He frowned. "Jordan always keeps them calm, but Jordan isn't here."

Lizzy put her hands to her mouth. "Something's wrong. I just know it."

Gabe considered her worry for only two seconds, then said, "Okay, just hang on, hon. I'm going in."

"How?"

For an answer, Gabe picked up a rock and tapped the glass out of a window. The howling and crying became louder with the window open—and then they smelled the smoke.

"Oh, God." Gabe jerked off his shirt, wrapped it around his hand and safely removed the broken glass. "Quickly, Lizzy. I'll go in and unlock the door. Use the cell phone in my car to call Morgan. He'll send people here. Hurry."

Lizzy ran off and Gabe carefully levered himself over the windowsill. The smoke wasn't very thick yet, but he could smell the acrid stench of burning plastic and paper. Gabe ran to the door and unlocked it, then pushed it wide open. He wasn't really given a chance to see what was burning or why, not with so many animals calling for attention. He hefted the first big cage he came to and hauled it outside.

Lizzy was back. "Morgan's on his way. What can I do?"

"Just pull these cages away from the house as I bring them out."

"But there's too many of them!"

"Just do it, Red. We don't have time to talk about it." Gabe didn't know how sick the animals were, if it was safe to open the cages… He raced inside and hauled two more out. He almost tripped over Lizzy. She had a big empty cage that she was dragging over the threshold. She had to pry open the double doors before it would fit through. Gabe frowned at her. "What the hell are you doing?"

Without answering, she ran in. She opened three pens filled with cats and began carrying the cats—without the bulky cages—outside. She got several scratches for her efforts, but the empty cage she'd taken outside was quickly filled. As Gabe worked he watched her make trip after trip, occasionally repeating the process of setting up an empty cage. The animals, penned together, might hurt each other in the excitement, but they wouldn't die.

The smoke was thicker, filling the air while frantic animal growls and cries echoed off every wall. Gabe hadn't seen any signs of an actual fire, but then the smoke tended to mask things. He had enough trouble just breathing. As Gabe struggled to release an older German shepherd, he tripped over a pile of feed and went down. His head hit the edge of a metal cage, and he saw stars.

"Gabe!"

As if from a distance he heard Lizzy calling him, and panic engulfed him. Was she hurt? He tried to raise himself, but everything spun around him. And then she was there, her arm supporting his head. She coughed several times before she was able to say, "Gabe, you have to stand."

Gabe could tell she was crying, and it cut him deeply. "Lizzy?"

"Please, Gabe. Please." She tugged on him and finally he managed to get his rubbery legs to work, leaning heavily against her. Something warm ran into his right eye, and he wondered vaguely what it was before Lizzy's insistence that he move forced him to concentrate on her demands. It was slow going, the smoke so thick he couldn't see at all.

Then blessedly clean air filled his lungs and he dropped to the ground. Lizzy knelt over him, her soft hands touching his face. "Oh, my God. You're bleeding."

Gabe said, "The animals…"

Elizabeth swabbed at his face with the hem of her dress, giving him a peek at her panties as she did so. "You've got a nasty cut."

"I'll be fine," he muttered.

She ran off but she was back within seconds. "Here, hold this against your head. Can you do that, Gabe?"

She handed him a soft pad, and he realized it was from the clinic. He pressed it hard to his head to stem the flow of blood.

"Don't you dare move, Gabriel Kasper." Her voice shook, thick with smoke and, he thought, perhaps emotion. "And don't you be seriously hurt, either." He saw her wipe tears from her face with a soot-covered hand, and he tried to smile at her, but his head was pounding painfully. "I'll never forgive you if you're seriously hurt."

Before he could reassure her she was gone and a new panic settled in. Dear God, she'd gone into the clinic! Gabe summoned all his strength to stand, to fetch her and keep her safe, and then he heard the sound of approaching sirens and knew Morgan was almost there. He'd take care of things. But Gabe was needed still; he had to help her....

Morgan's big hands settled on Gabe's shoulders. "Don't move, Gabe."

"It's just a knock on the head. Stupid cage got in my way."

Morgan pressed him down. "Damn it, I said don't move, you stubborn fool!" Speaking to someone else, Morgan said, "Go ahead. I'll take care of my brother. Get the animals out."

"Lizzy?" Already Gabe's head was starting to clear, even as a throbbing pain settled in. The sirens were blasting, not helping one bit, keeping the animals frenzied and his head pulsing. He glared at Morgan. "Get Lizzy."

"She's inside?" Morgan jerked to his feet, but at that moment Lizzy stumbled through the doorway, aided by two firemen. She had a box of mewling kittens in her arms, and she was a dirty mess. "Here she comes now."

Morgan went to her and took the box of kittens. "Sawyer was right behind me. He'll fix Gabe up good as new."

Gabe watched her lean against Morgan for just an instant, then she straightened and hurried to Gabe.

"Shh. It's all right, babe. I'm okay. I just got knocked silly." He pulled her to his side as he carefully sat up. "Morgan! Shut the damn sirens off."

Morgan barked a few orders, and one fireman rushed to do as he was told. When silence settled in, Gabe touched Lizzy's blackened face. "Are you all right?"

She wasn't listening to him. She'd spotted Sawyer and she ran to him, then practically dragged him to Gabe. He had Jordan with him, and Jordan looked frozen with shock.

"What the hell happened?" As Sawyer spoke he opened his bag and began swabbing off Gabe's face. To Lizzy he said, "Head wounds bleed like the very devil. If he's not hurt anywhere else then he should be fine."

Gabe took pity on Jordan. "I'm fine, Jordan. Go check your animals."

Jordan looked at Sawyer and got his nod of confirmation. "Looks like he'll need a few stitches, but that's all."

"Thank God." Jordan, still looking somewhat sick and so furious he could chew nails, headed for the clinic door.

An hour and a half later, everything had quieted down. There was a lot of smoke damage to the clinic, but very little had burned. It hadn't taken a large investigation to discover that a pet owner who'd come in earlier had evidently thrown a cigarette into the trash can in the bathroom. The can was metal, so other than the walls and floor in that room being singed, the damage was mostly smoke-related. It would take quite a bit of work, and a professional crew, to get everything clean again and to rid the clinic of the smell. Jordan had a strict no-smoking policy. Gabe couldn't remember ever seeing his brother look so ravaged, or so livid.

Gabe was propped up against a tree, his head bandaged, watching the proceedings with frustration since Sawyer had flatly refused to let him help out. Lizzy continued to work with Jordan until they had every animal accounted for and loaded into covered truck beds. Luckily, not a single animal had suffered a serious injury from the small fire, but they were frightened and skittish and Jordan was using his mesmerizing voice to calm them all. He looked like hell warmed over, but his tone didn't in any way match his expression. It was lulling and easy and sank into the bones, reassuring even the most fractious animal.

Lizzy returned to Gabe's side again and again, and each time he told her he was fine. Then she'd flit off to do more work. She had to be exhausted, but she kept on. He was so damn proud of her, he could barely contain himself.

As if she'd heard his thoughts, she glanced at him, then hurried to his side. "Do you need something to drink?"

On her knees beside him, she smoothed his hair and touched his cheek. Gabe caught her hand and carried it to his mouth. "Mm. You taste like charcoal."

She grinned. "I imagine I smell like it, too." She glanced at Jordan. "Sawyer recommended he move the animals into your garage until the clinic can be cleaned. It'll take a few days. Poor Jordan. He looks devastated."

"I know how he feels." She faced him, her brow puckered in confusion, and he said, "You scared the hell out of me, Lizzy, when you ran back in there without me. For all I knew, the place was burning to the ground. I kept thinking about you getting hurt...."

"I was careful."

"But what if you'd stumbled like I did? How the hell would I have gotten you out of there?" Her expression softened, and she leaned forward to gently kiss his mouth.

"I didn't mean to worry you."

"I love you." He hadn't said it again since she'd had her nightmare, and now he couldn't keep the words contained. Her eyes widened. "What?" he asked, sounding a little sarcastic. "You thought I made it up the first time? Not a chance."

"Oh, Gabe." Tears welled in her eyes, and Gabe held his breath, waiting to see what she would say.

Then Jordan appeared, and he hauled Lizzy to her feet. "I've been so busy trying to see to things, I haven't even thanked you yet."

Jealousy speared through Gabe as he watched Jordan lift Lizzy onto her tiptoes and kiss her soundly. She blushed, but she didn't pull away.

"This is going to be inconvenient as hell for a few days," Jordan said, hugging her tight, "but at least all the animals are safe."

Lizzy finally pulled back. She smiled and started to say, "Gabe's the real..." but then her words tapered off and she put a hand over her mouth.

Jordan raised a brow. "Real what? Hero? I'd say you both are. Not only did you get all twenty-three animals outside, you even managed to get my baby brother out with only a knock to his hard head. That took a lot of guts, sweetheart, and I want you to know how much I appreciate it."

After Jordan walked away, Gabe took pity on Lizzy and tugged her down beside him. She was mute, her dirty face blank. Gabe kissed her ear. "How's it feel to be a heroine? Will you add your own experiences to your thesis?"

She blinked owlishly at him. "But I didn't…"

"Didn't what?" He smoothed a long red sooty curl behind her ear. "Didn't risk your life for those animals? Didn't face injury without a thought? Didn't do what had to be done almost by instinct?"

"But…" She sucked in a deep breath. "I was so scared."

"For yourself?"

She stared into his eyes, bemused. "No, not at first. I was afraid for you, and for the poor animals. But now I'm shaking with nerves." She held out her hand to show him, and Gabe cradled it in his large hand.

"Only a fool wouldn't react after going through something like this. You think after that boating incident I wasn't something of a wreck?"

"You said you weren't afraid."

"I was mad as hell at that fool for falling out of his boat. I wanted to tear something apart, and since I couldn't get hold of him, I punched a hole in my wall, then had to repair it." He gave her a sheepish grin. "It's all just reaction. Anger, fear… I've even seen people start laughing and not be able to stop. You're trembling. I got violent. We're the same, sweetheart, but we're also different. And what you did today is no less significant than what I did a year ago."

She seemed to consider that for a long time, and Gabe was content to hold her. Finally, without quite looking at him, she said, "I don't want to be a coward, Gabe."

"You're not."

She bit her bottom lip. "Have you enjoyed spending your time with me these last few weeks?"

His heart started pounding. His palms got damp. Gabe didn't give away his reaction when he answered, keeping his tone mild. "I told you I love you. So of course I love spending time with you."

She nodded slowly, then curled tighter to his side, keeping her face tucked under his chin. "How many women have you loved?"

Wrapping a red curl around his finger, he said, "Hm. Let's see. There's my mother. And now Honey and Misty."

She punched his ribs. "No, I mean romantically."

"Just you, sweetheart."

"You've never told another woman that you loved her?"

"No. Though plenty of women have told *me* that."

She was so surprised, she leaned back to glare at him. "Really?"

Gabe flicked the end of her nose. "Really. Just not the one woman I wish would tell me."

She swallowed hard. Her blue eyes were round and filled with feminine daring. Gabe held his breath.

"What would you think," she asked slowly, "of me finishing school and coming back here to stay?"

Afraid to move, Gabe said, "Are you considering doing that?"

"I think, since you love me, and since I love you, it'd make sense."

He let his breath out in whoosh. "You little witch!" He laughed and squeezed her, then winced as his head pounded. "Why haven't you told me before now?"

"I wasn't sure if I'd dreamed it or if you'd want me around forever. I wasn't sure if I was making too much of things. I'm not very good at figuring out this whole romantic business. But I do love you. I can't think of much besides you."

Going for broke, Gabe said, "You know you'll have to marry me." He frowned at her just to let her know he was serious. "You can't tell a man you love him and then not marry him."

Her face lit up and her smile was radiant, despite the black soot on her cheeks and the end of her nose. "I have to finish out my semester first. But that won't be too long."

"I can wait. I don't want you to give up anything for me." Then he shook his head. "I take that back. I want you to give up your guilt. And your free weekends because I'll be coming to see you whenever you're off school. And I most definitely want you to give up any thoughts of other men, or—"

She touched his face. "Okay."

Gabe grinned so hard his head hurt. "I just love an agreeable woman."

Epilogue

"Quit looking so disgruntled."

Gabe frowned at Jordan, his face red, his fists clenched. "I can't believe you stole her right out from under my nose."

"She came to me willingly, Gabe. And besides, I need her."

"So do I!"

Jordan shrugged indifferently. "You can get anyone to answer your damn phones, but Elizabeth has the touch. The animals love her. More than they love me, sometimes, and that's a truth that hurts."

Gabe looked at his wife, all decked out in snowy white, her beautiful red hair hanging in long curls down her back. He wanted to get the damn reception over with so he could get her alone.

"Uh, Gabe, your lust is showing."

Gabe considered flattening his brother, but then he saw Lizzy smile and she looked so happy, he knew he had to give in gracefully. "All right, so she can be your assistant. I guess I can hire someone else." He had taken Sawyer's advice and opened a shop in town. He had more business than he could handle, but he enjoyed it so he wasn't complaining. He'd thought Lizzy would work with him, but she'd opted to sign on with Jordan, and he had to admit she had a way with animals.

She was so special she made his heart swell just looking at her.

"So magnanimous," Jordan uttered dryly. "I had no idea you had these caveman tendencies."

"I didn't, either, until I met Lizzy."

"She got a fantastic grade on her thesis. Did she tell you she's been approached about adding it to a text?"

Gabe scowled. "She's my wife. Of course she told me."

Jordan laughed, then quickly held up both hands. "All right, all right. Quit breathing fire on me. I'm sorry I mentioned it."

Thank God she'd kept his name anonymous, Gabe thought, disgruntled by the instant popularity of her *Mystique of Heroes.* He snorted. What a stupid subject. But evidently not everyone thought so; Lizzy had received several calls from men wanting her to interview them. Gabe would have liked to hide her away somewhere, but watching her bloom was a distinct pleasure, so he put up with all the other men ogling her and tamped down his jealousy.

After all, she'd married him.

Jordan nudged him with his shoulder. "She's getting

ready to throw the bouquet. This always cracks me up the way the women fight over it."

Ready to get back a little of his own, Gabe said, "I noticed all those women lining up are eyeing you like a side of beef. You'll be next, you know."

Jordan shook his head, then downed the rest of his drink. "You can forget that right now. I'm rather partial to my bachelor ways."

"You just haven't met the right woman yet. When you do, I bet you get knocked on your ass so quick you won't know what hit you."

Jordan was ready to refute that when suddenly the women all started shouting. He and Gabe looked up to see that Lizzy had thrown the bouquet, but her aim was off. It came sailing across the room in a dramatic arch. Right toward Jordan.

He almost dropped his drink he was so surprised, but when the flowers hit him in the chest, he managed to juggle everything, and was left standing there holding the flowers.

Gabe laughed out loud, Lizzy covered her mouth with a hand to stifle her giggles and Jordan, seeing a gaggle of women rushing toward him, muttered, "Oh, hell."

Gabe looked at his wife and winked, then whispered to Jordan, "You better make a run for it."

And he did.

Gabe smiled as Lizzy headed toward him, looking impish and beautiful and so sexy he decided the reception was well and truly over. He kissed her as soon as she reached him, then whispered against her lips, "That was a dirty trick to play on my brother."

She grinned. "I was tired of all the women here looking at you with broken hearts. It's time for Jordan to be the sacrificial lamb."

Gabe shook his head with mock sympathy. "Damn, I feel sorry for him."

Startled, Elizabeth leaned into his side and asked, "Why?"

Taking her by surprise, Gabe hoisted her up in his arms, which left her delicate white gown loose around her legs, giving everyone a sexy peek. Over the sound of the raucous applause from all the attending guests, Gabe whispered, "Because the prettiest, sexiest, smartest female is already taken—and I have her."

Elizabeth laughed. "You are a charmer, Gabe."

He started out of the room, holding her close to his heart. Right before he disappeared through the doorway, he looked up and saw Jordan backed against a wall, women surrounding him. Gabe shook his head.

He wished his only single brother all the same love that he'd just found.

The women looked determined enough to see that he got it.

* * * * *

Joss Wood loves books, coffee and traveling—especially to the wild places of Southern Africa and, well, anywhere. She's a wife and a mom to two young adults. She's also a slave to two cats and a dog the size of a small cow. After a career in local economic development and business, Joss writes full-time from her home in KwaZulu-Natal, South Africa.

Books by Joss Wood

Harlequin Desire

Murphy International

One Little Indiscretion
Temptation at His Door
Back in His Ex's Bed

Texas Cattleman's Club: Fathers and Sons

How to Handle a Heartbreaker

Harlequin Presents

South Africa's Scandalous Billionaires

How to Undo the Proud Billionaire
How to Win the Wild Billionaire

Visit the Author Profile page at Harlequin.com for more titles.

TAKING THE BOSS TO BED

Joss Wood

Chapter 1

Jaci Brookes-Lyon walked across the art deco, ridiculously ornate lobby of the iconic Forrester-Grantham Hotel on Park Avenue to the bank of elevators flanked by life-size statues of 1930s cabaret dancers striking dance poses. She stopped next to one, touching the smooth, cool shoulder with her fingertips.

Sighing through pursed lips, she looked at the dark-eyed blonde staring back at her in the supershiny surface of the elevator doors in front of her. Short, layered hair in a modern pixie cut, classic, fitted cocktail dress, perfect makeup, elegant heels. She looked good, Jaci admitted. Sophisticated, assured and confident. Maybe a tad sedate but that could be easily changed.

What was important was that the mask was in place. She looked like the better, stronger, New York version of herself, the person she wanted to be. She appeared to be someone who knew where she was going and how she was going to get there. Pity, Jaci thought, as she pushed her long bangs out of a smoky eye, that the image was still as substantial as a hologram.

Jaci left the elevator and took a deep breath as she walked across the foyer to the imposing double doors of the ballroom. *Here goes*, she thought. Stepping into the room packed with designer-dressed men and women, she reminded herself to put a smile on her face and to keep her spine straight. Nobody had to know that she'd rather stroll around Piccadilly Circus naked than walk into a room filled with people she didn't know. Her colleagues from Starfish were here somewhere. She'd sat with them earlier through the interminably long awards ceremony. Her new friends, Wes and Shona, fellow writers employed by Starfish, had promised to keep her company at her first film industry after-party, and once she found them she'd be fine. Between now and then, she just had to look as if she was having fun or, at the very least, happy to be surrounded by handsome men and supersophisticated women. Dear Lord, was that Candice Bloom, the multiple Best Actress award winner? Was it unkind to think that she looked older and, dare she even think it, fatter in real life?

Jaci took a glass of champagne from a tray that wafted past her and raised the glass for a taste. Then she clutched it to her chest and retreated to the side of the room, keeping an eye out for her coworkers. If she hadn't found them in twenty minutes she was out of there. She spent her entire life being a wallflower at her parents' soirees, balls and dinner parties, and had no intention of repeating the past.

"That ring looks like an excellent example of Georgian craftsmanship."

Jaci turned at the voice at her elbow and looked down into the sludge-brown eyes of the man who'd stepped up to her side. Jaci blinked at his emerald tuxedo and thought that he looked like a frog in a shiny suit. His thin black hair was pulled back off his forehead and was gathered at his neck in an oily tail, and he sported a silly soul patch under his thin, cruel mouth.

Jaci Brookes-Lyon, magnet for creepy guys, she thought.

He picked up her hand to look at her ring. Jaci tried to tug it away but his grip was, for an amphibian, surprisingly strong. "Ah, as I thought. It's an oval-faceted amethyst, foiled and claw-set with, I imagine, a closed back. The amethyst is pink and lilac. Exquisite. The two diamonds are old, mid-eighteenth century."

She didn't need this dodgy man to tell her about her ring, and she pulled her hand away, resisting the urge to wipe it on her cinnamon-shaded cocktail dress. Ugh. Creep factor: ten thousand.

"Where did you get the ring?" he demanded, and she caught a flash of dirty, yellow teeth.

"It's a family heirloom," Jaci answered, society manners too deeply ingrained just to walk off and leave him standing there.

"Are you from England? I love your accent."

"Yes."

"I have a mansion in the Cotswolds. In the village Arlingham. Do you know it?"

She did, but she wouldn't tell him that. She'd never

manage to get rid of him then. "Sorry, I don't. Would you exc—"

"I have a particularly fine yellow diamond pendant that would look amazing in your cleavage. I can just imagine you wearing that and a pair of gold high heels."

Jaci shuddered and ruthlessly held down a heave as he ran his tongue over his lips. Seriously? Did that pickup line ever work? She picked his hand off her hip and quickly dropped it.

She wished she could let rip and tell him to take a hike and not give a damn. But the Brookes-Lyon children had been raised on a diet of diplomacy and were masters of the art of telling someone to go to hell in such a way that they immediately started planning the best route to get there. Well, Neil and Meredith were. She normally just stood there with a mouth full of teeth.

Jaci wrinkled her nose; some things never changed.

If she wasn't going to rip Mr. Rich-but-Creepy a new one—and she wasn't because she had the confrontational skills of a wet noodle—then she should remove herself, she decided.

"If you leave, I'll follow you."

Dear God, now he was reading her mind? "Please don't. I'm really not interested."

"But I haven't told you that I'm going to finance a film or that I own a castle in Germany, or that I own a former winner of the Kentucky Derby," he whined, and Jaci quickly suppressed her eye roll.

And I will never *tell you that my childhood home is a seventeenth-century manor that's been in my family for over four hundred years. That my mother is a third cousin to the queen and that I am, distantly, related to most of the royal families in Europe. They don't impress me, so you, with your pretentious attitude, haven't a chance.*

And, just a suggestion, use some of that money you say you have to buy a decent suit, some shampoo and to get your teeth cleaned.

"Excuse me," Jaci murmured as she ducked around him and headed for the ballroom doors.

As she approached the elevators, congratulating herself on her getaway, she heard someone ordering an elderly couple to get out of the way and she winced as she recognized Toad's nasally voice. Glancing upward at the numbers above the elevator, she realized that if she waited for it he'd catch up to her and then she'd be caught in that steel box with him, up close and personal. There was no way he'd keep his hands or even— gack!—his tongue to himself. Thanks, but she'd rather lick a lamppost. Tucking her clutch bag under her arm, she glanced left and saw an emergency exit sign on a door and quickly changed direction. She'd run down the stairs; he surely wouldn't follow.

Stairs, lobby, taxi, home and a glass of wine in a bubble bath. Oh, yes, that sounded like heaven.

"My limousine is just outside the door."

The voice to her right made her yelp and she whirled around, slapping her hand to her chest. Those sludgy eyes looked feral, as if he were enjoying the thrill of the chase, and his disgusting soul patch jiggled as his wet lips pulled up into a smarmy smile. Dear God, he'd been right behind her and she hadn't even sensed him. Street smarts, she had none.

Jaci stepped to the side and looked past him to the empty reception area. Jeez, this was a nightmare… If she took the stairs she would be alone with him, ditto the elevators. Her only option was to go back to the ballroom where there were people. Across the room, the elevator doors opened on a discreet chime and Jaci watched as a tall man, hands in the pockets of his tuxedo pants, walked out toward the ballroom. Broad shoulders, trim waist, long legs. His dark hair was tapered, with the top styled into a tousled mess. He had bright, light eyes under dark brows and what she imagined was a three-day-old beard. She knew that profile, that face. Ryan?

Neil's Ryan? Jaci craned her neck for a better look.

God, it *was* the grown-up version—and an even more gorgeous version—of that young man she'd known so long ago. Hard, tough, sexy, powerful; a man in every sense of the word. Jaci felt her stomach roll over and her throat tighten as tiny flickers of electricity danced across her skin.

Instant lust, immediate attraction. And he hadn't even noticed her yet.

And she *really* needed him to notice her. She called out his name and he abruptly stopped and looked around.

"Limo, outside, waiting."

Jaci blinked at Mr. Toad and was amazed at his persistence. He simply wasn't going to give up until he got her into his car, into his apartment and naked. She'd rather have acid-coated twigs shoved up her nose. Seeing Ryan standing there, head cocked, she thought that there was maybe one more thing she could do to de-barnacle herself.

And, hopefully, Ryan wouldn't object.

"Ryan! Darling!"

Jaci stepped to her right and walked as fast as she possibly could across the Italian marble floor, and as she approached Ryan, she lifted her arms and wound them around his neck. She saw his eyes widen in surprise and felt his hands come to rest on her hips, but before he could speak, she slapped her mouth on his and hoped to dear Lord that he wouldn't push her away.

His lips were warm and firm beneath hers and she felt his fingers dig into her hips, their heat burning through the fabric of her dress to warm her skin. Her fingers touched the back of his neck, above the collar of his shirt, and she felt tension roll through his body.

Ryan yanked his head back and those penetrating eyes met hers, flashing with an emotion she couldn't identify. She expected him to push her away, to ask her what the hell she thought she was doing, but instead he yanked her closer and his mouth covered hers again. His tongue licked the seam between her lips and, without hesitation, she opened up, allowing him to taste her, to know her. A strong arm around her waist pulled her flush against him and then her breasts were flat against his chest, her stomach resting against his— *hello, Nelly!*—erection.

Their kiss might have lasted seconds, minutes, months or years, Jaci had no idea. When Ryan finally pulled his mouth away, strong arms still holding her against him, all she was capable of doing was resting her forehead on his collarbone while she tried to get her bearings. She felt as if she'd stepped away from reality, from time, from the ornate lobby in one of the most renowned hotels in the world and into another dimension. That had never happened to her before. She'd never been so swept away by passion that she felt as if she'd had an out-of-body experience. That it had happened with someone who was little more than a stranger totally threw her.

"Leroy, it's good to see you," Ryan said, somewhere above her head. Judging by his even voice, he was very used to being kissed by virtual strangers in fancy hotels. *Huh.*

"I was hoping that you would be here. I was on my way to find you," Ryan blithely continued.

"Ryan," Leroy replied.

Knowing she couldn't stay pressed against Ryan forever—sadly, because she felt as if she belonged there—Jaci lifted her head and tried to wiggle out of his grip. She was surprised when, instead of letting her go, he kept her plastered to his side.

"I see you've met my girl."

Jaci's head snapped back and she narrowed her eyes as she looked up into Ryan's urbane face. His girl?

His.

Girl?

Her mouth fell open. Bats-from-hell, he didn't remember her name! He had no idea who she was.

Mr. Toad pulled a thin cheroot from the inside pocket of his jacket and jammed it into the side of his mouth. He narrowed his eyes at Jaci. "You two together?"

Jaci knew that she often pulled on her Feisty Girl

mask, but she'd never owned an invisibility cloak. Jaci opened her mouth to tell them to stop talking about her as if she wasn't there, but Ryan pinched her side and her mouth snapped shut. Mostly from indignant surprise. "She's my girlfriend. As you know, I've been out of town and I haven't seen her for a couple of weeks."

Weeks, years... Who was counting?

Leroy didn't look convinced. "I thought that she was leaving."

"We agreed to meet in the lobby," Ryan stated, his voice calm. He brushed his chin across the top of her head and Jaci shivered. "You obviously didn't get my message that I was on my way up, honey."

Honey? Yep, he definitely didn't have a clue who she was. But the guy lied with calm efficiency and absolute conviction. "Let's go back inside." Ryan gestured to the ballroom.

Leroy shook his head. "I'm going to head out."

Thank God and all his angels and archangels for small mercies! Ryan, still not turning her loose, held out his right hand for Leroy to shake. "Nice to see you, Leroy, and I look forward to meeting with you soon to finalize our discussions. When can we get together?"

Leroy ignored his outstretched hand and gave Jaci another up-and-down look. "Oh, I'm having second thoughts about the project."

Project? What project? Why was Ryan doing business with Leroy? That was a bit of a silly question since she had no idea what business Ryan, or the amphib, was in. Jaci sent her brand-new boyfriend an uncertain glance. He looked as inscrutable as ever, but she sensed that beneath his calm facade, his temper was bubbling.

"I'm surprised to hear that. I thought it was a done deal," Ryan said, his tone almost bored.

Leroy's smile was nasty. "I'm not sure that I'm ready to hand that much money to a man I don't know all that well. I didn't even know you had a girlfriend."

"I didn't think that our *business* deal required that level of familiarity," Ryan responded.

"You're asking me to invest a lot of money. I want to be certain that you know what you are doing."

"I thought that my track record would reassure you that I do."

Jaci looked from one stubborn face to the other.

"The thing is… I have what you want so I suggest that if I say jump, you say how high."

Jaci sucked in breath, aghast. But Ryan, to his credit, didn't dignify that ridiculous statement with a response. Jaci suspected that Leroy didn't have a clue that Ryan thought he was a maggot, that he was fighting the urge to either punch Leroy or walk away. She knew this because his fingers were squeezing her hand so hard that she'd lost all feeling in her digits.

"Come now, Ryan, let's not bicker. You're asking for a lot of money and I feel I need more reassurances. So I definitely want to spend some more time with you—" Leroy's eyes traveled up and down her body and Jaci felt as if she'd been licked by a lizard "—and with your lovely girlfriend, as well. And, in a more businesslike vein, I'd also like to meet some of your key people in your organization." Leroy rolled his cheroot from one side of his mouth to the other. "My people will call you."

Leroy walked toward the elevators and jabbed a finger on the down button. When the doors whispered open, he turned and sent them an oily smile.

"I look forward to seeing you both soon," he said before he disappeared inside the luxurious interior. When the doors closed, Jaci tugged her hand from Ryan's, noting his thunderous face as he watched the numbers change on the board above the elevator.

"Dammittohellandback," Ryan said, finally dropping her hand and running his through his short, stylishly messy hair. "The manipulative cretin."

Jaci took two steps backward and pushed her bangs out of her eye. "Look, seeing you again has been... well, odd, to say the least, but you do realize that I can't do this?"

"Be my girlfriend?"

"Yes."

Ryan nodded tersely. "Of course you can't, it would never work."

One of the reasons being that he'd then have to ask her who she was...

Besides, Ryan, as she'd heard from Neil, dated supermodels and actresses, singers and dancers. His old friend's little sister, neither actress-y nor supermodelly, wasn't his type, so she shrugged and tried to ignore her rising indignation. But, judging by the party in his pants while he was kissing her, maybe she was his type...just a little.

Ryan flicked her a cool look. "He's just annoyed that you rebuffed him. He'll forget about you and his demands in a day or two. I'll just tell him that we had a massive fight and that we split up."

Huh. He had it all figured out. Good for him.

"He's your connection, it's your deal, so whatever works for you," she said, her voice tart. "So…'bye."

Ryan shoved his hand through his hair. "It's been interesting. Why don't you give him ten minutes to leave then use the elevators around the corner? You'd then exit at the east doors."

She was being dismissed and she didn't like it. Especially when it was by a man who couldn't remember her name. Arrogant sod! Pride had her changing her mind. "Oh, I'm not quite ready to leave." She looked toward the ballroom. "I think I'll go back in."

Jaci saw surprise flicker in his gorgeous eyes. He wanted to get rid of her, she realized, maybe because he was embarrassed that he couldn't recall who she was. Not that he looked embarrassed. But still…

"Interesting seeing you *again*, Ryan," she said in a catch-a-clue voice.

A puzzled frown pulled his brows together. "Maybe we should have coffee, catch up."

Jaci shook her head and handed him a condescending smile. "*Honey*, you don't even know who I am so what, exactly, would be the point? Goodbye, Ryan."

"Okay, busted. So who are you?" Ryan roughly demanded. "I know that I know you…"

"You'll work it out," Jaci told him and heard him mutter a low curse as she walked away. But she wasn't sure if he would connect her with the long-ago teenager who'd hung on his every word. She doubted it. Her mask was intact and impenetrable. There was no hint of the insecure girl she used to be…on the outside, anyway. Besides, it would be fun to see his face when he realized that she was Neil's sister, the woman Neil, she assumed, wanted him to help navigate the "perils" of New York City.

Well, she was an adult and she didn't need her brother or Ryan or any other stupid man doing her any favors. She could, and would, navigate New York on her own.

And if she couldn't, her brother and his old friend would be the last people whom she'd allow to witness her failure.

"Then how about another kiss to jog my memory?" Ryan called out just as she was about to walk into the ballroom.

She turned around slowly and tipped her head to the side. "Let me think about that for a minute… Mmm… no."

But hot damn, Jaci thought as she walked off, she was tempted.

Chapter 2

Jaci slipped into the crowd and placed her fist into her sternum and tried to regulate her heart rate and her breathing. She felt as if she'd just experienced a wild gorge ride on a rickety swing and she was still trying to work out which way was up. She so wanted to kiss him again, to taste him again, to feel the way his lips moved over hers. He'd melted all her usual defenses and it felt as if he was kissing her, the *real* her. It was as if he'd reached inside her and grabbed her heart and squeezed…

That had to be a hormone-induced insanity because stuff like that didn't happen and especially not to her. She was letting her writer's imagination run away with her; this was real life, not a romantic comedy. Ryan was hot and sexy and tough, but that was what he looked like, wasn't what he was. *As you do, everybody wears masks to conceal who and what lies beneath*, she reminded herself. Sometimes what was concealed was harmless—she didn't think that her lack of confidence hurt anybody but herself—and occasionally people, including her ex-fiancé, concealed secrets that were devastating.

Clive and his secrets... Hadn't those blown up in their faces? It was a small consolation that Clive had fooled her clever family, too. They'd been so thrilled that, instead of the impoverished artists and musicians she normally brought home to meet her family, she'd snagged an intellectual, a success. A *politician*. In hindsight, she'd been so enamored by the attention she'd received by being Clive's girlfriend—not only from her family but from friends and acquaintances and the press—that she'd been prepared to put up with his controlling behavior, his lack of respect, his inattention. After years of being in the shadows, she'd loved the spotlight and the new sparky and sassy personality she'd developed to deal with the press attention she received. Sassy Jaci was the brave one; she was the one who'd moved to New York, who walked into crowded ballrooms, who planted her lips on the sexiest man in the room. Sassy Jaci was who she was going to be in New York, but this time she'd fly solo. No more men and definitely no more fading into the background...

Jaci turned as her name was called and she saw her friends standing next to a large ornamental tree. Relieved, she pushed past people to get to them. Her fellow scriptwriters greeted her warmly and Shona handed her a champagne glass. "Drink up, darling, you're way behind."

Jaci wrinkled her nose. "I don't like champagne." But she did like alcohol and it was exactly what she needed, so she took a healthy sip.

"Isn't champagne what all posh UK It girls drink?" Shona asked cheerfully and with such geniality that Jaci immediately realized that there was no malice behind her words.

"I'm not an It girl," Jaci protested.

"You were engaged to a rising star in politics, you attended the same social events with the Windsor boys, you are from a very prominent British family."

Well, if you looked at it like that. Could she still be classified as an It girl if she'd hated every second of said socializing?

"You did an internet search on me," Jaci stated, resigned.

"Of course we did," Shona replied. "Your ex-fiancé looks a bit like a horse."

Jaci giggled. Clive did look a bit equine.

"Did you know about his…ah…how do I put this? Outside interests?" Shona demanded.

"No," Jaci answered, her tone clipped. She hadn't even discussed Clive's extramural activities with her family—they were determined to ignore the crotchless-panty-wearing elephant in the room—so there was no way she would dissect her ex–love life with strangers.

"How did you get the job?" Shona asked.

"My agent sold a script to Starfish over a year ago. Six weeks ago Thom called and said that they wanted to develop the story further and asked me to work on that, and to collaborate on other projects. So I'm here, on a six-month contract."

"And you write under the pen name of JC Brookes? Is that because of the press attention you received?" Wes asked.

"Partly." Jaci looked at the bubbles in her glass. It was easier to write under a pen name when your parent, writing under her *own* name, was regarded as one of the most detailed and compelling writers of historical fiction in the world.

Wes smiled at her. "When we heard that we were getting another scriptwriter, we all thought you were a guy. Shona and I were looking forward to someone new to flirt with."

Jaci grinned at his teasing, relieved that the subject had moved on. "Sorry to disappoint." She placed her glass on a tall table next to her elbow. "So, tell me about Starfish. I know that Thom is a producer but that's about all I know. When is he due back? I'd actually like to meet the man who hired me."

"He and Jax—the big boss and owner—are here tonight, but they socialize with the movers and shakers. We're too far down the food chain for them," Shona cheerfully answered, snagging a tiny spring roll off a passing tray and popping it into her mouth.

Jaci frowned, confused. "Thom's not the owner?"

Wes shook his head. "Nah, he's Jax's second in command. Jax stays out of the spotlight but is very hands-on. Actors and directors like to work for him, but because they both have a low threshold for Hollywood drama, they are selective in whom they choose to work with."

"Chad Bradshaw being one of the actors they won't

work with." Shona used her glass to gesture to a handsome older man walking past them.

Chad Bradshaw, legendary Hollywood actor. So that was why Ryan was here, Jaci thought. Chad had received an award earlier and it made sense that Ryan would be here to support his father. Like Chad, Ryan was tall and their eyes were the same; they could be either a light blue or gray, depending on his mood. Ryan might not remember her but she recalled in Technicolor detail the young man Neil had met at the London School of Economics. In between fantasizing about Ryan and writing stories with him as her hero inspiration, she'd watched the interaction between Ryan and her family. It had amused her that her academic parents and siblings had been fascinated by the fact that Ryan lived in Hollywood and that he was the younger brother of Ben Bradshaw, the young darling of Hollywood who was on his way to becoming a screen legend himself. Like the rest of the world, they'd all been shocked at Ben's death in a car accident, and his passing and funeral had garnered worldwide, and Brookes-Lyon, attention. But at the time they knew him, many years before Ben's death, it seemed as if Ryan was from another world, one far removed from the one the Brookes-Lyon clan occupied, and he'd been a breath of fresh air.

Ryan and Neil had been good friends and Ryan hadn't been intimidated by the cocky and cerebral Brookes-Lyon clan. He'd come to London to get a business degree, she remembered, and dimly recalled a dinner conversation with him saying something about wanting to get out of LA and doing something completely different from his father and brother. He visited Lyon House every couple of months for nearly a year but then he left the prestigious college. She hadn't seen him since. Until he kissed the hell out of her ten minutes ago.

Jaci pursed her lips in irritation and wondered how he kissed women whose names he *did* know. If he kissed them with only a smidgeon more skill than he had her, then the man was capable of melting polar ice caps.

He was *that* good and what was really, really bad was that she kept thinking that he had lips and that she had lips and that hers should be under his...*all the damn time*.

Phew. Problematic, Jaci thought.

Ryan "Jax" Jackson nursed his glass of whiskey and wished that he was in his apartment stretched out on his eight-foot-long couch and watching his favorite sports channel on the huge flat-screen that dominated one wall of his living room. He glanced at his watch, grateful to see that the night was nearly over. He'd had a run-in with Leroy, kissed the hell out of a sexy woman and now he was stuck in a ballroom kissing ass. He'd much rather be kissing the blonde's delectable ass... Dammit, who the hell was she? Ryan discarded the idea of flicking through his mental black book of past women. He knew that he hadn't kissed that mouth before. He would've remembered that heat, that spice, the make-him-crazy need to have her. So *who* was she?

He looked around the room in the hope of seeing her again and scowled when he couldn't locate her. Before the evening ended, he decided, he'd make the connection or he'd find her and demand some answers. He wouldn't sleep tonight if he didn't. He caught a flash of a blond head and felt his pants tighten. It wasn't her but if the thought of seeing her again had him springing up to half-mast, then he was in trouble. Trouble that he didn't need.

Time to do a mental switch, he decided, and deliberately changed the direction of his thoughts. What was Leroy's problem tonight? He'd agreed, in principle, to back the film and now he needed more assurances? *Why?* God, he was tired of the games the very rich boys played; his biggest dream was to find an investor who'd just hand over a boatload of money, no questions asked.

And that would be the day that gorgeous aliens abducted him to be a sex slave.

Still, he was relieved that Leroy had left; having his difficult investor and his DNA donor in the room at the same time was enough to make his head explode. He hadn't seen Chad yet but knew that all he needed to do was find the prettiest woman in the room and he could guarantee that his father—or Leroy, if he were here—would be chatting her up. Neither could keep his, as Neil used to say, pecker in his pants despite having a wife at home.

What was the point of being married if you were a serial cheater? Ryan wondered for the millionth time.

Ryan felt an elbow in his ribs and turned to look into his best friend's open face. "Hey."

"Hey, you are looking grim. What's up?" Thom asked.

"Tired. Done with this day and this party," Ryan told him.

"And you're avoiding your father."

Well, yeah. "Where is the old man?"

Thom lifted his champagne glass to his right. "He's at your nine o'clock, talking to the sexy redhead. He cornered me and asked me to talk to you, to intercede on his behalf. He wants to *reconnect.* His word, not mine."

"So his incessant calls and emails over the past years have suggested," Ryan said, his expression turning cynical. "Except that I am not naive to believe that it's because he suddenly wants to play happy families. It's only because we have something he wants." As in a meaty part in their new movie.

"He would be great as Tompkins."

Ryan didn't give a rat's ass. "We don't always get what we want."

"He's your father," Thom said, evenly.

That was stretching the truth. Chad had been his guardian, his landlord and an absent presence in his life. Ryan knew that he still resented the fact that he'd had to take responsibility for the child he created with his second or third or fifteenth mistress. To Chad, his mother's death when he was fourteen had been wildly inconvenient. He was already raising one son and didn't need the burden of another.

Not that Chad had ever been actively involved in his, or Ben's, life. Chad was always away on a shoot and he and Ben, with the help of a housekeeper, raised themselves. Ben, just sixteen months older than him, had seen him through those dark and dismal teenage years.

He'd idolized Ben and Ben had welcomed him into his home and life with open arms. So close in age, they'd become best buds within weeks and he'd thought that there was nothing that could destroy their friendship, that they had each other's backs, that Ben was the one person who would never let him down.

Yeah, funny how wrong he could be.

Ben. God, he still got a lump in his throat just thinking about him. He probably always would. When it came to Ben he was a cocktail of emotions. Betrayal always accompanied the grief. Hurt, loss and anger also hung around whenever he thought of his best friend and brother. God, would it ever end?

The crowds in front of him parted and Ryan caught his breath. There she was… He'd kissed that wide mouth earlier, but between the kiss and dealing with Leroy he hadn't really had time to study the compact blonde. Short, layered hair, a peaches-and-cream complexion and eyes that fell somewhere between deep brown and black.

Those eyes… He knew those eyes, he thought, as a memory tugged. He frowned, immediately thinking of his time in London and the Brookes-Lyon family. Neil had mentioned in a quick email last week that his baby sister was moving to New York… What was her name again? Josie? Jackie… Close but still wrong… Jay-cee! Was that her? He narrowed his eyes, thinking it through. God, it had been nearly twelve years since he'd last seen her, and he struggled to remember the details of Neil's shy sibling. Her hair was the same white-blond color, but back then it hung in a long fall to her waist. Her body, now lean, had still been caught in that puppy-fat stage, but those eyes... He couldn't forget those eyes. Rich, deep brown, almost black Audrey Hepburn eyes, he thought. Then and now.

Jesus. He'd kissed his oldest friend's baby sister.

Ryan rubbed his forehead with his thumb and index finger. With everything else going on in his life, he'd completely forgotten that she was moving here and that Neil had asked him to make contact with her. He'd intended to once his schedule lightened but he never expected her to be at this post-awards function. And he certainly hadn't expected the shy teenager to have morphed into this stunningly beautiful, incredibly sexy woman; a woman who had his nerve endings buzzing. On the big screen in his head he could see them in their own private movie. She'd be naked and up against a wall, her legs around his waist and her head tipped back as he feasted on that soft spot where her neck and shoulders met...

Ryan blew out a breath. He was a movie producer, had dabbled in directing and he often envisioned scenes in his head, but never had one been so sexual, so sensual. And one starring his best and oldest friend's kid sister? That was just plain weird.

Sexy.

But still weird.

As if she could feel his eyes on her, Jaci turned her head and looked directly at him. The challenging lift of her eyebrow suggested that she'd realized that he'd connected the dots and that she was wondering what he intended to do about it.

Nothing, he decided, breaking their long, sexually charged stare. He was going to do jack about it because his sudden and very unwelcome attraction to Jaci was something he didn't have time to deal with, something he didn't *want* to deal with. His life was complicated enough without adding another level of crazy to it.

Frankly, he'd had enough crazy to last a lifetime.

Jaci stumbled through the doors to Starfish Films at five past nine the next morning, juggling her tote bag, her mobile, two scripts and a mega-latte, and decided that she couldn't function on less than three hours of sleep anymore. If someone looked up the definition of *cranky* in the dictionary, her picture next to the word would explain it all.

It hadn't helped that she'd spent most of the night reluctantly reliving that most excellent kiss, recalling the strength of that masculine, muscular body, the fresh, sexy smell of Ryan's skin. It had been a long time since she'd lost any sleep over a man—even during the worst of their troubles she'd never sacrificed any REMs for Clive—and she didn't like it. Ryan was sex on a side plate but she wasn't going to see him again. Ever. Besides, she hadn't relocated cities to dally with hot men, or any men. This job was what was important, the only thing that was important.

This was her opportunity to carve out a space for herself in the film industry, to find her little light to shine in. It might not be as bold or as bright as her mother's but it would be hers.

Frowning at the empty offices, she stepped up to her desk and dropped the scripts to the seat of her chair. This was the right choice to make, she told herself. She could've stayed in London; it was familiar and she knew how to tread water. Except that she felt the deep urge to swim…to do more and be more. She had been given an opportunity to change her life and, although she was soul-deep scared, she was going to run with it. She was going to prove, to herself and to her family, that she wasn't as rudderless, as directionless—as useless—as they thought she was.

This time, this job, was her one chance to try something different, something totally out of her comfort zone. This was her time, her life, her dream, and nothing would distract her from her goal of writing the best damn scripts she could.

Especially not a man with blue-gray eyes and a body that made her hormones hum.

Shona peeked into their office and jerked her head. "Not the best day to be late, sunshine. A meeting has started in the conference room and I suggest you get there."

"Meeting?" Jaci yelped. She was a writer. She didn't do meetings.

"The boss men are back and they want to touch base," Shona explained, tapping a rolled-up newspaper against her thigh. "Let's go."

A few minutes later, Shona pushed through the door at the top of the stairs and turned right down the identical hallway to the floor below. Corporate office buildings were all the same, Jaci thought, though she did like the framed movie posters from the 1940s and 1950s that broke up the relentless white walls.

Shona sighed and covered her mouth as she yawned. "We're all, including the boss men, a little tired and a lot hungover. Why we have to have a meeting first thing in the morning is beyond me. Jax should know better. Expect a lot of barking."

Jaci shrugged, not particularly perturbed. She'd lived with volatile people her entire life and had learned how to fly under the radar. Shona stopped in front of an open door, placed her hand between Jaci's shoulder blades and pushed her into the room. Jaci stumbled forward and knocked the arm of a man walking past. His coffee cup flew out of his hand toward his chest, and his cream dress shirt, sleeves rolled up past his elbows, bloomed with patches of espresso.

He dropped a couple of blue curses. "This is all I freakin' need."

Jaci froze to the floor as her eyes traveled up his coffee-soaked chest, past that stubborn, stubble-covered chin to that sensual mouth she'd kissed last night. She stopped at his scowling eyes, heavy brows pulled together. Oh, jeez...*no.*

Just no.

"Jaci?" Coffee droplets fell from his wrist and hand to the floor. "What the hell?"

"Jax, this is JC Brookes, our new scriptwriter," Thom said from across the room, his feet on the boardroom table and a cup of coffee resting on his flat stomach. "Jaci, Ryan 'Jax' Jackson."

He needed a box of aspirin, to clean up—the paper napkins Shona handed him weren't any match for a full cup of coffee—and to climb out of the rabbit hole he'd climbed into. He'd spent most of last night tossing and turning, thinking about that slim body under his hands, the scent of her light, refreshing perfume still in his nose, the dazzling heat and spice of her mouth.

He'd finally dozed off, irritated and frustrated, hours after he climbed into bed, and his few hours of sleep, starring a naked Jaci, hadn't been restful at all. As a result, he didn't feel as if he had the mental stamina to deal with the fact that the woman starring in his pornographic dreams last night was not only his friend's younger sister but also the screenwriter for his latest project.

Seriously? Why was life jerking his chain?

His mind working at warp speed, he flicked Jaci a narrowed-eyed look. "JC Brookes? You're him? Her?"

Jaci folded her arms across her chest and tapped one booted foot. How could she look so sexy in the city's uniform of basic black? Black turtleneck and black wide-leg pants… It would be boring as hell but she'd wrapped an aqua cotton scarf around her neck, and blue-shaded bracelets covered half her arm. He shouldn't be thinking about her clothes—or what they covered—right now, but he couldn't help himself. She looked, despite the shadows under those hypnotically brown eyes, as hot as hell. Simply fantastic. Ryan swallowed, remembering how feminine she felt in his arms, her warm, silky mouth, the way she melted into him.

Focus, Jackson.

"What the hell? You're a scriptwriter?" Ryan demanded, trying to make all the pieces of the puzzle fit. "I didn't know that you write!"

Jaci frowned. "Why should you? We haven't seen each other for twelve years."

"Neil didn't tell me." Ryan, still holding his head,

kneaded his temples with his thumb and index finger. "He should've told me."

Now he sounded like a whining child. Freakin' perfect.

"He doesn't know about the scriptwriting," Jaci muttered, and Ryan, despite his fuzzy shock, heard the tinge of hurt in her voice. "I just told him and the rest of my family that I was relocating to New York for a bit."

Ryan pulled his sticky shirt off his chest and looked at Thom again. "And she got the job how?"

Thom sent him a what-the-hell look. "Her agent submitted her script, our freelance reader read it, then Wes, then me, then you read the script. We all liked it but you fell in love with it! Light coming on yet?"

Ryan looked toward the window, unable to refute Thom's words. He'd loved Jaci's script, had read it over and over, feeling that tingle of excitement every time. It was an action comedy but one with heart; it felt familiar and fresh, funny and emotional.

And Jaci, his old friend's little sister, the woman he'd kissed the hell out of last night, was—thanks to fate screwing with him—the creator of his latest, and most expensive, project to date.

And his biggest and only investor, Leroy Banks, had hit on her and now thought that she was his girlfriend.

Oh, and just for kicks and giggles, he really wanted to do her six ways to Sunday.

"Could this situation be any more messed up?" Ryan grabbed the back of the closest chair and dropped his head, ignoring the puddles of coffee on the floor. He groaned aloud. Banks thought that his pseudo girlfriend was the hottest thing on two legs. Ryan understood why. He also thought she was as sexy as hell.

She was also now the girlfriend he couldn't break up with because she was his damned scriptwriter, one of—how had Banks put it?—his key people!

"I have no idea why you are foaming at the mouth, dude," Thom complained, dropping his feet to the floor. He shrugged. "You and Jaci knew each other way back when, so what? She was employed by us on her merits, with none of us knowing of her connection to you. End of story. So can we just get on with this damn meeting so that I can go back to my office and get horizontal on my couch?"

"Uh...no, I suggest you wait until after I've dropped the next bombshell." Shona tossed the open newspaper onto the boardroom table and it slid across the polished top. As it passed, Ryan slapped his hand on it to stop its flight. His heart stumbled, stopped, and when it resumed its beat was erratic.

In bold color and filling half the page was a picture taken last night in the reception area outside the ballroom of the Forrester-Graham. One of his hands cradled a bright blond head, the other palmed a very excellent butt. Jaci's arms were tight around his neck, her mouth was under his, and her long lashes were smudges on her cheek.

The headline screamed Passion for Award-Winning Producer!

Someone had snapped them? When? And why hadn't he noticed? Ryan moved his hand to read the small amount of text below the picture.

Ryan Jackson, award-winning producer of *Stand Alone*—the sci-fi box office hit that is enthralling audiences across the country—celebrates in the arms of JC Brookes at the Television and Film Awards after-party last night. JC Brookes is a scriptwriter employed by Starfish Films and is very well-known in England as the younger daughter of Fleet Street editor Archie Brookes-Lyon and his multi-award-winning author wife, Priscilla. She recently broke off her longstanding engagement to Clive Egglestone, projected to be a future prime minister of England, after he was implicated in a series of sexual scandals.

What engagement? What sexual scandals? More news that his ever-neglectful friend had failed to share. Jaci had been engaged to a politician? Ryan just couldn't see it. But that wasn't important now.

Ryan pushed the newspaper down the table to Thom. When his friend lifted his eyes to meet his again, his worry and horror were reflected in Thom's expression. "Well, hell," he said.

Ryan looked around the room at the nosy faces of his most trusted staff before pulling a chair away from the table and dropping into it. It wasn't in his nature to explain himself but this one time he supposed, very reluctantly, that it was necessary. "Jaci and I know each other. She's an old friend's younger sister. We are not in a relationship."

"Doesn't explain the kiss," Thom laconically stated.

"Jaci, on impulse, kissed me because Leroy was hitting on her and she needed an escape plan."

That explained her first kiss. It certainly didn't explain why he went back for a second, and hotter, taste. But neither Thom nor his staff needed to know that little piece of information. *Ever.*

"I told him that she was my girlfriend and that we hadn't seen each other for a while." Ryan kept his attention on Thom. "I had it all planned. When next we met and if Leroy asked about her, I was going to tell him that we'd had a fight and that she'd packed her bags and returned to the UK. I did not consider the possibility that my five-minute girlfriend would also be my new scriptwriter."

Thom shrugged. "This isn't a big deal. Tell him that you fought and that she left. How is he going to know?"

Ryan pulled in a deep breath. "Oh, maybe because he told me, last night, that he wants to meet the key staff involved in the project, and that includes the damned scriptwriter."

Thom groaned. "Oh, God."

"Not sure how much help he is going to be." Ryan turned around and looked at a rather bewildered Jaci, who had yet to move away from the door. "My office. Now."

Well, hell, he thought as he marched down the hallway to his office. It seemed that his morning could, after all, slide further downhill than he'd expected.

Chapter 3

Jaci waited in the doorway to Ryan's office, unsure whether she should step into his chaotic space—desks and chairs were covered in folders, scripts and stacks of papers—or whether she should she just stay where she was. He was in his private bathroom and she could hear a tap running and, more worrying, the steady stream of inventive cursing.

Okay, crazy, crazy morning and she had no idea what had just happened. It felt as if everyone in that office had been speaking in subtext and that she was the only one who did not know the language. All she knew for sure was that Jax was Ryan and Ryan was Neil's friend—and her new boss—and that he was superpissed.

And judging by their collective horror, she also

knew that Banks's clumsy pass and her kissing Ryan had consequences bigger than she'd imagined.

Ryan walked out of the bathroom, shirtless and holding another dress shirt, pale green this time, in his right hand. He was coffee-free and that torso, Jaci thought on an appreciative, silent sigh, could grace the cover of any male fitness magazine. His shoulders were broad and strongly muscled as were his biceps and his pecs. And that stomach, sinuously ridged, was a work of art. Jaci felt that low buzz in her stomach, the tingling spreading across her skin, and wondered why it had taken her nearly twenty-eight years to feel true attraction, pure lust. Ryan Jackson just had to breathe to make her quiver...

"You used to be Ryan Bradshaw. Why Jackson?" Jaci blurted. It was all she could think of to say apart from "Kiss me like you did last night." Since she was already in trouble, she decided to utter the only other thought she had to break the tense, sexually saturated silence.

Ryan blinked, frowned and then shook his shirt out, pulling the fabric over one arm. "You heard that Chad was my father, that Ben was my brother, and you assumed that I used the same surname. I don't," Ryan said in a cool voice.

She stepped inside and shut the door. "Why not?"

"I met Chad for the first time when I was fourteen, when the court appointed me to live with him after my mother's death. He dumped my mother two seconds after she told him she was pregnant and her name appeared on my birth certificate. I'd just lost her, and I wasn't about to lose her name, as well." Ryan machine-gunned his words and Jaci tried to keep up.

Ryan rubbed his hand over his face. "God, what does that have to do with anything? Moving rapidly on…"

Pity, Jaci thought. She would've liked to hear more about his childhood, about his relationship with his famous brother and father, which was, judging by his pain-filled and frustrated eyes, not a happy story.

"Getting back to the here and now, how the hell am I going to fix this?" Ryan demanded, and Jaci wasn't sure whether he was asking the question of her or himself.

"Look, I'm really sorry that I caused trouble for you by kissing you. It was an impulsive action to get away from Frog Man."

Ryan shoved his other arm into his sleeve and pulled the edges of his shirt together, found the buttons and their corresponding holes without dropping his eyes from her face.

"He was persistent. And slimy. And he wouldn't take the hint!" Jaci continued. "I'm sorry that the kiss was captured on camera. I know what an invasion of your privacy that can be."

Ryan glanced at the paper that he'd dropped onto his desk. "You seem to know what you're talking about." Ryan tipped his head. "Sexual scandals? Engaged?"

"All that and more." Jaci tossed her head in defiance and held his eyes. "You can find it all online if you want some spicy bedtime reading."

"I don't read trash."

"Well, I'm not going to tell you what happened," Jaci stated, her tone not encouraging any argument.

"Did I ask you to?"

Hell, he hadn't, Jaci realized, as a red tide crept up her neck. *Jeez, catch a clue. The guy kissed you. That doesn't mean he's interested in your history.*

Time to retreat. What had they been talking about? Ah, their kiss. "Look, if you need me to apologize to your girlfriend or wife, then I will." She thought about adding "I won't even tell her that you initiated the second kiss" but decided not to fan the flames.

"I'm not involved with anyone, which is about the only silver lining there is."

Jaci pushed her long bangs to one side. "Then I really don't understand what the drama is all about. We're both single, we kissed. Yeah, it landed up in the papers, but who cares?"

"Banks does and I told him that you're my girlfriend."

Jaci lifted her hands in confusion. This still wasn't any clearer. "So?"

Ryan started to roll up his sleeves, his expression devoid of all emotion. But his eyes were now a blistering blue, radiating frustration and a healthy dose of anxiety. "In order to produce *Blown Away*, to get the story you conceived and wrote onto the big screen, to do it justice, I need a budget of a hundred and seventy million dollars. I don't like taking on investors, I prefer to work solo, but the one hundred million I have is tied up at the moment. Besides, with such a big budget, I'd also prefer to risk someone else's money and not my own. Right now, Banks is the only thing that decides whether *Blown Away* sees the light of day or gets skipped over for a smaller-budget film.

"I thought that we were on the point of signing the damn contract but now he just wants to jerk my chain," Ryan continued.

"But why?"

"Because he knows that I caught him hitting on my girlfriend and he's embarrassed. He wants to remind me who's in control."

Okay, now she got it, but she wished she hadn't. She'd put a hundred-million deal in jeopardy? With a kiss? When she messed up, she did a spectacular job of it.

Jaci groaned. "And I'm your screenwriter." She shoved her fingers into her hair. "One of the project's key people."

"Yep." Ryan sat down on the edge of his desk and picked up a glass paperweight and tossed it from hand to hand. "We can't tell him that you only threw yourself into my arms because you found him repulsive... If you do that, we'll definitely wave goodbye to the money."

"Why can't I just stay in the background?" Jaci asked. She didn't want to—it wasn't what she'd come to the city to do—but she would if it meant getting the film produced. "He doesn't know that I wrote the script."

Ryan carefully replaced the paperweight, folded his arms and gave her a hard stare. After a long, charged minute he shook his head. "That's problematic for me. Firstly, you did write that script and you should take the credit for it. Secondly, I don't like any forms of lying. It always comes back to bite me on the ass."

Wow, an honest guy. She thought that the species was long extinct.

Jaci dropped into the nearest chair, sat on top of a pile of scripts, placed her elbows on her knees and rested her chin in the palm of her hand. "So what do we do?"

"I need you as a scriptwriter and I need him to fund the movie, so we do the only thing we can."

"Which is?"

"We become what Leroy and the world thinks we are, a couple. Until I have the money in the bank, and then we can quietly split, citing irreconcilable differences."

Jaci shook her head. She didn't think she could do it. She'd just come out of a relationship, and she didn't think she could be in another one, fake or not. She was determined to fly solo. "Uh…no, that's not going to work for me."

"You got me into this situation by throwing yourself into my arms, and you're going to damn well help me get out of it," Ryan growled.

"Seriously, Ryan— "

Ryan narrowed his eyes. "If I recall, your contract hasn't be signed…"

It took twenty seconds for his words to sink in. "Are you saying that you won't formalize my contract if I don't do this?"

"I've already bought the rights for the script. It's mine to do what I want with it. I did want some changes and I would prefer it if you write those, but I could ask Wes, or Shona, to do it."

"You're blackmailing me!" Jaci shouted, instantly

infuriated. She glanced at the paperweight on his desk and wondered if she could grab it and launch it toward his head. He might not lie but he wasn't above using manipulation, the dipstick!

Ryan sighed and placed the paperweight on top of a pile of folders. "Look, you started all this trouble, and you need to figure out how to end it. Consider it as part of your job description."

"Don't blame this on me!"

Ryan lifted an eyebrow in disbelief and Jaci scowled. "At least not all of it! The first kiss was supposed to be a peck, but you turned it into a hot-as-hell kiss!" Jaci shouted, her hands gripping the arms of the chair.

"What the hell was I supposed to do? You plastered yourself against me and slapped your mouth on mine!" Ryan responded with as much, maybe even more, heat.

"Do you routinely shove your tongue into a stranger's mouth?"

"I knew that I'd met you, dammit!" Ryan roared. He sprang to his feet and stormed over to his window and stared down at the tiny matchbox cars on the street below. Jaci watched as he pulled in a couple of deep breaths, amazed that she was able to fight with this man, shout at him, yet she felt nothing but exhilaration. No feelings of inadequacy or guilt or failure.

That was new. Maybe New York, with or without this crazy situation, was going to be good for her.

"So what are we going to do?" Jaci asked after a little while. It was obvious that they had to do something because walking away from her dream job was not an option. She was not going to go back to London without giving this opportunity her very best shot.

Giving up now was simply not an option. She had to prove herself and she'd do it here in New York City, the toughest place around. Nobody would doubt her then.

"Do you want to see this film produced? Do you want to see your name in the credits?" Ryan asked without turning around.

Well, duh. "Of course I do," she softly replied. This was her big break, her opportunity to be noticed, to get more than her foot through the door. She'd been treading water for so long, she couldn't miss this opportunity to ride the wave to the beach.

"Then I need Banks's money."

"Is he the only investor around? Surely not."

"Firstly, they don't grow on trees. I've also spent nearly eighteen months thrashing out the agreement. I can't waste any more time on him and I can't let that effort be for nothing."

There was no way out of this. "And to get his money we have to become a couple."

"A fake couple," Ryan hastily corrected her. "I don't want or need a real relationship."

Jeez, chill. She didn't want a relationship, either.

"So I can see some garden parties in the Hamptons in our future. Maybe theater or opera tickets, dinners at upscale restaurants because Banks will want to show me how important he is and he'll want to show you what you missed out on."

"Oh, joy."

Ryan shoved his hands in his hair and tugged. "We don't have a choice here and we have to make this count."

Jaci rubbed her hands over her face. Who would've

thought that an impulsive kiss could lead to such a tangle? She didn't have a choice but to go along with Ryan's plan, to be his temporary girlfriend. If she didn't, months of work—Ryan's, hers, Thom's—would evaporate, and she doubted that Ryan and Thom would consider working with her again if she was the one responsible for ruining their deal with Banks.

She slumped in her chair. "Okay, then. It's not like we—I—have much of a choice anyway."

Ryan turned and gripped the sill behind him, his broad back to the window. He sighed and rubbed his temple with the tips of his fingers, his action telling her that he had a headache on board. Lucky she hadn't clobbered him with that paperweight; his headache would now be a migraine.

"For all we know, Leroy might change his mind about socializing and we'll be off the hook," Ryan said, rolling his head from side to side.

"What do you think are the chances of that happening?" Jaci asked.

"Not good. He doesn't like the fact that I have you. He'll make me jump through hoops."

"Because you're everything he isn't," Jaci murmured.

"What do you mean?"

You're tall, hot and sexy. Charming when you want to be. You're successful, an acclaimed producer and businessman. You're respected. Leroy, as far as she knew, just had oily hair and enough money to keep a third-world economy buoyant. Jaci stared at her hands. She couldn't tell Ryan any of that; she had no intention of complimenting her blackmailer. Even if he could kiss to world-class standards.

"Don't worry about it." Jaci waved her words away and prayed that he wouldn't pursue the topic.

Thankfully he didn't. Instead he reached for the bottle of water on his desk and took a long sip. "So, as soon as I hear from Banks I'll let you know."

"Fine." Jaci pushed herself to her feet, wishing she could go back to bed and pull the covers over her head for a week or two.

"Jaci?"

Jaci lifted her eyes off her boots to his. "Yes?"

"We'll keep it completely professional at work. You're the employee and I'm the boss," Ryan stated. That would make complete sense except for the sexual tension, as bright and hot as a lightning arc, zapping between them. Judging by his hard tone and inscrutable face, Ryan was ignoring that sexual storm in the room. She supposed it would be a good idea if she did the same.

Except that her feet were urging her to get closer to him, her lips needed to feel his again, her... God, this was madness.

"Fine. I'll just get back to work then?"

"Yeah. I think that would be a very good idea."

When Jaci finally left his office, Ryan dropped into his leather chair and rolled his head from side to side, trying to release the tension in his neck and shoulders. In the space of ten hours, he'd acquired a girlfriend and the biggest deal of his life was placed in jeopardy if he and Jaci didn't manage to pull off their romance. He hadn't been exaggerating when he told Jaci that Leroy would be furious if he realized that Jaci was just using him as an excuse to put some distance between her and his wandering hands…but hell, talk about being in the wrong place at the wrong time!

It was the kiss—that fantastic, hot, sexy meeting of their mouths—that caused the complications. And, dammit, she was right. The first kiss, initiated by her, had been tentative and lightweight and he was the one who'd taken it deeper, hotter, wetter. Oh, she hadn't protested and had quickly joined him on the ride. A ride he wouldn't mind taking to its logical conclusion.

Concentrate, moron. Sex should have been low on his priority list. It wasn't but it should have been.

When he'd come back down to earth and seen Banks's petulant face—pouty mouth and narrowed eyes—he'd realized that he'd made a grave miscalculation. Then he'd added fuel to the fire when he'd informed him that Jaci was his girlfriend. Banks wanted Jaci and didn't like the fact that Ryan had her, and because of that, Ryan would be put through a wringer to get access to Banks's cash.

Like his father, Banks was the original playground bully; he instantly wanted what he couldn't and didn't have. Ryan understood that, as attractive as he found Jaci—and he did think that she was incredibly sexy—for Leroy his pursuit of her had little to do with Jaci but, as she'd hinted at earlier, everything to do with him. With the fact that she was with him, that he had her…along with a six-two frame, a reasonable body and an okay face.

This was about wielding power, playing games, and

what should've been a tedious, long but relatively simple process would now take a few more weeks and a lot more effort. He knew Leroy's type—his father's type. He was a man who very infrequently heard the word *no*, and when he did, he didn't much care for it. In the best-case scenario, they'd go on a couple of dinners and hopefully Leroy would be distracted by another gorgeous woman and transfer his attention to her.

The worst-case scenario would be Leroy digging his heels in, stringing him along and then saying no to funding the movie. Ryan banged his head against the back of his chair, feeling the thump of the headache move to the back of his skull.

The thought that his father had access to the money he needed jumped into his brain.

Except that he'd rather drill a screwdriver into his skull than ask Chad for anything. In one of his many recent emails he'd skimmed over, his father had told him that he, and some cronies, had up to two hundred million to invest in any of his films if there was a part in one of his movies for him. It seemed that Chad had conveniently forgotten that their final fight, the one that had decimated their fragile relationship, had been about the industry, about money, about a part in a film.

After Ben's death, his legions of friends and his fans, wanting to honor his memory, had taken to social media and the press to "encourage" him—as a then-indie filmmaker and Ben's adoring younger brother—to produce a documentary on Ben's life. Profits from the film could be donated to a charity in Ben's name. It would be a fitting memorial. The idea snowballed and soon he was inundated with requests to do the film, complete with suggestions that his father narrate the nonexistent script.

He'd lost the two people he'd loved best in that accident, the same two people who'd betrayed him in the worst way possible. While he tried to deal with his grief—and anger and shock—the idea of a documentary gained traction and he found himself being swept into the project, unenthusiastic but unable to say no without explaining why he'd rather swim with great whites in chum-speckled water. So he'd agreed. One of Ben's friends produced a script he could live with and his father agreed to narrate the film, but at the last minute Chad told him that he wanted a fee for lending his voice to the documentary.

And it hadn't been a small fee. Chad had wanted ten million dollars and, at the time, Ryan, as the producer, hadn't had the money. Chad—Hollywood's worst father of the year—refused to do it without a financial reward, and in doing so he'd scuttled the project. He was relieved at being off the hook, felt betrayed by Ben, heartbroken over Kelly, but he was rabidly angry that Chad, their father, had tried to capitalize on his son's death. Their argument was vicious and ferocious and he'd torn into Chad as he'd wanted to do for years.

Too much had been said, and after that blowout he realized how truly alone he really was. After a while he started to like the freedom his solitary state afforded him and really, it was just easier and safer to be alone. He liked his busy, busy life. He had the occasional affair and never dated a woman for more than six weeks at a time. He had friends, good friends he enjoyed, but he kept his own counsel. He worked and he made excellent films. He had a good, busy, productive life. And if he sometimes yearned for more—a partner, a family—he ruthlessly stomped on those rogue thoughts. He was perfectly content.

Or he would be if he didn't suddenly have a fake girlfriend who made him rock-hard by just breathing, a manipulative investor and a father who wouldn't give up.

Chapter 4

Jaci, sitting cross-legged on her couch, cursed when she heard the insistent chime telling her that she had a visitor. She glanced at her watch. At twenty past nine it was a bit late for social visits. She was subletting this swanky, furnished apartment and few people had the address, so whoever was downstairs probably had the wrong apartment number.

She frowned and padded over to her front door and pressed the button. "Yes?"

"It's Ryan."

Ryan? Of all the people she expected to be at her door at twenty past nine—she squinted at her watch, no, that was twenty past ten!—Ryan Jackson was not on the list. Since leaving his office four days before, she hadn't exchanged a word with him and she'd hoped that his ridiculous idea of her acting as his girlfriend had evaporated.

"Can I come up?" Ryan's terse question interrupted her musings.

Jaci looked down at her fuzzy kangaroo slippers—a gag Christmas gift from her best friend, Bella—and winced. Her yoga pants had a rip in the knee and her sweatshirt was two sizes too big, as it was one of Clive's that she'd forgotten to return. Her hair was probably spiky from pushing her fingers into it and she'd washed off her makeup when she'd showered after her run through Central Park after work.

"Can this wait until the morning? It's late and I'm dressed for bed."

She knew it was ridiculous but she couldn't help hoping that Ryan would assume that she was wearing a sexy negligee and not clothes a bag lady would think twice about.

"Jaci, I don't care what you're wearing so open the damn door. We need to talk."

That sounded ominous. And Ryan sounded determined enough, and arrogant enough, to keep leaning on her doorbell if he thought that was what it would take to get her to open up. Besides, she needed to hear what he had to say, didn't she?

But, dammit, the main reason why her finger hit the button to open the lobby door was because she wanted to see him. She wanted to hear his deep, growly voice, inhale his cedar scent—deodorant or cologne? Did it matter?—have an opportunity to ogle that very fine body.

Jaci placed her forehead on her door and tried to regulate her heart rate. Having Ryan in her space, being alone with him, was dangerous. This apartment wasn't big—this was Manhattan, after all—and her bedroom was a hop, skip and a jump away from where she was standing right now.

You cannot possibly be thinking about taking your boss to bed, Jacqueline! Seriously! Slap some sense into yourself immediately!

Ryan's sharp knock on the door had her jerking her head back. Because her father had made her promise that she wouldn't open the door without checking first—apparently the London she'd lived in for the past eight years was free of robbers and rapists—she peered through the peephole before flipping the lock and the dead bolt on the door.

And there he was, dressed in a pair of faded jeans and a long-sleeved, collarless black T-shirt. He held a leather jacket by his thumb over his shoulder and, with the strips of black under his eyes and his three-day beard, he looked tired but tough.

Ryan leaned his shoulder into the door frame and kept his eyes on her face, which Jaci appreciated. "Hey."

Soooo sexy. "Hello. What are you doing here? It's pretty late," she said, hoping that he missed the wobble in her voice.

"Leroy Banks finally returned my call. Can I come in?"

Jaci nodded and stepped back so that he could walk into the room. Ryan immediately dropped his jacket onto the back of a bucket chair and looked around the room, taking in the minimalist furniture and the abstract art. "Not exactly Lyon House," he commented.

"Nothing is," Jaci agreed. Her childhood home was old and stately but her parents had made it a home. It had never been a showpiece; it was filled with antiques and paintings passed down through the generations but also packed with books and dog leashes, coffee cups and magazines.

"Did your mother ever get that broken stair fixed? I remember her nagging your father to get it repaired. She said it had been driving her mad for twenty years."

Did she hear longing in his voice or was that her imagination? Ryan had always been hard to read, and her ability to see behind the inscrutable mask he wore had not improved with age. And she was too tired to even try. "Nope, the stair is still cracked. It will never be fixed. She just likes to tease my father about his lack of handyman skills. Do you want something to drink? Coffee? Tea? Wine?"

"Black coffee would be great. Black coffee with a shot of whiskey would be even better."

She could do that. Jaci suggested that Ryan take a seat but instead he followed her to the tiny galley kitchen, his frame blocking the doorway. "So, how are you enjoying work?"

Jaci flashed him a quick smile at his unexpected question. "I'm loving it. I'm working on the romcom at the moment. You said that you want changes done to *Blown Away* but I need to spend some time with you and Thom to find out exactly what you want and, according to your PA, your schedules are booked solid."

"I'll try to carve out some time for you soon, I promise."

Jaci went up onto her toes to reach the bottle of whiskey on the top shelf. Then Ryan's body was flush up against hers, his chest to her back, and with his extra height he easily took the bottle off the shelf. Jaci expected him to immediately move away but she felt his nose in her hair, felt the brush of his fingers on her hip. She waited with bated breath to see if he'd turn her to face him, wondered whether he'd place those broad hands on her breasts, lower that amazing mouth to hers…

"Here you go."

The snap of the whiskey bottle hitting the counter jerked her out of her reverie, and then the warmth of his body disappeared. With a dry mouth and a shaking hand, Jaci unscrewed the cap to the bottle and dumped a healthy amount of whiskey into their cups.

Hoo, boy! And down, girl!

"It's a hell of a coincidence that you, the sister of my old friend, had a script accepted by me, by us," Ryan said, lifting his arms up so that he gripped the top of the door frame. The action made his T-shirt ride up, showing a strip of tanned, muscled abdomen and a hint of fabulous oblique muscles. Jaci had to bite her tongue to stop her whimper.

"Actually, I'm not at all surprised that you like the script. After all, *Blown Away* was your idea."

"Mine?" Ryan looked confused.

Jaci poured hot coffee into the cups and picked them up. She couldn't breathe in the small kitchen—too much distracting testosterone—and she needed some space between her and this sexy man. "Shall we sit?"

Ryan took his cup, walked back to the living room and slumped into the corner of her couch. Jaci took the single chair opposite him and immediately put her feet up onto the metal-and-glass coffee table.

Ryan took a sip of his coffee and raised his eyebrows. "Explain."

Jaci blew air across the hot liquid before answering him. "You came down to Lyon House shortly before you dropped out of uni—"

"I didn't drop out, I graduated."

Jaci shook her head. "But you're the same age as Neil and he was in his first year."

Ryan shrugged, looking uncomfortable. "Accelerated classes. School was easy."

"Lucky you," Jaci murmured. Unlike her siblings, she'd needed to work a lot harder to be accepted into university, which she'd flunked out of halfway through her second year. She thought that she and Ryan had that in common, but it turned out that he was an intellectual like her sister. And brother. And her parents. She was, yet again, the least cerebral person in the room.

Lucky she'd had a lot of practice at being that.

"So, the script?" Ryan prompted.

"Oh! Well, you came home with Neil and the two of you were playing chess. It was raining cats and dogs. I was reading." Well, she'd been watching him, mooning over him, but he didn't need to know that! Ever. "You were talking about your careers and Neil asked you if you were going into the movie business like your father."

Jaci looked down into her cup. "You said that your dad and Ben had that covered, that you wanted your own light to shine in." His words had resonated with her because she understood them so well. She'd wanted exactly the same thing. "You also said that you were going to go into business management and that you were going to stay very far away from the film industry."

"As you can see, that worked out well," Ryan said, his comment bone-dry and deeply sarcastic.

"Neil said that you were fooling yourself, that it was as much in your blood as it was theirs." Jaci quirked an eyebrow. "He called that one correctly."

"Your brother is a smart man."

As if she'd never noticed.

"Anyway, Neil started to goad you. He tossed out plots and they were all dreadful. You thought his ideas were ridiculous and started plotting your own movie about a burnt-out cop and his feisty female newbie partner who were trying to stop a computer-hacking serial bomber from taking a megacity hostage. I was writing, even then, mostly romances but I took some of the ideas you tossed out, wrote them down and filed them. About eighteen months ago I found that file and the idea called to me, so I sat down and wrote the script." Jaci sipped her coffee. "I'm not surprised that you liked the script but I am surprised that you own a production company and that I'm now working for you."

Ryan's eyes pinned her to her chair. "Me, too." He pushed his hand through his hair. "Talking of non-scriptwriting work—"

Jaci sighed. "Toad of Toad Hall—"

"—has issued his first demand." Jaci groaned but Ryan ignored her. "He's invited us to join him at the premiere of the New York City Ballet Company's new production of *Swan Lake.*"

Jaci groaned again but more loudly and dramatically this time.

"You don't like ballet? I thought all girls like ballet," he said, puzzled. "And didn't your family have season tickets to the Royal Opera House to watch both ballet and opera?"

"They did. They dragged me along to torture me." Jaci pulled a face. "I much prefer a rock concert to either."

"But you'll do it?"

Jaci wrinkled her nose. "I suppose I have to. When is it?"

"Tomorrow evening. Black tie for me, which means a ball gown, or something similar, for you." His eyes focused on the rip in her pants before he lifted amused eyes to hers. "Think you can manage that?"

Jaci looked horrified. "You're kidding me right? Tomorrow?"

"Evening. I'll pick you up at six."

Jaci leaned back in her chair and placed her arm over her eyes. "I don't have anything to wear. That one cocktail dress I brought over was it."

Ryan took a sip from his cup and shrugged. "Last time I checked, there are about a million clothes stores in Manhattan."

She'd made a promise to herself that, now that she was free of Clive and free of having her outfits picked apart by the fashion police in the tabloids, she could go back to wearing clothes that made her feel happy, more like herself. Less staid, more edgy. When she left London with the least offensive of the clothes that had been carefully selected by the stylist Clive employed to shop for her, she'd promised herself that she would overhaul her wardrobe. She'd find the vintage shops and the cutting-edge designers and she would wear clothes that were a little avant-garde, more edgy. And she wouldn't wear another ball gown unless someone put a gun to her head.

Unfortunately, risking so many millions wasn't a gun, it was a freaking cannon…

She'd thought she was done with playing it safe.

"You're still frowning," Ryan said. "This is not a big deal, Jaci. How difficult can shopping be?"

"Only a man would say that," Jaci replied, bouncing to her feet. She slapped her hands onto her hips and jerked her head. "What do you want me to wear?"

Ryan shrugged and looked confused. "Why the hell should I care?"

"It's your party, Ryan, your deal. Give me a clue… regal, flamboyant, supersexy?"

"What the hell are you talking about?" Ryan demanded. "Put a dress on, show up, smile. That's it. Just haul something out of your closet and wear it. You must have something you can wear."

He really didn't get it. "Come with me," she ordered.

Ryan, still holding his coffee, followed her down the supershort hallway to the main bedroom. Jaci stomped over to the walk-in closet and flung the doors open. She stepped inside and gestured to the mostly empty room. Except for the umber cocktail dress she'd worn the other night, nearly every single item hanging off the rod and on the shelves was a shade of black.

Ryan lifted an eyebrow. "Do you belong to a coven or something? Or did the boring stuff get left behind when they robbed you?"

"I have enough clothes to stock my own store," Jaci told him with frost in her voice. "Unfortunately they aren't on this continent."

Ryan looked at her empty shelves again. "I can see that. Why not?"

Jaci pushed her hair behind her ears. "They are in storage, as I wasn't intending to wear them anymore."

"I can't believe that I am having a conversation about clothes but...and again...why not?"

Jaci stared at the floor and folded her arms across her chest. After a long silence, Ryan put his finger under her chin and lifted her eyes to his. "Why not, Jace?"

"I only brought a few outfits with me to the city. I was going to trawl the vintage shops and edgy boutiques to find clothes that were me, clothes that I liked, that I wanted to wear, clothes that made me feel happy. Now I have to buy a staid and boring ball gown that I'll probably never wear again."

Ryan narrowed his eyes. "Why does it have to be staid and boring?"

"You're in the public eye, Ryan. And there's a lot riding on this deal," Jaci pointed out. "It's important that I look the part."

The corners of Ryan's mouth twitched. "If our deal rests on what you are wearing then I'm in bigger trouble than I thought. You're making too big a deal of this, Jace. Wear whatever the hell you want, wherever and whenever. Trust me, I'm more interested in what's under the clothes anyway."

He really wasn't taking this seriously. "Ryan, impressions matter."

"Maybe if you're a politician who has a stick up his ass," Ryan retorted, looking impatient.

He didn't understand; he hadn't been crucified in the press for, among other things, his clothes. He hadn't been found wanting. She'd had enough of that in the United Kingdom. She didn't want to experience it on two continents. That was why she was trying to stay out of the public eye, why she was avoiding functions exactly like the one Ryan was dragging her to. And if she had to go, and it seemed as if she had little choice in the matter, she'd wear something that didn't attract attention, that would let her fly under the radar.

She waved her hand in the air in an attempt to dismiss the subject. "I'll sort something out."

Ryan sent her a hot look. "I don't trust you… You'll probably end up buying something black and boring. Something safe."

Well, yes. That was the plan.

Ryan put his hands on his hips. "You want vintage and edgy?"

Where was he going with this? "For my day-to-day wardrobe, yes."

"And for the ball gown?" Jaci's shrug was his answer. "I'm taking you shopping," Ryan told her with a stubborn look on his face.

Ryan…shopping? With her? For a ball gown? Jaci couldn't picture it. "I don't think… I'm not sure."

"You need a dress, and I am going to get you into one that isn't suitable for a corpse," Ryan promised her, his face a mask of determination. "Tomorrow."

"It would be a lot easier if you just excused me from the ballet," Jaci pointed out.

"Not going to happen," Ryan said as his eyes flicked from her face to the bed and back again. And, just like that, her insecurities about her clothes—okay, about herself—faded away, replaced by hot, flaming lust. She saw his eyes deepen and darken and she knew what he was thinking because, well, she was thinking it, too. How would it feel to be on that bed together, naked, limbs tangled, mouths fused, creating that exquisite friction that was older than time?

"Jaci?"

"Mmm?" Jaci blinked, trying to get her eyes to focus. When they did she saw the passion blazing in Ryan's eyes. If that wasn't a big enough clue as to what he wanted to do then there was also the impressive ridge in his pants. "The only real interest I have in your clothes is how to get you out of them. I really want to peel off that ridiculous shirt and those ratty pants to see what you're wearing underneath."

Nothing—she wasn't wearing a damn thing. Jaci touched the top of her lip with her tongue and Ryan groaned.

"I'm desperate to do what we're both thinking," Ryan said, his voice even huskier coated with lust. "But that would complicate this already crazy situation. It would be better if I just left."

Better for whom? Not for her aching, demanding libido, that was for sure. Jaci was glad that she didn't utter those words out loud. She just stood there as Ryan brushed past her. At the entrance of her room, he stopped and turned to look back at her. "There's a coffee shop around the corner from here. Laney's?"

"Yes."

"I'll meet you there at nine to go shopping."

Jaci nodded. "Okay."

Ryan's smile was slow and oh so sexy. "And, Jace? I value authenticity above conventionality. Just an FYI."

Ryan left the coffee shop holding two takeout cups and looked right and then left, not seeing Jaci anywhere. The outside tables were full and he brushed past some suits to stand in a patch of spring sunshine, lifting his leg behind him to place his foot against the wall.

He had a million things to do this morning but he was taking a woman shopping. There was something very wrong with this picture. He had a couple of rules when it came to the women he dated: he never slept over, he never took the relationship past six weeks, and he never did anything that could, even vaguely, be interpreted as something a "couple" would do. Clothes shopping was right up there at the top of the list.

A hundred million dollars...

Yeah, that was a load of bull. Jaci could turn up in nipple caps and a thong and it wouldn't faze him. He didn't care jack about what Leroy, or people in general, thought. Yet Jaci seemed to be determined to hit the right note, sartorially speaking. Something about their conversation last night touched Ryan in a place that he thought was long buried. He couldn't believe that the sexy, stylish, so outwardly confident Jaci could be so insecure about what she wore and how she looked. Somebody had danced in her head, telling her that she wasn't enough exactly as she was, and that made him as mad as hell.

Maybe because it pushed a very big button of his own: the fact that, in his father's eyes, he'd never been or ever would be the son he wanted, needed, the son he lost. It was strange that he'd shared a little of his dysfunctional family life with Jaci; he'd never divulged any of his past before, mostly because it was embarrassing to recount exactly how screwed up he really was. That's what happened when you met your father and half brother for the first time at fourteen and within a day of you moving in, your father left for a six-month shoot across the country. He and Ben were left to work out how they were related, and they soon realized that they could either ignore each other—the house was cavernous enough that they could do that—or they could be friends and keep each other company. That need for company turned into what he thought was an unbreakable bond.

Ryan stared at the pavement and watched as a candy wrapper danced across the sidewalk, thinking that bonds could be broken. He had the emotional scars to prove it. All it took was two deaths in a car crash and the subsequent revelation of an affair.

"Hi."

The voice at his elbow came out of nowhere and the cups in his hands rattled. God, he'd been so deep in thought that she'd managed to sneak up on him, something that rarely happened. Ryan looked into her face, noticed the splash of freckles across her nose that her makeup failed to hide and handed her a cup of coffee. Today she was wearing a pair of tight, fitted suit pants and a short black jacket. Too much black, Ryan thought. Too structured, too rigid.

But very New York.

"Thanks." Jaci sipped her coffee and lifted her face to the sun. "It's such a gorgeous day. I'd like to take my laptop and go to the park, find a tree and bang out a couple of scenes." She handed him a puppy-dog look. "Wouldn't you rather have me do that instead of shopping?"

"Nice try, but no go."

Ryan placed his hand on her lower back and steered her away from the wall. He could feel the warmth of her skin through the light jacket, and the curve of her bottom was just inches away. He was so damn tempted. Screw writing and shopping. His idea of how to spend a nice spring morning was to take this woman to bed.

Boss/employee, fake relationship/Leroy Banks, friend's kid sister…there were a bunch of reasons why that wasn't a viable option. But, hellfire, he really wanted to.

Ryan lifted his fingers to his mouth and let out a shrill whistle. Seconds later a taxi pulled up next to them. Ryan opened the door and gestured Jaci inside.

"Where to?"

Ryan started to give the address of his apartment then mentally slapped himself and told the driver to take them to Lafayette Street in Soho. "If we don't find what we're looking for there, we'll head to Nolita."

He saw Jaci's frown. "Nolita?"

"North of little Italy," Ryan explained. "It's like a cousin to Soho. It also has curb-to-curb boutiques."

Her frown deepened. "I thought we were heading for Fifth Avenue and the department stores or designer stores there."

"Let's try something different," Ryan replied, cyeing her tailored jacket. The unrelenting black was giving him a headache. The plump, happy teenager he knew had loved bright colors, and he'd love to see her in those shades again. He operated in a fake world and if he had to be saddled with a girlfriend, pretend or not, then he wanted the real Jaci next to him, not the cardboard version of whom she thought she should be.

As he'd said, authenticity was a seldom-found commodity, and he wasn't sure why it was so important that he get it from her.

Ryan watched as the taxi driver maneuvered the car through the busy traffic. He was going shopping. With his fake girlfriend. Whom he wanted, desperately, to see naked.

All because a narcissistic billionaire also had the hots for her. Yes, indeed. There was something very wrong with this picture.

Chapter 5

Her previous visits to New York had always been quick ones and because of that, Jaci had never taken in the time to let the nuances of the city register. She'd visited Soho before but she'd forgotten about the elegant cast-iron architecture, the cobblestone streets, the colorful buildings and the distinct artistic vibe.

Obviously, the artists peddling their creations contributed to the ambience but she could also smell the art in the air, see it in the fabulous window displays, in the clothes of the people walking the streets. Jaci—for the first time in years—felt like the fish out of water. The old Jaci, the one she'd been before Clive and the stylist he insisted she used, dressed in battered jeans, Docs and her favorite Blondie T-shirt belonged in Soho. This Jaci in her funeral suit? Not so much.

Ryan, with his messy hair and his stubble and stunning eyes, would fit in anywhere. He wore a black-and-white plaid shirt under a black sweater, sleeves pushed up. His khaki pants and black sneakers completed his casual ensemble and he looked urban and classy. Hot.

Ryan paid the taxi driver and placed his hand on her back. He'd done that earlier and it was terrifying to admit how much she liked the gesture. His broad hand spanned the width of her back and it felt perfect, right there, just above the swell of her bottom.

Ryan gestured to the nearest boutique and Jaci sighed. Minimalistic, slick and, judging by the single black halter neck in the window, boring. But, she reluctantly admitted, it would probably be eminently suitable for an evening spent at the ballet.

Jaci followed Ryan to the shop window and he pulled the door open for her to enter. As she was about to step inside, he grabbed her arm to hold her back. "Hey, this isn't a torture session, Jace. If this isn't your type of place, then let's not waste our time."

Jaci sucked in her bottom lip. "It's the type of shop that Gail, my stylist, would take me to."

"But not your type of shop," Ryan insisted.

"Not my type of shop. Not my type of clothes. Well, not anymore," Jaci reluctantly admitted. "But I should just look around. The dress is for the ballet and I will be going with a famous producer and a billionaire."

Ryan let go of the door and pulled her back onto the pavement. He lifted his hand and brushed the arch of his thumb along her cheekbone. "I have a radical idea, Jaci. Why don't you buy something that you want to wear instead of wearing something you think you should wear?"

God, she wished she could. The thing was, her style was too rock-chick and too casual, as she explained to Ryan. "Tight Nirvana T-shirts didn't project the correct image for a politician's SO."

"Jerk." Ryan dropped his eyes to her breasts, lingered and slowly lifted them again. Jaci's breath hitched at the heat she saw in the pale blue gray. Then his sexy mouth twitched. "There is nothing wrong, in my opinion, with a tight T-shirt." Jaci couldn't help her smile. "The thing is…you're not his fiancée anymore and you're not in London anymore. You can be anyone you want to be, dress how you wish. And that includes any function we attend as a fake couple."

He made it sound so simple… She wished it was that easy. Although she'd made up her mind to go back to dressing as she wanted to, old habits were hard to break. And sometimes Sassy Jaci wasn't as strong as she needed her to be. She still had an innate desire to please, to do what was expected of her, to act—and dress—accordingly. When she dressed and acted appropriately, her family approved. When she didn't they retreated and she felt dismissed. She was outgrowing her need for parental and sibling approval, but sometimes she simply wished that she was wired the same as them, that she could relate to them and they to her. But she was the scarlet goat in a family of sleek black sheep.

"Hey." Ryan tipped her chin up with his thumb and made her meet his startling eyes. "Come on back to me."

"Sorry."

"Just find something that you want to wear tonight. And if I think it's unsuitable then I'll tell you, okay?"

Jaci felt a kick of excitement, the first she'd felt about clothes and shopping for a long, long time. It didn't even come close to the galloping of her heart every time she laid eyes on Ryan, but it was still there.

Jaci reached up and curled her hand around his wrist, her eyes bouncing between his mouth and those long-lashed eyes. She wanted to kiss him again, wanted to feel those clever lips on her, taste him. She wanted to—

Then he did as she'd mentally begged and kissed her. God, that mouth, those lips, that strong hand on her face. Kissing him in the sunlight on a street in Soho... Perfection. Jaci placed her hands on his waist and cocked her head to change the angle and Ryan, hearing her silent request, took the kiss deeper, sliding his tongue into her mouth to tangle with hers. Slow, sweet, sexy. He tasted of coffee and mint, smelled of cedar and soap. Jaci couldn't help the step that took her into his body, flush against that long, muscled form that welcomed her. She didn't care that they were in the flow of the pedestrian traffic, that people had to duck around them. She didn't hear the sniggers, the comments, the laughter.

There was just her and Ryan, kissing on a city street in the spring sunshine.

Jaci lost all perception of time; she had no idea how long it had been when Ryan pulled back.

Don't say it, Jaci silently begged. *Please don't say you're sorry or that it was a mistake. Just don't. I couldn't bear it.*

Ryan must have seen something on her face, must have, somehow, heard her silent plea, because he stepped away and jammed his hands into his pockets.

"I really need to stop doing that," he muttered.

Why? She rather liked it.

"We need to find you a dress," he said, in that sexy growl.

Jaci nodded and, wishing that she had the guts to tell him that she'd far prefer that he find them a bed, fell into step beside him.

They left another shop empty-handed and Jaci walked straight to a bench and collapsed onto it. Her feet were on fire, she was parched and was craving a cheeseburger. They'd visited more than ten shops and Ryan wouldn't let her buy any of the many dresses she'd tried on, and Jaci was past frustrated and on her way to irritated. "I'm sick of this. I need a vodka latte with sedative sprinkles."

Ryan sat on the bench next to her, and his cough sounded suspiciously like "lightweight." Jaci narrowed her eyes at him. "I would never have taken you for a shopaholic, Jackson."

"For the record, normally you couldn't get me to do this without a gun to my head."

Because there was a hundred million on the line…

"You're the one who is drawing this out," Jaci pointed out. "The second shop we visited had that black sheath that was imminently suitable. You wouldn't let me buy it."

"You hated it." Ryan wore an expression that Jaci was coming to realize was his stubborn face. "As I said, tonight I'd like you to wear something you feel sexy in."

I'd feel sexy wearing you… Moving the hell on.

"Denim shorts, a Ramones tee and cowboy boots?" Jaci joked, but she couldn't disguise the hopeful note in her voice.

His mouth quirked up in a sexy smile that set her hormones to their buzz setting. "Not tonight but I'd like to see that combination sometime."

Jaci crossed one leg over the other and twisted her body so that she was half facing him. Sick of discussing clothes, she changed the subject to something she'd been wondering about. "When did you open Starfish and why?"

Ryan took a long time to answer and when he started to speak, Jaci thought that he would tell her to mind her own business. "Neil was right, I couldn't stay away from the industry. I landed a job as business manager at a studio and I loathed it. I kept poking my nose into places it didn't belong, production, scripts, art, even direction. After I'd driven everybody mad, the owner took me aside and suggested I open up my own company. So I did." Ryan tipped his face up to the sun. "That was about six months before Ben died."

His dark designer shades covered his eyes, but she didn't need to see them to know that, on some level, he still mourned his brother. That he always would. "I'm so sorry about Ben, Ryan."

"Yeah. Thanks."

Jaci sucked in some air and asked the questions she, and a good portion of the world, still wondered about. "Why did they crash, Ryan? What really happened?"

Ryan shrugged. "According to the toxicology screen, he wasn't stoned or drunk—not that night, anyway. He wasn't suicidal, as far as we knew. Witnesses said that he wasn't driving fast. There was no reason why his Porsche left the road and plunged down that cliff. It was ruled a freak accident."

"I'm sorry." The words sounded so small, so weak. She bit her bottom lip. "And the woman who died along with him? Had you met her? Did you know her?"

"Kelly? Yeah, I knew her," Ryan replied, his voice harsh as he glanced at his watch. Subject closed, his face and body language stated. "It's nearly lunchtime. Want to hit a few more shops? If we don't find anything, we'll go back for that black sheath."

"Let's go back for that black sheath now," Jaci said as she stood up, pulling her bag over her shoulder. As they stepped away from the bench, she saw a young woman holding four or five dresses on a hanger, her arm stretched above her head to keep the fabrics from skimming the ground. The top dress, under its plastic cover, made her heart stumble. It was a striking, A-line floor-length dress in watermelon pink with a deep, plunging, halfway-to-her-navel neckline.

Without hesitation she crossed the pavement and tapped the young woman on her shoulder. "Hi, sorry to startle you." She gestured to the garments. "I love these. Are they your designs?"

The woman nodded. "They are part of a consignment for The Gypsy's Caravan."

Jaci reached out and touched the plastic covering the top dress. It was simple but devastatingly so, edgy but feminine. It was a rock-chick dress trying to behave, and she was in love. The corners of Ryan's mouth kicked up when she looked at him.

"What do you think?" she asked, not quite able to release the plastic covering of the dress, her dress.

"I think that you love it." Ryan flashed his sexy smile at the woman carrying the dresses and Jaci was sure that she saw her knees wobble. This didn't surprise her in the least. Her knees were always jelly-like around Ryan.

"It looks like we're going where you are," Ryan said as he reached for the dresses and took them from her grasp, then held them with one hand so that they flowed down his back. With his height they didn't even come close to the dirty sidewalk. He placed his other hand on Jaci's back.

Jaci shook her head, planting her feet. "I don't think it's suitable. It's too sexy… I mean, I couldn't wear a bra with it!"

After looking at her chest, Ryan lifted his eyebrows. "You don't need a bra." He grabbed her hand and tugged it. "It's the first time I've seen you remotely excited about a dress all morning. You're trying it on. Let's go."

"The black sheath is more appropriate."

"The black sheath is as boring as hell," Ryan whipped back. "Jace, I'm tired and sick of this. Let's just get this done, okay?"

Well, when he put it like that… He was still—despite their hot kisses and the attraction that they were trying, and failing, to ignore—the boss.

As an excuse, it worked for her.

* * *

In the end it was just the three of them who attended the ballet, and despite the fact that Ryan did his best to keep himself between her and Leroy, Jaci knew that he couldn't be her buffer all evening and at some point she would have to deal with Leroy on her own. The time, Jaci thought as she sent Ryan's departing back an anxious look, had come. It was intermission and Ryan, along with what seemed to be the rest of the audience, was making his way toward the bar for the twelve-year-old whiskey Leroy declared that he couldn't, for one more minute, live without.

Keeping as much distance as she could from him in the crowded, overperfumed space, she fixed her eyes on Ryan's tall frame, trying to keep her genial smile in place. It faltered when a busty redhead bumped her from behind and made her wobble on her too-high heels. She gritted her teeth when she felt Leroy's clammy grip on her elbow. *Ick.* Jaci ruthlessly held back her shiver of distaste as she pulled her arm from his grasp. Strange that Ryan, with one look, could heat her up from the inside out, that he could have her shivering in anticipation from a brief scrape of his hand against any part of her, yet Leroy had exactly the opposite effect. They were two ends of the attraction spectrum and she was having a difficult time hiding her reactions, good and bad, to both of them.

One because there was a hundred million on the line; the other because she was, temporarily, done with men and a dalliance with Ryan—her boss!—would not be a smart move. She wouldn't jeopardize her career for some hot sex…as wonderful as she knew that hot sex would be. Mmm, not that she'd ever had any hot sex, but a girl could dream. She'd had hurried sex and boring sex and blah sex but nothing that would melt her panties. Judging by the two kisses they'd shared, Ryan had a PhD in melting underwear.

Yep, just the thought had the thin cord of her thong warming; if she carried on with this train of thought she'd be a hot mess. Jaci straightened her back and mentally shook herself off. She was enough of a mess as it was. She was in New York to get a handle on her crazy life, to establish her career and to find herself. She was not supposed to be looking for ways to make it more complicated!

"I have a private investigator."

Jaci tucked her clutch bag under her arm and linked her fingers together. *Be polite, friendly but distant.* She could make conversation for ten minutes or so; she wasn't a complete social idiot. A private investigator? Why would he be telling her that? "Okay. Um…what do you use him for?"

"Background checks on business associates, employees," Leroy explained. His eyes were flat and cold and Jaci felt the hair on her arms rise. "When I was considering whether to go into business with Jackson, I had him investigated."

"He wouldn't have found anything that might have given you second thoughts," Jaci quickly replied.

Leroy cocked his head. "You seem very sure of that."

"Ryan has an enormous amount of integrity. He says what he means and means what he says." Jaci heard the heat in her voice and wished that she could dial it down. Leroy hadn't said anything to warrant her defense of Ryan but something in his tone, in his body language, had her fists up and wanting to box. This was very unlike her. She wasn't a fighter.

"Strange that you should be so sure of that since you've only known him for a few weeks," Leroy replied, his words silky. Leroy ran a small, pale hand down the satin lapels of his suit in a rhythmic motion. Where was he going with this? Jaci, deciding that silence was a good option, just held his reptilian eyes.

"So tell me, Jacqueline, how involved can you be with Ryan after knowing him for just seventeen days?"

"I broke up with my ex six weeks before that and sometimes love—" she tried not to choke on the word "—happens in unexpected places and at unexpected times." Jaci allowed herself a tiny, albeit cold, smile. "You really should hire better people, Leroy, because your PI's skills are shoddy. I've known Ryan for over twelve years. He attended university with my brother, and he was a guest in my parents' home. We've been in contact for far longer than two weeks." Jaci tacked on the last lie with minimal effort.

It was time for Sassy Jaci, she thought. She needed to throw politeness out the window, so she nailed Leroy with a piercing look. "Why the interest in me? And if you have to color outside the lines, there are hundreds of gorgeous, unattached girls, interested girls, out there you can dally with."

"My pursuit of you annoys Ryan and that puts him off guard. I like him off guard. But I do find you attractive and taking you from Ryan would be an added bonus." After a minute, he finally spoke again. "I like to have control in a relationship, whether that's business or personal."

That made complete sense, Jaci thought. "And Ryan won't be controlled."

"He will if he wants my money." Leroy's smile was as malicious as a snakebite. He lifted his hand and the tip of his index finger touched her bare shoulder and drifted down the inside of her arm. "He'll toe the line. They always do. Everyone has their price."

"I don't. Neither does Ryan."

"Everyone does. You just don't know what it is yet and neither do I."

There was a relentless determination in his eyes that made her think he was being deadly serious.

"This conversation has become far too intense," Leroy calmly stated. "You do intrigue me… You're very different from what I am used to, from the women I usually meet."

"Because I'm not rich, or plastic, or crazy?" Jaci demanded.

Leroy's laugh sounded like sandpaper on glass and it was as creepy as his smile. "At first, perhaps. But mostly you fascinate me because Ryan is fascinated by you. I want to know why."

There was that one-upmanship again, Jaci thought. What was with this guy and his need to feel superior to Ryan? The chip on his shoulder was the size of a redwood tree. Didn't he realize that few men could compete with Ryan? Ryan was a natural leader, utterly and completely masculine, and one of his most attractive traits was the fact that he didn't care what people thought about him.

Leroy had a better chance of corralling the wind than he did of controlling Ryan. Why couldn't he see that? Couldn't he see Ryan was never going to kowtow to him, that he would never buckle?

Ryan marched to the beat of his own drum.

"Everything okay here?"

Jaci whirled around at Ryan's voice and reached for the glass of wine she'd ordered. Taking a big sip, she looked at him over her glass, her expression confused and uneasy.

"Everything is fine," Leroy said.

Ryan ignored him and kept his eyes on Jaci's face. "Jace?"

Jaci drank in his strong, steady presence and nodded. He held her stare for a while longer and eventually his expression cleared. He finally handed over Leroy's glass into his waiting hand, accompanied by a hard stare. Ryan wasn't a fool. He knew that words had been exchanged and Jaci knew that he'd demand to know what they'd discussed. How serious was Leroy's need to control Ryan? Jaci wasn't as smart about these things as her siblings were, but with her career and Ryan's film on the line, she couldn't afford to shove her head in the sand and play ostrich.

The lights flickered and Ryan placed his hand on her lower back. "Time to head back in," he said.

As Ryan led her back to their seats, Jaci thought that they had to manage the situation and, right now, she was the only pawn on the chessboard. If she removed herself, Ryan and Leroy wouldn't have anything to tussle over. But they couldn't admit to their lie about being a couple; that would have disastrous consequences.

But what if they upped the stakes, what if they showed Leroy that she was, in no uncertain terms, off-limits forever? Right now, as Ryan's girlfriend, there was room for doubt… Maybe they should remove all doubt.

Not giving herself time to talk herself out of the crazy idea that popped into her head, she stopped to allow an older couple to walk into the theater in front of her and slipped her hand into Ryan's, resting her head on his shoulder. She sent Leroy a cool smile. "There is one other thing your PI didn't dig up, Leroy."

Ryan's body tensed. "PI? What PI?"

Jaci ignored him and kept her eyes on Leroy's face. She watched as his eyebrows lifted, those eyes narrowed in focus. "And what might that be?"

Here goes, Jaci thought. *In for a penny and all that, upping the stakes, throwing the curveball.* "He wouldn't know that Ryan and I are deeply in love and that we are talking about marriage." She tossed Ryan an arch look. "I expect to be engaged really soon and I can't wait to wear Ryan's ring."

Chapter 6

*W*hat.
   The.
   Hell?

Two hours and a couple of lukewarm congratulations from Leroy later, and Ryan was still reeling from Jaci's surprise announcement and "what the hell" or other variations of the theme kept bouncing around his head. Leaving the theater, back teeth grinding, he guided Jaci through the door, his hand on her back. She'd, once again and without discussion, flipped his world on its head. *Thinking about marriage?* Did she *ever* think before she acted?

On the sidewalk, Ryan saw a scruffy guy approaching them from his right, an expensive camera held loosely in his hands, and he groaned. He immediately recognized Jet Simons. He was one of the most relentless—and annoying—tabloid reporters on the circuit. Part journalist, part paparazzo, all sleaze. Ryan knew this because the guy practically stalked him in the month following Ben's death. Jet had witnessed his grief and every day Ryan would pray that Jet wouldn't capture his anger at Ben and his pain at being betrayed by his brother and Kelly. He definitely hadn't wanted Jet to capture how alone he felt, how isolated. Soul-sucking bottom-feeder.

Ryan sent a back-the-hell-off look in his direction, which, naturally, Simons ignored. Dammit, he needed him around as much he needed a punch in the kidneys. Ryan grabbed Jaci's hand, hoping to walk away before they were peppered with questions.

"Leroy Banks and Jax Jackson," Simons drawled, stepping up to them and lifting his camera, the flash searing their eyes. "How's it hanging, guys?"

"Get out of my face or I'm going to shove that camera where it hurts," Ryan growled, pushing the lens away. Unlike the actors he worked with who played a cat-and-mouse game with the press, he didn't need to make nice with the rats.

The flash went off another few times and Ryan growled. He was about to make good on his threat when Simons lowered the camera and looked over it to give Jaci a tip-to-toe look, his gaze frankly appreciative. Ryan felt another snarl rumble in his throat and reminded himself that Jaci was his pretend girlfriend and that he had no right to feel possessive over her. The acid in his stomach still threatened to eat a hole through its lining.

Just punch him, caveman Ryan said from his shoulder, *you'll feel so much better after.*

Yeah, but sitting in jail on assault charges would suck.

"So, you're Jaci Brookes-Lyon," Simons said, his eyes appreciative. "Not Jax's usual type, I'll grant you that."

Ryan squeezed Jaci's hand in a silent reminder not to respond. It was good advice, and he should listen to it, especially since he still wanted to shove that lens down Simons's throat or up his…

"Mr. Banks, how you doing? You still in bed with Jackson? Figuratively speaking, that is? Where's Mrs. Banks?" Simons machine-gunned his words. "What do you think about Jax's little sweetie here? Do you think she is another six-weeker or does she have the potential to be more?"

Ryan heard Jaci's squawk of outrage but his attention was on Leroy's face, and his slow smile made Ryan's balls pull up into his body. Dammit, he was going to dump them right in it. He knew it as he knew his own signature. Ryan's mind raced, desperate for a subject change, but before he could even try to turn the conversation Leroy spoke again. "They are talking about marriage, so maybe I suspect she does—" he waited a beat before speaking again "—have potential, that is."

Ryan let fly with a creative curse and shook his head when he realized that his outburst just added a level of authenticity to Banks's statement. He knew that a vein was threatening to pop in his neck and he released a clenched fist. Maybe he should just punch Leroy, as well, and make his jail stay worth his while.

"So you're engaged?" Simons demanded, his face alight with curiosity.

"Look, that's not exactly..." Jaci tried to explain but Ryan tightened his grip on her hand and she muttered a low "Ow."

"Stop talking," Ryan ordered in her ear before turning back to Simons and pinning him to the floor with a hard glance. "Get the hell out of my face."

Simons must have realized that he was dancing on his last nerve because he immediately took a step backward and lifted his hands in a submissive gesture. *Wuss*, Ryan internally scoffed as he watched him walk away. When Simons was out of earshot, Ryan finally settled his attention on Banks and allowed him to see how pissed he was with him, too. "I don't know what game you're playing, Banks, but it stops right now."

Leroy shrugged. "I am the one financing your film so you don't get to talk to me like that."

Wusses. He was surrounded by them tonight.

"I haven't seen any of your money so you're not in any position to demand a damn thing from me," Ryan said, keeping his voice ice cold. Cold anger, he realized a long time ago, was so much more effective than ranting and raving. "And even if we do still do business together, it'll always be my movie. You will never call the shots. Think about that and come back to me if you think those are terms you can live with."

Banks flushed under Ryan's hard stare and Ryan thought that it was a perfect time to throw in one last threat. "And this thing you have for my girlfriend stops right here. Leave her the hell alone."

"Ryan..." Jaci tried to speak as he pulled her toward a taxi sitting behind Leroy's limo and yanked the door open. He bundled her inside and when she was seated, he gripped the sides of the door and glared at her. This was all her and her big mouth's fault! What the hell had she been thinking by telling Leroy that they were talking about marriage? And how could he still be so intensely angry with her but still want to rip her clothes off? How could he want to strangle and kiss her at the same time?

He was seriously messed up. Had been since this crazy woman dropped back into his life.

"Not one damn word," he ordered before slamming the door closed and walking around the back of the cab. He slid inside and Jaci opened her mouth again.

"Ryan, I need you to understand why—"

God, she seriously wasn't listening. "What part of 'not one damn word' didn't you understand?" he growled after he tossed the address to her place to the driver up front.

"I understand that you are angry—"

"Shut. Up." Ryan felt as if a million spiders were dancing under his skin and that his temper was bubbling, looking for a way to escape. He'd spent his teenage years with a volatile father who didn't give a damn about him, and when he did pay him some attention, it was always negative. He'd learned to ignore the disparaging comments, to show no reaction and definitely no emotion. His father had fed off drama, had enjoyed baiting him, so he'd learned not to lose control, but

tonight he was damn close. Engaged? Him? The man who, thanks to his brother and Kelly, rarely dated beyond six weeks? Who would believe it? And he was engaged to Jaci, who wasn't exactly his type…mostly because she wasn't like the biddable, eager-to-please women he normally dated. God, he hadn't even slept with Jaci yet and he was halfway to being hitched? On what planet in what freaking galaxy was that fair?

"I need to explain. Leroy—"

Okay, obviously she had no intention of keeping quiet, and he had two options left to him. To strip sixteen layers of skin off her or to shut her up in the only way he knew how. Deciding to opt for the second choice, he twisted, leaned over and slapped his mouth on hers. He dimly heard her yelp of surprise, and taking advantage of her open mouth, he slid his tongue inside…

His world flipped over again as he licked into her mouth, his tongue sliding over hers. She tasted of mint and champagne and heated surprise. The scent of her perfume, something light but fresh, enveloped him and his hands tightened on her hips, his fingers digging into the fabric of the dress he'd helped her choose, the dress he so desperately wanted to whip off her to discover what lay underneath. The backs of his fingers skimmed the side of her torso, bumped up and over her ribs, across the swelling of her breasts. He wanted to cup her, to feel her nipple pucker into his hand, but he was damned if he'd give the taxi driver a free show. Knowing her, discovering her, could wait until later. He needed to delay gratification, even if his erection felt as if it was being strangled by his pants. He could do it but that didn't mean he had to like it.

He wanted her. He wanted all of her...

Jaci yanked him back to the present by whipping her mouth off his and pushing herself into the corner of the cab, as far away from him as possible. "What are you doing?"

That was obvious, wasn't it? "Kissing you."

Dark eyes flashed her annoyance. "You tell me to shut up and then you kiss me? Are you crazy?"

That was highly possible.

"You wouldn't shut up," Ryan pointed out, his temper reigniting as he remembered her stupid declaration.

"You wouldn't let me explain," Jaci retorted.

"Yeah, I can't wait to see what you come up with." Ryan retreated to his corner of the cab, knowing that a muscle was jumping in his cheek. "Why would you make up such a crazy story? Are you that desperate to be engaged, to show the world that someone wants to marry you, that you would just go off half-cocked? I don't want to be engaged. God, I've been battling to wrap my head around having a fake girlfriend, and now I have a fake fiancée? And that it's you? Jesus!"

Ryan would never have believed it possible if he didn't witness her already brown-black eyes darken to coals. Anger and pride flashed but he couldn't miss the hurt, couldn't help but realize that he'd pushed one button too many, that he'd gone too far. He fumbled for words as she turned away to stare out the window, her hands in a death grip in her lap.

But God, his work was *his life* and she was screwing with it. He wanted that hundred million, he wanted to share the risk with an investor. And the one he'd had on his hook he'd just cut loose because of this woman and her way of speaking without thinking, of screwing up his life.

And it killed him to know that if she made one move to sleep with him, even kiss him, he'd be all over her like a rash. He was a reasonably smart guy, a guy who'd had more than his fair share of gorgeous women, but this one had him tied up in knots.

Not.

Cool.

Thinking that he needed separation from her before he did something stupid—not that this entire evening hadn't been anything but one long stupidity—he reached across her and pushed her door open. Jaci seemed as eager to get away from him as he was from her, and she quickly scrambled out of the cab, giving him a superexcellent flash of a long, supple leg and the white garter holding up a thigh-high stocking. He felt the rush of blood to his groin and had to physically restrain himself from bolting after her and finding out whether the rest of her lingerie was up to the fantastic standard her garters set.

Ryan banged the back of his head on the seat as he watched Jaci walk toward the doormen standing on the steps of her building. She was trying to kill him, mentally and sexually.

It was the only explanation he could come up with.

Jaci, vibrating with fury, stood outside Ryan's swanky apartment building in Lenox Hill and stormed into the lobby, startling the dozy concierge behind the desk. He blinked at her and rubbed his hand over his face before lifting his hefty bulk to his feet.

"Help you?"

Jaci forced herself to unclench her jaw so that she could speak. "Please tell Ryan Jackson that Jaci Brookes-Lyon is here to see him."

Deputy Dog Doorman looked doubtful. "It's pretty late, miss. Is he expecting you?"

Jaci's molars ground together. "Just call him. Please?"

She received another uncertain look but he reached for the phone and dialed an extension. Within twenty seconds she was told that Ryan had agreed to see her— how kind of him!—and she was directed to the top floor.

"What number?" she demanded, turning on her spiked heel, wishing that she'd changed out of the dress she'd worn to the ballet before she'd stormed out of her apartment to confront him in his.

"No number. Mr. Jackson's apartment is on the top floor, *is* the top floor." The doorman sighed at her puzzled expression. "He has the penthouse apartment, miss."

"The penthouse?"

"Mr. Jackson recently purchased one of the most sought-after residences in the city, ma'am. Ten thousand square feet, four bedrooms with a wraparound terrace. Designer finishes, with crown moldings, high ceilings and custom herringbone floors," the concierge proudly explained.

"Good for him," Jaci muttered and headed for the elevator, the doorman on her heels. At the empty elevator, the doorman keyed in a code on the control panel on the wall and gestured her inside. "The elevator opens directly into his apartment, so guests need to be authorized to go up."

Whatever, Jaci thought, as the doors started to close.

"Have a good evening, miss."

She heard the words slide between the almost closed doors and she knew that she was about to have anything but. She'd been heading up to her apartment, intending to lick her wounds, when she'd suddenly felt intensely angry. It made her skin prickle and her throat tighten. How dare Ryan treat her as if she was something he'd caught on the bottom of his shoe? He'd refused to let her speak, had ignored her pleas to allow her to explain and had acted as if she were an empty-headed bimbo who should be grateful to spend any time she could in his exalted presence. And how stupid was he to challenge Leroy like that? It was entirely possible that he'd decimated any chance of Leroy funding *Blown Away* with his harshly uttered comments... And he accused *her* of acting rashly!

Unable to enter her apartment and stay there like a good little woman, she'd headed downstairs, hailed a cab and headed for Ryan's apartment, seething the whole way. Maybe he could afford to let *Blown Away* blow away but she couldn't! She wasn't going to allow him to lose this chance to show the world, her family—to show herself—that she could be successful, too. It was a good script and she was determined that the world would see it!

Jaci released her tightly bunched hands and flexed her fingers; for an intensely smart man, Ryan could be amazingly stupid. And Jaci was going to tell him so—no man was going to get away with dismissing her again. She didn't care if he was her boss, or her fake boyfriend or her almost, albeit fake, fiancé. There was too much at stake: the film, her career and, most important right now, her pride.

Jaci rested her forehead against the oak-paneled interior of the elevator.

Unlike in her arguments with Clive, this time she would scream and shout. She'd do anything to be heard, dammit! And Ryan, that bossy, alpha, sexy sod, was going to get it with both barrels! Jaci had barely completed that thought when the elevator doors opened and she was looking into Ryan's living room, which was filled with comfortable couches and huge artwork. He stood in front of the mantel, and despite her anger, Jaci felt the slap of attraction. How could she not since he looked so rough and tough in his white dress shirt that showed off the breadth of his shoulders, his pants perfectly tailored to show off his lean waist and hips, his long, muscled legs.

The top two buttons of the shirt were open and the ends of his bow tie lay against his chest, and she wanted her hands there, on his chest, under his shirt, feeling that warm, masculine skin.

Focus. She wasn't here to have sex with him… but, dear God with all his angels and archangels, she wanted to. She wanted to as she wanted her heart to keep beating.

If she was a man at least she would have the excuse of thinking with the little head, but because she was a woman she was out of luck.

"What do you want, Jaci?" Ryan demanded, jamming his hands into his suit pockets.

You. I want you. So much.

Jaci shook her head to dislodge that thought. This wasn't about a tumble, this was about the way he had treated her. Her third-grade teacher, Mrs. Joliet, was correct: *Jacqueline is too easily distracted.* Nothing, it seemed, had changed.

Jaci licked her lips.

"God, will you stop doing that?" Ryan demanded, his harsh voice cutting through the dense tension between him.

"What?" Jaci demanded, not having a clue what he was talking about. Her eyes widened as he stalked toward her, all fierce determination and easy grace, his eyes on her mouth.

"Licking your lips, biting your lip! That's my job." He grabbed her arms and jerked her up onto her toes. It was such a caveman-like action, but she couldn't help the thrill she felt when her chest slammed into his and her nipples pushed into his chest. If she wasn't such a sap she would be protesting about him treating her like a ditsy heroine in a romcom movie, but right now she didn't care. She was pressed so close to him that a beam of light couldn't pass through the space between them, and his mouth was covering hers.

And, God, then her world tipped over and flipped inside out. The kisses she'd shared with him before were a pale imitation of the passion she could taste on the tongue that swept inside her mouth, that she could feel in the hand that made a possessive sweep over her back, in the appreciative, low groans that she could hear in the back of his throat. In a small, rarely used part of her brain—the only cluster of brain cells that weren't overwhelmed by this fantastically smoking-hot kiss—she was in awe of the fact that Ryan wanted her like this.

It almost seemed as if kissing her, touching her, was more important to him than breathing. Actually, Jaci agreed, breathing was highly overrated. Her hands drifted up his chest, skimmed the warm skin beneath the collar of his shirt and wound around the back of his strong neck, feeling his heat, his strength. Then his hand covered her breast and he rubbed his palm across her nipple and, together with feeling the steel pipe that was pressing into her stomach, those last few brain cells shut down.

Ryan jerked his head back and, when she met them, his light eyes glittered down at her. "So, we're engaged, right?"

Jaci half shrugged. "Probably. At least we will be, in the eyes of the world, when the news breaks in a few hours."

"Well, in that case…" Ryan bent his knees and ran his hands up the outside of her thighs, her dress billowing over his forearms. "It's a damn good excuse to do this."

Jaci gasped as he played with the lace tops of her garters, danced up and across her hip bone and slid down to cover her bare butt cheek.

"Garters and a thong. I've died and gone to heaven," Ryan muttered, sliding his fingers under that thin cord.

Ryan sucked the soft spot where her jaw and neck

met, and she whimpered in delight. "God, Ryan…is this a good idea?"

Ryan pulled his head up and frowned down at her. "Who the hell knows? But if I'm going to be bagged and tagged, then I'm going to get something out of the deal. Stop playing with my hair and put your hands on me, Jace. I'm dying here."

Jaci did as she was told and she placed her hand flat against his sex. He jumped and groaned and she wanted more. She wanted him inside her, filling her, stretching her…but she had to be sensible.

"Just sex?" she asked, unable to stop her hand from pulling down the zipper to his pants and sliding on inside. She pushed down his underwear and there he was, hot and pulsing and hard and…oh, God, his hands were between her legs and he'd found her. Found that most magical, special, make-her-crazy spot…

"Yeah, one night to get this out of our systems. You okay with that? One night, no strings, no expectations of more?"

How was she supposed to think when his fingers were pushing their way inside? Her thumb rubbed his tip and she relished the groan she pulled from him. They were still fully dressed yet she was so damn close to gushing all over his hand. If he moved his thumb back to her hot nub, she'd lose it. Right here, right now.

"I'm supposed to be fighting with you right now," Jaci wailed.

Ryan responded by covering her mouth with his. After swiping his tongue across the indents her teeth marks made, he lifted his head to speak. "We can fight later. So, are we good? If not, now is the time to say no, and you'd better do it fast."

His words and attitude were tough but she couldn't miss the tension she felt in his body, in the way his arms tightened his hold on her, as if he didn't want to let her go. She should say no; it was the clever thing to do. She couldn't form the word, so she encased him in her fist and slid her hand up and then down his shaft in a low, sensuous slide.

Ryan responded by using his free hand to twist the thin rope of her underwear. She felt it rip, felt the quick tug, and then the fabric drifted down her leg to fall onto her right foot.

"This dress is killing me," he muttered, trying to pull the long layers up so that he could get as close to her as possible, while nudging her backward to the closest wall. She wasn't this person, Jaci thought. She didn't have sex up against a wall, she didn't scream and moan and sigh. She'd never been the person to make her lovers shout and groan and curse.

But, unless she was having a brilliant, mother of a hallucination, she was being that person right now. And...yay!

"It would be a lot easier if we just stripped," Jaci suggested, feeling the cool wall against her back. She leaned forward to push Ryan's pants and underwear down his thighs.

"That'll take too long." Ryan leaned his chest into hers, gripped the back of her thighs and lifted her. With unerring accuracy, his head found her channel and he slid along her, causing her to let out a low shriek of pleasure. "I can't wait for you, I can't leave...but God, we need a condom."

Jaci banged her head against the wall as he probed her entrance. "On the pill and I've been tested for every STD under the sun," she muttered.

"I'm clean, too." Ryan choked the words out.

"I need you now. No more talking, no more fighting, just you and..." She lifted her hips and there he was, inside her, stretching her, filling her, completing her.

Ryan's mouth met hers and his tongue mimicked the movement of his hips, sliding in and out, leaving no part of her unexplored. Jaci felt hyperaware, as if her every sense was jacked up to maximum volume. She yanked his shirt up and ran her hands over his chest, around his ribs and down his strong back, digging her nails into his buttocks when he tilted his hips and went even deeper. She cried out and he yelled, and then suddenly she was riding a white-hot wave. In that moment of magical release, she felt connected to all the feminine energy in the world and she was its conduit.

She felt powerful and uninhibited and so damn wild. When she came back to herself, back to the wall and to Ryan's face buried in her neck, his broad hands were still holding her thighs.

Jaci dropped her face into his neck and touched her tongue to the cord in his neck. "Take me to bed, Ryan. We can fight later."

"I can do that, and we most likely will," Ryan muttered as he pulled out of her and allowed her to slide down his body. He kicked off his pants and pulled her,

her hair and dress and mind tangled, down the hallway to his bedroom. "But, for now, I can't wait any longer… I've got to see you naked."

Chapter 7

Jaci pushed back the comforter and left the bed, glancing down at her naked body. Clothes would be nice and she wrinkled her nose at the pile of fabric in a heap on the floor, just on this side of the door. Pulling that on was going to be horrible, as was the walk of shame she'd be doing later as she headed back to her apartment in a wrinkled dress and with messy hair.

Then Jaci saw the T-shirt and pair of boxer shorts on Ryan's pillow. They hadn't been there earlier so Ryan must have left them for her to wear. Sweet of him, she thought, pulling the T-shirt over her head. It was enormous on her, the hem coming to midthigh. It was long enough for her to be decent without wearing underwear but there was no way that she was going commando. She couldn't even pull on the thong she wore last night since Ryan had, literally, ripped it off her.

Sighing, she pulled up his boxers, rolling the waistband a couple of times until she was certain they wouldn't fall off her hips.

"Mornin'."

Jaci yelped and spun around, her mouth drying at the sight of a rumpled, unshaven Ryan standing in the doorway, dressed only in a faded pair of jeans, zipped but not buttoned. She was so used to seeing him impeccably, stylishly dressed that observing him looking like a scruffy cowboy had her womb buzzing. She started to bite her lip and abruptly stopped.

"Hi," she murmured, unable to keep the heat from flaring on her cheeks. She'd kissed those rock-hard abs, raked her fingers up those hard thighs, taken a nip of those thick biceps. And if he gave her one hint that he'd like her to do it again, she'd Flash Gordon herself to his side.

But Ryan kept his face impassive. "Coffee?"

"Yeah." Jaci made herself move toward the door and took the cup from his hand, being careful not to touch him. She took a grateful sip, sighed and met his eyes. His shoulder was against the door frame and he looked dark and serious, and she quickly realized that playtime was over. "I guess you want to talk?"

What about? Being engaged? Leroy? The script? The amazing sex they'd shared?

"Since we are the leading story in the entertainment world, I think that would be a very good idea." Ryan peeled himself from the door and walked down the hallway. Well, that answered that question. Good thing, because while she knew that she was old enough to have a one-night stand with her fake boyfriend, she doubted that she could talk about it. Jaci followed, trying but not succeeding at keeping her eyes off his tight, masculine butt.

"I have a million messages on my mobile and in my inbox, from reporters and friends, asking if it's true," Ryan said, heading across his living room to the luxurious open-plan kitchen. He grabbed the coffeepot and refilled a cup that had been sitting on the island in the center of the kitchen. Judging by the fact that the coffeepot was nearly empty, he'd been up for a while and this was his third or fourth cup.

Jaci took a sip from her own cup of coffee and wrinkled her nose at the bitter, dark taste. "What do you want to do? Deny or confirm?"

Ryan rested his bottom against the kitchen counter and pushed a hand through his hair. "I suppose that depends on your explanation on why you made such an asinine comment."

Jaci swallowed down her retort and another sip of coffee. Taking a seat on one of the stools that lined the breakfast bar, she put her cup on the granite surface and placed her chin in the palm of her hand. "I tried to explain last night."

"Last night there was only one thing I wanted from you and it wasn't an explanation." He waved his coffee cup. "Go."

Jaci rubbed her forehead with her fingertips in an effort to ease the headache that was gaining traction. Too much sex and not enough sleep. "Leroy hired a PI to investigate me, and you, by the way. He obviously found out about my broken engagement and was questioning how quickly I moved on."

Ryan's focus on her face didn't waver. "Okay. I presume that you had a very good reason for leaving the politician?"

"You still haven't done your own digging?" Jaci asked, surprised.

"I'm waiting for your version," Ryan replied. "Not important now… Go back to explaining how we got engaged."

"Right." Jaci sipped and sighed. "I asked Banks why me, what this was all about. I mean, this makes no sense to me… I'm nothing special. He said that it didn't matter why he wanted me, only that he always gets what he wants. That he's now using me to get a handle on you." Jaci ran a fingertip around the rim of her cup. "I thought that we needed to take me out of the equation, to remove me as a pawn. That can only happen if we break up or if he thinks that the relationship between us is more serious than he realized. So I thought that if I told him that we were thinking of marriage—thinking of, not that we were engaged— he'd back off."

Ryan shook his head. "Marriage, fidelity, faithfulness mean nothing to him. He's married to a sweet, sexy, lovely woman whom he treats like trash. You just handed him more ammunition to mess with me by suggesting we're that deeply involved. You poured blood into the water and the sharks are going to come and investigate."

Jaci looked bleak. "You mean the press."

"Yep. There's a reason why I keep a low profile, Jaci, and I've appeared more in the press since I've met you than in the last few years." Ryan banged his coffee cup as he placed it on the counter and rubbed the back of his neck. "They were relentless when Ben died, and I had so much else I was dealing with that the last thing I needed was to read the flat-out fiction they were printing in the papers. And the last thing I need right now is dealing with the press as I deal with Banks."

Jaci tilted her head. "And you smacked him down last night… Are you worried about the consequences? Think he might bail?"

Ryan lifted a powerful shoulder in an uneasy shrug. "We'll have to wait and see."

"Wait and see?" Jaci demanded, her face flushing. "Ryan, this is my career we're talking about, my big break. You might be able to afford to let this project go down the toilet but I can't. If I have any chance of being recognized as a serious scriptwriter, I need this film to be produced, I need it to be successful."

"I know that!" Ryan slapped his hands on his hips and scowled at her. "I don't want this project to fail, either, Jaci. I'll lose millions of my own money, money that I've paid into the development of this film. It'll take a good while for me to recover that money if I lose it."

"This is such a tangled mess," Jaci said in a low voice. She flipped him a look. "I shouldn't have kissed you. It was an impulsive gesture that has had huge consequences."

Ryan looked at her for a long time before replying. "Don't beat yourself up too much. I am also to blame. You didn't deepen that kiss, I did, and I told Leroy that you were my girlfriend."

"Okay, I'll happily let you accept most of the blame."

"*Some* of the blame. It wasn't my crazy idea to say that we were thinking of getting married." Ryan shook his head at her when she opened her mouth to argue. "Enough arguing, okay? I need sustenance."

Ryan walked over to the double-door, stainless steel fridge and yanked open a door and stared inside. "You're wrong, you know," he said, and Jaci had to strain to hear his words.

"Since I've been wrong so many times lately you're going to have to be more specific," Jaci told him.

"About not being special." Ryan slammed the door shut and turned around, slowly and unwillingly and, it had to be said, empty-handed. "You are the dream within the dream."

Jaci frowned. "Sorry?"

Ryan cleared his throat and she was amazed that this man, so confident in business and in bed, could look and sound this uneasy. "Banks has everything money can buy except he wants what money can't buy. Happiness, normality, love."

"But you've just said that he has a stunning, lovely wife—"

"Thea was a top supermodel and Banks knows that she is far too good for him." Ryan folded his arms and rocked on his heels. "Look, forget about it…"

Jaci shook her head, thinking that she needed to know where he was going with this. "Nope, your turn to spill. Are you telling me that I am more suited to Banks than his gorgeous, sweet, stunning wife?"

"Jesus, no!" Ryan looked horrified and he cursed. "But he knows that you are different from the women he normally runs into."

Oh, different, yay. Generally in her experience that meant less than. "Super," she said drily.

"Look, you're real."

"Real?" Jaci asked, confused.

"Yeah. Despite your almost aristocratic background, you seem to have your feet planted firmly on the ground. You aren't a gold digger or a slut or a party girl or a diva. You're as normal as it comes."

"Is normal higher up on the attractiveness ladder than real?" She just couldn't tell.

Ryan muttered a curse. "You are determined to misunderstand me. I'm just trying to explain why your openness, lack of bitchiness and overall genuineness is helluva attractive."

"Oh, so you *do* think that I am attractive?" Jaci muttered and heard Ryan's sharp intake of breath.

"No, of course not. I just made love to you all last night because I thought you were a troll." Ryan sent her one of those male looks that clearly stated he thought she was temporarily bat-lolly insane.

"Oh." Jaci felt heat creep across her face. She noticed him clenching and releasing his fists as if he were trying to stop himself from reaching for her. And in a flash she could feel the thump-thump-thump of her own heart, could hear the sound as clearly as she could read the desire in his eyes.

Ryan Jackson hadn't had nearly enough of her or, she had to admit, her of him. One more time, Jaci told herself, she could give herself the present of having, holding, feeling Ryan again. He wanted her, she wanted him, so what was the problem?

Career, Banks, sleeping with your boss? Jaci ig-

nored the sensible angel on her shoulder and slid off
her chair, her body heating from the inside out and her
stomach and womb taking turns doing tumbles and
backflips inside her body.

"One more time," she muttered as she stroked her
hand up Ryan's chest to grip his neck and pull his
mouth down to hers.

"Why do I suspect that's not going to be enough?"
Ryan muttered, his lips a fraction from hers.

"It has to be. Shut up and kiss me," Jaci demanded,
lifting herself up on her toes.

Ryan's lips curved against hers. "Just as long as we
won't be married when we come up for air."

"Funny." Jaci just got the words out before Ryan
took possession of her mouth, and then no words were
needed.

Jaci, sitting in Ryan's office four days later, was
struggling to keep her pretend-you-haven't-licked-me-
there expression, especially now that their conversation
had moved on from discussing the script changes he
and Thom wanted. She hadn't seen Ryan since she left
his apartment the morning after the ballet; he hadn't
called, he hadn't texted.

And that was the way it should be, she told herself. What they'd shared was purely bedroom based.
It meant nothing more than two adults succumbing to
a primal desire that had driven mankind for millennia.
He'd wanted her, she'd wanted—God, that was such a
tame word for the need he'd aroused in her!—him and
that was all it was.

Then why did she want to ask him why his eyes

looked bleak? Why did she want to climb into his lap, place her face into his neck and tell him that it would all work out? She wanted to massage the knots out of his neck, smooth away the frown between his heavy brows, kiss away the bracket that appeared next to his mouth. He was off-the-charts stressed and it was all her fault.

She'd put his relationship with his investor on the line. It was amazing that she was still discussing script changes, that he hadn't fired her scrawny ass.

"Have you heard anything from Banks yet?" she demanded, pulling her gaze away from the view of the Hudson River.

Ryan looked startled at the sudden subject change. He exchanged a long look with Thom and after their silent communication, Thom stood up. "Actually…"

Thom lifted a hand and he ambled to the door. "You can explain. Later."

Jaci's eyebrows rose. "Explain what?"

Ryan tapped the nib of a pen on the pad of paper next to his laptop. "We've been invited to join a dinner on a luxury yacht tonight. The invitation came from Banks's office. Apparently Leroy's just bought himself an Ajello superyacht and this is its initial voyage. Lucky Leroy, those are only the best yachts in the world."

Jaci stood up and walked toward the floor-to-ceiling window, shoving her hands into the back pockets of her pants.

"I like your outfit," Ryan commented.

Jaci looked down at the deep brown leather leggings she'd teamed with a flowing white top and multiple strands of ethnic beads. It was nice to wear something other than black, she thought, and it made her feel warm and squirmy that Ryan approved. "I must be doing something right because a random man complimented my outfit in a coffee shop yesterday, as well."

"Honey, any man under dead would've noticed those stupendous legs under that flirty skirt." She saw the flare of heat in his eyes and looked down at her feet encased in knee-high leather boots. Damn but she really wanted to walk over to him and kiss him senseless. Her fingers tingled with the need to touch and her legs parted as if… Dear Lord, this was torture!

"I'm glad that the furor over our possible engagement has died down," she said, trying to get her mind to stop remembering how fantastic Ryan looked naked.

"It was nothing that my PR firm couldn't handle," Ryan said, leaning back in his chair and placing his hands on his flat stomach. "As of the columns this morning, we're still seeing each other, but any talk of marriage is for the very distant future."

Jaci felt her shoulders drop and quickly pulled them up again. She had no reason to feel let down, no reason at all. She wasn't looking for a relationship, not even a pretend one. She'd been engaged, had talked incessantly about marriage—and what did she get out of that? Humiliation and hurt. Yeah, no thanks.

"As for Leroy's silence, you know what they say, no news is good news." Ryan picked up a file from his desk and flipped it open.

"Shouldn't you call him, say something, do something?" Jaci demanded, and his eyes rose at her vehement statement.

Ryan closed his file and leaned back in his chair. "It's a game, Jaci, and I'm playing it," he replied, linking his fingers on his stomach. Then his eyes narrowed. "You don't like the way I'm playing it?"

"I don't know the flipping rules!" Jaci snapped back. "And it's my future that's at stake, too. I have a lot to lose, but I can't do anything to move this along."

Ryan frowned at her outburst. "It's not the end of the world, Jace. Don't you and your siblings have a big trust fund that's at your disposal? It's not like you'll be out on the streets if this movie never gets produced. And you'll write other scripts, have other chances."

Could she tell him? Did she dare? She'd hinted at how important this was to her before, but maybe if he understood how crucial it really was, he'd understand why this situation was making her stress levels redline. And it wasn't as if he was a stranger; she had known him for years.

"This script means more to me than just a break into the industry, Ryan. It's more than that. It's more than my career or my future…" She saw him frown and wondered how she could explain the turbulent, churning emotions inside. "It's a symbol, a tipping point, a fork in the road."

She expected him to tell her to stop being melodramatic, but he just sat calmly and waited for her to continue. "You buying my script and offering me a job to work on *Blown Away* was—is—more than a career opportunity. It was the catalyst that propelled me into a whole new life." Jaci gestured to her notes on the desk. "That's all mine…my effort, my words, my script. This is something I did, without my parents' knowledge or without them pulling any strings. It's the divide between who I was before and who I am now. God, I am so not explaining this well."

"Stop editing yourself and just talk, Jace."

"On one side of the divide, I was the Brookes-Lyon child who drifted from job to job, who played at writing, maybe to get her mother's attention. Then I became Clive's fiancée and an object of press attention and I had to grow a spine, fast. I couldn't have survived what I did without it. When I left London, I vowed that I wasn't going to fade into the background again."

"Yeah, you used to do that as a kid. Your family would take over and dominate a room, a conversation, yet you wouldn't contribute a thing." His mouth twitched. "Now you won't shut up."

"It's because I'm different in New York!" Jaci stated, her face animated. "I'm better here. Happier, feistier!"

"I like feisty." Ryan murmured his agreement in a low voice, heat in the long, hot glance he sent her.

It was so hard to ignore the desire in his voice. But she had to. "I don't want to go backward, Ry. If I lose this opportunity…"

Ryan frowned at her and leaned forward. "Jaci, what you do is not who you are. You can still be feisty without the job."

Could she be? She didn't think so; Sassy Jaci needed to be successful. If she wasn't then she'd just be acting. She didn't want to skate through her life anymore. She wanted to live and feel and be this new Jaci. She *liked* this new Jaci.

Ryan pinned her to the floor with his intense blue-gray stare. "Have a little faith, Jace. It will all work out."

But what if it didn't? Who would she be if she couldn't be New York Jaci? She didn't know if she could reinvent herself again. She saw Ryan looking over his desk, saw his hand moving toward the folder he'd discarded minutes before and read the silent message. It was time to go back to work, so she started for the door.

Ryan's phone rang and he lifted his finger to delay her. "Hang on a sec. We still need to talk about the yacht thing tonight."

Oh, bats, she'd forgotten about that. Jaci stopped next to his desk.

"Hey, Jax." The voice of Ryan's PA floated through the speakers of the phone. "Jaci's mother is on the phone and she sounds…determined. I think Jaci needs to take this."

"Sure, put her through."

Jaci shot up and pulled her hand across her throat in a slashing motion. Dear Lord, the last person in the world she wanted to talk to was her mother. She still hadn't told them that she was working as a scriptwriter, that she was pseudo-dating Ryan…

"Morning, Priscilla."

Jaci glared at him and grabbed the pen out of his hand and scribbled across the writing pad in front of him. *I'm NOT here*; she underlined the *not* three times.

He cocked an eyebrow at her and quickly swung his right leg around the back of her knees to cage her between his legs. Jaci sent him her death-ray glare, knowing that she couldn't struggle without alerting her mother to her presence. As it was she was certain that Priscilla could hear her pounding heart and shaky breathing as she stood trapped between Ryan's legs.

"Ryan, darling boy." Priscilla's voice was as rich and aristocratic as ever. "How are you? It's been so long since we've seen you. I can't wait to see you at Neil's wedding next weekend."

Jaci slapped her hand against her forehead and stifled her gasp of horror. She'd forgotten all about Neil's blasted wedding. It was next weekend? Good Lord! How had that happened?

Jaci quickly drew a hanging man on the pad, complete with a bulging tongue, and she felt the rumble of laughter pass through Ryan as he exchanged genialities with her mother, quickly explaining that Jaci had just left his office. Ryan was talking about his duties as best man when she felt him grip the waistband of her pants and pull her down to sit on his hard thigh. Jaci sent him a startled look. Being this close was so damn tempting…

Oh, who was she kidding? Being in the same room as Ryan was too damn tempting. Jaci closed her eyes as his hand moved up her back and gripped the nape of her neck. His other hand briefly rested on her thigh before he pulled the pen from her hand and scribbled on the pad with his left hand. Huh, he was left-handed… She'd forgotten.

Jaci looked down at the pad, and it took a moment for her to decipher his scrawl. *Why don't you want to talk to your mother?*

"Yes, I have my suit and Neil told me, very clearly

and very often, that he didn't want a stag party. He couldn't take the time away from work."

Jaci grabbed another pen from his container of stationery and scribbled her reply. *Because she doesn't know what I am doing in New York and that we're... you know.*

Why not? & what does "you know" mean? Sleeping together? Pretending to date?

Jaci kept half an ear on her mother's ramblings. After nearly thirty years of practice, she knew when she'd start slowing down, and they had at least a minute.

All of it, she replied. *She—they—just think that I'm licking my wounds. They don't take my work—*

Jaci stopped writing and stared at the page. Ryan tapped the page with the pen in a silent order for her to finish her sentence. She sent him a small smile and lifted her shoulders in an it-doesn't-matter shrug. Ryan's glare told her it did.

"Anyway, what on earth is this nonsense I'm reading in the press about you and Jaci?"

Ah, her mother was upset. Jaci, perfectly comfortable on Ryan's knee, sucked in her cheeks and stared at a point beyond Ryan's shoulder.

"What have you heard?" Ryan asked, his tone wary. The hand moved away from her neck to draw large, comforting circles on her back. Jaci felt herself relax with every pass of his hand.

"I have a list," Priscilla stated. Of course she did. Priscilla would want to make sure that she didn't forget anything. "Firstly, is she working as a scriptwriter for you?"

"She is."

"And you're paying her?" There was no missing the astonishment in her voice.

"I am." Jaci heard the bite in those two words as he drew three question marks on the pad.

Not serious writing, Jaci replied. Ryan's eyes narrowed at her response, and she felt her stomach heat at his annoyance at her statement. Nice to be appreciated.

"She's a very talented writer," Ryan added. "She must have got that from you."

Thanks, Jaci wrote as his words distracted her mother and she launched into a monologue about her latest book, set in fourteenth-century England. Jaci jumped when she felt his hand on the bare skin of her back. His fingers rubbed the bumps on her spine and Jaci felt lightning bolts dance where he touched her.

Concentrate! she wrote.

Can do two things at once. God, your skin is so soft. We're not doing this again!

And you smell so good.

"Anyway, I'm getting off the subject. Are you and Jaci engaged or not?" Priscilla demanded.

"Not," Ryan answered, his eyes on Jaci's mouth. She knew that he wanted to kiss her and, boy, it was difficult to resist the desire in his eyes, knowing the amount of pleasure he was capable of giving her.

"Good, because after that louse she was engaged to, she needs some time to regroup. *That stuffed cloak-bag of guts!*" Ryan's eyebrows flew upward at Priscilla's venomous statement. *Shakespeare*, Jaci scribbled. *Henry IV.*

"Jaci was far too good for him!" Jaci jerked her eyes

away from Ryan's to stare at the phone. Really? And why couldn't her mother have told *her* this?

"That business with the Brazilian madam was just too distasteful for words, and so stupid. Did he really think he wouldn't get caught?"

Brazilian? Madam?

My ex liked a little tickle and a lot of slap.

Ryan stared down at the page before lifting his eyes back to Jaci's rueful face. "Jesus," he muttered.

"I do hope that she got herself tested after all of that but I can't ask her," Priscilla stated in a low voice. "We don't have that type of relationship. And that's my fault."

Jaci's mouth fell open at that statement. Her mother wished that they were closer? Seriously?

"And what's going on between you? Are you dating? Is it serious? Are you sleeping together?" Priscilla demanded.

Jaci opened her mouth to tell her that it was none of her damn business, but Ryan's hand was quicker and he covered her mouth with his hand. She glowered at him and tried to tug his hand away.

"It's complicated, Priscilla. I'm involved in a deal and, bizarrcly, I needed a girlfriend to help me secure it. Jaci stepped up to the plate." Ryan kept his hand on her mouth. "It's all pretend."

"Well, I'm looking at a photograph of the two of you and it doesn't look like either of you are pretending to me."

Ryan dropped his hand but not his eyes. "We're good actors, it seems," he eventually replied.

"Huh. Well, I hope this mess gets sorted out soon,"

Priscilla said. "Not that I would mind if you and Jaci were involved. I have always liked you."

"Thank you," Ryan replied. "The sentiment is returned."

Such a suck-up, Jaci scribbled and gasped when his arm pulled her against his chest. Against her hip she could feel his hard erection, and she really couldn't help nestling her face into his neck and inhaling his scent. Damn, she could just drift away, right here, right now, in his arms.

"I must go. Take care of my baby, Ryan."

Ryan's arms tightened around Jaci and she sighed. "Will do, Priscilla."

"Bye, Ryan. Bye, my darling Jaci."

"Bye, Mom," Jaci replied lazily, the fingers of her left hand diving between the buttons of his dress shirt to feel his skin. Then her words sank in and she shot up and looked at Ryan in horror as the call disconnected.

"She knew that I was here. The witch!"

Ryan just laughed.

Chapter 8

That evening, Leroy, too busy showing off his amazing yacht, ignored them, and Ryan was more than happy with that. He and Jaci stood at the back of the boat, where there was less of a crowd, and watched the city skyline transition from day to night. Dusk was a magical time of the day, Ryan thought, resting his forearms on the railing and letting his beer bottle dangle from his fingers over the Hudson River. It had the ability to soothe, to suggest that something bolder and brighter was waiting around the next corner. Or maybe that was the woman standing next to him.

Ryan stood up and looked at her. Tonight's dress was a frothy concoction with beads up top, no back and a full skirt that ended midthigh. He wanted to call it a light green but knew that if he had to ask Jaci to tell him what color it was she'd say that it was pistachio or sea foam or something ridiculous. Equally ridiculous was his desire to walk her down to one of the staterooms below deck and peel her out of it. His nights had been consumed with thoughts and dreams—awake and asleep—about her. He wanted her again, a hundred times more. He'd never—he ran his hand over his face—*craved* anyone before.

Ryan rubbed the back of his neck and was grateful that his heavy sigh was covered by the sound of the engine as it pushed the yacht and its fifty-plus guests through the water. Jaci had him tied up in every sailor knot imaginable. In his office this morning, it had taken every atom of his being to push her out of his lap so that he could get back to work. He was watching his multimillion-dollar deal swirling in the toilet bowl, Jaci's career—her big break and, crazily, her self-worth—was on the line, and all he could think about was when next he could get her into bed.

Despite wanting her as he wanted his next breath, he also wanted to go back to being the uncomplicated person he'd been before Jaci hurtled into his life. And it had been uncomplicated: he had an ongoing love–hate relationship with his dead brother, a hate–hate relationship with his father and, thanks to Kelly's lack of fidelity, a not-getting-involved attitude to women.

Simple, when you looked at it like that.

But Jaci made him feel stuff he didn't want to feel. She made him remember what his life had been like before Ben's death. He'd been so damn happy, so confident and so secure in the belief that all was right with his world. He'd accepted that his father was a hemorrhoid but that he could live with it; at the time his best mate was also his brother and he was engaged to the most beautiful girl in the world. He was starting to taste success…

And one evening it all disappeared. Without warning. And he learned that nothing lasted forever and no one stuck around for the long haul. It was just a truth of his life.

God, get a grip, Jackson. You sound like a whiny, bitchy teenager. Ryan turned his attention back to Jaci, who'd been content to stand quietly at his side, her shoulder pressed into his, her light perfume dancing on the breeze.

"So, whips and chains, huh?" It was so much easier to talk about Jaci's failures than his own.

Jaci sent him a startled look and when his words made sense, her expression turned rueful. "Well, I'm not so sure about the chains but there definitely were whips involved."

Dipstick, Ryan thought, placing his hand in the center of Jaci's back. She sent him a tentative smile but her expressive eyes told him that she'd been emotionally thrown under a bus. He nodded to a padded bench next to him and guided Jaci to it, ordering another glass of wine for Jaci and a whiskey for himself. Jaci sat down, crossed one slim leg over the other and stared at the delicate, silver high heel on her foot.

"Talk to me," Ryan gently commanded. He was incredibly surprised when she did just that.

"I was impressed by him and, I suppose, impressed by the idea that this rising-star politician—and he really was, Ryan—wanted to be with me. He's charismatic and charming and so very, very bright."

"He sounds like a lightbulb."

His quip didn't bring the smile to her face he'd hoped to see. "Did you love him?"

Jaci took a long time to answer. "I loved the fact that he said that he loved me. That everyone seemed to adore him and, by extension, adored me. Up to and including my family."

Another of the 110 ways family can mess with your head, Ryan thought. It had been a long time since he'd interacted with the Brookes-Lyon clan but he remembered thinking that, while they were great individually, together they were a force of nature and pretty much unbearable. "My family loved him. He slid right on in. He was as smart and as driven as them, and my approval rating with them climbed a hundred points when I brought him home and then skyrocketed when I said yes to getting married."

The things we do for parental and familial approval, Ryan thought with an internal shake of his head. "But he wasn't the Prince Charming you thought he was."

Jaci lifted one shoulder in a shrug. "We got engaged and it was a big deal, the press went wild. He was a tabloid darling before but together with the fact that he was gaining political power, he became the one to watch. And they really watched him."

Ryan frowned, trying to keep up. "The press?"

"Yeah. And their doggedness paid off," Jaci said in a voice that was pitched low but threaded with embarrassment and pain. "He was photographed in a club chatting up a Brazilian blonde, looking very cozy. The photos were inappropriate but nothing that couldn't be explained away."

She pushed her bangs out of her eyes and sighed. "About two weeks after the photographs appeared, I was at his flat waiting for him to come home. I'd prepared this romantic supper, I'd really pulled out the stops. He was running late so I decided to work on some wedding plans while I waited. I needed to contact a band who'd play at the reception and I knew that Clive had the address in his contacts, so I opened up his email program."

Ryan, knowing what was coming, swore.

"Yep. There were about sixteen unread emails from a woman and every one had at least four photos attached." Jaci closed her eyes as the images danced across her brain. "They were explicit. She was known as the Mistress of Pain."

He winced.

Jaci stared across the river to the lights of Staten Island. When she spoke again, her words were rushed, as if she just wanted to tell her story and get it done. "I knew that this could blow up in our faces so I confronted Clive. We agreed that we would quietly, with us little fuss as possible, call it quits. Before we could, the story broke that he was seeing a dominatrix and the bomb blew up in our faces." Ryan lifted his eyebrows as Jaci flicked her fingers open, mimicking the action of a bomb detonating.

"Ouch."

"Luckily, a month later a crazy producer made me an offer to work in New York as a scriptwriter and I jumped at the chance to get the hell out of, well, hell."

"And you didn't tell your family that you had a job?"

"It's not like they would've heard me, and if they

did, they wouldn't have taken it seriously. They'd think my writing is something I play at while I'm looking to find what I'm really going to do with the rest of my life."

Ryan heard the strains of a ballad coming from the band on the front deck and stood up. Pulling Jaci to her feet, he placed his hand on her hip and gripped her other hand and started to sway. She was in his arms, thank God. He rubbed his chin through her hair and bent his head so that his mouth was just above her ear. He thought about telling her how sorry he was that she'd been hurt, that she deserved none of it, how much he wanted to kiss her…everywhere. Instead, he gathered her closer by placing both his hands on her back and pulled her into him.

"For a bunch of highly intellectual people, your family is as dumb as a bag of ostrich feathers when it comes to you."

Jaci tipped her head and he saw appreciation shining in those deep, hypnotic eyes. "That's the nicest thing you've ever said to me."

He was definitely going to have to try harder, Ryan thought as he held her close and slowly danced her across the deck.

Leroy didn't bother to engage with them, Jaci thought, when they were back in the taxi and making their way from the luxury marina in Jersey City back to Manhattan. She wasn't sure whether that was a good or a bad thing.

She sighed, frustrated. "God, the business side of moviemaking gives me a headache."

"It gives me a freakin' migraine," Ryan muttered. "I've got about a two-week window and then I need to decide whether to pull the plug on the project or not."

Two weeks? That was all? Jaci, hearing the stress in Ryan's voice, twisted her ring around her finger. Who could magic that much money out of thin air in less than two weeks? This was all her fault; if she hadn't kissed him in that lobby, if she hadn't gone to that stupid party, if she hadn't moved to New York… It was one thing messing up her own life, but she'd caused so much trouble for Ryan, this hard-eyed and hard-bodied man who didn't deserve any of this.

"I'm so, so sorry." Jaci rested her head on the window and watched the buildings fly past. "This is all my fault."

Ryan didn't respond and Jaci felt the knife of guilt dig a little deeper, twist a little more. She thought about apologizing again and realized that repeating the sentiment didn't change the facts. She couldn't rewrite the past. All she could do was try to manage the present. But there was little— actually nothing—that she could do to unravel this convoluted mess, and she knew that Ryan would tie her to a bedpost if he thought that there was a minuscule chance of her complicating the situation any further.

Out of the corner of her eye she saw him dig his slim cell phone out of the inner pocket of his gray jacket. He squinted at the display. His long fingers flew across the keypad and she saw the corners of his mouth twitch, the hint of a smile passing across his face.

Ryan lifted his eyes to look at her. "Your brother just reamed me a new one for sleeping with you."

Jaci ignored the swoop of her stomach, pushed away the memory of the way Ryan's arms bulged as he held himself above her, the warmth of his eyes as he slid on home. "He thinks that we're sleeping together?"

"Yep," Ryan responded. "And if you check your cell, you'll probably find a couple messages from the rest of your family." Ryan placed a hand on her thigh, and her breath hitched as his fingers drew patterns on her bare skin. "Priscilla has a very big mouth."

"Oh, dear Lord God in heaven." Jaci resisted the desire to slap her mouth against his and made herself ignore the heat in his eyes, the passion that flared whenever they were breathing the same air. She grabbed her evening bag, pulled out her own phone and groaned at the five missed calls and the numerous messages on their family group chat.

Oh, this was bad, this was very bad.

Jaci touched the screen to bring up the messages.

Meredith: You have some explaining to do, sunshine.

Priscilla: Screenwriting? Really? Since when? Why don't you tell me anything?

Ryan moved up the seat so that his thigh was pressed against hers, and her shoulder jammed into his arm. She inhaled his scent and when heat dropped into her groin, she shifted in the seat. Ryan moved her phone so that he could see the screen.

Neil: Ryan? I was expecting you to have coffee with him, not an affair!

Meredith: Admittedly, anyone is better than the moron, but I don't think you should be jumping into a relationship this quickly!

Archie: Ryan? Who the hell is Ryan?

Neil: My Yank friend from uni, Dad.

Archie: The Hollywood one? The pretty boy?

Jaci rubbed her fingertips across her forehead. Damn, the Atlantic Ocean might be between them but her family still managed to exacerbate her headache. She looked at Ryan and shrugged. "Well, you *are* pretty."

Ryan dug an elbow into her side. "Your opinion on how I look is a lot more important than your father's," he said, his tone low and oozing sex.

Jaci deliberately lifted her nose in a haughty gesture, her eyes twinkling. "You'll do."

Ryan squeezed her thigh in response. "I suppose I asked for that." He nodded to the phone in her hands. "So, what are you going to tell them?"

Jaci tapped her finger against her lips. "The same thing you told my mother—that it was a pretend thing, that we aren't in a relationship, that this isn't going anywhere." She turned her head to look out the window. "Basically the truth."

Ryan's finger and thumb gripped her chin and turned her face to look at him. Jaci stifled a sigh at his gorgeous eyes and gripped her phone with both hands to keep them from diving into his hair, from rubbing his neck, his shoulders. Her mouth wanted to touch his, her legs wanted to climb onto his lap...

Ryan looked at her mouth and she felt his fingers tighten on her chin. He was fighting the urge to kiss her, as well, she realized. His rational side was barely winning and that realization made her feel powerful and feminine and so wanted. She'd never felt this desired. No man had ever looked at her the way Ryan was looking at her right now, right here.

"Your family is thinking that we are sleeping together," Ryan stated, his thumb moving up from her chin to stroke her full bottom lip.

Well, that was obvious. She glanced at her phone in confusion. "Well, yeah."

"Not that I give a rat's ass what your family thinks, but…"

Jaci felt her breath stop somewhere on the way to her lungs. "But?"

"Screw this, we don't need to explain this or justify this or make excuses for this."

For what? Jaci frowned, confused. "What are you trying, very badly, to say, Ryan?"

"I want you. I want you in my bed. Screw the fact that you work for me and the film and all the rest of the craziness. I just want you. Come home with me, Jace. Be mine for as long as this madness continues."

Be his. Two words, two syllables, but so powerful. How was she supposed to be sensible, to back away, to resist? She wasn't an angel and she definitely wasn't a saint. Jaci quickly justified the decision she was about to make. He wanted her, she—desperately—wanted him. They were both single and this was about sex and passion and lust… No love was required. They weren't hurting anyone…

If you fall in love with him, you'll hurt yourself.

Then I won't fall in love with him, Jaci told herself. But a little part of her doubted that statement and she pulled back, wondering if she shouldn't just take a breath and get oxygen to her brain. *You've been hurt enough*, that same cautious inner voice told her. And Ryan would take what was left of her battered heart and drop-kick it to the moon.

"I can't get enough of you," Ryan muttered before slanting his mouth over hers and pushing his tongue between her parted lips. One swipe, another lick and all doubts were gone, all hesitation burned away by the heat of his mouth, the passion she tasted on her tongue. His arm pushed down between her back and the seat, and his other hand held her head in place so that he commanded the kiss. And command he did, and Jaci followed him into that special, magical place where time stood still.

Under his touch… This was where she felt alive, powerful, connected to the universe and sure of her place in it. When she kissed him she felt confident and desired and potent. Like the best version of herself. Ryan's mouth left hers and he feathered openmouthed kisses across her cheekbone, along her jaw, down her neck. Jaci shivered when he tasted the hollow of her collarbone.

"We've got to stop making out in cabs," Ryan murmured against her skin.

"We've got to stop making out, full stop," Jaci tartly replied.

"News flash, honey, that's probably not going to happen." Jaci felt Ryan's lips curve into a smile against her neck. The backs of his fingers brushed her breast as he straightened and moved away from her, his expression regretful. He looked past her and Jaci finally noticed that they were parked outside Ryan's swish apartment building.

"Come inside with me, please."

How could she resist the plea in his eyes, the smidgen of anxiety she heard in his voice? Did he really think that she was strong enough to say no, that she was wise enough to walk away from this situation, to keep this as uncomplicated as it could possibly be? Well, no chance of that. Her brain thought that she should stay in the cab and have the driver deliver her home, but the need to erase the distance between them, to feel every naked inch of him, was overpowering. She wanted Ryan, she needed him. She was going to take him and have him take her.

The morning and its problems could look after themselves. Tonight was hers. He was hers. Jaci opened the door and left the cab, teetering on her heels as she spun around and held out her hand to Ryan.

"Take me to bed, Ry."

Ryan enjoyed women; he liked their curves, their soft-feeling, smooth skin, the small, delicate sounds they made when his touch gave them pleasure. He loved the sweet-spicy taste of their skin, their pretty toes, the way their tantalizing softness complemented his hard, rougher body.

Yeah, he liked women, but he adored Jaci, he thought as he slowly pulled her panties down her hips. Naked at last. Ryan, minus his jacket and black tie, was still dressed and liking the contrast. He dropped the froth of lace to the floor and sat on the side of the bed, his hand stroking her long thigh, watching how her small nipples puckered when he looked at them. He'd had more than his share of women but none of them reacted to his look as if it was a touch. There had never been this arc of desire connecting them. He'd never felt a driving need to touch anyone the way he wanted to touch her.

It was both terrifying and amazingly wonderful.

"What are you thinking?" Jaci asked him, her voice low and sexy. Ryan usually hated that question, thought it was such an invasion of his privacy, but this time, and with this woman, he didn't mind.

"I'm thinking that you are absolutely perfect and that I'm desperate to touch you, taste you." Ryan was surprised to hear the tremble in his voice. This was just sex, he reminded himself. He was just getting caught up in the moment, imagining more than what was actually there.

Except that Jaci was naked, open to his gaze, her face soft and her eyes blazing with desire. And trust. He could do anything right now, suggest anything, and she'd probably acquiesce. She was that into him and he was that crazy about her.

Jaci sat up and placed an openmouthed kiss on his lips. He put his hand on the back of her head to hold her there as her fingers went to the buttons on his black-and-white checked shirt, ripping one or two off in her haste to get her hands on his skin. Then her small hands, cool and clever, pushed the shirt off his shoulders and danced across his skin, over his nipples, down his chest to tug on the waistband of his pants. Her mouth lifted off his and he felt bereft, wanting—no, needing—more.

"Need you naked." Jaci tugged on his pants again.

He summoned up enough willpower to resist her,

wanting to keep her naked while he explored her body. He'd had a plan and that was to torture Jaci with his tongue and hands, kissing and loving those secret places and making her scream at least twice before he slid on home...

He shrugged out of his shirt and removed his socks and shoes, but his pants were staying on because discovering Jaci, pleasing Jaci, was more important than a quick orgasm. It took all of his willpower to grab her hand and pull it from his dick. He gently gripped her wrists and pushed them behind her back, holding them there while he dropped his head to suck a nipple into his mouth. From somewhere above him Jaci whimpered and arched her back, pushing her nipple against the roof of his mouth. Releasing her hands, he pushed her back and spent some time alternating between the two, licking and blowing and sucking.

He could make her come by just doing this, he realized, slightly awed. But he wanted more for her, from her. Leaving her breasts, he trailed his mouth across her ribs, down her stomach, probed her cute belly button with his tongue. He licked the path on each side of her landing strip and, feeling her tense, dipped between her folds and touched her, tasted her, circling her little nub with the tip of his tongue.

It all happened at once. He slid his finger inside her hot channel, Jaci screamed, his tongue swirled in response and then she was pulsing and clenching around his fingers, thrusting her hips in a silent demand for more. He sucked again, pushed again and she arched her back and hips and shattered, again and again.

Ryan pulled out and dropped a kiss on her stomach

before hand-walking his way up the bed to look into her feverish eyes. "Good?" he asked, balancing himself on one hand, biceps bulging, to push her hair out of her eyes.

"So good." Jaci linked her hands around his neck, her face flushed with pleasure and...yeah, awe.

He'd made her scream, he'd pushed her to heights he was pretty sure—judging by the dazed, surprised look on her face—that she hadn't felt before. Mission so accomplished.

Jaci's hands skimmed down his neck, down his sides to grip his hips, her thumbs skating over his obliques before she clasped him in both hands. He jerked and sighed and pushed himself into her hands. "Let me in," he begged. Begged! He'd never begged in his life.

"Nah." Jaci smiled that feminine smile that told him that he was in deep, deep trouble. The best type of trouble. "My turn to drive you crazy."

He knew that he was toast when, in the middle of fantastic, mind-altering sex he realized that this wasn't just sex. It was sex on steroids and that happened to him only when he became emotionally attached. Well, that had to stop, immediately. Well, maybe after she'd driven him crazy.

Maybe then.

Chapter 9

Sunlight danced behind the blinds in Ryan's room as Jaci forced her eyes open the next morning. She was lying, as was her habit, on her stomach, limbs sprawled across the bed. And she was naked, which was not her habit. Jaci squinted across the wide expanse that was Ryan's chest and realized that her knee was nestled up against a very delicate part of his anatomy and that her arm was lying across his hips, his happy-to-see-you morning erection pressing into her skin.

She gazed at his profile and noticed that he looked a lot younger when his face was softened by sleep and a night of spectacular sex. Spectacular sex… Jaci pulled in a breath and closed her eyes as second and third and tenth thoughts slammed into her brain.

Why was she still lying in bed with him in a tangle of limbs and postorgasmic haze? She was smart enough to know that she should've taken the many orgasms he'd given her last night, politely said thank you and hightailed it out of his apartment with a breezy smile and a "see you around." She shouldn't have allowed him to wrap his big arm around her waist or to haul her into a spooning position, her bottom perfectly nestled in his hips. She shouldn't have allowed herself to drift, sated and secure, feeling his nose in her hair, reveling in the soft kisses he placed on her shoulders, into her neck. She shouldn't have allowed herself the pleasure of falling asleep in his arms.

Straight sex, uncomplicated sex, wham-bam sex she could handle; she knew what that was and how to deal with it. It was the optional extras that sent her into a spiral. The hand drifting over her hip, his foot caressing her calf, his thick biceps a pillow under her head. His easy affection scared the pants off her—well, they would if she were wearing any—and generated thoughts of *what if* and *I could get used to this*.

This wouldn't do, Jaci told herself, and gently—and reluctantly—removed her limbs from his body. Nothing had changed between them. They had just shared a physical experience they'd both enjoyed. She was not going to get too anal about this. She wasn't going to overthink this. This was just sex, and it had nothing to do with the fact that they were boss and employee or even that they were becoming friends.

Sex was sex. Not to be confused with affection or caring or emotion or, God forbid, love. She'd learned that lesson and, by God, she'd learned it well. Jaci slipped out of bed, looking around for something to wear. Unable to bear the thought of slipping into her dress from the night before—she'd be experiencing another walk of shame through Ryan's apartment lobby soon enough—she picked up his shirt from the night before and pulled it over her head, grimacing as the cuffs fell a foot over her hands. She was such a cliché, she thought, roughly rolling back the fabric. The good girl in the bad boy's bedroom, wearing his shirt...

After checking that Ryan was still asleep, Jaci rolled her shoulders and looked around Ryan's room, taking in the details she'd missed before. The bed, with its leather headboard, dominated the room and complemented the other two pieces of furniture: a black wing-back chair and four-drawer credenza with a large mirror above it. Jaci tipped her head as she noticed that there were photograph frames on the credenza but they were all facedown and looked as if they'd been that way for a while. Curious, she padded across the room, past the half-open door that led to a walk-in closet, and stood in front of the credenza. Her reflection in the mirror caused her to wince. Her hair was a mess. She had flecks of mascara on her eyelids, and on her jaw she could see red splotches from Ryan rubbing his stubble-covered chin across her skin. Her eyes were baggy and her face was pale with fatigue.

The morning after the night before, she thought, rubbing her thumb over her eyes to remove the mascara. When the mascara refused to budge, she shrugged and turned her attention back to the frames. Silver, she thought, and a matching set. She lifted the first one up and her breath caught in her throat as the golden image of Ben, bubbling with life, grinned back at her. He looked as if he was ready to step out of the frame, handsome and sexy and so, well, alive. Hard to believe that he was gone, Jaci thought. And if she found it hard, then his brother would find it impossible, and she understood why Ryan wouldn't want to be slapped in the face with the image of Ben, who was no more real than fairy dust.

And photograph number two? Jaci lifted up the frame and turned it over, then puzzled at the image of a dark-haired, dark-eyed woman who looked vaguely familiar. Who was this and why did she warrant being in an ornate, antique silver frame? She couldn't be Ryan's mother. This was a twenty-first-century woman through and through. Was she one of Ryan's previous lovers, possibly one who got away? But Ryan, according to the press, didn't have long-term relationships and she couldn't imagine that he'd keep a photo of a woman he'd had a brief affair with. Jaci felt the acid burn of jealously and wished she could will it away. You had to care about someone to be jealous and she didn't want to care about Ryan…not like that, anyway.

Jaci replaced the frame and when she looked at her reflection in the mirror, she saw that Ryan was standing behind her and that a curtain had fallen within his fabulous eyes. Her affectionate lover was gone.

"Don't bother asking," Ryan told her in a low, determined voice. He was as naked as a jaybird but his emotions were fully concealed. He might as well have been wearing a full suit of armor, Jaci thought. She couldn't help feeling hurt at his back-off expression; she found it so easy to talk to him but he, obviously, didn't feel the same.

Maybe she'd read this situation wrong; maybe they

weren't even friends. Maybe the benefits they'd shared were exactly that, just benefits. The thought made her feel a little sad. And, surprisingly, deeply annoyed. How dare he make incredible, tender-but-hot love to her all night and then freeze her out before she'd even said good-morning?

The old Jaci, Lyon House Jaci, would just put her tail between her legs, scramble into her dress and apologize for upsetting him. New York Jaci had no intention of doing the same.

"That's it?" she demanded, hands on her hips. "That's all you're going to say?"

Ryan pushed a hand through his dark hair and Jaci couldn't miss his look of frustration. "I am not starting off the morning by having a discussion about her."

"Who is she?" Jaci demanded.

Ryan narrowed his eyes at her. "What part of 'not discussing this' didn't you hear?" He reached for a pair of jeans that draped across the back of his chair and pulled them on.

Jaci matched his frown with one of her own. "So it's okay for you to get me to spill my guts about my waste-of-space ex and his infidelities but you can't even open up enough to tell me who she is and why she's on your dresser?"

"Yes."

Jaci blinked at him.

"Yes, it's okay for you to do that and me not to," Ryan retorted. "I didn't torture you into telling me. It was your choice. Not telling you is mine."

Jaci pressed the ball of her hands to her temples. How had her almost perfect night morphed into something so… She wanted to say *ugly* but that wasn't the right word. Awkward? Unsettling? Uncomfortable? She desperately wanted to argue with him, to insist that they were friends, that he owed her an explanation, but she knew that he was right; it was his choice and he owed her nothing. He'd given her physical pleasure but there had been no promises to give her his trust, to let her breach his emotional walls. His past was his past, the girl in the photograph his business.

If his reluctance to talk, to confide in her, made her feel as if she was just another warm body for him to play with during the night, then that was her problem, not his. She would not be that demanding, insecure, irritating woman who'd push and pry and look to him to give more than he wanted to.

He'd wanted sex. He'd received sex and quite a lot of it. It had been fun, a physical release, and it was way past time for her to leave. Jaci dropped her eyes from his hard face, nodded quickly and managed to dredge up a cool smile and an even cooler tone. "Of course. Excuse me, I didn't mean to pry." She walked across the room, picked up her dress and her shoes, and gestured to the door to the en suite bathroom. "If I may?"

Ryan rubbed the back of his neck and sent her a hot look. "Don't use that snotty tone of voice with me. Just use the damn bathroom, Jace."

Hell, she just couldn't say the right thing this morning, Jaci thought. It was better if she just said nothing at all. Jaci walked toward the bathroom without looking at him again, silently cursing herself and calling herself all kinds of a fool.

Stupid, stupid, stupid. She should've left last night

and avoided this morning-after-the-night-before awkwardness.

Lesson learned.

Stupid, stupid, stupid.

Ryan gripped the edge of the credenza with white-knuckled hands and straightened his arms, dropping his head to stare at the wooden floor beneath his bare feet. *You handled that with all the sophistication of a pot plant, moron.* She'd asked a simple question to which there was a simple answer.

Who is she?

There were many answers to that, some simple, some a great deal more complicated. *She was someone who was, once, important to me.* Or… *She was an ex-girlfriend.* Or that, *She was my fiancée.* Or, if he really wanted to stir up a hornets' nest, he could've said that she was Ben's lover.

All truth.

What a complete mess of the morning, Ryan thought, straightening. He stepped over to the window and yanked up the blind and looked down onto the greenery of Central Park in spring. It was a view he never failed to enjoy, but this morning he couldn't even do that, his thoughts too full of the woman—who was probably naked—in the next room.

Instead of slipping out of bed and getting dressed long before his lover woke up, this morning he'd opened his eyes on a cloud of contentment and had instinctively rolled over to pull her back into his arms. The empty space had been a shock to his system, a metaphorical bucket of icy water that instantly shriveled his morning erection. She'd left him, he'd thought, and the wave of disappointment that followed was even more of a shock. He did the leaving, he was in control, and the fact that he was scrambling to find his mental equilibrium floored him. He didn't like it.

At all.

He'd long ago perfected his morning-after routine, but nothing with Jaci was the same as those mindless, almost faceless encounters in his past. Last night had been the most intense sexual experience of his life to date and he hated that she'd had such an effect on him. He wanted to treat her like all those other encounters but he couldn't. She made him want things that he'd convinced himself he had no need for, things such as trust and comfort and support. She made him feel everything too intensely, made him question whether it was time to remove the barbed wire he'd wrapped his heart in.

Seeing her holding Kelly's photograph made him angry and, worse, confused. There was a damn good reason why he kept their photographs in a prominent place. Seeing them there every morning, even facedown, was like being flogged with a leather strap, but after the initial flash of pain, it was a good and solid reminder of why he chose to live his life the way he did. People couldn't be trusted; especially the people who were supposed to love you the most.

Yet a part of him insisted that Jaci was not another Kelly, that she'd never mangle his heart as she'd done, but then his common sense took over and reminded him that he couldn't take the chance. Love and trust—

he'd never run the risk of having either of those emotions thrown back at him as if they meant nothing.

They meant something to him and he'd never risk them again.

It was better this way, Ryan told himself, sliding a glance toward the still-closed bathroom door. It was better that he and Jaci put some distance between them, allowed some time to dilute the crazy passion that swirled between them whenever they were alone. Because passion had a sneaky way of making you want more, tempting you to risk more than was healthy.

No, they needed that distance, and the sooner the better. Ryan walked into his closet, grabbed a T-shirt and shoved his feet into a pair of battered athletic shoes. He raked his hands through his hair, walked back into his bedroom and picked up his wallet from the credenza, in front of the now-upright photo of Ben.

"Hey, Jaci?" Ryan waited for her response before speaking again in an almost jovial voice. God, the last thing in the world he felt was jovial. He felt horny, and frustrated and a little sick, but not jovial. "I'm running out for bagels and coffee. I'll be back in ten."

He already knew how she'd respond and she didn't disappoint. "I won't be here when you get back. I've got a…thing."

She didn't have a thing any more than he wanted bagels and coffee but it was an out and he'd take it. "Okay. Later."

Later? Ryan saw that his hand was heading for the doorknob and he ruthlessly jerked it back. He was not going in there. If he saw Jaci again he'd want to take her to bed and that would lead to more confusing… well, feelings, and he didn't need this touchy-feely crap.

Keep telling yourself that, Jackson. Maybe you'll start to believe it sometime soon.

It was spring and the sprawling gardens at Lyon House, Shropshire, had never looked so beautiful with beds of daffodils and bluebells nodding in the temperate breeze. At the far edge of the lawn, behind the wedding tent, it looked as if a gardener had taken a sponge and dabbed the landscape with colored splotches of rhododendron and azalea bushes, a mishmash of brilliant color that hurt the eyes.

It was beautiful, it was home.

And she was miserable.

Sitting in the chapel that had stood for centuries adjacent to Lyon House, Jaci rolled her head to work out the kinks in her neck. If she looked out the tiny window to her left, she could see the copse of trees that separated the house from the chapel, and beyond that the enormous white designer fairy-tale tent—with its own dance floor—that occupied most of the back lawn. It was fairly close to what she'd planned for her own wedding, which had been scheduled for six weeks from now. Like the bride, she would've dressed at Lyon House, in her old room, and her mother would've bossed everyone about as she had been doing all day. The grounds would have been as spectacular, and she would've had as many guests. Like Neil, her groom would've been expectant, nervous, excited.

Her only thought about her canceled wedding was that she'd dodged a bullet. And then she'd run to the

States, where she'd fallen into the flight path of a freakin' bazooka. Jaci blew her frustration out and sneaked another look at Ryan. So far she'd spent a lot of the ceremony admiring his broad shoulders, tight butt and long legs, and remembering what he looked like naked. Jaci wiggled in her seat, realizing that it was very inappropriate to be thinking of a naked man in a sixteenth-century English church. Or, come to think of it, *any* church, for that matter…

Jaci crossed her legs and thought that she should be used to seeing him in a tuxedo, but today he looked better than he had any right to. The ice-blue tie turned his eyes the same color and she noticed that he'd recently had his hair trimmed. He'd spent the week avoiding her since their—what could she call it?—*encounter* in LA, and while her brain thought that some time apart was a wonderful idea, every other organ she possessed missed him. To a ridiculous degree. She sighed and sent another longing look at his profile. So sexy, and when he snapped his head around and caught her looking, she flushed.

No phone call. No email. No text. Nothing, she reminded herself. It was horrifying to realize that if he so much as crooked his baby finger she'd kick off her shoes, scramble over the seats and, bridal couple be damned, fly into his arms.

She wanted him. She didn't want to want him.

A slim arm wrapping around her waist had her turning, and she sighed at the familiar perfume. Meredith, her big sister, with her jet-black, geometric bob, red lipstick and almost oriental eyes looked sharp and sleekly sexy in a black sheath that looked as if it had been painted on her skinny frame. Twelve-year-olds had thighs fatter than hers, Jaci thought.

Merry gave her shoulders a squeeze. "Hey, are you okay?"

Jaci lifted one shoulder. How should she answer that? *No, my life is an even bigger mess now than it was when I left. I might not have a job soon and I think I might be in love with my fake boyfriend, who has the communication skills of a clam. That's the same fake boyfriend who left New York the morning after a night of marvelous sex. The same one whom I haven't spoken to or had an email or a text or a smoke signal from.*

Not that she was sure she wanted to talk to the moronic, standoffish, distant man who used a stupid excuse to run out of his apartment as quickly as he could. As if he could fool her with that bagels-and-coffee comment. After Clive she had a master's degree in the subject of crap-men-say.

Merry spoke in her ear. "So…you and Ryan."

"There is no me and Ryan," Jaci retorted, her voice a low whisper.

Merry looked at Ryan and licked her lips. "He is a *babe*, I have to admit. Mum thinks you're having a thing."

"The supposed relationship between us has been wildly exaggerated." Nobody could call a few hot nights a relationship, could they?

"Come on, tell me." Meredith jammed an elbow in her ribs.

The elderly aunt on her other side nudged her in the ribs. "Shh! The reverend is trying to give his sermon!"

"And I'm trying not to fall asleep." Merry yawned.

Ryan shifted his position and subtly turned so that he was practically facing her and she felt his eyes, like gentle fingers, trace her features, skim her cheekbones, her lower lips, down to her mouth. When his eyes dropped to look at her chest, her nipples responded by puckering against the fabric of her dress. The corners of Ryan's mouth lifted in response and she flamed again. Traitorous body, she silently cursed, folding her arms across her chest and narrowing her eyes.

"Some of your attention should be on your brother," Merry said out of the side of her mouth. "You know, the guy who is getting married to the girl in the white dress?"

"Can't help it, he drives me batty," Jaci replied, sotto voce. "He's arrogant and annoying and…annoying. The situation between us is…complicated."

"Complicated or not he is, holy bananas, *so* sexy."

Priscilla, on the bench in front of them, spun around in her seat and sent them her evil-mother laser glare. Her purple fascinator bounced and she slapped a feather out of her eye. Her voice, slightly quieter than a foghorn, boomed through the church. "Will you two please be quiet or must I put you outside?"

If Jaci hadn't been so embarrassed she might have been amused to see her ever-cool and unflappable world-class-journalist sister slide down in her seat and place her hand over her eyes.

Chapter 10

The band was playing those long, slow songs that bands played for the diehard guests who couldn't tear themselves away from the free booze or the dance floor or, as was Merry's case, the company of a cousin of the bride. Her sister looked animated and excited, Jaci thought, watching them from her seat at a corner table, now deserted. She hoped that the man wasn't married or gay or a jerk. Her sister deserved to have some fun, deserved a good man in her life. Always so serious and so driven, it would be good for her to have someone in her life who provided her with some balance. And some hot sex. You couldn't go wrong with some hot sex.

Well, you could if you were on the precipice of falling in love with the man who, up to a couple of days ago, had provided you with some very excellent sex. Jaci closed her eyes and rested her temple against her fist. She couldn't be that stupid to be falling in love with Ryan, could she? Maybe she was just confusing liking with love. Maybe she was confused because he made her feel so amazing in bed.

If so, why did she miss him so intensely when he wasn't with her? Why did she think about him constantly? Why did she wish that she could provide him with the emotional support he gave to her by just standing at her side and breathing? Why did she want to make his life better, brighter, happier? She couldn't blame that on sexual attraction or even on friendship.

Nope, she was on the verge of yanking her heart out and handing it over to him. And if she did that, she knew that if he refused to take it, which he would because Ryan didn't do commitment in any shape or form, it would be forever mangled and never quite the same. She had to pull back, had to protect herself. Hadn't her heart and her confidence and her psyche endured enough of a battering lately? Why would she want to torture herself some more?

A strong, tanned hand placed a cup full of hot coffee in front of her and she looked up into Ryan's eyes. "You look like you need that," he said, taking the chair next to her and flipping it so that he faced her, his long legs stretched out in front of him.

"Thanks. I thought you were avoiding me."

"Trying to." Ryan sent her a brooding look before looking at his watch. "I managed it for six hours but I'm caving."

Jaci lifted her eyebrows. "That's eight days and six hours. I heard you went to LA."

Ryan glowered at her. "Yeah. Waste of a trip since I spent most of my time thinking of you. Naked."

Lust, desire, need swirled between them. How was she supposed to respond to that? Should she tell him that she'd spent less time writing and more time fantasizing? *He's still your boss*, she reminded herself. Maybe she should keep that to herself.

"I've spent most of the evening watching you talk to your ex." Ryan frowned.

Now, that was an exaggeration. She'd spoken to Clive, sure, but not for that long and not for the whole evening.

"You're not seriously considering giving him another chance, are you?" Ryan demanded, his eyes and voice hot.

No calls, no text messages, no emails and now stupid questions. Jaci sighed. Going back to Clive after being with Ryan would be like living in a tiny tent after occupying a mansion. In other words, completely horrible. But because he'd been such a moron lately, she was disinclined to give him the assurance his question seemed to demand. Or was she just imagining the thread of concern she heard in his voice?

That was highly possible.

"Talk to me, Jace," Ryan said when she didn't answer him.

Jaci's lips pressed together. "You're joking, right? Do you honestly think that you can sleep with me and then freeze me out when I ask a personal question? Do you really think it's okay for you not to call me, to avoid me for the best part of a week?"

Ryan released a curse and rubbed the back of his neck. "I'm sorry about that."

Jaci didn't buy his apology. "Sure you are. But I bet that if I suggest that we go back to your B and B you'd be all over that idea."

"Of course I would be. I'm a man and you're the best sex I've ever had." Jaci widened her eyes at his statement. The best sex? Ever? *Really?*

"Dammit, Jace, you tie me up in knots." Ryan tipped his head back to look at the ceiling of the tent. The main lights had been turned out and only flickering fairy lights illuminated the tent, casting dancing shadows on his tired face. What was she supposed to say to that? *Sorry that I've complicated your life? Sorry that I'm the best sex you've ever had?*

She'd apologized for too many things in her life, many of them that weren't her fault, but she would be damned if she was going to apologize to Ryan. Not about this. She liked the fact that she, at least, had some effect on the man. So Jaci just crossed her legs and didn't bother to adjust her dress when the fabric parted and exposed her knee and a good portion of her thigh. She watched Ryan's eyes drop to her legs, saw the tension that skittered through his body and the way his Adam's apple bobbed in his throat.

Another knot, she thought. Good, let him feel all crazy for a change.

Instead of touching her as she expected, Ryan sat up, took a sip of her coffee and, after putting her cup back in its saucer, tapped his finger on the white damask tablecloth. "I'm not good at sharing my thoughts, at talking."

That didn't warrant a response, so Jaci just looked at him.

"I have a messed-up relationship with my family, both dead and alive." Ryan stared off into the distance. "My mother is dead, my father is a stranger to me, someone who always put his needs above those of his kids. I'm not looking for sympathy, I'm just telling you how it was." Ryan stopped talking and hauled in another breath. It took a moment for his words to sink in, to realize that he was talking to her. Jaci's heart stopped momentarily and then it started to pound. He was *talking* to her? For real?

"I don't talk to people because I don't want them getting that deep into my head," Ryan admitted with a lot of reluctance. He closed his eyes momentarily before speaking again. "That girl in the picture? Well, she died in the same car accident as Ben."

"Ben's fiancée? I'm sorry but I don't remember her name." And why did he have a photograph of Ben's fiancée in his bedroom? Facedown, but still…

"Kelly. Everyone thought that she was engaged to Ben because she was wearing an engagement ring," Ryan said, but something in his voice had Jaci leaning forward, trying to look into his eyes. Judging by his hard expression, and by the muscle jumping in his cheek, talking about Ben and this woman was intensely difficult for Ryan. Of course, they were talking about his brother's death. It had to be hard, but there was more to this story than she was aware of.

Ryan stared at the ground between his knees and pulled in a huge breath, and Jaci was quite sure that he wasn't aware that his hand moved across the table to link with hers. "Kelly wasn't Ben's fiancée, she was mine."

Jaci tangled her fingers in his and held on. "What?"

Ryan lifted his head and dredged up a smile but his eyes remained bleak. "Yeah, we'd got engaged two weeks earlier."

Jaci struggled to make sense of what he was saying. "But the press confirmed that they had spent a romantic weekend together." Jaci swore softly when she realized what he was trying to tell her. "She was *cheating*. On you." She lifted her hand to her mouth, aghast. "Oh, Ryan!"

How horrible was that? Jaci felt her stomach bubble, felt the bile in the back of her throat. His fiancée and his brother were having an affair and he found out when they both died in a car crash? That was like pouring nitric acid into a throat wound. How…how… how dare they?

How did anyone deal with that, deal with losing two people you loved and finding out they were having an affair behind your back? What were you supposed to feel? Do? Act? God, no wonder Ryan had such massive trust issues.

Fury followed horror. Who slept with her fiancé's brother, who slept with their brother's fiancée? *Who did that?* She was so angry she could spit radioactive spiders. "I am so mad right now," was all she could say.

The corners of Ryan's mouth lifted and his eyes lightened a fraction. "It was a long time ago, honey." He removed his fingers from her grasp and flexed his hand. "Ow."

"Sorry, but that disloyalty, that amount of selfishness—"

Ryan placed the tips of his fingers on her mouth to stop her talking. Jaci sighed and yanked her words back. It didn't matter how angry she was on his behalf, how protective she was feeling, the last thing he needed was for her to go all psycho on him. Especially since Ben and Kelly had paid the ultimate price.

"Sorry, Ry," she muttered around his fingers.

"Yeah. Me, too." Ryan dropped his hand. "I never talk about it—nobody but me knows. Kelly wanted to keep the engagement secret—"

"Probably because she was boinking your brother."

"Thank you, I hadn't realized that myself," Ryan said, his voice bone-dry.

Jaci winced. "Sorry." It seemed as if it was her go-to phrase tonight.

"Anyway, you're the first person I've told. Ever." Ryan shoved his hand through his hair. "You asked who she was and I wanted to tell you, but I *didn't* want to tell you and it all just got too…"

Jaci waited a beat before suggesting a word. "Real?"

Ryan nodded. "Yeah. If I explained, I couldn't keep pretending that we were just…friends."

What did that mean? Were they more than friends now? Was he also feeling something deeper than passion and attraction, something that could blossom and grow into…something deeper? Jaci wished she had the guts to ask him, but a part of her didn't want to risk hearing his answer. It might not be what she was looking for or even wanting. Her heart was in her hands and she was mentally begging him to take it, to keep it. But she wanted him to keep it safe and she wasn't sure that he would.

Ryan closed his eyes and rubbed his eyelids with his thumb and forefinger. "God, I'm tired."

"Then go back to the B and B," Jaci suggested.

"Will you come with me?"

Jaci cocked her head in thought. She could but if she did she knew that she would have no more defenses against him, that she would give him everything she had, and she knew that she couldn't afford to do that. And, despite the fact that he'd opened up, he wasn't anywhere near being in love with her and he didn't want what she did. Oh, she was in love with him. He had most of her heart, but she was keeping a little piece of that organ back, and all of her soul, because she needed them to carry on, to survive when he left.

Because he would leave. This was her life, not a fairy tale.

He stood up and held out his hand. "Jace? You coming?"

"Sorry, Ry."

Ryan frowned at her and looked across the room to where Clive stood, watching them. Watching *her*. Creepy. "You've got something better to do?" Ryan demanded, his eyes dark with jealously.

"Oh, Ryan, you are such an idiot!" she murmured.

She was tempted to go with him, of course she was. Despite his opening up and letting her a little way in, they weren't in a committed relationship, and the more she slept with him the deeper in love she would fall. She had to be sensible, had to keep some distance. But she didn't want to make light of the fact that he'd confided in her and that she appreciated his gesture, so Jaci reached up and touched her lips to his cheek. Then she held her cheek against his, keeping her eyes closed as she inhaled his intoxicating smell. "Thank you for telling me, Ry."

The tips of Ryan's fingers dug into her hips. He rested his forehead on hers and sighed heavily. "You drive me nuts."

Jaci allowed a small laugh to escape. "Right back at you, bud. Are you coming to the family breakfast in the morning?"

"Yeah." Ryan kissed her nose before stepping back. He tossed a warning glance in Clive's direction. "Don't let him snow you, Jace. He's a politician and by all reports he's a good one."

"So?"

"So, don't let him con you," Ryan replied impatiently. "He cheated on you and lied to you and treated you badly. Don't get sucked back in."

Jaci looked at him, astounded. She wasn't a child and she wasn't an idiot and she knew, better than anybody, what a jerk Clive was. Did she come across that naive, that silly, that in need of protection? She was a grown woman and she knew her own mind. She wasn't the weak-willed, wafty, soft person Ryan and her family saw her as. Sometimes she wondered if anyone would ever notice that she'd grown up, that she was bigger, stronger, bolder. Would they ever see her as she was now? Would anyone ever really know her?

She didn't need a prince or a knight to run to her rescue anymore.

She'd slay her own dragons, thank you very much, and she'd look after herself while she did it.

The next morning Jaci, her mother and Merry sat on the terrace and watched as the people from the catering company dismantled the tent and cleared up the wedding detritus. When Ryan got there they would haul Archie out of his study and they'd rustle up some breakfast. The bride and groom would arrive when they did—they weren't going to wait for them—but for now she was happy to sit on the terrace in the spring sunshine.

"One down, two to go," Priscilla stated without looking up. Her mother, wearing an enormous floppy hat, sat next to her, a rough draft of her newest manuscript in her hands.

"Don't look at me," Merry categorically stated, placing her bare feet on the arm of Jaci's chair.

"It should've been my marriage next," Jaci quietly stated.

"Speaking of," Merry said, "I saw you talking to Clive last night. You looked very civilized. Why weren't you slapping his face and scratching his eyes out?"

Jaci rested her cup of coffee on her knee. "Because I don't care about him anymore. He's coming here today. I stored some things of his in my room that he needs to collect." Jaci pushed her sunglasses up her nose. "Once that's done I'll be free of him, forever."

Merry snorted her disbelief and Jaci wanted to tell her that it was true because she was in love with Ryan, but that was too new, too precious to share.

"So what did you talk about?" Merry asked. "Your relationship?"

"A little. He was very apologetic and sweet about it. He groveled a bit and that was nice."

"I don't buy it," Merry stated, her eyes narrowed. "Clive isn't the type to grovel."

Merry was so damn cynical sometimes, Jaci thought. "Look, he tried to talk me into trying again but I told him about New York, about everything that happened there and how happy I was. He eventually gave up and said that he understood. He wished me well and we parted on good terms."

"Clive doesn't like hearing the word *no*," Merry stated, her lips in a thin line. "I don't trust him. Be careful of him."

Merry really was overreacting, thought Jaci, bored with talking about her ex.

"And Ryan?" Merry asked.

Ryan? Jaci rested her head on the back of her chair. "I don't know, Merry. He has his own issues to work through. I don't know if we will ever be anything more than just friends."

"He doesn't look at you like you're just friends," Merry said.

"That's just because we are really good in bed together," Jaci retorted, and sent her mother a guilty look. "Sorry, Mum."

"I know you had sex with him, child," Priscilla drily replied. "I'm not that much of a prude or that oblivious. I have had, and for your information, still do have, a sex life."

"God." Jaci placed her hand over her eyes and Merry

groaned. "Thanks for putting that thought into my head. Eeew. Anyway, coming back to Ryan…he's a closed book in so many ways. I take one step forward with him and sixty back. I thought we took a couple of steps forward last night."

"I thought you said that things are casual between you," Merry said.

"They are." Jaci tugged at the ragged hem of her denim shorts. "Sort of. As I said, I think we turned a corner last night but, knowing me, I might be reading the situation wrong." She pulled her earlobe. "I tend to do that with men. I'm pretty stupid when it comes to relationships."

"We all are, in one way or another," Merry told her.

"Yeah, but I tend to take stupidity to new heights," Jaci replied, tipping her face up to the sun. She'd kissed Ryan impulsively, agreed to be his pretend girlfriend, slept with him and then fell in love with him. *Stupid* didn't even begin to cover it.

Well, she'd made those choices and now she had to live the consequences…

Jaci jerked when she heard the slap of paper hitting the stone floor and she winced when the wind picked up her mother's manuscript and blew sheets across the terrace. Before her mother could get hysterical about losing her work, Jaci jumped up to retrieve the pages, but Priscilla's whip-crack voice stopped her instantly. "Sit down, Jacqueline!"

"But…your papers." Jaci protested.

"Leave them," Priscilla ordered and Jaci frowned. Who was this person and what had she done with her mother? The Priscilla Jaci knew would be having six kittens and a couple of ducks by now at the thought of losing her work.

Priscilla yanked off her hat and shoved her hand into her short cap of gray hair. She frowned at Jaci but her eyes looked sad. "I don't ever want to hear those words out of your mouth again."

Jaci quickly tried to recall what she'd said and couldn't pinpoint the source of her ire. "What words?"

"That you are stupid. I won't have it, do you understand?"

Jaci felt as if she was being sucked into a parallel universe where nothing made sense. Before she could speak, Priscilla held up her hand and shook her head. "You are not stupid, do you understand me?" Priscilla stated, her voice trembling with emotion. "You are more intelligent than the rest of us put together!"

No, she wasn't. "Mum—"

"None of us could have coped with what Clive put you through with the grace and dignity you did. We just shoved our heads in the sand and ignored him, hoping that he would go away. But you had to deal with him, with the press. The four of us deal with life by ignoring what makes us unhappy and we're selfish, horrible creatures."

"It's okay, Mum. *I'm* okay."

Jaci flicked a look at Merry, who appeared equally uncomfortable at their mother's statement. "It's not okay. It's not okay that you've spent your life believing that you are second-rate because you are not obsessive and selfish and driven and ambitious."

"But I'm not smart like you." Jaci stared at her intertwined fingers.

"No, but you're smart like you," Merry quietly said. "Instead of falling apart when Clive raked you, and your relationship, through the press, you picked yourself up, dusted yourself off and started something new. You pursued your dream and got a job and you started a new life, and that takes guts, kid. Mum's right. We ignore what we don't understand and bury ourselves, and our emotions, in our work."

Jaci let out a low, trembling laugh. "Let's not get too carried away. I'm a scriptwriter. It's not exactly *War and Peace*."

"It's a craft," Priscilla insisted. "A craft that you seem to excel at, as I've recently realized. I'm sorry that you felt like you couldn't share that with us, that you thought that we wouldn't support you. God, I'm a terrible mother. I'm the failure, Jaci, not you. You are, by far, the best of us."

Merry reached out and squeezed her shoulder. "I'm sorry, too, Jace. I haven't exactly been there for you."

Jaci blinked away the tears in her eyes and swallowed the lump in her throat. What a weekend this had been, she thought; she'd fallen in love and she'd realized that she was a part of the Brookes-Lyon family—quite an important part, as it turned out. She was the normal one. The rest of her family were all slightly touched. Clever but a bit batty.

It was, she had to admit, a huge relief.

"And you are not stupid when it comes to men," Priscilla stated, her voice now strong and back to its normal no-nonsense tone. "Ryan is thick if he can't see how wonderful you are."

She wished she could tell them about Ben and Kelly's betrayal, but that was Ryan's story, not hers. Maybe they had made some progress last night, but how much? Jaci knew that Ryan wasn't the type to throw caution to the wind and tumble into a relationship with her; he might have told her the reasons for his wariness and reserve but he hadn't told her that he had any plans to change his mind about trusting, about loving someone new. She knew that he would still be the same guarded, restrained, unable-to-trust person he currently was, and she didn't know if she could live with that...long term. How did you prove yourself worthy of someone's trust, someone's love? And if she ignored these concerns and they fell back into bed, she'd be happy until the next time he emotionally, or physically, disappeared. And she would be hurt all over again. She could see the pattern evolving before her eyes, and she didn't want to play that game.

She wanted a relationship, she wanted love, she wanted forever.

Jaci gnawed at her bottom lip. "I don't know where I stand with him."

Priscilla sent her a steady look. "As much as I like Ryan, if you can't work that out, and if he won't tell you, then maybe it's time that you stopped standing and started walking."

Stop standing and start walking... Jaci felt the truth of her mum's words lodge in her soul. Would Ryan ever let her be, well, more? Was she willing to stand around waiting for him to make up his mind? Was she willing to try to prove herself worthy of his love? His trust?

But did she have the strength to let him go? She didn't think so. Maybe the solution was to give him a little time to get used to having someone in his life again. After all that he'd suffered, was that such a big ask? In a month—or two or three—she could reevaluate, see whether he'd made any progress in the trust department. That was fair, wasn't it?

Jaci had the niggling thought that she was conning herself, that she was delaying the inevitable, but when she heard the sound of a car pulling up outside she pushed out her doubts and jumped to her feet, a huge smile blossoming.

"He's here!" she squealed, running to the edge of the railing and leaning over to catch a glimpse of the car rolling up the drive. Her face fell when she recognized Clive's vintage Jaguar. She pouted. "Damn, it's Clive."

Merry caught Priscilla's eye. "Music to my ears," she said, sotto voce.

Priscilla smiled and nodded. "Mine, too."

Chapter 11

Ryan, parking his rental car in the driveway of Lyon House, felt as if he had a rope around his neck and barbed wire around his heart. He looked up at the ivy-covered, butter-colored stone house and wondered which window on the second floor was Jaci's bedroom. The one with frothy white curtains blowing in the breeze? It would have been, he thought, a lot easier if they'd spent the night having sex instead of talking. Sex, that physical connection, he knew how to deal with, but talking, exposing himself? Not so much.

If he wanted to snow himself, he supposed he could try to convince himself that he'd told her about Ben and Kelly's deception, their betrayal, as a quid pro quo for her telling him about her disastrous engagement to Horse-face. But he'd had many women bawl on his shoulder while they told him their woes and he'd never felt the need to return the favor.

Jaci, unfortunately, could not be lumped into the masses.

Ryan leaned his head against the headrest and closed his eyes. What a week. In his effort to treat her like a flash-in-the-pan affair, he'd kept his distance by putting the continent between them, but he'd just made himself miserable. He'd missed her. Intensely. His work and the drive and energy he gave it made his career his primary focus, but he'd had only half his brain on business this past week. Not clever when so much was at stake.

He had to make a decision about what to do with her, about her, soon. He knew that she wasn't the type to have a no-strings affair. Her entire nature was geared to being in a steady relationship, to being committed and cared for. She was paying lip service to the idea of a fling but sooner or later her feelings would run deeper... His might, too.

He'd put his feelings away four years ago, and he didn't like the fact that Jaci had the ability to make him feel more, be more, made him want to be the best version of himself, for her. She was becoming too important and if he was going to walk, if he was going to keep his life emotionally uncomplicated, then he had to walk away *now*. He couldn't sleep with her again because every time they had sex, every moment he had with her, with every word she spoke, she burrowed further under his skin. He had to act because his middle ground was fast disappearing.

Ryan picked up his wallet and mobile from the console and opened his door on a large sigh. It was so much easier to remain single, he thought. His life had been so uncomplicated before Jaci.

Boring, admittedly, but uncomplicated. Ryan turned to close the car door and saw Jaci's father turning the corner to walk up the steps. "Morning, Archie," he said, holding out his hand for Jaci's father to shake. "Have you seen Jaci?"

Archie, vague about anything that didn't concern his newspaper or world news, thought for a moment. "In her room, with the politician," he eventually said.

Blood roared through Ryan's head. "Say what?" he said, sounding as if he was being strangled. What the hell did that mean? Had Whips and Chains spent the night? With Jaci?

What the...

"Ryan!"

Ryan looked up as Jaci's slim figure walked out of the front door of Lyon House, her ex close on her heels. He had a duffel bag slung over his shoulder and his hand on Jaci's back, and he sent Ryan a look that screamed *Yeah, I did her and it was fantastic, dude.* Ryan clenched his fist as Jaci skipped down the stairs. He could watch her forever, he thought, as she approached him with a smile on her face that lit her from the inside out. God, she was beautiful, he thought. Funny, smart, dedicated. Confident, sexy and, finally, starting to realize who she was and her place in the world.

Clive greeted Archie as he walked back into the house, then he kissed Jaci's cheek, told her to give him a call and walked toward his car. Jaci stared at Clive's departing back for more time than Ryan was comfortable with and when she turned to look at him she was—damn, what was the word?—*glowing*. She looked—the realization felt like a fist slamming into his stomach—soft and radiant, the way she looked after they'd shared confidences, exactly the way she looked after they made love. Her eyes were a gooey brown, filled with emotion. He could read hope there and possibilities and…love. He saw love.

Except that *they* hadn't made love. He hadn't made love…

Jesus, no.

Maybe she *had* slept with Whips and Chains again, Ryan thought, his mind accelerating to the red zone. It was highly possible; three months ago she'd loved him, was planning to marry him. Those feelings didn't just disappear, evaporate. He was a politician and he probably talked her around and charmed her back into bed. Had he read too much into whatever he and Jaci had? Had it just been a sexual fling? Maybe, possibly…after all, Jaci hadn't given him the slightest indication of her desire to deepen this relationship, so was he rolling the wrong credits? They'd slept together a couple of times. For all he knew, she might just regard him as a way to pass some time until her ex came to his senses.

Did Jaci still love Clive? The idea wasn't crazy; yeah, the guy was a jerk-nugget, but love didn't just go away. God, he still loved Ben despite the fact that he'd betrayed him, and a part of him still loved Kelly, even after five years and everything that happened.

But, God, it stung like acid to think of Jaci and Clive in bed, that moron touching her perfect body, pulling her back into his life. He'd shared a woman before and he would *never* do it again. Ryan felt the bile rise up in his throat and he ruthlessly choked it down. God, he couldn't be sick, not now.

Feeling sideswiped, he looked down and noticed that his mobile, set to silent, was ringing. He frowned at the unfamiliar number on the screen. Thinking that taking the call would give him some time to corral his crazy thoughts, he pushed the green button and lifted the phone to his ear.

"Jax? This is Jet Simons."

Ryan's frown deepened. Why would Simons, the slimiest tabloid writer around, be calling him and how the hell did he get his number? He considered disconnecting, blowing him off, but maybe there was a fire he needed to put out. "What the hell do you want? And how did you get my number?"

"I have my sources. So, I hear that you and Jaci Brookes-Lyon think that Leroy Banks is a slimy troll and that you two are pretending to be in a relationship to keep him sweet. What did you two call him, 'Toad of Toad Hall'?"

Ryan's eyes flew to Jaci's face. The harsh swear left his mouth, and only after it was out did he realize that it, in itself, was the confirmation Simons needed.

"No comment," he growled, wishing he could reach through the phone and wrap his hand around Simons's scrawny neck. Strangling Jaci was an option, too. She was the only person who used that expression. He sent her a dark look and she instinctively took a step back.

"So is that a yes?" Simons persisted.

"It's a 'no comment.' Who did you get that story from?" Ryan rested his fist against his forehead.

Simons laughed. "I had a trans-Atlantic call earlier. Tell Jaci that you can never trust a politician."

"Egglestone is your source?" Ryan demanded, and Simons's silence was enough of an answer.

Yep, it seemed that Jaci had shared quite a bit during their pillow talk. Ryan sent her another blistering look, deliberately ignoring her pleading, confused face. Ryan felt the hard, cold knot of despair and anger settle like a concrete brick in his stomach. He remembered this feeling. He'd lived with it for months, years after Ben and Kelly died. God, he wanted to punch something. Preferably Simons.

He was furiously angry and he needed to stay that way. This was why he didn't get involved in relationships; it was bad enough that his heart was in a mess and his love life was chaotic. Now it was affecting his business. Where had this gone so damn wrong?

He hated to ask Simons a damn thing, but he needed to know how much time he had before he took a trip up that creek without a paddle. "When are you running the story?"

"Can't," Simons said cheerfully. "Banks threatened to sue the hell out of my paper if we so much as mentioned his name and my editor killed it. That's why I feel nothing about giving up my source."

"You spoke to Banks?" Ryan demanded. He felt a scream starting to build inside him. This was it, this was the end. His business had been pushed backward and Jaci's career was all but blown out of the water.

"Yeah, he was…um, what's the word? *Livid*?" Ryan could hear the smile in his voice. The jackass was enjoying every second of this. "He told me to tell you to take your movie and shove it—"

"Got it." Ryan interrupted him. "So, basically, you just called me to screw with me?"

"Basically," Simons agreed.

Ryan told him to do something physically impossible and disconnected the call. He tossed his mobile through the open window of the car onto the passenger seat and linked his hands behind his neck.

"What's happened?" Jaci asked, obviously worried.

"That must have been a hell of a cozy conversation you had with Horse-face last night. It sounds like you covered a hell of a lot of ground."

Jaci frowned. "I don't understand."

"Your pillow talk torpedoed any chance of Banks funding *Blown Away*," he stated in his harshest voice.

Jaci looked puzzled. "What pillow talk? What are you talking about? Has Banks pulled his funding?" Jaci demanded, looking surprised.

"Your boyfriend called Simons and told him the whole story about how we snowed Banks, how we pretended to be a couple because he repulsed you. Nice job, kid. Thanks for that. The movie is dead and so is your career." He knew that he should shut up but he was so hurt, so angry, and he needed to hurt her, needed her to be in as much pain as he was. He just wished he was as angry at losing the funding as he was at the idea of Jaci sleeping with that slimy politician. Of losing Jaci to him.

Jaci just stood in the driveway and stared at him, her dark eyes filled with an emotion he couldn't identify. "Are you crazy?" she whispered.

"Crazy for thinking you could be trusted." Ryan tossed the statement over his shoulder as he yanked open the door to the car and climbed inside. "I should've run as hard and as fast as I could right after you kissed me. You've been nothing but a hassle. You've caused so much drama in my life I doubt I'll ever dig myself out of it. You know, you're right. You are the Brookes-Lyon screwup!"

Ryan watched as the poison-tipped words struck her soul, and he had to grab the steering wheel to keep from bailing out of the car and whisking her into his arms as she shrunk in on herself. He loved her, but he wanted to hurt her. He didn't understand it and he wasn't proud of it, but it was true. Because, unlike four years ago, this time he could fight back.

This time he could, verbally, punch and kick. He could retaliate and he wouldn't have to spend the rest of his life resenting the fact that death had robbed him of his chance to confront those who'd hurt him. He could hurt back and it felt—dammit—good!

"Why are you acting like this? Yes, I told Clive about Banks, about New York, but I never thought that he would blab to the press! I thought that we were friends again, that we had come to an understanding last night."

"Yet you still hopped into bed with that horse's ass."

"I did not sleep with Clive!" Jaci shouted.

Sure, you didn't, he mentally scoffed. Ryan started the engine of the car. He stared at the gearshift before jamming it into Reverse. He backed up quickly and pushed the button to take down the window of the passenger door. On the other side of the car stood

Jaci, tears running down her face. He couldn't let her desperate, confused, emotional expression affect him. He wouldn't let anything affect him again…not when it came to her, or any other woman, either.

He didn't trust those tears, didn't trust her devastated expression. He didn't trust her. At all. "Thanks for screwing up my life, honey. I owe you one."

"Have you been fired?" Shona asked, perching her bottom on the corner of the desk Jaci was emptying.

It was Wednesday. Jaci'd been back in New York for two days and she'd sent Ryan two emails and left three voice mails asking him to talk to her and hadn't received a reply. Ryan, she concluded, was ignoring her.

She'd reached out five times and he'd ignored her five times. Yeah, she got the message.

"Resigned. I'm saving them the hassle of letting me go," Jaci said, tossing her thesaurus into her tote bag. "Without funding, *Blown Away* is dead in the water and I'm not needed."

Shona tapped her fingernails on her desk in a rat-a-tat-tat that set Jaci's teeth on edge. "I hear that Jax has been in meetings from daybreak to midnight trying to get other funding."

Jaci wasn't one to put any stock in office rumors. No, Ryan had moved on. It was that simple.

Thanks for screwing up my life, honey…

Moron man! How *dare* he think that she'd slept with Clive? Yes, she told Clive about Leroy, but only because a part of her wanted him to see that she was happy and content without him, that she had other men in her life and that she wasn't pining for him. But she'd forgotten that Clive hated to share and that he still, despite everything, considered her his. Under those genial smiles was a man who had still been hell-bent on punishing her; payback for the fact that she'd had the temerity to move on to Ryan from him. But while she knew that Clive could be petty, she'd never thought that he'd be so vengeful, so malicious as to call up a tabloid reporter and cause so much trouble for her and Ryan.

Oh, she was so mad. How dare Ryan have so little faith in her? How could he think that she would sleep with someone else, and just after they'd shared something so deep, as important as they had earlier that night? She might have a loose mouth and trust people too easily and believe that they were better than they were, but she wouldn't cheat. She'd been cheated on, so had he, and they both knew how awful it made the other person feel. How could he believe that she was capable of inflicting such pain?

She got it, she did. She understood how much it had to have hurt to be so betrayed by Ben and Kelly and she understood why he shied away from any feelings of intimacy. She understood his reluctance to trust her, but it still slayed her that Ryan didn't seem to know her at all. How could he believe that she would do that, that she would hurt him that way after everything they'd both experienced? Didn't he have the faintest inkling that she loved him? How could he be so blind?

"I'm so sorry, Jaci," Shona said and Jaci blinked at her friend's statement. She'd totally forgotten that she was there. "Are you going back to London?"

Jaci lifted her shoulders in a slow shrug. "I'm not sure."

"Sorry again." Shona squeezed her shoulder before walking back to her desk.

So was she, Jaci thought. But she couldn't make someone love her. Her feelings were her own and she couldn't project them onto Ryan. She could, maybe, forgive his verbal attack in the driveway of Lyon House, but by ignoring her he'd shown her that he regretted sharing his past with her, that he didn't trust her and, clearly, that he did not want to pursue a relationship with her. It hurt like open-heart surgery but she could deal with it, she *would* deal with it. She was never going to be the person who loved too much, who demanded too much, who gave too much, again.

When she loved again, *if* she ever loved again, it would be on her terms. She would never settle for anything less than amazing again. She wanted to be someone's sanctuary, her lover's soft place to fall. She wanted to be the keeper of his secrets and, harder, the person he confided his fears to. She wanted to be someone's everything.

Walking away from another relationship, from this situation that was rapidly turning toxic, wasn't an easy decision to make, but she knew that it was the right path. It didn't matter that it was hard, that she felt the brutal sting of loss and disappointment. She couldn't allow it to dictate her life. She was stronger and braver and more resilient than she'd ever been, and she wouldn't let this push her back into being that weak, insecure girl she'd been before.

It was time that she started protecting her heart, her feelings and her soul. It was time, as her mum had suggested, to stop standing and start walking.

* * *

Because he'd spent the past week chasing down old contacts and new leads, Ryan quickly realized that there was no money floating around to finance *Blown Away. We're in a recession, we don't have that much, it's too risky, credit is tight.* He'd heard the same excuses time and time again.

This was the end of the line. He was out of options.

Not quite true, he reluctantly admitted. He still had his father's offer to finance a movie, but he'd rather wash his face with acid than ask him. He could always come back to *Blown Away* in the future, but Jaci's career would take a hit…

Jaci… No, he wasn't going to think about her at all. It was over and she had—according to the very brief letter she'd left with his PA—released him from her contract.

She was out of his life, and that was good. But his mind kept playing the last scenes of their movie in his head. Instead of fighting the memory, as he had been doing, instead of pushing it aside, he let it run. It wasn't as if he was doing any work, and maybe if he just remembered, properly, the events of that night, he'd be able to move *on*. He *had* to get his life back to normal.

He remembered the wedding, how amazing Jaci looked in that pale pink cocktail dress with the straps that crisscrossed her back. Her eyes looked deep and mysterious and her lips had been painted a color that matched her dress. He'd kept his eyes on her all night, had followed her progress across the tented room, watched her talk to friends and acquaintances, noticed how she refused the many offers to dance. After the meal, the horse's ass had approached her and she'd looked wary and distant. They'd talked and talked and Clive kept moving closer and Jaci kept putting distance between them.

Ryan frowned. She *had* done that. He wasn't imagining that. Clive had eventually left her, looking less than happy. Then he'd joined her at that table and they'd chatted and the pinched look left her eyes. Her attention had been on him, all on him; her eyes softened when they looked at *him*. Her entire attention had been focused on him; she hadn't looked around. Clive had been forgotten when they were together.

She'd been that into me...

So how had she gone from being so into him to jumping into bed with Whips? *Did she? Are you so sure that she did?* Ryan picked up his pen and tapped it against his desk. He had no proof that Jaci had slept with Clive, just his notoriously unreliable gut instinct. And his intuition was clouded by jealously and past insecurities about being cheated on...

He wished he could talk to someone who would tell him the unvarnished, dirty truth.

Jaci's ball-breaker sister would do that. Merry had never pulled her punches. Ryan picked up his mobile and within a minute Meredith's cut-glass tones swirled around his office. "Are you there, you ridiculous excuse for a human being?"

Whoa! Someone sounded very irritated with him. That was okay because he was still massively irritated with her sister. "Did she sleep with Whips and Chains?" he demanded.

"We video chatted last night and she looked like death warmed up. I have never seen her so unhappy, so…so…so heartbroken. She cries herself to sleep every night, Ryan, did you know that?"

Ryan's heart lurched. "Did. She. Sleep. With. Him?"

There was a long, intense silence on the other end of the phone and Ryan pulled the receiver away, looked at it and spoke into it again. "Are you there?"

"Oh, dear Lord in heaven," Merry stated on a long sigh. Her voice lost about 50 percent of its tartness when she spoke again. "Ryan Jackson, why would you think that Jaci slept with Clive?"

"That morning she looked…" Ryan felt as if his head was about to explode. "… God, I don't know. She… glowed. She looked like something wonderful had happened. Your dad told me that they were in her bedroom so I presumed that they'd…reconciled."

"You are an idiot of magnificent proportions," Merry told him, exasperated. "Now, listen to me, birdbrain. Clive came to pick up some stuff of his she was storing at Lyon House. That's the only reason he was there. Yes, she told him about New York, how happy she was there. Because she's a girl and she has her pride, she wanted Clive to know how happy and successful she was, how much she didn't need him. She told Clive about Banks, and you, because she wanted to show him that there were other men out there, rich, powerful and successful men, who wanted and desired her. She wanted him to know that she didn't need him anymore because she was now a better version of who she used to be with him."

Ryan struggled to keep up. "She told you all that?"

"Yeah. She's proud of who she is now, Ryan, proud of the fact that she picked herself up and dusted herself off. Sure, she should never have told Clive what she did but she never thought that he would talk to the press… I would've suspected him but she's not cynical like me. Or you."

"I'm not cynical," Ryan objected but he knew that he was. Of course he was.

Merry snorted. "Sure, you are. You thought Jaci slept with her ex because she looked *happy.* Anyway, Jaci blames herself for you losing the funding. She blames herself for all of it. Her dream is gone, Ryan."

He'd made a point of not thinking about that because if he did, it hurt too damn much. He rubbed his eyes with his index finger and thumb. "I know."

"But worse than that, she's shattered that you could think that she slept with Clive, that she would cheat on you. She feels annihilated because she never believed that you could think that of her."

Ryan rested his elbow on his desk and pushed the ball of his hand into his temple. He felt as if the floor had fallen out from under his feet. "Oh." It was the only word he could articulate at the moment.

"Fix this, Jackson," Merry stated in a low voice that was superscary. "Or I swear I'll hurt you."

He could do that, Ryan thought, sucking in air. He could…he could fix this. He *had* to fix this. Because Jaci had been hurt and no one, especially not him, was allowed to do that.

The fact that Merry would—actually—hurt him was just an added incentive.

* * *

There was only one person in the world whom he would do this for, Ryan thought, as the front door to Chad's house opened and his father stood in the doorway with an openly surprised look on his face.

Ryan held his father's eyes and fought the urge to leave. He reminded himself that this was for Jaci, this was to get her the big break that she so richly deserved. Shelving *Blown Away* meant postponing Jaci's dream. He couldn't do that to her. Once the world and, more important, other producers saw the quality of her writing, she'd have more work than she could cope with and she'd be in demand, and maybe then they could find a way to be together. Because, God, he missed her.

He loved her, he needed her, and there was no way that he could return to her—to beg her to take him back—without doing everything and anything he could to resurrect her dream. She'd probably tell him to go to hell, and he suspected that he had as much chance of getting her back as he did of having sex with a zombie princess, but he had to try. Writing made her happy and, above all, he wanted her happy.

With or without him.

"Are you going to stand there and stare at me or are you going to come in?" Chad asked, that famous smile hovering around his lips.

Yeah, he supposed he should. Bombshells shouldn't be dropped on front porches, especially a porch as magnificent as this one. Ryan walked inside the hall and looked around; nothing much had changed since the last time he was here. What was different, and a massive surprise, was the large framed photograph of Ben and himself, arms draped around each other's shoulders, wearing identical grins, that stood on a hall table. Well…huh.

"Do you want to talk in the study or by the pool?" Chad asked.

Ryan pushed his hand through his hair. "Study, I guess." He followed his father down the long hallway of the sun-filled home, catching glances of the magnificent views of the California coastline through the open doors of the rooms they passed. He might not love his father, but he'd always loved this house.

Chad opened the door to the study and gestured Ryan to a chair. "Do you want a cup of coffee?"

Ryan could see that Chad expected him to refuse but he was exhausted, punch-drunk from not sleeping for too many nights. He needed caffeine so he quickly accepted. Chad called his housekeeper on the intercom, asked for coffee and sat down in a big chair across the desk from him. "So, what's this about, Ryan? Or should I call you Jax?"

"Ryan will do." Ryan pulled out a sheaf of papers from his briefcase and slapped them on the table. "According to the emails you've sent me in the past, you are part of a group prepared to invest in my films. I'd like to know whether you, and your consortium, would like to invest in *Blown Away*."

Chad looked at him for a long time before slowly nodding. "Yes," he eventually stated, quietly and without any fanfare.

"I need a hundred million."

"You could have more if you need it."

"That'll do." Ryan felt the pure, clean feeling of

relief flood through him, and he slumped back in his chair, suddenly feeling energized. It had been a lot easier than he expected, he thought. He was prepared to grovel, to beg if he needed to. Asking his father for the money had stung a lot less than he expected it to. Because Jaci, and her happiness, was a lot more important to him than his pride.

It was that simple.

"That's it? Just like that?" Ryan thought he should make sure that his father didn't have anything up his sleeve, a trick that could come back and bite him on the ass.

Chad linked his hands across his flat stomach and shrugged. "An explanation would be nice but it's not a deal breaker. I know that you'd rather swallow nails than ask me for help, so it has to be a hell of a story."

Ryan jumped to his feet and walked over to the open door that led onto a small balcony and sucked in the fragrant air. He rested his shoulder against the doorjamb and looked at his father. In a few words he explained about Banks and Jaci's part in the fiasco. "But, at the end of the day, it was my fault. Who risks a hundred million dollars by having a pretend relationship with a woman?"

"Someone who desperately wanted a relationship but who was too damn scared to admit it and used any excuse he could to have one anyway?"

Bull's-eye, Father. Bull's-eye. He had been scared and stupid. But mostly scared. Scared of falling in love, of trusting someone, terrified of being happy. Then scared of being miserable. But hey, he was miserable anyway, and wasn't that a kick in the pants?

"As glad as I am that you've asked me to help, I would've thought that you'd rather take a hit on the movie than come to me," Chad commented, and Ryan, from habit, looked for the criticism in his words but found none. Huh. He was just sitting there, head cocked, offering his help and not looking for a fight. What had happened to his father?

"Why are you being so nice about this?" he demanded. "This isn't like you."

Chad flushed. With embarrassment? That was also new. "It isn't like the person I used to be. Losing Ben made me take a long, hard look at myself, and I didn't like what I saw. Since then I've been trying to talk to you to make amends."

Now, that was pushing the feasibility envelope. "And you did that by demanding ten million for narrating the documentary about Ben's life?" He shot the words out and was glad that his voice sounded harsh. Anger he could deal with, since he was used to fighting with his father.

Chad didn't retaliate and he remained calm. A knock on the door broke the tension and he turned to see Chad's housekeeper in the doorway, carrying a tray holding a carafe and mugs. She placed it on his desk, smiled when Chad politely thanked her and left the room. Chad, ignoring Ryan's outburst, poured him a cup and brought it over to him.

Ryan took the mug and immediately lifted the cup to his lips, enjoying the rich taste. He needed to get out of this room, needed to get back to business. He gestured to the contract. "There's the deal. Get it to your lawyers but tell them that they need to get cracking. I don't have a lot of time."

"All right." Chad nodded. "Let's go back a step and talk about that demand I made for payment for narrating that movie."

"We don't have to... What's done is done."

"It really isn't," Chad replied. His next question was one Ryan didn't expect. "Did you want to do that documentary? I know that Ben's friends were asking you to, that you were expected to."

God, how was he supposed to answer that? If he said yes, he'd be lying—the last thing he'd wanted at the time was to do a movie about his brother, who died on his way back from a dirty weekend with his fiancée— and if he said no then Chad would want an explanation as to why not. "I don't want to talk about this."

"Tough. I think it's time that you understood that I made that demand so that you couldn't do the movie... to give you an out."

Ryan frowned, disconcerted. Chad jammed his hands into the pockets of his shorts and looked Ryan in the eye. "I knew that Ben was fooling around with Kelly and I told him to stop. It wasn't appropriate and I didn't approve. You didn't deserve that amount of disloyalty, especially not from Ben."

Chad's words were like a fist to his stomach, and he couldn't get enough air to his brain to make sense of his statements. "What?"

"Ben told me that they were just scratching an itch and I told him to scratch it with someone else. He promised me that that weekend would be the last time, that they'd call it off when they got back. I wanted to warn you about marrying her but I knew that you wouldn't have listened to me."

"I wouldn't have," Ryan agreed. He and Chad had been at odds long before the accident.

Chad dropped his eyes. "My fault. I was a useless father and terrible role model. I played with women and didn't take them seriously. Ben followed my example." He walked back to his desk, poured coffee into his own cup and sipped. "Anyway, to come back to the documentary… I knew that asking you to make that film would've been cruel so I made damn sure that the project got scuttled."

Ryan wished he could clear the cobwebs from his head. "By asking for that ridiculous fee."

"Yeah. I knew that you didn't have the cash, that you wouldn't borrow the money to do it and that you wouldn't ask anyone else to narrate it." Chad shrugged. "That being said, I still have the script and if you ever want to take on the project, I'll narrate it, for free."

Ryan slid down the door frame to sink to his haunches. "God." He looked up. "I came to ask you for a hundred million and I end up feeling totally floored."

Chad rubbed the back of his neck. "Neither you nor your mother deserved any of the pain I put you through. I've been trying to find a way to say I'm sorry for years." His jaw set and he looked like the stubborn, selfish man whom Ryan was used to. "And if I have to spend a hundred million to do it then I will." He grabbed the stack of papers, flipped to the end page and reached for a pen. Ryan watched, astounded, as he dashed his signature across the page.

"Don't you have to talk to your partners?" Ryan asked.

"I'm the only investor," Chad said, quickly initialing the pages.

Well, okay, then. "Don't you think your lawyers should read the contract or, at the very least, that you should?" Ryan asked as he stood up, now feeling slightly bemused. He was still trying to work through the fact that his father had been trying to protect him from further hurt, that Chad seemed to want a relationship with him, that it seemed as if his father had, to some measure, changed.

"No, no lawyers. We'll settle this now and before you leave town I'll do a direct deposit into your account for half of the cash. I'll need some time to get you the other half. A week, maybe. Besides, if you take me for a hundred million then it's no less than what I deserve for being the worst father in the world."

Ryan picked his jaw up from the floor. "Chad, hell... I don't know what to say."

"Say that you'll consider me for a part in the movie...any part," Chad retorted, as quick as lightning.

Ryan had to laugh and felt strangely relieved knowing that his father hadn't undergone a total personality change.

"I'll consider it."

Chad lifted his head and flashed him a smile. "That's my boy."

Chapter 12

In all honesty, Jaci was proud of her heart. It had been kicked, battered, punched, stabbed and pretty much broken but it still worked...sort of, kind of. It still pumped blood around her body but, on the downside, it still craved Ryan, missed him with every beat.

This was the height of folly because his silence over the past ten days had just reinforced her belief that he'd been playing with her, possibly playing her. If he felt anything for her, apart from sex, he would've contacted her long before this, but he hadn't and that was that.

Ryan aside, she had other problems to deal with. Her career as a screenwriter was on the skids and there was absolutely nothing she could do about that. Before she'd left Starfish the office rumors had been flying, and even if she took only 5 percent of what was being said as truth, then she knew that there was more chance of the world ending this month than there was of *Blown Away* reaching the moviegoing public. And with that went her big break, her career as a screenwriter. She would have to start again with another script and see if her agent could get lucky a second time around. She wasn't holding her breath...

Being the scriptwriter for a blockbuster like *Blown Away*—and it would have been a blockbuster, of that she had no doubt—would have got her noticed and she would have been on her way to the success that she'd always craved.

She didn't crave it so much anymore. Since her conversation with her mother and Merry on the terrace at Lyon House, the desire to prove herself to her family, to herself, had dissipated. She knew that she was a good writer, and if it took another ten years for her to sell a script, she'd keep writing because this was what she was meant to do. This was what made her happy, and writing scripts was what she was determined to stick with. She'd keep on truckin' and one day, someday, her script would see the big screen.

It was wonderfully liberating to be free of that choking need to prove herself... She was Jaci and she was enough. And if that stupid, moron man couldn't see that, then he was a stupid moron man.

And who was leaning on her doorbell at eleven thirty at night? What was so important that it couldn't wait until morning?

Jaci hauled herself to her feet and walked to her door. When she pressed the intercom button and asked who was there, there was silence. Yay, now she had a creepoid pressing random doorbells. Well, they could carry on. She was going to bed, where she was determined to not think about stupid men in general and a moronic man in particular.

A hard rap had her spinning around, and she glared at her door. Frowning, she walked back to the door and looked through the peephole and gasped when she saw Ryan's distorted face on the other side. Now he wanted to talk to her? Late at night when she was just dressed in a rugby jersey of Neil's that she'd liberated a decade ago, fuzzy socks and crazy hair? Was he insane?

"Let me in, Jace."

At the sound of his voice, her traitorous heart did a long, slow, happy slide from one side of her rib cage to the other. Stupid thing. "No."

"Come on, Jaci, we need to talk." Ryan's voice floated under the door.

Jaci, forgetting that she looked like an extra in a vampire movie, jerked the door open and slapped her hands on her hips. She shot him a look that was hot and frustrated. "Go away. Go far, far away!"

Ryan pushed her back into her apartment, shut the door behind him and shrugged out of his leather jacket. Despite her anger, and her disappointment, Jaci noticed that Ryan looked exhausted. He had twin blue-black stripes under his eyes and he looked pale. So their time apart hadn't been easy on him, either, she realized, and she was human enough to feel a tiny bit vindicated about that. But she also wanted to pull him into her arms, to soothe away his pain.

She loved him, and always would. Dammit.

Jaci slapped her hands across her chest. "What do you want, Ryan?"

Ryan shoved his hands into the front pockets of his jeans and rocked on his heels. "I came to tell you that I've secured another source of funding for *Blown Away*."

Really? Oh, goodie! Jaci realized that he couldn't hear her sarcastic thoughts, so she glared at him again. "*That's* why you're here?"

Ryan looked confused. "Well, yeah. I thought you'd be pleased."

Jaci brushed past him, yanked her door open and waved her arm to get him to walk out. When he didn't, she pushed the words through her gritted teeth. "Get out."

"The funding isn't from Banks, it's from…" he hesitated for a moment before shaking his head. "…someone else."

"I don't care if it's from the goblins under the nearest bridge."

"Jaci, what the hell? This is your big break. This is what you wanted." Ryan looked utterly confused and more than a little irate. "I've been busting my ass to sort this out, and this is your response?"

"Did I ask you to?" Jaci demanded. "Did I ask you to roar off, ignore me for days, refuse to take my calls and keep me in the dark?"

"Look, maybe I should've called—"

"Maybe?" Jaci kicked the door shut with her foot and slapped her hands on his chest, attempting and failing to push him back. "Damn right you should've called! You don't get to fall in and out of my life. I'm not a doll you can pick up and discard on a whim."

"No, you're just an enormous pain in my ass." Ryan

captured her wrists with one hand and gripped her hip with his other hand, pulling her into his rock-hard erection. "You drive me mad, you're on my mind first thing in the morning and last thing at night and, annoyingly, pretty much any minute in between." He dropped his mouth onto hers and slid his tongue between her lips. Jaci felt her joints melt and tried not to sink into him. He was like the worst street drug she could imagine— one hit and she was addicted all over again.

She felt Ryan's hands slide up her waist to cover her breasts and she shuddered. One more time, one more memory. She needed it and she needed him.

One more time and then she'd kick him out. Of her apartment and her life.

"There you are," Ryan murmured against her mouth. "I needed you back in my arms."

He needed *her*? Back in his arms? Oh, God, he wasn't back because he loved her or missed her. He was back because he loved the sex and he missed it. Stiffening, she pulled her mouth from his and narrowed her eyes. "Back off," she muttered.

Ryan lifted his hands and took a half step away. He ran a hand around the back of his neck and blew air into his cheeks. "Jace, I—"

Jaci shook her head and pushed past him, thinking that she needed some distance, just a moment to get her heart and head under control. She walked into the bathroom and gripped the edge of the sink, telling herself that she had to resist temptation because she couldn't kid herself anymore; Ryan wanted to have sex and she wanted to make love. Settling for less than she wanted wasn't an option anymore. She didn't want to settle for a bouquet of flowers when she needed the whole damn florist. Jaci placed her elbows on the bathroom counter and stared at her pale reflection in the mirror.

She needed more and she had to tell him. It was that simple. And that hard. She'd tell him that she loved him and he'd walk, because he wasn't interested in anything that even hinted at permanence.

Her expiration date was up.

"You can do this, you are stronger than you think." Jaci whispered the words to herself.

"You can do what?"

Jaci stood up and slowly turned around to Ryan standing in the entrance to the bathroom, holding the top rim of the door. He looked hot and sexy and rumpled. Still tired, she thought, but so damn confident. God, she needed every bit of willpower she possessed to walk away from him, but if she didn't do it now she never would.

Jaci pulled in a deep breath. "I'm walking away… from you, from this."

Ryan tipped his head to the side and Jaci saw the corners of his mouth twitch in amusement. Ooh, that look made her want to smack him silly.

"No," he calmly stated. He dropped his hands and crossed his arms over that ocean of a chest and spread his legs, effectively blocking her path out of the bathroom.

That just made her mad. "What do you mean *no*? I am going to leave New York and I am definitely leaving you."

"No, you are not leaving New York and you are definitely not leaving me."

Jaci leaned back against the counter and thought that it was ridiculous that they were having this conversation in the bathroom. "I refuse to be your part-time plaything."

"You're not my plaything and, judging by the space you take up in my head, you're not a part-time anything."

"You run, Ryan. Every time I need you to talk to me, you run," Jaci cried.

To her surprise, he nodded his agreement. "Because you scare me. You scare the crap out of me."

"Why?" Jaci wailed, not understanding any of it.

Ryan lifted one powerful shoulder in a long shrug. "Because I'm in love with you."

No, he wasn't. He *couldn't* be. "You're not in love with me," Jaci told him, her voice shaky. "People in love don't act like you did. They don't accuse people of having affairs. They don't try to hurt the people they love!"

Horror chased pain and regret across his face. "Sorry. God, I'm so sorry that I hurt you," Ryan said in a strangled voice. "I'd just heard that you discussed us with that horse's butt and you looked all dewy, and soft, and in love. I thought that you'd gone back to him."

"Why did you think that?"

"Because it's the way you look after I make love to you!" Ryan shouted, his chest heaving. "I was jealous and scared and I didn't want to be in love with you, to expose myself to being hurt. You loved him three months ago, Jaci."

"That was before I learned that he liked S&M and that he cheated on me. It was before I grew stronger,

404 *Taking the Boss to Bed*

bolder. It was before I met you. How could you think that, Ryan? How could you believe that I would hurt you like that?"

"Because I'm scared to love you, to be with you." Ryan's jaw was rock hard and his eyes were bleak. When he spoke again, his words sounded as if he was chipping them from a mound of granite. "Because all the people who I loved have let me down in some way or the other. I love you, and why would life treat me any different now?" He shrugged and he swallowed, emotion making his Adam's apple bounce in his strong throat. "But I'm willing to take the chance. You're that important."

No, he wasn't, and he couldn't be in love with her. It sounded far too good to be true.

"You don't love me," Jaci insisted, her voice shaky. Yet she could hear, and she was sure he could, too, the note of hope in her voice.

"Yeah, I do. I am so in love with you. I didn't want to be, didn't think I ever would fall in love again, but I have. With you." He didn't touch her, he didn't try to persuade her with his body because his eyes, his fabulous eyes, radiated the truth of that statement. He loved her? Good grief. Jaci gripped the counter with her hands in an effort to keep from hurtling herself into his arms.

"But you run, every time. Every time we get close, you bolt."

"And that's something I will try to stop doing," Ryan told her, a smile starting to flirt with his eyes and mouth. He held out his broad hand to her and waited until she placed hers in it. Jaci sighed at the warmth of his fingers curling around hers. She stared down at their intertwined hands and wondered if she was dreaming. But if she was, surely she would've chosen a more romantic setting for this crazy conversation? It was a tiny bathroom in a tiny apartment… It didn't matter, she'd take it. She'd take him.

Ryan's finger under her chin lifted her face up and she gasped at the love she saw in his eyes. No, this was too good to be a dream. "I really don't want to carry on this conversation in the bathroom, but you're not getting out of here before I hear what I need to."

Jaci grinned and picked up her spare hand and ran her finger over his collarbone, down his chest, across those ridges in his abdomen, stopping very low down. "What do you want to hear? That I love your body? I do," she teased and saw his eyes darken with passion.

Ryan gripped her finger to stop it going lower. "You know what I want to hear, Jace. Tell me."

When Jaci saw the emotion in his eyes, all thoughts of teasing him evaporated. He looked unsure and a little scared. As if he was expecting her to reject him, to reject them. Her heart, bottom lip and hands trembled from excitement, from love…

"Ryan, of course I love you. I have for a while."

Ryan rested his forehead on hers and she could feel the tension leaving his body. "Thank God."

"How could you not know that?" Jaci linked her arms around his neck and placed her face against his strong chest. "Honestly, for a smart man you can be such an idiot on occasion."

"Apparently so," Ryan agreed, his arms holding her tightly. He pulled his head back to smile at her, relief and passion and, yes, love dancing in his eyes. "Come back to bed, darling, and let me show you how much I love and adore you."

"You've just missed sex," Jaci teased him on a happy laugh.

Ryan pushed her bangs off her forehead and rubbed the pad of his thumb across her delicately arched brow. "No, sweetheart, I've just missed you." He grinned. "But hey, I'm a guy, and if you're offering…"

Jaci launched herself upward and he caught her as she wrapped her legs around his waist. "Anywhere, anyhow, anytime."

Ryan kissed her open mouth, and Jaci's body sighed and shivered in anticipation. "Can I add that to your contract?" he asked as he backed out of the bathroom into the bedroom.

Lover, friend, boss…there wasn't much she wouldn't do for him, Jaci thought as he lowered her onto the bed and covered her body with his.

Anything. Anywhere. Anytime.

Much, much later Ryan was back in his jeans and Jaci was wearing his button-down shirt and they were sitting cross-legged on her bed, digging chocolate chip ice cream from the container she'd abandoned earlier.

What an evening, Jaci thought, casting her mind back over the past few hours. She felt as if she'd ridden a crazy roller coaster of emotion, stomach churning, heart thumping adrenaline, and she'd come out the other side thrilled. Happy. Content. Dopey. Oh, they still had a lot to talk about, but they'd be fine.

Had he really said that he'd secured funding for

Blown Away? Her spoon stopped halfway to her mouth and she didn't realize that ice cream was rolling off the utensil and dropping to her knee. "Did I hear you say that you have funding for *Blown Away*?"

Ryan leaned forward, maneuvered the spoon in her hand to his mouth and ran his thumb over the ice cream on her knee, licking his digit afterward. "Uh-huh."

"Do I have to pretend to be your girlfriend or your wife this time?" Jaci teased.

"No pretending needed this time," Ryan said, peering into the empty container. "Is that it? Damn! I'm still starving. Don't you have any real food in this house?"

"No, I was on the I-hate-men diet. Ice cream and wine only." Jaci tossed her spoon into the container and placed her elbows on her knees. "Who is your investor, Ry? Did you make nice with Banks?"

"Hell no! However, I did meet with him. I felt I owed him that."

"And?"

"He ripped into me, which I expected. Afterwards he offered me half of the money, told me that he wanted you off the project and that he wanted creative control."

"And you said no. You'd never give him control."

Ryan sent another longing look at the empty ice cream container. "That was part of it but not having you as part of the project was the deal breaker. I need real food."

He was trying to change the subject, Jaci realized. *No chance, buddy.* "Ok, so who is this new investor that you found so quickly?"

Ryan stretched his legs out and placed them on each side of her hips. He leaned forward and dropped his head to nibble on her exposed collarbone. Jaci frowned, pushed his head away and leaned back so that she could see his face. "Stop trying to distract me, Jackson, and keep talking to me."

Ryan twisted his lips and tipped his face up so that he was looking at the ceiling. Okay, it didn't take a rocket scientist to realize that he didn't want to talk about this, but the sooner he learned that she was the one person he could talk to, the easier the process would get.

"Chad Bradshaw," he reluctantly admitted.

Jaci gasped. "What? Chad? Your father?"

"You know any other Chad Bradshaw?" Ryan muttered.

Jaci rubbed her forehead with the tips of her fingers. "Wait, hold on a second, let me catch up. Your father, the father you don't talk to, is financing your movie?"

"Yep."

Oh, right, so she was going to have to drag this out of him. Well, she would, if she had to. "Ryan, we're in a relationship, right?"

Ryan smiled and it warmed every strand of DNA in her body. "Damn straight," he replied.

"Okay, then, well, that means that we get to have spectacular sex—" Jaci glanced at her messy bed and nodded "—check that—and that we talk to each other. So talk. Now."

"I went to go see him," Ryan eventually admitted in a low voice. "I needed the money, I knew that he wanted to invest in one of my projects, so I made it happen."

That didn't explain a damn thing. "But why? You

told me that if Banks bailed, you would mothball *Blown Away*."

Ryan squeezed her hips with the insides of his calves. "My and Thom's careers would withstand the hit, but yours wouldn't."

It took a minute for her to make sense of those words, and when she did, she tumbled a little deeper and a little further into love. She hadn't thought it possible, but this was just another surprise in a night full of them. "But you hate your father."

"Well, *hate* is a strong word." He pulled his long legs up and rested his elbows on his knees. "Look, Jace, the reality is that your career is on a knife's edge. Your script is stunning but if nobody sees your work, it could be months, years before you get another shot at the big leagues. I don't want you to have to wait years for another chance, so I made it happen."

Jaci placed her hands on his strong forearms and rested her forehead on her wrists. "Oh, Ryan, you do love me."

His fingers tunneled into her hair. "Yep. An amazing amount, actually."

Jaci's heart sighed. She lifted her head and pulled back. "Did he make you grovel?"

Ryan shook his head. "He was…pretty damn cool, actually." Ryan took a deep breath and Jaci listened intently as he explained how Chad had known about Ben's affair with Kelly and how Chad had clumsily, Jaci thought, tried to protect Ryan. It was so Hollywood, so messed up, but sweet nonetheless.

"Chad tried to explain that they, Ben and Kelly and Chad himself, looked at affairs differently than I did.

That to them sex was just sex, an itch to scratch, I think he said. That they didn't mean to hurt me."

"It shouldn't have mattered how they felt about sex. They knew how you felt and they should've taken that into account," Jaci said, her voice hot. She looked at Ryan's bemused face and reined her temper in. "Sorry, sorry, it just makes me so angry when excuses are made."

"I've never had anyone defend me before."

"Well, just so you know, I'll always be in your corner, fists up and prepared to fight for you," Jaci told him, ignoring the sheen of emotion in his eyes. Her big, tough warrior-like man…emotional? He'd hate her to comment on it so she moved the conversation along briskly. "What else did Chad have to say?"

"That he would narrate the documentary on Ben if I ever chose to do it. For free this time. But I don't know if I can make that film."

"You'll know when you're ready."

Ryan's hand gripped her thigh. "It's not because I care about their affair or care about her anymore, Jace. You understand that, don't you? It feels like another life, another time, and I'm ready to move on, with you. It's just that he was…"

"Your hero. Your brother, your best friend." Jaci touched his cheek with her fingertips. "Honey, there is no rule that you have to make a movie on him. Maybe you should remember him like you'd like to remember him and let everyone else do the same."

Ryan placed his hand on top of hers and held it to his cheek. He closed his eyes and Jaci looked at him, her masculine, strong, flawed man. God, she loved him. She saw his Adam's apple bob and knew that he was fighting to keep his emotions from bubbling up and over.

"Don't, Ry, don't hide what you're feeling from me," she told him, her voice low. "I know talking about Ben hurts. I'm sorry."

Ryan jerked his head up and his eyes blazed with heat, and hope, and love. "I'm not thinking about him. I'm thinking about you and us and this bright new life we have in front of us. I'm so damn happy, Jace. You make me."

Jaci cocked her head. "You make me...what?"

"That's all. You just make me."

Jaci sighed as he kissed the center of her palm and placed her hand on his heart. "I never realized how alone I was until you hurtled into my life. You've put color into my world, and I promise I'll make you happy, Jace."

Jaci blinked away her happy tears. "For how long?" she whispered.

Ryan pushed her long bangs out of her eyes and tucked them behind her ear. "Forever...if you'll let me."

Jaci leaned in for a kiss and smiled against his mouth. "Oh, Ry, I think we can do better than that. Amazing love stories last longer than that."

* * * * *

SPECIAL EXCERPT FROM

⬦ **HARLEQUIN**
DESIRE

*Learning he's the secret heir to a business mogul,
Kenan Rhodes has a lot to prove. His best friend,
lingerie designer Eve Burke, agrees to work with him...
if he'll help her sharpen her dating skills.
Soon, fake dates lead to sexy nights...*

Read on for a sneak peek of
The Perfect Fake Date,
by USA TODAY *bestselling author Naima Simone.*

The corridor ended, and he stood in front of another set of towering doors. Kenan briefly hesitated, then grasped the handle, opened the doors and slipped through to the balcony beyond. The cool April night air washed over him. The calendar proclaimed spring had arrived, but winter hadn't yet released its grasp over Boston, especially at night. But he welcomed the chilled breeze over his face, let it seep beneath the confines of his tuxedo to the hot skin below. Hoped it could cool the embers of his temper...the still-burning coals of his hurt.

"For someone who is known as the playboy of Boston society, you sure will ditch a party in a hot second." Slim arms slid around him, and he closed his eyes in pain and pleasure as the petite, softly curved body pressed to his back. "All I had to do was follow the trail of longing glances from the women in the hall to figure out where you'd gone."

He snorted. "Do you lie to your mama with that mouth? There was hardly anyone out there."

"Fine," Eve huffed. "So I didn't go with the others and watched all of that go down with your parents and brother. I waited until you left the ballroom and went after you."

"Why?" he rasped.

He felt rather than witnessed her shrug. The same with the small kiss she pressed to the middle of his shoulder blades. He locked his muscles, forcing his head not to fall back. Ordering his throat to imprison the moan scrabbling up from his chest. Commanding his dick to stand down.

"Because you needed me," she said.

So simple. So goddamn true.

He did need her. Her friendship. Her body.

Her heart.

But since he could only have one of those, he'd take it. With a woman like her—generous, sweet, beautiful of body and spirit—even part of her was preferable to none of her. And if he dared to profess his true feelings, that was exactly what he would be left with. None of her. Their friendship would be ruined, and she was too important to him to risk losing her.

Carefully, he turned and wrapped her in his embrace, shielding her from the night air. Convincing himself if this was all he could have of her—even if it meant Gavin would have all of her—then he would be okay, he murmured, "You're really going to have to remove 'rescue best friend' off your résumé. For one, it's beginning to get too time-consuming. And two, the cape clashes with your gown."

She chuckled against his chest, tipping her head back to smile up at him. He curled his fingers against her spine, but that didn't prevent the ache to trace that sensual bottom curve.

"Where would be the fun in that? You're stuck with me, Kenan. And I'm stuck with you. Friends forever."

Friends.

The sweet sting of that knife buried between his ribs.

"Always, sweetheart."

Don't miss what happens next in
The Perfect Fake Date *by Naima Simone,*
the next book in the Billionaires of Boston series!

Available January 2022 wherever
Harlequin Desire books and ebooks are sold.

Harlequin.com

Love Harlequin romance?

DISCOVER.

Be the first to find out about promotions,
news and exclusive content!

f Facebook.com/HarlequinBooks

y Twitter.com/HarlequinBooks

⊙ Instagram.com/HarlequinBooks

⊚ Pinterest.com/HarlequinBooks

You Tube YouTube.com/HarlequinBooks

ReaderService.com

EXPLORE.

Sign up for the Harlequin e-newsletter and
download a free book from any series at
TryHarlequin.com

CONNECT.

Join our Harlequin community to
share your thoughts and connect
with other romance readers!
Facebook.com/groups/HarlequinConnection

HARLEQUIN

Heartfelt or thrilling, passionate or uplifting—Harlequin is more than just happily-ever-after.

With twelve different series to choose from and new books available every month, you are sure to find stories that will move you, uplift you, inspire and delight you.

SIGN UP FOR THE HARLEQUIN NEWSLETTER

Be the first to hear about great new reads and exciting offers!

Harlequin.com/newsletters